THE MEMORY OF MIDNIGHT

One hot day in Elizabethan York, young Nell Appleby is trapped in a wooden chest, and a horror of the stifling dark – and of the man who trapped her – dogs her the rest of her life. Wed to the sadistic Ralph Maskewe, Nell must find joy where she can, until the return of her childhood sweetheart offers a chance of flight to the New World. Will Nell escape the dark at last? Four and a half centuries later, Tess and her small son Oscar move to York. But time in York has a way of shifting strangely, and memories of a past that is not her own begin to surface with disturbing effect.

THE MEMORY OF MIDNIGHT

THE MEMORY OF MIDNIGHT

by

Pamela Hartshorne

Magna Large Print Books
Long Preston, North Yorkshire,
BD23 4ND, England.

British Library Cataloguing in Publication Data.

Hartshorne, Pamela
The memory of midnight.

A catalogue record of this book is
available from the British Library

ISBN 978-0-7505-3892-3

First published in Great Britain in 2013 by Pan Books
an imprint of Pan Macmillan,
a division of Macmillan Publishers Limited

Published in Large Print 2014 by arrangement with
Pan Macmillan Publishers Ltd.

Magna Large Print is an imprint of Library Magna Books Ltd.

Printed and bound in Great Britain by
T.J. (International) Ltd., Cornwall, PL28 8RW

For Diana, best of friends, with love

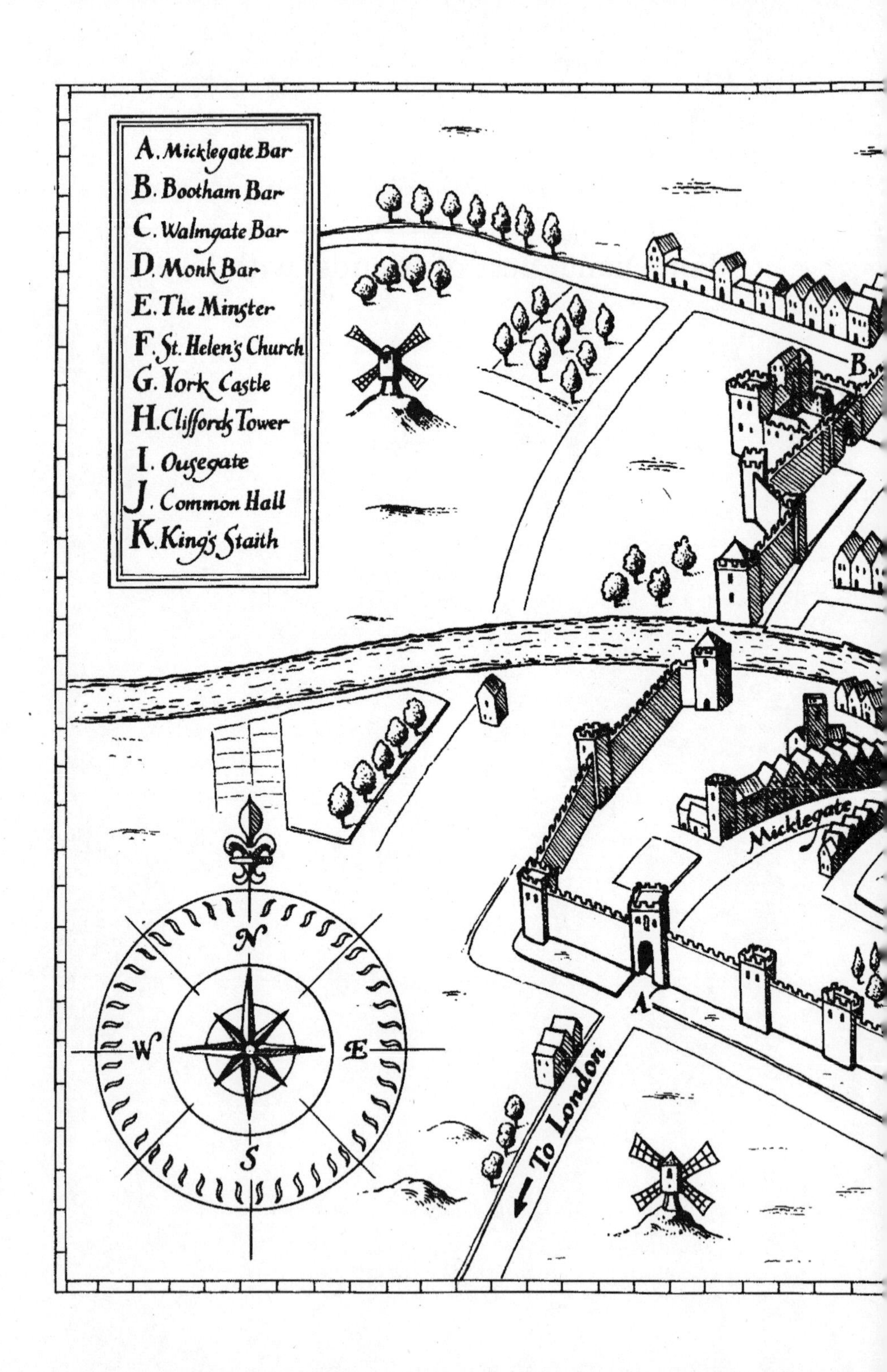
A. Micklegate Bar
B. Bootham Bar
C. Walmgate Bar
D. Monk Bar
E. The Minster
F. St. Helen's Church
G. York Castle
H. Clifford's Tower
I. Ousegate
J. Common Hall
K. King's Staith
B
Micklegate
A
To London
N
S
E
W

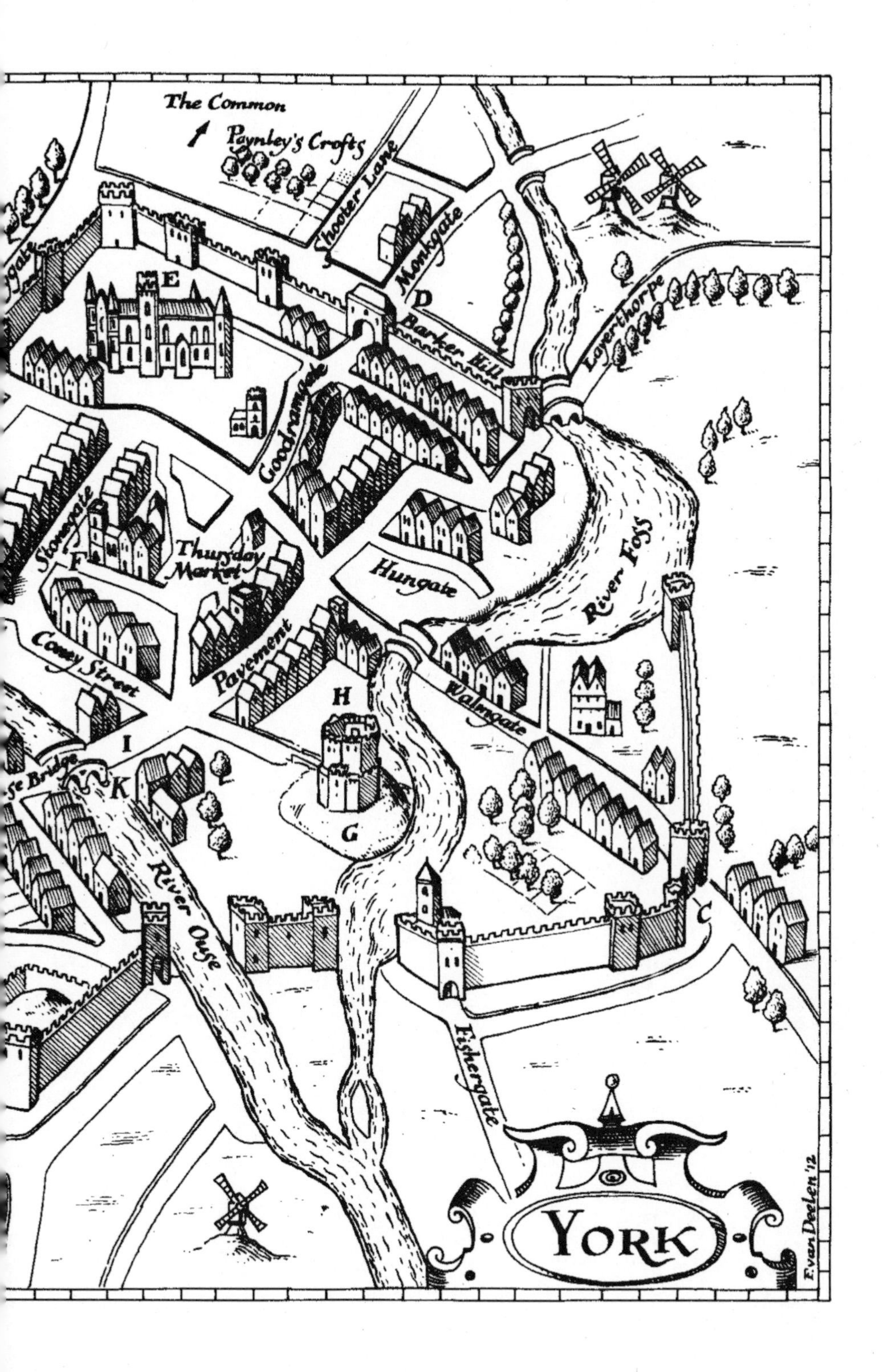

The Common
Paynley's Crofts
Shooter Lane
Monkgate
E
D
Barker Hill
Layerthorpe
Goodramgate
Stonegate
F
Thursday Market
Hungate
River Foss
Coney Street
Pavement
Walmgate
H
I
K
G
River Ouse
C
Fishergate
YORK
F.van Deelen '12

Chapter One

York, August 1561

She had to hide.

'One ... two...'

Nell didn't wait to hear more. Dashing across the yard and through the main door, she skidded to a halt in the dim passage while her eyes darted around in search of somewhere Tom wouldn't find her.

A wooden staircase led up to the first floor, where Mistress Maskewe was lying in, and a door to the right opened into the buttery, the pantry and the kitchen, but otherwise the passage offered nothing in the way of a hiding place.

'Three ... four...'

Instinctively, Nell headed towards the kitchen, only to hesitate with her hand on the latch. There would likely be servants there: Joan, the Maskewes' rabbit-faced maid, perhaps, and certainly Fat Peg, the brawny cook whose temper was unpredictable, to say the least. If she caught a glimpse of Nell, she might laugh her fat laugh and offer a scraping from the sugarloaf. Or she might buffet Nell's ears till they rang and raise a clamour that would bring Tom running straight to her.

Which would mean that Nell would lose *again*. She always lost to Tom. Her face darkened at the thought. It wasn't fair. This time she was determined to show him that she was just as good as him.

'Five ... six ... seven...'

Dropping her hand to her side, she nibbled at her bottom lip. Perhaps it had been a mistake to come inside? Outside there were stables in the garth at the back, and a hay chamber, a wood store and a dairy. Good places to hide, all of them, but the first that Tom would look.

No, she needed somewhere different. Somewhere small and secret. Somewhere he would never find her.

She put a foot on the bottom stair. Did she dare go up? If her stepmother saw her, she'd be scolded and made to sit quietly in the stifling chamber where the gossips were cooing over Tom's new brother. Nell had hunched a shoulder uncomprehendingly when called upon to admire it. It was only a baby, she thought. It just lay in its cradle and cried sometimes. No need for everyone to sit around and make a fuss about it. She had slipped away as soon as she could to find Tom.

They weren't supposed to play upstairs. Nell knew that. But didn't that make it the perfect place to hide? Tom would never think she would be brave enough to go up there on her own.

Outside in the yard, he was beginning to gabble through the numbers and Nell's soft mouth set disapprovingly. He was cheating, but she couldn't tell him so or she would give herself away.

Her shoulders straightened. Enough! This time, *this* time, she would hide so well he would have to admit that she was cleverer. *This* time she would win.

Without allowing herself to think any more on it, Nell grabbed her skirts and ran up the stairs, remembering just in time to jump over the fifth step from the bottom that always creaked and groaned horribly if you trod on it. The house was quiet apart from an occasional murmur of desultory conversation from the great chamber, and the slap, slap, slap of her small leather soles rang loud in the silence, but it was too late to change her mind now.

Her heart was beating hard when she reached the top and she paused, the sound of her breathing loud in her ears, waiting for one of the women to look out and demand to know what all the noise was about. But no one bothered. Perhaps it was too hot for them to move.

The summer heat was slumped over the city, as it had been all week, and the air was so thick and soupy it was an effort to drag it in for breath. Everyone except Tom and Nell seemed to be seized with a kind of torpor. They moved lethargically, plucking at their collars and wiping the sweat from their foreheads. Even the dogs lying in the dust could barely rouse themselves to bark.

At the top of the stairs, Nell hesitated, one hand on the intricately carved post, before tiptoeing across the threshold of the great hall. She loved this room, so different from her father's cramped hall where despondence seemed to hang next to the cheap painted cloths. Here the walls were covered with richly coloured tapestries, their edges thronging with flowers and birds and insects, the way the hedgerows did in June when the grass grew long and lush and the air was soft and humming with the promise of summer to come. It was Nell's favourite time of year and she couldn't resist reaching out and touching a butterfly. The tapestry rippled beneath her fingers, and the butterfly's wings seemed to beat in flight.

Tom's father was an important man, an alderman, one of the warmest in the city, they said. You could see it in the pewter that gleamed on the cupboards and the Turkey-work carpets spread plush and vibrant on the tables; in the glazed windows and the cushions embroidered with gold thread. You could smell it in the opulent air.

A burst of laughter from the women's chamber along the passage made Nell start just as she heard Tom sing out 'One hundred!' down in the yard.

'I'm coming to ge-et you, Nell Appleby,' he called. 'Ready or not!'

Nell stiffened. She mustn't let herself be diverted. What if Tom came running inside after her? He would find her in an instant.

But then she heard him clatter through the passage below and out into the garth and her shoulders relaxed. So she had read him right. Sidling over to the window, she peered down to see him running towards the stables.

He wouldn't find her there.

That meant she had plenty of time to look for a really good hiding place.

Pleased, Nell turned back to survey the hall, only to still once more at the sound of sharp footsteps in the yard below and a voice calling for ale.

Ralph Maskewe.

Nell wrinkled her nose. She didn't like Ralph, for all his smiles and soft words. Tom's half-brother was tall, and well favoured of shape and countenance. He had a smooth face with a full, red mouth, and a set of strong teeth that were the envy of many. Nell thought they were too big for his mouth. He could barely close his lips over them, and when he smiled, instead of admiring how white they were, Nell found herself remembering the stories old Agnes, her father's servant, would tell about ghoulies and ghosties and bones in the moonlight. She avoided him whenever she could.

She strained to hear what was going on in the yard below. There was a mumble in response to Ralph's shout – doubtless Joan sliding shyly out of the kitchen. What if Ralph wanted her to bring the ale up to the hall?

Nell bit her knuckle, thinking. She didn't want Ralph to find her there alone. But if she scuttled back down to the yard, Tom would be bound to find her straight away and he would crow like a cock on a dung heap again. She was only a little maid, but just once she would like to beat him.

Besides, she might meet Ralph on the stairs. Better to stay where she was.

Behind the turned chair? In the corner beside the cupboard? She could squeeze into the shadowy space, and if she stayed very still, no one would notice her.

Or there was Mr Maskewe's closet in the far

corner of the hall. The door stood invitingly ajar. It was almost as if it was beckoning her inside.

Even more than the hall, the closet was a special room. It was for men's business. It was not a place for small children.

Tom would never think of looking for her in there.

The telltale creak of the fifth stair decided her. Ralph was coming up. Scurrying over to the closet door, Nell peered around it. The room was empty, waiting. She could hear the drone of a fly and the murmur of women's voices from the suffocating chamber along the passage where the babe lay, but otherwise there was silence.

The closet held a table, upon which sat a gilded leather writing box and a heavy ledger in which Mr Maskewe kept his accounts. Next to the table stood a chair and a stool. And a long cypress chest, a kist bought at the same time as the new wainscot that covered the walls. Tom had whispered to Nell that the wainscot had been put up to hide a priest hole, but Nell thought he was making that up to seem important. She couldn't see any sign of a door in the walls. Besides, Mr Maskewe was an alderman, and attended divine service for all to see. Mistress Maskewe was less often seen in church, it was true, but why would Tom's father go to such trouble and expense to indulge his wife?

Of course, if it *were* true, the priest hole would be an excellent place to hide. Tom would never find her there. A gleam of excitement bloomed on Nell's face. She had already forgotten Ralph. She pushed the door open wider, but just as she went to step inside, horror dropped over her like a net, pinning her to the threshold. For a moment she couldn't breathe with it, but the room looked just as it did before, panelled, still. The casement window was wedged open in the vain hope of allowing in some air to stir the heavy heat, and she could make out the sounds of Tom searching for her in the outhouses.

'I know you're in there,' he called, snatching open a door.

The horror lifted from her mind as suddenly as it had gripped her, and she stepped inside the room, shaking the feeling aside as she smirked at the idea that she had got the better of him at last.

The smell of freshly cut wood thickened the hot air. It was a smell Nell associated with the Maskewe house, where there were always new rooms, new furniture, new cladding on the walls. Unlike her father's house, where everything was old and worn.

The desk drew her towards it. Daringly, she opened the writing box, intrigued by its cunning little cubby holes and by the special places for the inkpot and quill. The ledger was almost as tall as Nell herself, and almost as heavy, she guessed. Tentatively, she put her hands on either side of the book and tried to lift it, but her face reddened with the effort and she let it fall back on the table with a dull thud. She had to make do with lifting the cover instead, and peering at the columns of figures. She wished that she could read better. Her stepmother was teaching her, but she was still not as good as Tom, who went to school to learn his ABC.

The thought of Tom, who was a year older and better than her at almost everything, reminded Nell of her task. She had to find the perfect hiding place. She tried to imagine where she would put a priest hole, but she had little knowledge of such things. Her father and stepmother didn't hold with the old faith the way some did and had no need to hide a priest.

She spread her small hands over the wainscot and felt her way around the room, but she could find no sign of a secret door. Absorbed in her task as she was, the stillness of the closet started to make her uneasy after a while. It was as if she had stepped into a different world, cut off from the women passing the baby between them in the chamber down the hall and the servants laughing in the kitchen below, far from the street outside and the city that was all she had ever known. Distant even from Tom down in the garden, kicking the woodhouse door in frustration.

Her hands fell from the panelling and she stood very still. Only her eyes moved around the room, from the chest to the window to the desk where the massive ledger sat, and as she looked, there was a strange ringing in her ears and a whirling in her head; the light shifted and shivered, and in place of the wainscot were shelves filled with tiny, narrow books. Where the table had stood was now a truckle bed of some kind, its coverlet so oddly coloured and patterned that Nell blinked. A black cat was curled up on it, but when she stepped towards it, it lifted its head to stare at her with great yellow eyes before its ears flattened in fright and it leapt from the bed.

A movement behind Nell made her swing round with a gasp, but there was nothing there, and when she looked back, the cat had vanished, along with the shelves and the bed. It was all gone.

Puzzled, a little giddy, she stared at the desk, the ledger, the new wainscot on the walls. Everything was as it should be. She must have imagined it, Nell decided, but she felt jolted and on edge until a crash and a screech from below snapped her firmly back to the present.

'Tom Maskewe! You get out of my kitchen, you rascal! Them were my apples stewing for tonight!'

Fat Peg. Nell spared Tom a grimace of sympathy. He would be lucky if he escaped with a buffet to his ear. If he had any sense, he would slip out of the kitchen while he could, and that meant he would soon be on his way upstairs.

Reminded of the game, Nell looked around the room. She would have to give up on the idea of the priest hole, she decided reluctantly, and find somewhere else to hide. But where?

Her eye fell on the kist. It would be too small for him, but she would be able to squeeze inside. *I give up*. She couldn't wait to hear Tom say it. How sweet it would be! He would grind his teeth and scowl, but he would have to say the words, and then she would spring out of the chest and he would have to admit that she, Nell Appleby, was cleverer than him.

It was too delightful a prospect to resist. Nell hauled up the lid of the chest. It was heavier than she had imagined, but when she peered inside, there were just a few papers at the bottom.

There was a moment of foreboding, a darkness flitting across her mind, but she pushed it aside as she climbed into the chest, and let the lid lower over her. It was dark inside the box, and the smell of new wood was very strong. It was stoutly made, with hardly any chinks.

At first she was so pleased with herself for finding such a good hiding place that she didn't mind the closeness, but it wasn't long before she began to feel stifled. It was even hotter than before. Nell shifted around in the chest, wriggling to ease the laces in her bodice. A pin from her sleeve had come loose and was sticking into her. She wished Tom would hurry up and admit that he couldn't find her.

Straining to listen, she heard him clatter up the stairs at last, and then the sharp chiding of the women. She smiled. She didn't get caught. She wondered how long it would take Tom to think to look in his father's closet. He wouldn't believe she would dare.

Footsteps nearby made her still, and she felt a flicker of pride in him for finding her so quickly. Perhaps he thought she was braver than she had imagined.

Brave? Foolish more like! Tom would say, she knew. She could practically hear him saying it, picture his expression exactly. For all he was son to one of the wealthiest merchants in York, Tom looked like an urchin, or so his mother was always telling him. He was scrawny and scrappy, but Nell liked his face, homely as it was. He had springy hair that never lay flat and bright eyes that looked out on the world with such keen interest that it didn't matter that he was less handsome than his older brother Ralph.

The footsteps paused, and for no reason Nell could put her finger on, her smile faded in the darkness. These footsteps were too stealthy. Tom didn't move like that. Tom was eager and noisy. He clattered and ran. He didn't put his shoes carefully down on the rush matting, one after the other.

All at once, Nell wished she hadn't got into the chest. She was hot and uncomfortable and bored of the game. What did it matter if Tom always won, after all? But she couldn't get out now until the owner of the footsteps had gone. If anyone other than Tom found out she had been in the closet, there would be trouble. Tom's father was quick to beat him. Nell might not want Tom to win, but she didn't want him to suffer for her clever choice either.

She was still fretting when the whole chest jumped as a heavy weight was dumped on the lid without warning. Nell sucked in a breath of fright at the thump of it against the wood and without thinking she pushed at the lid with the flat of her hands. It wouldn't budge, and panic scuttled through her.

'I'm in here!' she shouted, careless of being found out now. She wanted to get out. She *needed* to get out, right now. 'Let me out!'

There was no reply.

The weight on the lid was pressing the darkness around her face, pressing it onto her chest so that she couldn't breathe. Dread blocked her throat.

'Let me out!' she tried again. 'Help me!' But her voice was thin and when she cried out, the sound was muffled by the box and the wainscot in the room beyond. The women along the passage couldn't hear her. Tom couldn't hear her.

But surely whoever had put the weight on the chest could hear her?

'Tom!' Terror pushed a real scream from her throat now. 'Tom, help me!'

Her fists beat frantically at the wooden lid. She had to get out or she would die in this box. If she died, she would never see Tom again. Never lift her face to the sky or run to her father to rub her cheek against his whiskery beard. Never wake to the sound of the city or watch the sunlight ripple over the river or juggle a hot pie between her fingers. Nell normally scorned to weep but now she was gasping and gulping as the tears came and she thrashed her head from side to side.

'Please,' she whimpered. 'Please, please, please.' But the darkness only tightened inexorably around her and soon she wasn't thinking about pies or Tom, or anything but the need to get out of the chest. Her hands were raw. She was suffocating, gulping for air, drumming her heels on the end of the box. It was a perfect-sized coffin for a seven-year-old girl. They could bury her in it and save themselves the trouble of sewing her a shroud.

Oh, she would be good always if only someone would find her! She would say her prayers every day and sit still and not be pert. But first she had to breathe.

Nell was crying seriously now, so loudly that she didn't hear the footsteps coming back, didn't hear the weight being lifted from the lid. She was beside herself with terror.

'Mamma!' she cried, forgetting that her mother had been dead these two years.

'Nell!' Through the harsh labour of her breath, Nell heard Tom calling for her, but he was too far away. He wouldn't have heard her.

'Eleanor!' It was her stepmother's voice now, taut with impatience. 'Eleanor, where are you?'

'Here, here, I'm here!' Nell was choking and gasping, too weak to scream.

Her stepmother was still complaining. 'Where has that girl gone? God's bodkin, that child is nothing but trouble.'

'Wait, I heard something!' That was Tom.

'Tom, Tom!' Feebly Nell banged against the lid, but she was barely whispering by then.

The next instant the lid was thrown open, and she arched out of the chest in search of air, an arrow released from a bow, dragging in a desperate, ragged breath, and then another, and another, not even aware of the shocked exclamations, needing only the sweetness of air.

'Eleanor!' Her stepmother bustled forward. 'You foolish child! What are you doing in that chest?'

Ungently she hauled Nell out of the kist, but Nell was still frantically gulping in air and didn't care what happened as long as they let her breathe. She caught a glimpse of Tom's white, shocked face and that brought her back to herself more than her stepmother's scolding.

'Couldn't ... couldn't get out...' she stammered.

'Why didn't you just push the lid? It's not that heavy.'

'Somebody put something on it.' Nell was bent

over, gasping and choking still, but a quality in Tom's silence made her look up. 'Didn't you see?'

'There was nothing on the chest,' he said at last.

'But I heard him!' Tears of frustration filled her eyes. She looked around the room and spied the heavy ledger on the desk. 'That! He put that on the chest! He knew I was in there, and he put it on so I couldn't get out.'

Tom looked horrified. 'Who did?'

'I don't know. I couldn't see. But I heard him. I did!'

'Nonsense!' Her stepmother was brushing her down efficiently. 'Who would do such a thing? You just frightened yourself, you beetle-headed child! I'm not surprised you imagined things, stuck in a dark box.'

Was that all it had been? Nell looked at the ledger and tried to remember where it had been on the desk when she came in, but her mind hurt with the effort of it. It had moved, she was sure it had, but how could she remember now when her breath was still coming in hoarse rasps and her heart was galloping in her chest? The more she tried to remember, the more her memory slipped and slithered away. The truth was, she couldn't be certain.

There was a splinter in her palm and her fingers stung where she had hammered at the lid.

'What in the name of Our Lady were you thinking to get in there in the first place?' Anne Appleby went on. Having satisfied herself that her stepdaughter was in one piece, her mind was running on to how to explain to Henry Maskewe that his papers were crushed by Nell's panic. Her husband had obligations to Mr Maskewe. They couldn't afford to alienate him. Why else would she be here, attending his wife in childbed on a day like this? She had business enough in her own home.

Anne's mouth tightened as she looked at Nell in exasperation. The child was a hoyden and no amount of beating seemed to quench her spirit. Everything about her was unruly: the thick coppery hair that curled out irrepressibly from under her cap, the freckles on her snub nose, the wilful gleam in her green eyes. Anne had done her best to teach her husband's daughter to be obedient and demure, but Eleanor seemed possessed by an unchristian energy. Get the child to sit still, but yet she simmered, ready to burst into action the moment she took her eyes off her. It was very unrestful.

She had a good heart, Anne could see that, but this latest escapade would have to be punished. Her husband was inclined to be indulgent of his only daughter, but Anne had their future to think of. They needed Mr Maskewe's good opinion, and Nell's friendship with Tom Maskewe could not be allowed to undo it.

'We were playing,' Nell answered hoarsely. Her throat was burning as she heaved in one delicious, agonizing breath after another.

'You were told not to get into trouble.' Anne clicked her tongue. 'Why can you not play quietly like good children?'

Nell and Tom didn't bother to answer this.

'I'm sorry, Mother,' Nell tried after a moment.

'Sorry is as sorry does,' Anne snapped back. She looked anxiously at the crushed rolled documents at the bottom of the chest. 'Now what is to be done?'

'Is there a problem?'

They all swung round to see Ralph Maskewe in the doorway. He was smiling, but Nell found herself shrinking from the sight of all those teeth. Instinctively, she drew towards Tom and slipped her hand into his.

Her stepmother explained that the children had been playing a game. 'I fear your father will not be pleased to hear that Eleanor came into his closet. She knows better, but you know what children are...'

If she hoped Ralph would let the matter go, she was disappointed. The smile evaporated and he looked grave. 'I will send for my father,' he said.

Recalled from his warehouse, Tom's father was in a black mood. 'What's this?' he demanded, his gaze darting round the closet and his brows snapping together at the sight of the open chest.

Nell and Tom had scrambled to their feet at his approach and were standing with their heads hung. It was Ralph who explained the situation this time.

'By cock!' Henry Maskewe roared at Tom when he was done. 'Is there no end to the trouble you will put me to, boy?' He pulled a switch from his doublet and tested it against his hand. 'Come here, Thomas.'

Nell quailed but she couldn't let Tom take the blame. 'It was not Tom's fault,' she protested, her voice quavering as she stepped forward. 'You should punish me, not him.'

'No, Nell, it was my idea to play hide-and-seek,' said Tom, stepping ahead of her and holding out his hand.

'Tom, no, you didn't come in here!'

'Since you're both so happy to share the punishment, I'm happy to oblige,' growled Henry Maskewe.

'But sir–' Tom started to protest.

'Enough!' His father snarled at him. 'How many times have you been told not to come into the closet? It is not a place for children, as this brat should know too. And as for you, madam,' he added with a glare at Anne Appleby, 'I suggest you teach your daughter better manners than to go poking around in other people's houses!'

'Indeed, I am sorry for her behaviour.' Anne swallowed her humiliation with a resentful glance at Nell. 'She will be punished, you can be sure.'

'I will punish her now since she is so ready for it. Step forward, girl.'

Exchanging a look with Tom, Nell lifted her chin and took a step towards Mr Maskewe, but her legs were not very long and she had to take three more before she stood before him.

'Hold out your hand.'

She swallowed but did as he told her. Her palms were still torn and red from the chest, but she knew better than to resist.

Beside Mr Maskewe, Ralph stood alert. He was watching Nell avidly, his pale eyes gleaming, and she knew without being told that he was enjoying this. She looked away, taking her bottom lip between her teeth as she braced herself. The pain that already clamoured in her hands was nothing compared to what was to come.

The switch sliced through the air with a rushing noise and lashed her palm. In spite of herself, her body jerked, but she wouldn't let herself cry. That would be letting Tom down.

Swish, sting. Swish, sting. There were great red weals across her palm, and Nell's face was screwed up with the effort of not whimpering at the pain of it.

Swish, sting. Swish, sting. Swish, sting.

Five strikes and it was done. Nell's knees were unsteady as Mr Maskewe made a noise of disgust and waved her away.

Stepping back, she caught Ralph's eye again and this time he smiled, showing those big, even teeth. Perhaps it was meant to be a smile of sympathy. To anyone watching, it might indeed seem so, but that was not sympathy Nell saw in his eyes. She might only be seven but she knew pleasure, and excitement, when she saw it.

Tom was beaten too. He set his mouth and he didn't say a word, but Nell could see how it hurt him. Her hands throbbed in sympathy.

This was her fault. Guilt made it too hard to look any more and she shifted her gaze to Ralph instead. She watched him watching his brother. Something ran over his face whenever Tom flinched, something convulsive and unpleasant that she couldn't put a name to, but which made her shudder, and when he glanced her way and smiled again, she could tell that he knew she had understood his expression and he didn't care. For who would ever believe her? And what could she say anyway? *I don't like the way he looked when Tom was being beaten?* She was a girl, and he was sixteen, the elder son of the house, and his father's favourite. Ralph was always being held up as a model for Tom to follow.

At last it was done, and Tom's hands were as red and painful as her own. 'I've had enough of trying to tame you,' Henry Maskewe told his son. 'You are eight now. Old enough to put off childish games like this. It's time you had other things on your mind. I spoke to William Todd the other day. He is willing to take you as his apprentice. Perhaps when you have work to do, you will be less trouble.'

Nell was taken home in disgrace.

Their house lay across the street in Stonegate. Nell was desolate. Her hands hurt, but worse was the thought that Tom would be her playmate no more. He was happy at the thought of going to Mr Todd's, she knew. William Todd was a merchant adventurer and did business overseas. If Tom did well, he could go on a ship, just as he had always wanted to do.

And she would be left alone.

Nell couldn't remember a time when Tom wasn't there. They knew the back ways into each other's houses, how to slip in and out without being seen and given a job to do. Together, they had run out through the bar or over the crumbling city walls to the crofts and the common beyond. They had jumped over gutters and splashed in the river and listened wide-eyed to the stories of the mariners down on the staithes. To Nell, they had played and fought together forever, and even though Tom was a stupid boy at times, she could not conceive of life without him.

But now, it seemed, she must.

Everything was changing, she thought, scuffing her shoes miserably against the cobbles and earning herself a cuff of reprimand from Anne. After her mother's death, her father had been too stricken with grief to care what she did and Nell had got used to running free. But a year ago, he remarried, and her stepmother made it her business to take both her husband and his daughter in hand. Nell had no objection to her stepmother as such, except that Anne was set on curbing her freedoms. She talked endlessly of proper behaviour, and reputation. She wanted Nell to sit still and silent, not run and jump as she was wont to do with Tom.

Now Anne was increasing. Her father hoped for a son, and Nell hoped that it would take her stepmother's mind off her, but today she had succeeded in capturing her attention once more.

'Your father has been too indulgent with you,' Anne chided as they crossed the street. Stonegate was divided into blocks of light and shade, with a narrow strip of sunlight laid between the gutters. When Nell looked up, she could see a thin slice of fierce blue between the jostling gables, and she screwed up her eyes, blinded by the contrast of dazzling light and the deep shade beneath the overhanging jetties. Normally the shade would be cool, but it had been hot for so long that the heat had crept into the darkest corners and there was no relief anywhere.

Splatters of horse dung had dried to crisp

trenchers on the street. Clouds of flies hovered over a dead pigeon and, without rain for so long, the gutters were clogged with weeds and dead leaves, with nettles and filthy straw and other ramell that rotted with the rubbish, their combined stench mingling with the stink of the festering cesspits. The inhabitants of Stonegate prided themselves on their street, but the heat had been so wearisome for so long that each complained about the state of their neighbours' doors without rousing themselves to clear their own.

'Something should be done about it.' Nell had heard her stepmother grumbling to her father. 'You must speak to the chamberlains again. What if the sickness comes?'

Nell didn't care about the pestilence or about the smell. She wished only to be out of her stiff skirts and scratchy cap. If only she could strip down to her shift and paddle in the river the way Tom did sometimes.

The thought of Tom reminded her of that day's news and her heart sank. Her stepmother was still talking, her hands spread against her hips to support her swollen belly.

'He has let you run wild like a heathen, and what is the result? Mr Maskewe is angered, who must be kept sweet. Your father already owes him too much,' Anne fretted, pushing Nell before her, past the shop with its stall and tattered pentice and down the narrow passage to the yard.

'I will be confined soon, and there will be no one to mind you again. You will have to help with your new brother or sister, and then you will go into service like Tom. Your father will find a family where you can learn how to go on when I do not have the time to teach you.'

Nell brightened. 'Can I go to Mr Todd's too and be in service with Tom?' She wouldn't mind that.

Anne sighed. 'You must learn to live without Tom, Eleanor.'

'But he is my friend!'

'You will have other friends. Maids like yourself. You'll soon forget Tom when you don't see him every day.'

Nell's face darkened. 'I won't!'

'We all have to do things we don't want to do,' snapped Anne, impatient with her stepdaughter's show of temper. 'Even you, Eleanor.'

'I'll never forget Tom.' Nell set her chin and shook her head stubbornly. 'Never, never, never!' She looked at her stepmother and her green eyes were bright with defiance. 'Never,' she said.

Chapter Two

York, present day

'I can't believe you're going to live here!' Vanessa stood in the doorway of the kitchen and looked around her with distaste. 'It's a horrible flat. Dark and poky and dingy. Ugh.'

'It's characterful,' said Tess, determinedly unpacking pasta and milk and not looking at the stained sink or grubby tiles.

'It's dirty!'

'Then I'll clean it.' Tess kept her voice even, the way she had learnt to do when she was talking to Martin. The thought of him snagged in her mind, caught on the barbed wire of memory, and she shook it free. She didn't need to be careful now. She could say what she thought. The realization still caught her unawares sometimes, making her giddy with a strange combination of relief and apprehension. It was so long since she had been able to open her mouth without thinking that she wasn't quite sure what to do with her newly found freedom.

No more gauging a mood before she spoke. No more quick readjustment of her opinions in response to a drawing together of Martin's brows. The slightest tightening of his lips could set her mind scrambling for a way out of the conversation without provoking him further.

'I like it,' she told Vanessa for the thrill of disagreeing, although the truth was that she had been dismayed when she unlocked the door at the top of the narrow stairs and let herself in. The flat felt different without Richard's cheerfully chaotic presence. Before, it had seemed cosy and comfortable, the perfect refuge, but now the air smelt stale, sour, and the warm tranquillity she had liked so much when Richard showed her round had evaporated into an uneasy silence.

It wouldn't be silent when Oscar was here, she reminded herself. All it needed was a good airing. It would be fine. She *would* like it.

Vanessa pulled the scrunchie from her hair, bent over, shook her head and then tied the glossy mass back in a ponytail, all in one practised move. She had the intimidating glow of an exercise addict and was as slim and sparklingly pretty as she had been when they were at school. Next to her, Tess always felt drab and limp, and although she was glad to have a friend again, it was impossible not to feel suffocated sometimes by Vanessa's insistence on helping her do everything.

Tess wanted to manage by herself. Nobody seemed to think that she would be able to, and how could she prove them wrong when Vanessa kept sweeping in and taking over?

'Seriously, Tess, I think you're making a mistake,' Vanessa said now as she smoothed the last strands back from her face. 'Stonegate is no place to live with a child. It might be picturesque, but it's noisy and there are tourists everywhere and you won't have proper neighbours and there's nowhere to park.'

'I don't have a car.' Frustration feathered Tess's voice, but Vanessa didn't notice.

'Yes, and look what a hassle it's been just bringing some shopping in,' she said. 'I'd never live on a pedestrianized street like this. You've got to wait until cars are allowed in, sit for hours behind delivery vans, park on the pavement…'

A sense of despair, all too familiar, began to wash over Tess but she brushed it aside. She was grateful to her friend, of course she was, but she could have got a taxi from her mother's as planned. It was Vanessa who had insisted on helping her move in, and in the end, it had been easier just to give in than to argue.

As it had always been with Martin.

Humiliation bloomed under Tess's skin, and she felt herself redden as she turned away to put the milk in the fridge.

How many times do I have to tell you? The milk should be kept in the door of the fridge, Theresa, with the label facing the front. It's simple enough. Even you should be able to remember that.

Why hadn't she laughed at Martin when he insisted on something so petty? Surely a new wife should have been able to tease her husband out of a mood? But it hadn't seemed to matter much at first. Tess didn't care which way round the milk faced, but if it was important to Martin, why not do as he asked?

Besides, she had adored him. She had wanted to make him happy. He was so attractive, so tender, so loving. He told her she was beautiful. He made her *feel* beautiful. He made her feel safe. For a while it had been lovely to be cossetted. He said he wanted to look after her and that they would be together forever. Overlooking a few foibles about the arrangement of the fridge hadn't seemed too much to ask of her in return.

But the fridge had been just the beginning.

Defiantly, Tess put the pints of milk on the shelf and turned them to face in different directions. *What a rebel*, she thought to herself.

'I don't need a car,' she told Vanessa.

'What about Oscar?'

'People managed to get around perfectly well before cars were invented, Vanessa,' she said, trying not to show her annoyance. 'Oscar is quite capable of walking to school. It'll be good for him.'

'It's not just school. It's after-school clubs and swimming and music lessons and football practice and sleepovers... Believe me, I've been through all this with Sam. You've got no idea!'

Tess pulled a packet of cereal out of the carrier bag and set it on the counter, only just managing to stop herself straightening it. Vanessa had never liked being argued with, she remembered. Even at school it had been easier just to let her have her own way. Tess had been grateful for her friendship then, scarcely able to believe that the coolest girl in the class would take a shy, gawky girl like Tess under her wing.

Until Luke. Vanessa hadn't been pleased when Tess refused to listen to sense and it had taken Tess's ignominious return to York more than a decade later for all to be forgiven. Proved right about Luke as about so much else, it again seemed that there was nothing Vanessa wouldn't do for her.

As long as Tess did it Vanessa's way.

Tess had only just escaped from doing it Martin's way. This time, she wanted to do it her own way.

Vanessa had been a huge help since her return, Tess couldn't deny that. She had helped sort out a school, a doctor, all the red tape of moving and claiming child support. She looked after Oscar whenever Tess needed time on her own and he was always happy to play with her two children, Sam and Rosie. She made Tess feel welcome and wanted, and took her away from the disappointment that simmered in the air in Tess's own mother's house.

Tess hated feeling ungrateful, hated the creeping guilt of it and the familiar, awful doubt as to whether *she* was the one being unreasonable. Martin had been very good at making her feel that until the resentment that built up inside her corroded everything. She didn't want to feel the same about her old friend.

Frowning a little, not liking the way her thoughts were going, Tess carried on unpacking. Peanut butter, jam, bread. Eggs and cheese. There would be time enough to try and get some fresh vegetables down Oscar. For now it would be enough for the two of them to be alone, away from her baffled mother's resentment.

Away from Martin.

Doing it her own way.

'Oscar's only five,' she pointed out at last. 'I don't need to think about any of that just yet.'

'Well, I think you're mad!'

A wry smile touched the corner of Tess's mouth. 'Funny, that's exactly what Mum says.'

Her mother couldn't understand it. 'I don't know how you can leave Martin,' she complained at least once a day. 'A charming husband who adores you ... plenty of money ... a lovely house in London ... what more could you possibly want, Theresa?'

Tess had tried to explain, but Susan Frankland would not be consoled over the humiliating return of the daughter whose wealthy and successful husband she had boasted so much about over the years. She took Tess's new status as a single mother with a failed marriage as a personal affront. It had been a long two weeks before Richard

Landrow went off on research leave and handed over the key to his flat.

Now Tess looked down at the empty carrier bags that she was automatically folding into neat squares, and deliberately scrumpled them up into a ball so that she could toss them in the bin. Drawing a breath, she turned back to Vanessa.

'This is a fresh start for me, Van,' she tried to explain. 'The flat's perfect as far as I'm concerned. Come on,' she went on quickly before Vanessa could argue further, 'I'll show you round.'

Vanessa, proud owner of a new four-bedroom executive home, was unimpressed by the front room. 'It's going to be noisy,' she said, wandering over to the bay window that jutted out over the street and craning her head to look down at the tourists thronging Stonegate. 'It's bad enough now, but think what it'll be like when the pubs close!'

Tess thought about the immaculate house in Chiswick where silence clung to her face and the long days trembled with tension.

'It's just people. I don't mind a bit of noise.'

Vanessa turned to survey the room. 'Can you get rid of all these books while you're here? It's all a bit dreary, isn't it?'

It *was* dreary, but Tess wasn't going to admit it.

Vanessa wanted her to move into a house on the same estate as her. 'It'd be much handier for babysitting if you live nearby,' she had tried to persuade Tess. 'Oscar can play with Sam and Rosie and you know Graham and I would always be there for you.' Richard's flat wasn't her idea, so she wasn't going to like it.

My decision, my way, Tess reminded herself as she pushed open one of the top windows to let in some air. Some sunshine would have been nice but it had been an unseasonably cold May and outside a fine mizzle was dampening the paving stones. Perhaps it was the grey sky that was making the room feel so oppressive.

It certainly wasn't the books. 'I'm keeping the books,' she told Vanessa, picking up a Latin dictionary and riffling through it. It had been so long since she had worked on any documents it was going to take some time to get her eye in again. 'I'll be needing them anyway.'

'Oh, yes. Your job.'

Tess set her teeth. She could hear the virtual inverted commas Vanessa put around the last word. The job hadn't been Vanessa's idea either, but for Tess, living with her disappointed mother, transcribing and translating the sixteenth-century assize court records that had been recently unearthed in the city's archives was a dream assignment. The dapper Richard Landrow had supervised her MA dissertation at Warwick. After Tess had graduated he'd taken up a professorship a York and she had kept in contact with him until her marriage. Martin hadn't liked her talking about her life before she met him, and Tess had lost touch with Richard, like so many other friends. But he had been easy to find again when she moved back to York and she had emailed him for advice about using her old skills. Typically generous, Richard had responded straight away. It had been strange seeing him in York, but when he'd offered her the job, it had been a lifeline.

Tess had worked it all out. Together with tax credits and child benefit, the hourly rate Richard could pay for research assistance meant that she could survive financially. Nearing retirement now, he had a research grant for a year to work on a new book on Tudor crime and criminality, and was going to base himself in London. Tess, he said, could have his flat for free in return for looking after his beloved cat, Ashrafar.

'She'd hate London,' he said, and I don't want strangers in here.'

'Are you sure?' she had asked, hardly able to believe her luck.

'Of course I'm sure. There's plenty of room for you and your little boy. It suits me very well – and it's high time you used that brain of yours again.'

'It's the perfect job for me,' she told Vanessa as she had before. 'I can work from photographs and do it all at home. Reading documents is what I'm trained for, after all. Besides, it's fascinating stuff.'

'If you say so.'

More daunted by her friend's lack of enthusiasm than she wanted to admit, Tess put down the dictionary and brushed her hands on her jeans. 'Come and see the rest of the flat,' she said, determinedly cheerful.

She was hoping that the other rooms would be as charmingly quirky as she remembered them, but the sense of disquiet that had prickled in the front room only grew stronger as she led Vanessa along the narrow book-lined passage. The flat was on the first floor above a gift shop, and it stretched long and thin back from the street. The other rooms overlooked a dingy yard, and even on the brightest of days would get little light. Tess couldn't imagine how it had all seemed so cheerful before. Richard had left all his furniture, all his books and pictures. Nothing had changed.

'You should swap these light bulbs,' Vanessa said, flicking at the overhead shade in what would be Oscar's room. 'You can't see a thing with so few watts.' She shivered. 'It's cold too. It's like winter in here.'

Tess was finding it hard to keep sounding positive. She looked around the room dubiously. 'I suppose I could get him an electric radiator. I can hardly put the heating on in May! The trouble is, these old houses don't get much light. The gloominess is part of their charm,' she said, as she closed the door and showed Vanessa the spartan bathroom.

'Charm?' said Vanessa, missing Tess's lame attempt at humour. She cast a disparaging glance at the clawfoot tub with its rusty stains under the taps. 'Right.' She withdrew her head. 'How old is this place anyway?'

'I'm not sure.' Tess reached out to run her fingers down an exposed beam but the touch of the old wood sent a tiny shock darting through her and she jerked her hand back.

Puzzled, she shook her wrist to relieve the sensation. Since when did wood give you an electric shock? 'I'm not an architectural historian, but I'd say that most of this is sixteenth-century,' she said, eyeing the lumpy walls but not touching them. Her whole arm was still tingling. 'The facade is probably later. Seventeenth or eighteenth century, maybe. Of course, Stonegate's been one of the most important streets in York since Roman times, so it's more than likely there's been a house here since then.'

'You're kidding!'

'Not like this – there's always been renovation and rebuilding – but on this site; yes, I'd say so.'

Vanessa gave an exaggerated shiver. 'It would give me the creeps to live somewhere this old.'

'I like it,' said Tess, forcing a smile to her voice. Trying to make herself sound as if she did. And she *had* liked it before. 'History's my thing, remember, and it's not as if I believe in ghosts.'

She broke off at the involuntary twitch between her shoulder blades. 'This is Richard's study,' she said quickly, opening the next door to distract Vanessa from the silly little shudder that had wriggled down her spine.

'Oh my God!' Vanessa stared, aghast, at the piles of books covering the floor. 'What happened?'

Tess couldn't help smiling at her expression. 'The floor's so uneven that Richard had to wedge all his bookshelves against the wall with paper, but he's finally given in and arranged for a joiner to come in and build him some proper shelves while he's away. The walls are so wonky that it's going to be quite a job.' She tapped her forehead. 'I mustn't forget that he's coming in. Richard's given him a key so he can let himself in and out.'

'Do you think that's a good idea?' said Vanessa. 'He could be anybody!'

'Richard wouldn't have given his keys to a serial killer, Vanessa!'

'You don't always know,' Vanessa said darkly.

'You can't tell what people are really like when you first meet them.'

Tess's smile faded. She thought about Martin as he had seemed at first. Golden, glowing, dazzling her with his good looks and his charm and his romantic gestures. A fairy-tale hero to sweep her off her feet and adore her forever.

Should she have suspected that there was a dark side behind all that light and lustre?

'I know,' she said.

Abruptly she turned and led the way down to the very end of the passage. 'This is my room.'

She pushed open the door and a black cat that had been curled up on the bed lifted its head as if affronted by the interruption, only to flatten its ears and shoot off the bed and out past their ankles. At the same moment, a cold, clammy wall of despair seemed to heave away from the walls and roll over Tess, making her gag with the horror of it.

'God, that gave me a fright!' Vanessa patted her chest. 'Where on earth did that cat come fr–' She broke off as she caught sight of Tess's white face. 'Are you OK? Tess?' she added after a moment when Tess didn't reply.

The ghastly feeling receded, sucked away like a tide, leaving Tess trembling. Drawing a shaky breath, she licked her lips. 'I'm ... fine,' she managed, but she kept a hand to her throat, where her heart was still pounding.

'I nearly had a fit when that cat bolted too,' said Vanessa. 'I just wasn't expecting it.'

It hadn't been the cat. Tess forced herself to look around the room, moving her head very cautiously in case that horrible sensation rolled over her again, but there was nothing there. It was just a room. Everything was as it should be. A double bed, covered in a colourful counterpane. A chest of drawers set into what had once been a deep fireplace. More shelves crammed with tatty paperbacks. A wardrobe with a wad of newspaper stuck under the legs on one side to counteract the uneven floor. All exactly as Richard had shown her the other day.

She even looked up, half-expecting to see something slimy and unpleasant looming, but there were only the exposed beams and plaster and an old-fashioned lampshade hanging precariously low and badly in need of a dust.

You're highly strung, Theresa. Wasn't that what Martin was always telling her? *You imagine things. I sometimes think you live in a fantasy world.*

Carefully, Tess cleared her throat. Let Vanessa think she had been spooked by the cat.

'That was Richard's cat. Ashrafar.'

'*Ashrafar?*' Vanessa echoed disapprovingly. 'What kind of name is that?'

'I've no idea. When I asked Richard why he'd called her that, he just smirked.' She was beginning to feel a bit steadier. Of course there was nothing there.

Now that the sensation of dread had gone, Tess could hear a faint sound, somewhere between a scrape and a thud, reverberating around the room. Something about it made her nerves twitch and tense. 'What's that noise?' she asked Vanessa, who was fussily brushing cat hairs from the bedcover and tutting at the mess.

'What noise?'

Tess opened her mouth to describe it but was interrupted by the unmistakable whine of a drill starting up on the other side of the wall and her shoulders slumped with a disproportionate sense of relief.

What did you think it was, Tess?

'Oh, yes. Richard said they were doing up the house next door.' She had to raise her voice over the sound of the drilling until they could close the door behind them.

'For heaven's sake, Tess,' said Vanessa, heading back to the front door. 'This place is dingy and dirty and a *dump!* You've got to share it with an unknown joiner and a filthy cat, and to top it off, you've got builders next door so you won't be able to hear yourself think! Why don't you get somewhere decent?'

Because that's what you *want me to do. This time I'm doing what* I *want to do.*

Tess bit down on the words. 'Because I can't afford it,' she said evenly instead.

The door of the flat opened straight onto a steep flight of stairs that led down to the nondescript street door. Vanessa was right: it was dingy. Richard was interested in his records. He didn't care about his surroundings. He'd bought the flat when he moved to York and Tess suspected he hadn't done anything to improve it.

But she had made the decision and she was going to stick by it.

'Besides,' she said as Vanessa gathered up her bag and hunted for her car keys, 'I promised Richard I would stay and look after Ashrafar. If it hadn't been for Richard, I'd still be looking for a job and living with Mum. As it is, I've got a free flat in a great location and I can work at home so I can fit in with picking Oscar up from school. He's thrilled at the idea of having a cat.'

Which was true, Tess reminded herself, wishing that she didn't sound as if she was talking herself into it. Oscar loved animals but Martin wouldn't have them in the house. Once, Tess had steeled herself to suggest that a cat wouldn't be too much trouble.

A cat? Martin's lip had curled in disgust. *Revolting creatures, covered in spit and hair. It's out of the question, Theresa.*

'I feel really lucky,' she told Vanessa. And she *was* lucky. Tess forced herself to shake off the uneasiness she had felt ever since she let herself in. It was nothing a bright day wouldn't cure. 'It's going to be great.'

'Sam and Rosie got a trampoline.'

'Mmm'. Tess wiggled the key into the lock and opened the door so that Oscar could slip under her arm. Since Oscar had met Vanessa's children she had heard a lot about what Sam and Rosie had. 'Sam and Rosie also have a garden. But you know what they *don't* have?' she added quickly, before he could object to the limitations of his new home.

'What?'

'A cat.' It didn't sound much compared to a trampoline, but Tess infused her voice with as much enthusiasm as she could. 'Remember I told you about how we're going to look after Ashrafar?'

Oscar's face lit up. 'Will she sleep on my bed?'

'That's up to her.' There was no point in making promises on behalf of a cat, after all.

Tess was feeling better about the flat. After Vanessa had left, she had finished putting away the shopping. She had opened all the windows in spite of the drizzle, and cleaned the kitchen and the bathroom. She had unpacked the suitcase which held all that she had brought from London. She had made up Oscar's bed, and set Bink, his stuffed monkey, against his pillow so he would see him as soon as he came in. She had set up the two computers she needed to work on the records, and she hadn't let herself think about the way terror and despair had boiled out of nowhere in the back bedroom.

All day she had heard the builders next door: drilling, banging, shouting to each other over the sound of the radio. The ordinariness of the noise was comforting. Tess told herself that she had imagined the atmosphere earlier. It was just part of the strangeness of moving into a new place. The air was not condensed. It was not gathering itself together, bunching as if ready to pounce. There was nothing wrong.

By the time she had left to pick Oscar up from school, she had convinced herself that she had imagined her earlier unease.

'Why don't you go and see if you can find her?' she said to Oscar, helping him out of his jacket which was damp with mizzle. 'Be quiet, though!' she called after him as he turned and charged up the narrow stairs. 'You don't want to frighten her.'

She was smiling, her hands filled with his jacket and his Spiderman lunchbox, as she watched him climb eagerly up to the inner door. One palm was flat against the wall for support, and his sweatshirt was bright in the dingy light of the naked bulb hanging in the hallway. It was good to see him growing in confidence, rushing instead of hanging back timidly the way he had done before.

But just as Oscar reached for the door, foreboding whipped in out of nowhere and grabbed Tess by the throat. The certainty that something terrible awaited her son on the other side of the door pushed a shout of fear from her mouth. '*No!*' she cried, and at the top of the stairs, Oscar spun round on the narrow stair in fright and teetered on the edge.

'No! Wait!' Tess cried again, stumbling up the stairs to catch him before he could fall. 'I mean ... I'm sorry, pip,' she said unsteadily as his mouth trembled. The vision of him tumbling into darkness was still crowding her mind, but she could tell that she was frightening him, and she made herself loosen her grip on his hand. She swallowed. 'It's just ... you can't get in without a key. I'll need to unlock the door.'

Moving the jacket and lunchbox under her arm, she fumbled in her bag for the key. Her fingers shook as she tried to slot it into the door and ignore the voice in her head that was shouting at her to take Oscar and run back down the stairs.

To go where? Back to her mother? Back to Martin? The key was cold, smooth metal between her clenched fingers. Tess made herself take a breath. She was *not* going back. She had been through this. There was nothing bad waiting inside the flat. She was getting spooked by nothing.

You're overimaginative, Martin's voice whispered in her head and she shook it away.

Resolutely, she shoved the key into the lock, turned it and pushed open the door before she could change her mind.

'Here we are,' she said brightly. Too brightly. 'Let's get you some juice and then you can look at–'

She broke off, sucking in a gasp of fright as a figure loomed in the doorway of Richard's study, and she and Oscar both shrank back instinctively against the door.

'Sorry.' The figure stepped into the hallway so that she could see him. 'I didn't mean to frighten you.'

She hadn't seen him for eleven years, but she recognized him straight away.

Clutching the lunchbox and coat in one arm, Tess grabbed hold of Oscar's hand with the other and stared. She couldn't catch her breath. Her heart was still ricocheting off her ribs, her mind scrabbling to deal with the lurch from nameless fear to panic to stunned surprise.

'Luke!' Her voice was thin with shock.

He was tougher now, bigger than she had remembered somehow and more solid, but the shaggy hair and lean, beaky features were the same. It should have been an ugly face with that big nose and those slashing brows but something about the set of his mouth and the sharp intelligence in his eyes made you want to look twice.

'Hello, Tess,' he said.

'Wh-what are you doing here?'

She hated the waver in her voice. It had been impossible not to think of Luke when she came back to York, of course. Memories of him were inscribed on every street corner where she had ever waited for him; in the dull gleam of the river and the slanting shadows beneath the Minster; in every place where being with him had been enough and life had shimmered with possibilities.

Luke was long gone, Tess had known that. He hadn't been able to wait to leave York. Still, she had imagined what it would be like to bump into him again, imagined how cool and composed she would be, how *he* would be the one to stutter and stammer in shock.

She hadn't imagined *this*, the painful jerk of her heart or the swoop of her breath or the jumble in her head. She had wanted to look as if Luke's rejection had been the best thing that had ever happened to her, not drawn and tense and drab, as if every one of her possibilities had long ago disappeared.

Luke's eyes had narrowed at her expression. She must look dreadful, Tess realized. And sound pathetic with her tremulous voice. So much for cool and composed.

'Measuring up for shelves,' he said. 'Didn't Richard tell you?'

'*You're* the joiner?'

At least she managed not to stammer that time, but the sound of her middle-class vowels made her flinch inwardly. Did she always sound that ladi-dah? Martin approved of the way she spoke, but Luke had always teased her about her prim upbringing and her 'affected' voice. He'd always exaggerated his own Yorkshire accent when he talked to her mother, knowing how much it irritated her. Susan Frankland had abhorred his scruffy clothes and unshaven face. No wonder she had been so delighted with Martin, who was always immaculately groomed and wore a suit and tie. Tess looked at the dark stubble prickling Luke's jaw, at the ripped jeans and faded T-shirt, and was obscurely glad to see that he hadn't succumbed to conventionality after all.

'Yeah, I'm a joiner.' His lip still curled in the same defensive way too. 'Is that a problem?'

Oh, God, now she had offended him... Ever-present guilt clutched at Tess's gut, which was still swooping with the shock of seeing him so unexpectedly on top of that strangeness on the stairs. He thought she was sneering, and when she remembered that last bitter exchange, when she had accused him of not wanting to make anything of his life, Tess couldn't quite blame him. Luke wasn't to know just what a mess she had made of her own.

What did he see when he looked at *her?* Was he remembering the awkward girl who had plunged so desperately in love with him, or the one who had slimmed down and smartened up at university, who had opted for convention after all?

Or was he shocked by the way she looked now: brittle thin, with a bruised look under her eyes and the long, dark hair he had loved so much now cut short and choppy?

And why should she care?

'Of course it's not a problem.' Tess let go of Oscar's hand and pressed her fingers against her temple while she struggled to contain her swirling thoughts. 'I'm sorry,' she said after a moment. 'I just moved in this morning. I don't know if I'm coming or going, and I wasn't expecting to see you.'

To her relief the grim expression relaxed very slightly. 'I thought Richard would have warned you.'

'He didn't give me a name. He just said that someone would be here.'

An awkward silence fell. At least, it felt awkward to Tess. Luke seemed unbothered by it, but then it had always been hard to tell exactly what he was thinking.

They appeared to have dealt with the initial misunderstanding, but there were so many more questions swirling in Tess's head that she didn't know where to start. Why had Luke come back to York? What had happened to his determination to be a photojournalist? Had he settled down with a wife and family or was he still restless and impatient? Did he remember her as well as she remembered him? Had he thought about her over the years? What was he thinking now?

If only they could have both laughed at the coincidence and relaxed straight away into do-you-remember? Once she had found him easy to talk to; now she stood stiffly, clutching the lunch-box under one arm and Oscar with the other. Silent and owl-eyed, Oscar had shrunk into her side at the sight of Luke. When Luke looked at him, he hid his face against Tess's stomach and tugged at her jeans.

She bent down to hear what he was saying. 'Speak up, Oscar,' she said. 'And say hello to Luke. He's ... an old friend of mine.'

Oscar only shook his head and clung tighter, whispering something about finding the cat.

Forcing a smile, Tess straightened to look at Luke again. 'Look, Oscar hasn't been here before and it's all new to him.' She sounded brittle, she knew, but at least it was better than quavery. 'I need to get him settled in first. Would you excuse me a minute?'

'Sure.'

'Would you like some tea?'

Amusement flashed in his face at her formal tone and Tess fought the blush that mottled her throat. She might be coming across as an uptight executive's wife, but Luke wouldn't have forgotten a time when there had been no need for politeness.

Anyone would think they had never tugged at each other's clothes, or tumbled frantically onto his bed, never rolled together in the dunes with the North Sea wind brushing sand along the beach. In spite of herself, Tess's blood heated at the memory of how it had been between them. They'd been so different, Luke a biker, playing his bad boy image to the hilt, she the shy solicitor's daughter who'd broken training for a brief, glorious period of rebellion.

Convention had won out in the end, of course, the way Luke had always said it would. He wouldn't be at all surprised to see her now, offering tea with frigid formality, Tess knew. She half-expected him to roll his eyes and tell her to take the stick out of her arse, but he was turning back to work already.

'Sure,' he said again. 'When you're ready. No hurry.'

'Sorry about that.' It was some time before Tess elbowed open the study door, holding two mugs of tea. Luke was leaning over, measuring a skirting board. His T-shirt had ridden up to give her a glimpse of bare back. She could see the bumps in his spine. Martin didn't like to be seen less than immaculately dressed, even by his own wife, and for Tess the sight of Luke's exposed skin felt shockingly intimate now. Hastily, she averted her eyes.

'I had to find the cat. Oscar's been desperate to meet her, and of course she chose now to go out. But fortunately she comes when you shake her biscuit box, and she let him stroke her, so he's thrilled and...' She was babbling. Tess made herself stop and take a breath. This was Luke. There was no reason to be nervous. 'Anyway, here's your tea.'

Luke straightened at her words, scribbled a measurement down with the stump of a pencil, then took the mug she held out with a nod of thanks. He always had been a man of few words.

She had left Oscar watching television with Bink tucked under his arm. He had climbed up onto the sofa and sat with his legs stuck straight out in front of him. He hadn't liked Luke. He was wary of all men, Tess had noticed, but it wasn't hard to see why he found Luke particularly unapproachable, with those scowling brows and the surly expression she remembered so well. It was a shame Oscar couldn't see him smile. Luke looked quite different then.

He wasn't smiling now as he took a sip from the mug. 'You remembered how I take my tea,' he said.

Her face warmed. 'My head's full of useless information like that.'

It had seemed easy in the kitchen. Take Luke tea. Have a chat about ground rules. Be adult. But now she was there, facing him, the room was jangling with memories of the things they'd done together, the things they'd said to each other.

The things they'd felt for each other.

She studied him surreptitiously over the rim of her own mug. He had filled out over the past ten years and grown into that beaky nose. Where once he had been thin and wiry, now he was lean and hard. But that shuttered, self-contained air was exactly the same. He was leaning back against an empty bookcase, drinking his tea, and something about the way he filled the space set a burn spreading from her chest to her throat.

She swallowed, made a big thing of drinking her own tea. 'So…' She cleared her throat. 'How are you, Luke?'

'I'm good. You?'

'Fine.' She smiled a brittle smile and knew he didn't believe her. She had looked in the mirror. There were shadows under her eyes and she looked gaunt and older than her thirty years. Funny how she had used to long to be thin. Now she would happily trade her hollow cheeks and jutting shoulder blades for the bloom a few extra pounds would give her.

She kept the smile. Just because they'd once been lovers didn't mean they couldn't be polite. 'How long have you been a joiner?' She hated the way her voice came out with that undercurrent of unconscious condescension. *A joiner? How marvellous.* She hadn't actually said it, but that was the way it would sound to Luke, she knew. He had always had a massive chip on his shoulder about her solidly middle-class background. He would have had her down as a yummy mummy the moment he saw Oscar.

It hadn't mattered before, not to her. But now she was so attuned to gauging how Martin was going to react that she existed in a state of constant fretfulness, wondering if she had said the right thing or the wrong thing. Look at her now, Tess thought, exasperated with herself, tying herself into knots wondering what Luke thought of her. What did it *matter* what he thought? Chances were he wasn't thinking of her at all.

His expression hadn't even flickered. 'Just since I came back to York,' he said. 'My mum died last year, and Dad's not managing very well on his own. He had a stroke a couple of years ago, and refused to have any help, so one of us had to be around. I flipped a coin with my brother, and I lost.' He shrugged. 'I was freelance so it was easier for me.'

'I'm sorry about your mum,' said Tess honestly. She remembered Betty Hutton, a sparrow of a woman with shrewd eyes and a disconcerting cackle of laughter. 'I always liked her.'

'So did I. Dad ... well, he's the same miserable old bugger.'

A miserable old bugger he had put his life on hold for, thought Tess. Luke hadn't been able to disguise the rough affection lurking in his voice.

There was a tiny pause.

'You're still taking photographs?' she persevered. Luke had always taken the most wonderful pictures. She had liked to listen to him talk about the work he would do as a photojournalist, his sullen features lit with passion at the outrages he would expose.

'When I can,' he said. 'I specialized in travel – couldn't hack it on the news desk in the end – but it's not so easy at the moment. I've finally persuaded Dad to have a carer twice a week, but I still need to be around. I pick up the odd freelance job and joinery helps in the meantime. It beats doing weddings and babies. I won't touch those.'

'Now there's a surprise.' The words popped out before Tess could stop them and she took a quick step back as Luke raised his brows at the snippiness of her tone. His frown at her unthinking reaction had her opening her mouth to apologize before she remembered with a flicker of exhilaration that she could be snippy if she liked. She wasn't surprised. Why shouldn't she say so?

She lifted her chin with an edge of defiance. 'Well, commitment was never your thing, was it?'

'Wasn't it?'

He had unsettling eyes, strikingly pale in his dark face, and when they looked straight into Tess's the past wavered between them, too far and too murky to see clearly.

And what did it matter anyway? The past was over.

Still, her eyes slid from his, her momentary defiance evaporating into the churning uncertainty that felt so much more familiar. She was used to being wrong now. What if she had been wrong about Luke too?

Desperately, she drained her tea and scrambled for a way out of a conversation that would take her round in circles if she let it. Forcing briskness into her voice, she changed the subject.

'How long do you think you'll be working here?' she asked.

'A week or so. It's a big job, and I need to fit it around various other work I've got on. Richard said he's in no hurry. That's why he gave me the key so I could come and go when it suited me.'

Luke slanted a glance up at Tess as he put down his own mug and bent back to the skirting board. 'I'll try not to get in your way,' he said. 'There might be a bit of drilling and hammering, but most of the time you won't even know I'm here.'

Tess just wished she could believe it.

Chapter Three

It took a long time for Oscar to settle that night. Exhausted but too hyped up to sleep herself, Tess wandered restlessly around the flat for the remainder of the evening. Her blood was racing with adrenalin, and her mind kept lurching and swerving through the events of the day. One moment she was thinking about Oscar, the awe on his face as he stroked Ashrafar's plushy fur, the intent way he had clambered onto the sofa and made himself at home in front of the television, and the next her mind had tumbled back to Martin.

Martin who hadn't allowed Oscar to watch television at all. 'It's brainwashing,' he declared. 'They're sending out subliminal messages all the time. I've got contacts who know about these things.'

Once Tess had dared to ask why it wasn't dangerous for Martin himself to watch television in that case and he had looked at her as if she were stupid. 'Because I'm an adult. My brain is fully formed. I'm not susceptible the way a child is. Besides, I'm only watching the news. I have to keep abreast of current events in my business.'

She had always been careful to switch off the television long before Martin was expected back. Once he had come home early and the set had still been warm. That had been a bad day.

Tess could still hardly believe how easily she had got away in the end. She had been braced for Martin's fury, had strategies to cope if he tried to force her back to London, but when he turned up on her mother's doorstep, his calm assumption that she would change her mind and go back to him had been almost more frightening. Only a twitch under his right eye had betrayed the control he was keeping over his temper.

'I'm not coming back,' Tess had said. The door pressed into her fingers where she clung to it but she kept her voice steady. 'I'm sorry, Martin.'

'You want to spend some time with your mother. I understand.' He nodded agreeably and smiled the smile that had once made her go weak at the knees with longing. 'Why didn't you say? Anyone would think I was some kind of ogre!' he said, twinkling at her in a way that made the fine hairs stand up on the back of Tess's neck.

She had fallen for that twinkle before. She had wanted to believe in the charm, in the protestations of undying love. She had let herself be convinced that she was the unreasonable one.

No longer, Tess had promised herself.

Still, it was hard to break the habit of appeasement and Tess had to swallow and force the conciliatory words back down her throat. 'My solicitor will be in touch with you.'

It was as if they were having two different conversations. Martin sighed and rolled his eyes. 'Oh, very well. If you're going to be difficult... I'll come back in a week or so and take you home.'

'No,' she said, stronger this time, irritated by his certainty. Irritated by how often she had given in, ensuring that he would always get his own way. 'No, I'm not coming home.'

'Of course you are,' said Martin. 'We're married. You promised we'd be together forever.'

God help her, she had. Nobody had forced her to marry him. She had chosen Martin. She had promised: for better, for worse. It was all her own fault, just as he was always telling her.

But she had Oscar. Tess held on to that. It was worth it all to have her son. She had stayed for Oscar, and now she was leaving for Oscar. She would hold firm for him.

In the end she had let Martin believe that her stay in York was temporary. It had seemed the easiest way to get him to go, but then he had come in and sat down and had tea while Tess and Oscar sat silently and her mother tried to make amends for Tess's stupidity by smoothing over any cracks and pretending that they were just an ordinary happy family on a visit home. It had been ghastly.

Tess had been desperate to move out before Martin came again. Richard's offer was too good for her not to stay in York, but she knew it would make her easier to find. She stood in the bay window and watched a busker braving the rain in a doorway below while she gnawed at her knuckle, a bad habit Martin had done his best to break her of. What would she do if Martin turned up here?

When he turned up. 'I never give up,' Martin was fond of saying. 'That's why other businesses fall by the wayside but Nicholson's just keeps getting stronger. I ride the bumps and I keep on going. I never, ever give up.'

Tess had made her mother promise not to tell him where she was, but even if she kept her word, Martin had the resources to track her down. Nicholson Electronics gave him access to some shadowy contacts. He was always boasting about the importance of the company's government contracts and the secrecy of his negotiations. He had spent some time in the army, he'd told her when they first met.

'I know guys who can get things done,' he had said and he'd smile and she, she had been impressed. Tess hated remembering how pathetic and naive she had been.

Digging her nails into her palm, she turned away from the window. She would never sleep if she started thinking about Martin. She would read one of Richard's books instead, but even as she reached for a battered paperback lying on an even more battered sideboard her mind was already jumping on to bookshelves and from there careening straight to Luke and the shock of seeing him again. She had thought she'd forgotten him, but one look and the memories had come slamming back – of his hard hands on her flesh, of the heat of his mouth. Of the contemptuous curl of his lip when he had turned and walked away.

Abandoning the idea of reading as hopeless, Tess let her arm fall and she rubbed it absently. It wasn't exactly hurting, but it hadn't felt *right* since that strange jolt from the beam. She kept jiggling it around to try and find a comfortable position to hold it.

And that, of course, sent her mind to the place

she had refused to let it go all day – the back bedroom and that dreadful roil of anguish she had felt when she stepped inside. She had pushed the memory back down every time it threatened to surface, but there had always been a good excuse not to go in there again. She couldn't put it off any longer, though. There was a perfectly good bed waiting for her there. She could hardly spend the next year sleeping on the sofa.

Abruptly she switched off the lamps in the front room and walked back to the bedroom. From the threshold, her eyes darted round the room as if she could see the dread uncoiling in the air, but the room stayed still, almost sullen.

Tess took a tentative step inside, then another. Nothing happened. She made it to the centre of the room before realizing how ridiculous she must look. Her shoulders unlocked and she laughed. 'See?' she said to Ashrafar, who had padded companionably down the passage after her. 'There's nothing here.' She patted the bed, glad of the cat's warm presence. 'Come on, puss,' she said.

Trying not to think about how quiet it was, she opened her suitcase. Unpacking didn't take long. She had brought hardly anything from London, where Martin had bought her the frilly, feminine clothes he liked her to wear. Most of her T-shirts and tops were ones she had left at home when she first moved to London. They could be quickly shoved in the chest of drawers rather than hung up or immaculately folded as Martin insisted.

When she had finished, Tess pushed the bottom drawer closed and stood with an armful of sheets to make up the bed. It was only then that she noticed Ashrafar. The cat hadn't followed her into the room. She was crouched at the open door, tail twitching, and the fur slowly stiffening on her back.

'Don't be silly.' Tess clutched the sheets to her chest. Her voice sounded thin and high in the silent room. 'It's fine. You were in here before.' What was she doing, trying to reason with a cat? 'Come here, puss.'

But Ashrafar only backed away, cautiously at first, and then with a sudden burst of speed turned and bolted down the passage. 'Be like that,' Tess shouted after her childishly. 'See if I care.' A few seconds later, she heard the clatter of the cat flap.

There was nothing wrong with the room. *Nothing.* Tess kept telling herself that as she lay rigidly under the duvet, her ears straining into the silence, her scalp prickling. She didn't know what she was listening for. The builders had long gone from next door, and back here there were none of the muted sounds from the street you could hear in the front room.

Come to think of it, there ought to be sounds in an old building like this, surely? Tess would have been glad to hear the comforting click of pipes, the creak of timber settling, or even the hum of a fridge, but the silence was oddly thick, broken only by the uneven sound of her breathing.

Scrape, scrape, scrape.

Out of nowhere, the noise rasped through the darkness and Tess sat bolt upright in bed, her hands clutching the duvet, her heart banging high in her throat.

Thud, thud, thud.

'Stop it,' she whispered, not sure who she was talking to.

It was a horrible sound, a scrabbling, scratching, clawing sound alternating with a pounding, with such a desperate undercurrent to it that Tess whimpered and covered her ears to block it out. She sat like that, her hands clamped to her head and her eyes squeezed shut, praying that it would stop, until a picture of herself cowering in the bed filtered into her brain. This was what she did when she didn't like what was happening, wasn't it? She closed down and pretended that it wasn't happening at all. It was what she had done with Martin, and it was what she was doing now she was on her own. When had she become so pathetic?

Slowly, Tess dropped her hands. She couldn't just sit here being frightened. Reaching out, she switched on the bedside light. The sudden glare made her screw up her eyes.

Scrape, thud, scrape, scrape.

It was more of a scratching sound now, and the answer hit Tess so suddenly that she slumped back against her pillow with relief.

Rats. Of course. It must be rats. Didn't they say that no one in a city was more than six feet from a rat at any time? Rats would have been breeding in these old roofs and drains for centuries.

Did they live in walls? Tess sat up again and looked at the fireplace. She was sure the sound was coming from there. They must be behind the plaster. First thing in the morning, she was going to contact the pesticide people. Oscar was only five. They would have to do something.

Scratch, scrape, scrape. Scrape, scrape, SCRAPE.

Feeling a little embarrassed by her fear now, Tess got out of bed, stomped across to the fireplace and banged on the plaster. 'Stop it!' she shouted, but not loud enough to wake up Oscar. 'Go away!'

The noise stopped.

'OK.' Oddly deflated by her success, Tess climbed back into bed and huddled into the duvet. May or not, she was going to get a radiator the next day. The room was so damp she could almost smell the river. Her face above the duvet felt clammy, and she fell asleep at last with the air clinging to it like fog.

Nell groped her way down Water Lane towards the staithe. She could barely see a few feet in front of her. All day the fog had hung dense and low, muffling the city in an eerie light. The air was thick, white, clammy. It wrapped itself around her face, stifling her, pressing against her nose and mouth. It made Nell think about the way the darkness had squeezed around her in the kist that day in Mr Maskewe's closet, and remembered panic squirmed in her belly, making her breath stutter.

Catching her bottom lip between her teeth, she made herself breathe in and out, the way she had learnt to do.

There was nothing to fear. She was not shut in a chest. She could breathe.

Above, the sun was a bright disc trying to break through the blanket of fog. Nell kept her eyes fixed on it. There was a blankness to everything that day. The familiar sounds of the city, the bangings and shoutings and clatterings and clangings of everyday life, had been swallowed up by the mist and even the birds were silent. One of her clogs skidded on the damp cobbles and she thrust out a hand to the warehouse wall to steady herself while the basket in her other hand swung wildly. Her heart was beating high in her throat.

She couldn't see the river, but she could smell it: dank and rank, all fish and slimy mud.

On King's Staithe, the keelboats loomed ghostly in the mist. They were drawn up against the quayside, waiting for the tide, watched over by a lone seagull hunched headily on a post. The staithe, normally bustling, was quiet. The mariners had taken refuge from the damp in the alehouse, and only Jack Brown, beaten to the colour of his name by the sea winds, was sitting on an uptight barrel, a clay pipe clamped between his teeth, watching Tom wrestle with a rope.

The tight band around Nell's chest loosened at the sight of Tom. The air seemed less dense, less threatening, and she breathed easily again. Tom knew that she was afraid of dark, tight places, but he never teased her. When a loutish apprentice had tried to push her into an empty barrel for his amusement and she had screamed and screamed and screamed, Tom had leapt at him with his fists even though the apprentice was twice his size. The boy had ended up with a black eye and cut lip and a thrashing from his master, but Nell had been able to wriggle free.

She was safe as long as Tom was there.

'What are you doing?' The fog forgotten, Nell

stepped over a pile of fish guts and peered at the rope in Tom's hands. He was twisting the cord carefully around itself.

'Tying a monkey's fist.' Tom was used to the way she appeared without warning and he barely glanced up.

Nell didn't mind. She liked watching his frown of concentration. When Tom wanted to learn something, he was fierce with focus. The bright eyes would narrow and his smiling mouth would set in a firm line, the restless energy that was so much part of him directed at the task in hand.

'Look.' He held up the rope with its misshapen lump to show her when he had finished. 'What do you think of that?'

She took it and weighed it in her hands. It was heavier than she expected. 'What is it for?'

'It gives weight to the heaving line,' said Tom importantly. He liked to impress her with his knowledge of the ships that plied between Hull and the great ports of the Low Countries. Taking the rope back, he swung it around his shoulder and made as if to throw it from a deck to a quay. 'See?'

Five years had passed since Nell had shut herself in the chest, and now she too was in service. At eleven she had joined the Harrison household, and since then she had been learning to wash and to brew and to bake, to dress meat and to cast accounts, but Mrs Harrison was an indolent mistress, unlike Anne Appleby, and it was easy for Nell to slip away when she was supposed to be running errands.

It had been strange at first to leave home and her

two small brothers, but she knew she was fortunate. Mr Harrison was a rich draper, although his wealth could not compare to Mr Maskewe's, and the house was much more comfortable than Nell's father's. There were two other maids to giggle with and, best of all, the Harrisons lived in Ousegate near William Todd's house, so she saw Tom nearly every day. Nell was well content with her lot.

She had known she would find Tom at the staithe. Even when he had nothing to do in Mr Todd's warehouses, Tom would be hanging around by the river, as if by wishing hard enough he could magic up a ship. For years now, Tom had yearned to go to sea, but so far his master had only taken him to Hull on the riverboats. Still, it was further than Nell had been.

Tom showed the rope to Jack, and at his brusque nod of approval began to loosen the knot with deft fingers so that he could start again.

'Got anything to eat in there?' he asked Nell, nodding at her basket. Tom was always hungry.

'No,' she said regretfully. She was always hungry too. 'My mistress just sent me for some pins and thread and ... oh, Tom, I heard hard news at the pinner's,' she said, remembering the reason she had come to find him. 'Do you remember your mother's little maid, Joan?'

'The clumsy one?' Tom grunted, intent once more on the rope in his hands. It was five years since he had lived in the house on Stonegate. The Todd house on Pavement was home to him now. 'What's she broken now?'

'Nothing,' said Nell. 'She's dead.' Distress

puckered her face. 'They're saying that she killed herself last night, God rest her soul.'

'What?' Tom's head jerked up in shock. Death could come calling at any time, but to kill oneself was a mortal sin. '*Why?*'

'Who knows why anyone does such a thing?'

Jack took the pipe from his mouth. He hawked and spat, and the seagull flapped its wings as if affronted. ''Tis common enough,' he said. 'There's many a servant as doesn't like the way life is.'

Nell and Tom knew that. They had had their share of beatings, but they had families behind them. Girls like Joan had no one to speak for them, and some masters were harsher than others. All the same, Nell had never known anyone to kill themselves before.

'They say she threw herself in the Ouse and drowned.'

Nell shivered as she looked at the river. It lay oily and still under the weight of the fog, and out of nowhere horror flapped in her face like a great black bird, making her reel back with a gasp and grope for the wall.

Tom didn't notice. He was staring down at the rope, pulling it between his hands, a muscle in his cheek working convulsively. 'Joan,' he muttered. He didn't know what else to say. 'She never did anyone any hurt except herself.'

With difficulty, Nell nodded. The feeling had lifted and she could breathe again, but her heart was still galloping. She remembered the last time she had seen Joan. The Maskewes' maid had been scuttling down Stonegate with her basket. She was a pale, timid girl with protuberant eyes that slid away from you when you talked to her. Nell wouldn't have said that she was unhappy, but what did she know?

Something had made Joan walk into the implacable grip of the Ouse. Its stillness was deceptive. Only the night before it had been running high after the recent rains, and once the current took her, Joan would have had little chance. Did she change her mind as the cold brown waters closed round her? Nell wondered. Did she try to go back? Or had she been seduced by the Devil and condemned herself to haunt the riverside forever?

Nell swallowed and crossed herself surreptitiously at the thought. They wouldn't bury Joan in the churchyard now. They would take her out to a crossroads at midnight and drive a stake tipped with iron through her heart to stop her rising again. Nell tried to imagine Joan with a stake embedded in her, but she couldn't do it.

She couldn't imagine feeling such despair. True, there were times when work was hard, times when life was cruel and uncertain, but for Nell there were more times when it was good. When the rooftops rimed with glassy frost glittered in the winter sunlight, or one of her small brothers squealed with delight as she swung him round and round. When there was laughter in the market, or Tom to meet down by the river, and her blood ran quick and eager.

True, the Maskewe house must have been a dull place since Tom's mother died with his little brother. Mother and babe had succumbed to the fever barely a week after Nell had been shut in the chest, and Mr Maskewe had not married again. He was comfortable enough with Fat Peg to run the house, and with no mistress to harry her, Joan's day couldn't have been so hard, could it? Nell herself could think of lots of things she would do if her mistress wasn't waiting for her to come home. Indolent as she was, even Mistress Harrison would notice if Nell spent all day there on the staithe with Tom.

Abandoning his knot, Tom sighed and brushed his hands on his breeches. Nell wished she could wear breeches too. She would much rather be a boy. As a girl she had to be clean and neat. She had to lower her eyes and walk slowly. She had to wear stiff skirts and lace a bodice across her flat chest.

She would have to stay home, while Tom went adventuring. One day before too long he would go, and she would be left behind.

She wouldn't think of it. Not yet.

'I'd better go and see my father,' said Tom. 'And Ralph, too, I suppose,' he added as an afterthought. 'It is a poor homecoming for him.'

Ralph had been in Antwerp for the past two years on his father's business, but the English had fallen into a great quarrel with the Spaniards, and Mr Maskewe had summoned him back to York until the merchants of England could find a more certain home in the Low Countries, where the Spanish presence wasn't so strong.

Nell had only seen Ralph once since he had been back. She had been visiting her stepmother and chasing little Harry and Peter round the yard, making them shriek with laughter, when the men came out of the hall. Immediately, Anne shushed Nell and the boys, and Nell turned, her face flushed, to see her father flanked by Mr Maskewe and Ralph.

Her father always looked diminished when Mr Maskewe was there, and the strain was there for everyone to see, for all his great professions of love and friendship. Harry, his firstborn son, was named after Mr Maskewe, who was Harry's godfather. The connection was an important one. Still, no one was ever quite comfortable when the Maskewes were present.

Except Tom, of course. Tom was different.

Whenever Nell looked at Tom, her heart lifted. It was hard to believe that he shared any blood with Ralph. They were not at all like brothers. It wasn't that Tom was unhandsome – indeed, Nell liked his face – but he was small and wiry and dark, with a quicksilver smile and a zest for life in his expression, while Ralph was tall and solid with a ruddy complexion and eyes as pale and hard as pebbles.

They said Ralph was a fine-looking man, and perhaps he was, but something about him curdled the blood in Nell's veins. She hadn't forgotten the day she got stuck in the chest, or the way Ralph had smiled when the switch lashed across her palm, when she flinched in pain and had to bite hard on her lip to stop the tears.

The sight of him suddenly in her father's yard after his years away was jarring and Nell sank into a curtsey and lowered her eyes so that she didn't have to look at his teeth.

Her stepmother apologized for the noise. Mr

Maskewe grunted, but Ralph was charming. Who could object to the sound of happy children? he had asked. Or to the sight of a pretty maid?

Nell kept her eyes lowered but she could feel his eyes on her. She could hear the lie in his voice, imagined him moving the words about his mouth, turning them like pebbles until they dropped smooth and deceitful from his lips. She was not a pretty girl, she knew that. She was too boyish with her flat chest and her freckled nose and the wild brown hair that no amount of pins could tame. Tom would scoff if he heard Ralph say that she was pretty.

There was something sly about Ralph, for all his fair features, and Nell remembered again the careful footsteps that crossed the floor while she hid in the chest in Mr Maskewe's closet, the leaden thump of the ledger on the lid. Had that been Ralph? Or had she imagined it all, as Tom and her stepmother had said?

Anne Appleby would hear nothing against Ralph after he and his father had gone. He was a sober, sensible man, she said. He was comely and full of compliments. 'And he will be rich,' she added with a meaningful glance at Nell, who looked blankly back at her.

'He is twenty-one,' Anne said to Nell's father. 'He will be looking for a wife one of these days.'

'Nell is only twelve. Too young to be thinking of marriage.'

'She will grow older. It would be a great connection for us. If she catches Ralph's eye...' Her stepmother trailed off significantly.

Nell had been following the conversation with

dismay. 'I'm not going to get married!' she burst out.

'Go to, Miss Eleanor! Then what will you do?'

She stuck out her bottom lip. 'I will stow away on a ship and make my fortune at the cloth markets in Antwerp.'

'Antwerp is overrun by the Spanish,' her father sighed. 'You will have no luck there as an Englishwoman.'

'Do not encourage her to think of it,' Anne scolded. 'Eleanor is not going anywhere. Her life is in York.'

'I will look after Harry and Peter,' said Nell defiantly, her eyes falling on her little brothers.

'Harry and Peter will have wives of their own, God willing. You must marry to have a home of your own.'

Nell sighed. 'Then I will marry Tom if I must marry someone.'

'Tom is a younger son, and still but a child. He will be in no position to marry for years.'

Nell was thinking of this conversation as she and Tom climbed the lane up from the staithe. The cobbles were uneven and slimy beneath their feet but the fog didn't feel as menacing with Tom there.

'Tom,' she said, 'do you think you will ever marry?'

'Marry?' Tom stared at her as if she had asked if he would grow a head with a single eye in the forehead, like the Cyclops in the book of travellers' tales Mistress Harrison sometimes read out loud in the evenings. 'What makes you think of marriage?'

'Oh, it was just something my stepmother said.' She scuffed at the edge of a pothole with her clogs. 'She said you were a younger son and that you wouldn't marry for a long time.'

'I dare say I won't,' said Tom cheerfully. 'I will be adventuring overseas. I will join Captain Drake and sail to the Indies and bring back sugar and spices and Spanish gold. What use will I have for a wife?'

'I wish I could go with you,' Nell said, her green eyes wistful.

'Well, if I do come home a rich man and want a wife, I will marry you,' Tom offered generously, and her face lit up.

'I wish it could be so!'

'I'll have to finish my apprenticeship first, mind,' Tom warned. 'And then I'll go to sea. It won't be for a while.'

'That's all right,' said Nell. 'It's not as if anyone else will want to marry me.' An image of Ralph watching her in the yard slithered into her mind, and she twitched it off as she would a fly. 'I have little dowry, and it's not as if I'm pretty.'

Tom didn't bother to correct her. 'You can run fast for a girl,' he said. 'That's something.'

Her eyes snapped open and she stared into the darkness, aware only of the blood drumming in her ears. And the fear snapping and crackling under her skin.

What had happened? One minute she had been trudging up the lane with Tom, and the next it was dark. Was she back in the kist? At the thought, horror shook her like a terrier with a rat, and her hands shot up as if to push frantically against the lid, but they met only air.

No kist.

The panic receded and the tightness in her chest relaxed a little as her eyes adjusted to the darkness. There was a faint, fuzzy light coming through a window, and a yellowy glow striping across the room from the open door. She wasn't in the kist. Thank God she wasn't shut up. She could breathe. Jerky, shallow breaths, but she could breathe.

And she could remember.

A dream. That's all it had been. *Tess*, she was Tess, not Nell, and she was in York. She remembered now. She was in Richard's flat, and Oscar was sleeping in the other room.

Oscar! The thought of her son jerked Tess upright. Muddled by the lingering fear of waking and not knowing who she was, she almost fell out of the bed and stumbled along the passage, careening off the walls in her exhaustion.

Oscar was sound asleep, his arms flung high on the pillow. Tess laid her hand lightly on his body and let the steady rise and fall of his chest calm her. She was properly awake now, but her mind was jangling still from the vividness of the dream.

She could remember exactly the eerie light, the dampness clinging to her lashes, the smell of wet rope and river and dried fish. Tom, his thin, homely face alight with a longing to explore the world. And herself as a girl, restless and brimming with energy. Tess could still feel the roughness of the linen shift against her skin, the weight of the sturdy clogs encasing her feet, the way they skidded slightly on the slimy cobbles.

Tess had never dreamt that clearly before.

In her dream, she had had memories. Of poor, rabbity Joan. Of Ralph's teeth. Of the terror of being shut up in a box. Was that normal? Tess wrapped her arms around herself and chewed the inside of her cheek as she stood looking down at Oscar in the darkness. Dreams didn't work like that, did they? This hadn't felt like a dream at all. It felt as if she had been there, lived there. It felt like a memory.

Which it couldn't be, of course. Immediately, Tess started to rationalize. She was a historian of sorts, after all. The sixteenth century was her period, and the clothes, the houses in her dream were familiar to her. It wasn't surprising she had dreamt of that time, especially given the work she was going to be doing for Richard. Moving into his flat had obviously been a catalyst. This house would have been standing in the sixteenth century. Perhaps not in the form Nell and Tom would have recognized, but it had been here.

In fact, it would have been surprising if she *hadn't* dreamt of Elizabethan York.

How strange to muddle it up with some garbled knowledge of vampires, though. Tess wondered where all that about poor Joan's burial had come from. As far as she knew, there had been no belief in vampires at the time ... but why was she trying to make sense of a dream anyway? Perhaps a psychologist could make something of it but she wasn't going to waste any more thought on it. It was just a dream. It didn't matter, and she had other things to think about.

Still, she wouldn't sleep now. She was churning with a mixture of fear and fascination. She couldn't get the dream from her mind: the fog hanging low over the river, her horrified fascination with the dead girl who would be buried with a stake through her heart, and how easily her young mind had jumped to other concerns.

Tess pulled a hoodie over her vest and shorts and padded restlessly through to the front room without turning on the lights. In the glow from the shop fronts outside, she booted up her main laptop. If she couldn't sleep, she might as well do some work.

The clock at the bottom of the screen read 03.14. *The dead of night*, Tess thought and then wished she hadn't. Something about the word 'dead' struck cold between her shoulder blades.

The street below was empty. It had stopped raining but the air was still damp and she huddled into her hoodie. She should have put on some tracksuit bottoms as well, but they were in the chest of drawers in the back bedroom and she didn't want to go back there.

Not in the dead of the night.

'Stop it,' Tess told herself out loud, but her voice came out shakily.

Pressing her lips together, she opened the document with Richard's notes on editing conventions for the records. How to indicate text that had been omitted by the clerk, or that had been deleted. Whether a fine was squeezed between lines, or words written in the left- or right-hand margin. Working steadily, Tess set them up on a clipboard, ready for her to start work the next day.

It was just the mindless task she needed, she decided, but as she worked she kept stopping to lift her head and listen to the silence. She couldn't shake the conviction that it was thickening, growing denser by the second, until it became a tangible thing that was creeping up behind her. Several times she actually glanced over her shoulder.

Her palms were damp. She wiped them on her thighs, just as the shrill of the phone beside her ripped through the heavy silence without warning. Tess's whole body jolted in shock, and it was a moment before her lungs started to work again and she could remember how to breathe.

Brrr, brrr. Brrr, brrr. Brrr, brrr.

It had to be an emergency for someone to ring at this time of night. Tess stared at the phone as if it were a living thing, her heart still jerking frantically. It was Richard's landline, she realized. What if a relative was trying to get in touch with him? Shakily, she picked up the unfamiliar phone and struggled to focus. Her thumb was so unsteady that it took several goes before she pressed the right button firmly enough to answer.

'Hello?' she croaked.

In reply she could hear breathing, quiet and steady.

'Hello?'

Nothing, just a dull burring in her ear as the connection was cut and the line went dead.

As dead as the dead of night.

Chapter Four

'I didn't tell Martin anything!' Sue Frankland's voice rose plaintively.

'Then how did he know how to get in touch with me?' Tess knuckled her eyes. They were gritty from lack of sleep. Oscar was safely at school, and she was walking back towards Monk Bar, her mobile pressed to her ear.

She should have known her mother would be the weak link.

'For heaven's sake, Theresa! You said there was nobody on the other end of the line. It was probably a wrong number.'

'At half past three in the morning?'

'Exactly. Why on earth would Martin ring you at that time and not say anything?'

To scare me. To let me know that he knows exactly where I am.

'I know it was him,' said Tess stubbornly.

She had a new mobile phone. She had changed her email address and shut down her Facebook account. She had done everything she could think of to cover her traces. And yet within a few hours of her moving out of her mother's house, somehow Martin had been able to find out Richard's number, which meant he not only knew how to contact her, he knew where she was.

If it *had* been him.

Maybe it hadn't. Even Martin couldn't have

access to that kind of information that quickly, could he?

Could he?

'Have you spoken to him at all?' she asked her mother, who huffed and puffed and finally admitted that Martin had rung the night before.

'So he knows we're still in York?'

'Of course he knows you're still here. I had to tell him that, at least.' Her mother sounded huffy. 'Martin's very concerned about you, Theresa, and about Oscar.' Sue was the only person apart from Martin who called her Theresa. 'He's Oscar's father. He has a right to know where his son is.'

'You said you didn't tell him!'

'There's no need to snap. I didn't give him your address, since you made such a fuss about it, but it was very awkward. I don't know why you've got it into your head that you can't trust Martin. He was charm itself when he rang yesterday, even though I could tell how disappointed he was not to be able to talk to you.'

'He *can* be charming when he wants to be,' Tess said wearily. She was never going to convince her mother that Martin wasn't the best thing that had ever happened to her. And that was her fault. For the first couple of years she had believed it herself.

Sue sucked in a breath. 'I don't understand you sometimes, I really don't. You had a wonderful life in London. Martin *adores* you.'

'Mum...'

'It's true! You can tell by the way he talks about you.' Her mother's voice began to wobble in distress. 'You had that lovely home, everything you could ever want ... if you ask me, you're spoilt! And now you throw it all away just because you've got some idea in your head about Martin being controlling.'

Tess was wishing she hadn't called her mother, but she needed to know what she had told Martin. She set her teeth. 'It's not an idea, Mum,' she said.

'The trouble with you, Theresa, is that you've always been overimaginative,' Sue went on as if Tess hadn't spoken.

That was always Martin's line too.

Tess pinched the bridge of her nose. 'Mum, I was a historian. I deal with facts, evidence. I'm the least imaginative person I know.'

'You were *always* imaginative,' Sue insisted. 'It could be quite embarrassing at times. Remember that time we took you to Rievaulx Abbey?'

'No.'

'Yes, you do. You ran around pointing out monks and trying to talk to them.'

A memory glimmered into life. Tess holding her father's hand, pulling him out of the way as the monks went about their business, puzzled rather than frightened when nobody else seemed to be able to see them.

'I was just a kid,' she said uncomfortably. 'I can't have been much older than Oscar then.'

'Then there was the time you started screaming because you could see heads stuck up on Micklegate Bar.' Her mother seemed determined to prove her point.

Tess took the phone away from her ear and

looked at it. Another incident she appeared to have wiped from her mind, but now her mother mentioned it, she did remember the bloated, rotting heads spiked to the top of the bar, the ghastly grimaces glimpsed between clouds of flies. Her stomach heaved. No wonder she had blocked out that particular memory.

She frowned. 'We must have been doing something at school about how they used to display traitors' heads on the bars or something.'

'That's exactly what I mean!' said her mother triumphantly. 'Barbara Jessop always said you were a sensitive, but I think you just took something you'd read or been told, and then exaggerated it out of all proportion.'

Well, thanks for that ringing endorsement, Mother, thought Tess. *Good to know that your own mother thinks you're hysterical, neurotic and obsessive.*

'Now you're doing the same with Martin,' Sue said. 'You've read some silly magazine article or something and you've decided that you're a victim too.'

'Where have you been?' Martin, grabbing her the moment she stepped through the door, shaking her.

'Just the supermarket.' Trying to free her arm so that she could manoeuvre the pram in.

'What for?'

'Some milk. Martin, let me go. You're hurting me.'

Releasing her reluctantly. 'Who did you meet while you were there?'

'No one.'

'There must have been someone. You met that guy, didn't you?'

'What guy?'

'The one I saw you talking to the other weekend. Young guy. Earring. Ponytail.' Spitting out the description.

And she, lacking the energy to argue, but trying anyway. 'Martin, he was a shelf-stacker. I wasn't talking to him. I was asking him where the caster sugar was.'

'Don't lie to me!' His voice rising without warning. 'You were flirting with him. I saw you smiling and chatting and he was lapping it up!'

Oscar, whimpering at the noise. Tess, flinching at the rage boiling in the air.

'You're frightening Oscar.'

'Oscar? Oscar? What about me? You've had all day with the child. Is it too much to ask for you to be here when I get home after a hard day? It's not as if you have anything else to do. Well, is it?'

Her head throbbing with tension. Picking up the baby, who was crying in earnest now. Not knowing what to deal with first. Taking the easy way out. Agreeing with him. Telling herself she would stand up to him next time.

It always ended the same way. Martin would retreat into a monumental sulk, until she couldn't stand it any longer and cajoled him out of it, at which point he would beg for her forgiveness in a voice choked with emotion.

'It's just because I love you so much, Theresa. You know that, don't you?'

After a while, it was easier not to go out in case he rang. Easier to give in when he suggested ordering online so that she didn't need to go to the supermarket at all. Easier to make sure Oscar was in bed before he came home.

Easier to lose contact with her own friends rather than have to make excuses about why Martin didn't want to socialize with them. Once or twice she had made the effort to go out on her own, but she had spent the whole time worrying about whether she would get home on time, and after Oscar's birth it had been clear that insisting on going out and leaving Martin alone with a baby after he had been at work all day would be monumentally selfish and irresponsible.

Easier to make her life smaller and smaller until it had almost disappeared.

Tess had never told anyone what it had been like. She was too ashamed.

'It's not as if Martin hit you or anything awful like that,' her mother said.

'No,' Tess agreed dully. 'He never hit me.'

He never had. Not physically. It was no use trying to explain to her mother, though. Sue saw Martin as the rest of the world saw him, as Tess herself had seen him at first: bright, articulate, successful, good-looking, oozing charm and confidence. When he looked at you, you felt you were the only person in the world he was interested in, that nobody else mattered.

It had been flattering at first. To be so wanted, so loved. To be the absolute centre of someone's world. Lonely and overwhelmed by London, Tess had been dazzled by him. Somewhere along the line, though, the flattering had become bullying, and the centre of Martin's world a more and more uneasy place to be.

Tess took a breath, tried to push back the headache grinding behind her eyes. 'What exactly did you tell Martin, Mum?'

Sue puffed out an offended sigh. 'I said Oscar was fine, and that you just needed a little time.'

'You didn't give him my new address or phone number?'

'No, and I didn't give him your new mobile number either, because I don't *know* it,' Sue reminded her. Tess hadn't wanted to give her mother any of her contact details, but her lack of trust had led to such a scene that she had had to give in, able to keep only the mobile number to herself. Even that obviously rankled. 'Satisfied?'

'All right. I'm sorry, Mum, I just...' Tess trailed off. What was the point of explaining? 'Next time Martin gets in touch, can you please just tell him to contact me through my solicitor?'

The headache had her brain in a vice by the time she got back to Stonegate. Fumbling with the key, she could smell cut wood from the builders who were refurbishing the shop next door. It reminded her of Mr Maskewe's closet, and that hot afternoon when she had felt her way along the new wainscot and then turned to see the chest. Her stomach clenched at the memory.

How could she have thought it was a good place to hide?

Tess put a hand to her head as she leant against the stair wall, suddenly dizzy. That wasn't *her* memory. She was remembering a memory in a dream. It wasn't real.

She just needed to lie down for a bit.

Somehow she made it up the stairs and let herself into the flat. Inside, the air felt taut, trembly with anticipation, and there was an edge to the silence that made her nerves prickle.

Not enough sleep, that was all.

She'd woken that morning, stiff and uncomfortable, with her head on the desk by the laptop. Oscar had dragged his feet, wanting to stay with Ashrafar rather than go to his new school, and Tess had underestimated how much time it would take to walk there with him dawdling all the way. Then the conversation with her mother, unearthing memories of monks and severed heads. Was it any wonder her head ached?

Her pulse boomed and thudded in her ears, adding to the thumping in her skull. She would lie down for a bit, close her eyes.

Sometime later, Tess woke with a panicky sense of suffocation. There was a great weight pressing down on her, and she struggled up, only to find that the cat had made itself at home on her chest and was regarding her with great yellow eyes, mildly irritated by her wriggles. In the end she had to lift him off bodily before she could sit up.

She felt better. Her headache had mostly gone, and by the time she had washed her face and made herself a cup of coffee, she was feeling almost normal and ready to start work. Settling at the desk in the window, she opened both computers so that she could see them side by side and called up a photograph of the first page of the manuscript. The yellowing pages were covered in a typical sixteenth-century scrawl. The ink was a little faded but otherwise the manuscript was in remarkably good condition.

These fragments of the coroner's inquest records had been discovered in the city's archives only the year before, and would be an important new source for Richard's study on Tudor crime. It was Tess's job to transcribe them accurately and translate from the Latin where necessary.

Drone work. She could almost hear Martin spitting out the words. He'd been contemptuous of her work – *It's not as if copying is a real job* – and she'd let him persuade her that there was no need to carry on working after their marriage. *We don't need the money. If you loved me, you'd want to be there for me. My work is so stressful, I need you at home.*

Determinedly, Tess shook off the memory. Martin was a distraction she didn't need.

It was slow going until her eyes adjusted to the unfamiliar script. *Anno regni Elizabeth regne viii*^{mo} ... 1566. Well, a date was a start. Tess wriggled her shoulders and settled more comfortably in her chair.

Ashrafar had found a patch of sun by the window and was sitting sphinx-like on the desk, watching the tourists taking photographs below. The ends of her black fur shimmered gold in the sunlight. Every now and then Tess reached out to run her hand along her back, and she would flex her spine and vibrate with a purr. She made for a peaceful companion.

Tess worked to the end of the page, closed down the image, and pulled up the next one, and then the next. It became easier as she got used to the vagaries of the clerk's hand, and she was able to work faster. It felt good to be using her skills again, and she was feeling confident as she pulled up the fourth page and the name Maskewe leapt out at her like a punch from the screen, driving the breath from her lungs in a cough of shock.

Coincidence, she told herself as she patted her throat and got her breathing back in order.

Focusing on the entry, she made herself work through it carefully, transcribing word by word and translating as she went along. The inquest jury had been sworn in to enquire into the death of one Joan Beck. Joan was servant to Mr Henry Maskewe, merchant, and her body was found on the riverbank at St George's Close.

Joan had drowned.

The tiny hairs on the back of Tess's neck lifted. She took a steadying breath and read the lines again, checking that she hadn't made a mistake, but no, the names were clear.

Coincidence, she reassured herself again. *It must be*. She had never read this account before. As far as she knew, no one had looked at it properly since the sixteenth century. The records had been shoved in the back of another manuscript and lost in the city's archives for four hundred years.

But if that were the case, how was it that she could remember so vividly standing on King's Staithe in the fog and telling Tom about Joan's death? How did she know about Joan's buck teeth and the way her head hunched down between her shoulders as if cringing away from a blow?

She *didn't* remember, Tess reminded herself desperately. It had been a *dream*.

There had to be an explanation for the coincidence of names. Perhaps she had glanced at the page when sorting the images into a folder and subconsciously registered the names? She knew enough about sixteenth-century York to fill in other details. Tess clutched at the idea, refusing to give in to the objections clamouring at the back of her mind. *Yes, that must be it. Poor Joan probably drowned accidentally.*

Trying not to notice that her hand wasn't quite steady on the mouse, she read on. Various witnesses testified to the fact that Joan had been of good character, but that a week or so before her death she had suffered a great heaviness of spirit. A neighbour, Margery Wrightson, who had seen Joan wandering by the river, opined that Joan had 'fallen in fere of worldly shame' and chosen to 'rydde herself from lyf for werynes'. Joan, the court found, had killed herself.

A strange wavery feeling rippled through Tess. She felt light-headed and insubstantial, as if she had peered into a dizzying chasm, and, as if through a gauze, she saw Ashrafar flatten her ears and jump off the desk, spitting in alarm. She was gripping the top of the desk, pressing the wood between her thumb and fingers until her flesh turned white. There was a chip in the varnished edge of the table and she could feel the splintery unevenness pressing into her skin. The table was real; *she* was real. Tess tried to hold onto that, but the harder she gripped, the more she felt herself receding. There was a strange, sucking sensation in her head, and she barely had time to feel frightened before her eyes blurred and the world seemed to tip away from her.

She stepped out of the cool darkness of the barbican into the sunlight, and into a jostling press of vagrants. 'A penny, sweet mistress!' they begged, feral-eyed, rank with dirt and desperation. 'For charity!'

'Ignore them,' said Alice but Nell was already digging into the purse at her girdle for a coin. She couldn't ignore them. There were too many of them, and they were too close, too loud. She caught the eye of a girl about her own age with a gaunt face and bitter eyes, two small boys clinging to her skirts, and she threw the penny to her. Snatching it out of the air, the girl ran away with the boys before the other vagrants surrounded her like a pack of snarling dogs.

Nell watched her go. 'Poor lass. Those boys can't be much older than Harry and Peter. I wonder how I would fare if I had to care for my brothers? If I had to beg for a crust of bread so they could eat?'

'For pity's sake, Nell.' Alice clicked her tongue and took Nell firmly by the arm. 'Now they will all want something. Come, walk quickly.'

'Did you hear they found another girl down by the river?' Nell shivered even though the sun struck warm across her shoulders. 'They say she was so savagely beaten, none could tell who she was or what she looked like. That is four now.'

'Four what?'

'Four vagrant girls who have been killed over the last year or so. Nobody seems to care.'

Alice shrugged. 'They are idle and shiftless,' she pointed out. 'They just make trouble. Nobody does care.'

'But who would do such a thing?'

'Nell, it is not for you to worry about such things,' said Alice, rolling her eyes. 'It is a holiday.

Can you not think about something merrier?'

Nell chewed her lip. It disturbed her that nobody worried about those girls whose bodies had been beaten so savagely and discarded so carelessly. The neighbourhood shrugged the way Alice did. It was distasteful, yes, but no one cried for an inquest. The girls were harlots and vagrants – rough, idle sorts. They might as well be dead as spend their lives begging outside the bars or spreading their legs in stinking alleys behind the alehouses.

Outside the bar, the calsey was wide and crowded. It was Whit Sunday, and apprentices and maids and servants, all dressed in their holiday best, were funnelling through the barbicans and out beyond the city walls, where supervision was not so strict and there were assignations to be had and quiet places to meet.

There were no plays to watch that year. In the past they would have stood in the streets as the wagons trundled past, or squeezed their way through the crowds to see Christ pinned to the cross, but no more. Belief was a fraught business these days. The Harrisons, Nell's master and mistress, went to church every Sunday, but who knew what they believed in their hearts? To be an alderman, as Mr Harrison was, was to be a Protestant. It was only sensible. Mr Maskewe was an alderman too, though. Nell found herself remembering the priest hole Tom swore was in his father's closet, and she wondered if it was ever used.

Letting Alice steer her away from the press of poor at Monk Bar, Nell lifted her face to the sun.

They had seen little enough of it recently and it was good to get out of the narrow streets. She and Alice had been to divine service and now they had the day to themselves.

In the past, she would have spent the day with Tom. It would never have occurred to her to do any different. As children, they had slipped out through the postern gate to sneak apples from the orchards in Paynley's Crofts or pick wild raspberries from the hedgerows, stuffing them in their mouths until their hands were stained and their lips blotched and red. They would chase each other along the paths and out to the common, and hang on the fence of the penfold, daring each other to touch the bull. Or they would head for the Foss to swing from the overhanging trees or paddle by its shallow banks. Nell could still remember the feel of the mud oozing between her toes.

It was a long time since she had been able to take off her stockings and go barefoot. She was sixteen. She wore a kirtle now, her best blue today, and a velvet hat. Her thick hair was plaited as best as she could manage, although it still sprang out wildly from under her coif. No longer was she a wild, romping girl, a tomboy with a flat chest. Her breasts had grown and even though she tried to walk straight and tall, still her hips swung from side to side in spite of herself, and she could feel the way men's eyes followed her down the street. It made Nell uncomfortable. She had put off childish things as she must, but oh, she missed them.

She missed Tom.

A year past, his master, Mr Todd, had announced that he would take him to Hamburg to teach him how to merchant.

Tom was wild to go, and Nell tried to make herself pleased for his sake, but it was hard not to feel left behind. He was gone for nigh on six months, and she missed him dreadfully. She waited and waited for him to come home, but when he did, everything was different.

He looked different, for a start. He was taller, his shoulders broader. His neck had thickened out and he had a new assurance that made Nell shy with him for the first time in her life. She wanted him to go back to being the Tom she knew, the Tom who tugged her hair and teased her. She wanted him to be a boy again, but instead he was a young man. A man who avoided her when he could, who wounded her with his silence.

Now when they met, their conversation was awkward, and the words clogged on their tongues. Where once they would have fought and tussled and laughed, now there was a silence fraught with uncertainty. Now instead of shoving easily at him, Nell was agonizingly aware of his deft hands. She couldn't meet his eyes any more.

He was utterly familiar, and yet a stranger. She knew the shape of his shoulders, the quick way he turned his head, but it was as if she had never noticed his mouth before, never noticed the line of his cheek, the angle of his jaw. Had never seen how easily he filled the air. How many times had he smiled before? Why was it only now that every time his lips quirked her heart barrelled around her ribs, the air evaporated from her lungs and her blood started to thrum restlessly?

Hurt by the way his gaze slipped away from hers now, Nell pretended that she had changed too. When he was near, she laughed and slanted looks at the other young men under her lashes the way she had seen Alice do. She tossed her head; she dimpled a smile. But the instant Tom appeared the air was charged with his presence, and no matter how fixedly she watched another, no matter how determinedly she chattered, her skin twitched under his bright, blue gaze and her throat grew hot and thick. It was exhausting. She had to be continually alert in case Tom should happen to find her looking as lost and lonely as she felt.

So today, instead of finding Tom as she used to, Nell was with Alice, who was also maidservant to the Harrisons. A pert wench a year or two older than Nell, Alice yearned for William Carter. William was a journeyman to a bladesmith and Nell didn't care overmuch for him. She didn't like his swagger, the cock o' the walk smirk that played around his lips, but he was handsome, yes, she could see that.

Alice was determined to find him. William would not be lurking in any quiet corners. Where most people were, there William would be, surrounded by giggling maids and cocksure boys.

So Alice tugged Nell towards St Maurice's churchyard where a cheering throng was gathered around a wrestling match. There was much betting going on, and as much attention on the money changing hands as on the two men struggling to pin each other to the ground.

'There he is!' Alice pinched Nell's arm as she spied William Carter through the crowd. 'Let's move over there where he can see us.'

Nell winced as a clodhopping countryman stood on her foot, and an elbow landed in her side, but they managed to squeeze their way to the front. By the time she got there, Nell's hat was askew and she was ruffled and red-faced, while Alice looked as if she might have strolled along an empty street. Her coif was in place, her skirts perfectly ordered, her smile demure.

The crowd whistled and jeered and catcalled while the wrestlers grunted. They were locked together, naked apart from their breeches, and Alice nudged Nell, momentarily distracted from William Carter. Both wrestlers were young and lean and fit, and although one was much slighter than the other, they were so equally matched they hardly seemed to be moving at all.

And then the smaller wrestler flipped the larger one onto his back so elegantly that no one saw quite how it was done. There was a shout of approval from the crowd, and the victor raised a fist in triumph. He turned round to acknowledge the applause with a blazing smile, and Nell sucked in a breath.

It was Tom, but Tom as she had never seen him before, and her mouth dried.

He had a bloody lip and a bruise on his cheek, but his body was sleek and muscled and sheened with sweat. Where had the thin boy she used to play with gone? In his place was a man, a stranger. A stranger who set her heart slamming painfully against her ribs.

Alice followed Nell's gaze. 'That's never *Tom?*'

'Yes,' Nell said, but there didn't seem to be enough breath in her lungs, and the word came out as little more than a wheeze.

As if he had heard them, Tom's gaze swung round, and when his eyes caught Nell's, the triumph in his face faded with his smile, leaving an expression that Nell couldn't identify but that made her heart clench in her chest. Nell wanted to look away but she couldn't. She wanted to give him a casual wave, to turn to Alice, pretend she didn't really care, but all she could do was look back at Tom through the crowd that was seething around them, eager for the next fight.

Alice looked from Nell to Tom and then back to Nell again. She smiled knowingly. 'Oho! So that's how it is,' she said with a wink.

'What? No! How what is?' Flustered, Nell wrenched her eyes from Tom's but Alice only smirked.

'I see William,' she said, and pointed back at the churchyard. 'I will wait for you by the stile there at seven of the Minster clock. We can go back to the house together.' Reaching out, she straightened Nell's hat. 'Be good!' she said.

'Wait, Alice–' Nell began, but Alice was already sauntering towards William Carter, and there seemed nothing to do but wait dumbly for Tom. He had grabbed his shirt and was dragging it over his head as he pushed his way towards her, accepting congratulatory pats on his shoulder on his way through. And suddenly there he was, standing right in front of her, dabbing at the blood on his split lip.

'Nell,' he said, and something inside her crumbled at the sound of her name in his mouth. She ran her tongue over her lips and swallowed the dryness in her throat.

'Tom,' she said, and then, realizing that no sound had come out, she cleared her throat and tried again. 'Good day, Tom.'

A new pair of wrestlers were taking a turn, to renewed whistles and catcalls from the crowd, but Nell hardly heard them. It was as if the raucous crowd had receded behind an invisible curtain, there but not really there, while she and Tom were isolated in a pool of sunlight where every sense was intensified. His hair was slick with sweat, his eyes dark with an expression that made her blood pound. She could smell the grass crushed beneath her feet, feel the tickle of the ruffled linen at her throat, the padded roll at her waist.

Very carefully, she let out the breath she was holding and managed to look away from him.

'Where did you learn to wrestle?' she said at last.

A smile cracked Tom's face as he slapped his hat back on his head. 'One of the sailors on the *Little George* from Hull taught me some tricks. He said I'd need it if I wanted to survive the ports, and he was right. They are no places for raw boys who can't defend themselves.'

'And it comes in useful now you are back in York too,' she said, pleased to find that her breath was steadier now, her voice clearer. She nodded towards the ram that was tied up, glowering, as it waited to be awarded to the victor of the wrestling. 'Will you stay and fight for the prize?'

'What would I do with a ram?'

'You could sell it.'

'True, but where would I keep it until I had negotiated a good price for it? I am a merchant trained,' he reminded her, his eyes laughing. 'I cannot just give it away to the first who offers. I must make a good profit, and consider my costs in feeding it and housing it, and it is too nice a day to think about such things. Are you hungry?'

'Hungry?' Nell was thrown by the abrupt change of subject.

'You used to be hungry all the time.'

She put up her chin, stung by the idea that he thought of her as a child still. 'Perhaps I have changed.'

'You have,' he agreed. 'I have noticed.'

She didn't mean to, but somehow she was looking at him again, and the air evaporated around them as their gazes tangled once more, like sheep in a briar patch. Nell's heart had stopped plunging and had settled instead to a slow, steady thud that made her ears bang like the waits' drum. What started out as a little silence stretched, then yawned alarmingly.

Nell swallowed and fiddled with the purse hanging from her girdle. This was silly. It was just Tom.

'But it is a long time since I have eaten,' she offered. 'I *am* quite hungry.'

'Then I will buy you a pie,' said Tom. 'Come.' He touched her arm to steer her away, and she felt his fingers burn through her worsted sleeve, through her Holland smock, and onto her bare skin.

The pie seller lifted the tray from his head as he saw them approach and hung it around his neck so that they could choose. Nell could smell browned butter and gravy. 'Fresh from the oven,' the pie man promised and indeed the pies were hot. Nell and Tom had to juggle them between their fingers to cool them down before they could eat them.

Nell bit into the pastry at last, careless of the crumbs falling on her bodice, only to realize that the inside was still hot enough to burn her tongue. 'Ah ... ah ... hot!' she gasped, laughing, and it helped to break the tension between them.

'Serves you right for being greedy,' said Tom, smiling.

'Good, though,' she mumbled through her mouthful.

'Come on, let's get away from the crowds.'

Eating their pies, they wandered up Monkgate towards the bridge. The calsey was broad and dusty between the posts and rails outside the houses there. A pig ambled along the gutter, snouting through the refuse. The dung hill outside Mr May's tenements stank in the warmth, but Nell hardly noticed. The stench was cancelled out by the freshness of the grass, the lush green growth along the roadside, the smell of orchards and gardens. The thorn trees were heavy with blossom. They looked as if a white cloth had been thrown over them to dry in the sun.

At last, Nell thought, she and Tom could talk easily again. It was better now that they were walking side by side, and had their pies to occupy them. 'Is it like this in Hamburg?' she asked him.

A smile creased his eyes. 'York is just a country town compared to the Hansa towns,' he said.

He told her about his life there, about the things he had seen and the things he had learnt. When he talked about the journey, the snap and crack of the sails filling with wind, the creaking of the timbers and the groan of the ropes, his face lit up. Some men clutched their stomachs the moment they set foot on a ship, but Tom was born, it seemed, to brace his feet against the swell of the ocean and feel the deck roll beneath his feet.

'I wish I could see the sea,' Nell sighed as they stopped on the bridge and looked down into the Foss. She dropped the last bit of pastry into the river and the swans below set up a clamour as they squabbled over the crumbs.

The Foss was not a pretty river. The water was goose-turd green and sluggish, the banks overgrown with bushes, but Nell had always had a fondness for it. She still remembered the hideaway she and Tom had built on the riverbank when they were children. It was little more than a few branches piled together, but it had been their very own. Those days were gone, Nell reminded herself. The hideaway had long rotted. Tom had followed the river down to Hull, across the sea, leaving her alone.

But now he had returned, and they were together once more. Just the two of them.

Chapter Five

They had left the crowds behind. In the distance, the jeers and cheers could be heard faintly, but the busy cheeping of the birds was louder. Nell looked at the river, so sleepy and still. So different from the sea Tom had crossed. 'York must seem tame to you now,' she said.

Tom looked around him as he brushed the crumbs from his fingers, then allowed his gaze to settle on Nell's profile. 'Sometimes,' he said. 'But it is home. And you are here.'

Warmth trembled in her stomach. 'I did not think you had noticed me,' she confessed.

'I was shy,' he said. 'You have grown up, Nell. I hardly recognized you when I came back.'

A little huff of relief escaped her. 'That is what I thought about you.'

They smiled at each other, and happiness rose in Nell's chest, a rolling swell that pushed almost painfully against her ribs and into her throat so that for a moment she could not speak with it. 'Come on,' said Tom, taking her hand just as he used to do when they were small. 'Let's go and find our old place.'

They followed the riverbank as it meandered up towards the mill. Their shelter had long gone, of course, but that meant they could argue about exactly where it had been. In the end they settled on a little clearing where the grass was long and sweet, and dappled in the shade of the elders that crowded the bank. It felt natural to throw themselves down there, to pull off their shoes and stockings so they could dangle their feet in the water. Nell pulled up her skirts and wriggled her toes in the cool river.

'I haven't done this for a long time.' She looked at Tom who was leaning back on his hands, watching her. 'I've missed you,' she said.

'And I you,' he said, and the air between them sang with the truth of it, with the sudden, sharp knowledge of what was between them and what could be said at last.

There was a silence, but it was not an uncomfortable one. It shimmered with promise. No longer did Nell's gaze have to slide away from Tom's face. Instead she could look into his blue, bright eyes and let anticipation flutter in her belly.

'When I was on the ship or at the markets, I thought of you and how much you would enjoy it,' Tom went on after a moment, easy now. 'You would like the feel of the salt spray stinging your cheeks and the sound of the waves against the hull. I know you would. You would have liked the quaysides at Hamburg. You might hear men talk in every language there.'

'What do they talk of?' Nell asked, not because she really cared, just to hear Tom's voice, just to know that he was there, that he had missed her.

'The merchants boast of their deals and the mariners boast of the voyages they have made. They say they have felt wind hot enough to melt men's bones and seen many marvels. They say they have been to the lands where peppers and cloves grow, far to the east, and that they have been west too, to the New World. Oh, they are full of it! I dare say not a twentieth man among them has actually been, but they have such stories, and every time I listened, I thought of how much you would have liked to listen to them too.

'And I would have liked it more if you had been with me,' he added and his voice deepened until it was like a caress on Nell's skin.

A water boatman paused as if listening, leaving tiny indents on the still water.

'I thought about you,' said Tom. 'I bought you a gift.'

'A gift?' Nell sat up straighter. 'For me?'

'For you.' He shifted onto one hip so that he could dig in the purse at his belt, and he drew out a plain gold ring set with a garnet that flashed a deep, dark red in the dappled light.

Nell drew a long breath as she took it from him and slid it onto her finger, tipping her hand from side to side so that she could admire it while a feeling like sunshine on a May morning spilled through her.

'Like it?' he asked, carefully casual.

'Oh, Tom...' Her voice had a catch in it. 'I will wear it always,' she vowed. 'I promise.' She raised her eyes to his. 'I thought you had forgotten me,' she admitted.

'Forget you? How could I? There is nobody like you, Nell.'

He smiled but the easy familiarity was leaking out of the air between them and she struggled to claw it back. 'What, no Easterling girls with green eyes?'

'Some,' he said, 'but none as green as yours.' He plucked a blade of grass and tickled her nose with it, making her laugh in spite of herself. 'Your eyes are as green as this grass, as green as the sea, as green ... as green as emeralds!'

'And I dare say they had beautiful brown hair like mine, instead of being fair and lovely?'

'Your hair isn't brown.' Somehow he was unpinning her cap, unpinning her hair so that the plaits tumbled down her back, and she was doing nothing to stop him. He fingered them and the bindings unravelled so that he could spread her hair over her shoulders and still she made no protest. She just sat, mouse still, and watched him.

'It's not brown,' he said again. 'It is the colour of nuts and the colour of honey. I see gold and bronze and copper here. I see the corn ripened by the sun. I see flames, hot and red. I see no brown.' He lifted a lock so that he could breathe in the scent of her. 'I smell gillyflowers.'

Nell swallowed. 'You have become a poet.'

'I would that I could find the words for how you make me feel, Nell,' he said in a low voice as he smoothed her hair back into place. 'I didn't think of you before. You were always there. You were just Nell. But when I came back and saw you, I felt as if I had taken a blow to my stomach. You were the same, but not the same. I thought I had changed, but I hadn't expected you to change too.'

'You ignored me.' A sliver of remembered hurt

speared the tremble of happiness.

'I was angry with you for changing,' Tom said.

There was a pause. Nell felt her hair soft against her neck. In the dappled sunlight it was very quiet. 'We haven't changed that much, have we?' she said.

Tom's smile was twisted as he lifted a lock of her hair and rubbed it between his fingers. 'I fear we have, Nell. We are not the boy and girl we were.'

Darkness swept over her face. 'I don't want things to change,' she said and his smile twisted tighter.

'I do,' he said and he leant closer. Very carefully, he licked his finger and pressed it against the swell of her breast where a pastry crumb clung to the edge of her shift. Nell sucked in an unsteady breath, her eyes darkening.

Tom leant closer still, until his mouth was almost on hers. 'There is no going back now,' he said and then she felt his lips touch hers. It was startling, this feeling of being at once gripped by an entirely new sensation and the certainty that she was made for this moment.

No shyness now, no hesitation. If they fumbled, it was with eagerness and inexperience, but Tom's fingers were as deft as ever, unlacing her bodice, unwinding and unravelling her until there was nothing but the shock of flesh against flesh. Their bodies fitted together so naturally. It was as if his hands had skimmed her many times; as if she already knew the texture of his skin, the bone-melting delight of losing herself in the insistent slide of flesh and muscle, of hardness and heat and hunger. Nell had often wondered how it would feel. She hadn't wanted to ask just how it would work, although she was certain Alice would have been able to tell her. And now she knew. In spite of their lack of experience, it all made perfect sense.

And afterwards, there was no shame – only breathless, incredulous laughter that it was so easy.

And so good.

There was a ringing in her head. On and on it went, pulling her up and out of sleep, until she groped for the alarm. She didn't want to wake up. She wanted to stay with Tom in the sweet grass, their limbs tangled, her hand on his belly, feeling the rise and fall of his breath while her body hummed with pleasure.

She didn't want it to be a dream.

Her flailing hand hit a mug, knocked it over. Cold coffee pooled on the desk as she straightened groggily. She blinked at the mug on its side, at the puddle of liquid, not understanding. Everything looked profoundly alien. The metal boxes with their uncannily shifting patterns. The piles of glaring white paper. The unnaturally regular shapes. She picked up a strange, slender object.

Pen. The word materialized in her brain, but it didn't make sense. It wasn't like any pen she had ever seen. There was a wrongness to it that made her drop it back onto the table with a shudder.

Her eyes skittered from side to side. She was frightened. This wasn't right. She'd thought she was waking from a dream, but she didn't recognize anything. Instinctively, she reached for Tom's hand, but Tom wasn't there, and desolation tore through her.

Tom had gone.

A monstrous headache was pressing behind her eyes. Tess put her head between her hands.

'What's happening?' she whispered. She could hear the ringing again. Was it real or in her mind?

Phone. Like pen, the word formed itself unbidden, but this time it made sense. Fumbling, she found the phone on the desk and somehow managed to press the right button.

'Hello?' Her voice wavered horribly. She had remembered where she was, *who* she was, but the transition from dream to wakefulness had left her feeling sick and shaken, and still uncertain as to what was reality.

'Hello,' she said again, but there was no reply. There was a deadened quality to the silence at the end of the line. 'Who is this?' she said more sharply, but the only response was the muffled click as the phone at the other end was put down.

Martin?

Tess dropped the phone back onto the desk as if it had bitten her, and slumped back in the chair. She felt boneless, fuzzy, on the brink of tears. The endlessly circling screensavers blurred before her eyes. She didn't want to be there. She wanted to be back in the dream, with Tom beside her. She was still tingling and throbbing in the aftermath of making love but at the same time there was a hollowness inside her, an aching void of loss. She felt wretched. Perhaps she was coming down with something? That would explain her pounding head and the lingering, faintly feverish feeling of frustration, of something lost and nearly found.

And the hallucination.

Tess struggled to her feet and went to find a cloth to mop up the mess on her desk.

It had to be a hallucination. What else could it be?

Somehow she had taken last night's dream and the names in the records and woven them together into a story in her mind.

The records must have triggered some kind of fit. She had been reading them just before she had blanked out. Tess swallowed a couple of paracetamol and stood looking at her laptop, remembering how the sight of those names had made her head ring with recognition; how one minute she had been sitting at the desk, the next walking out of the barbican with Alice.

Would it happen again?

Did she want it to?

Of course she didn't. What was she thinking? She was a historian. It hadn't been *real*.

Drawing a deep breath, she pulled out the chair and sat back down at the desk. She took hold of the mouse, and after a moment's hesitation, she clicked. The screen sprang back to life. There was the record, just as she had been reading it.

Tess made herself read it again. Nothing happened.

Straightening the second laptop so that she could see the other screen, Tess placed her fingers carefully on the keyboard, poised to snatch them away if anything untoward happened, but the cursors on both screens just blinked stolidly back at her.

She started to type. Nothing happened.

She transcribed to the bottom of the screen, and pulled up the next image as Ashrafar padded back into the room. The cat leapt up onto the desk and settled down to a thorough wash. Sticking her leg straight in the air, she cleaned carefully between her spread toes, barely pausing to lift her head when Tess laid a hand on her back. Her warm, living presence was insensibly reassuring.

She had just been tired, Tess decided. Not enough sleep, that was all, she told herself again, but even as she tried to reassure herself, she was aware that it was an excuse that was beginning to wear thin.

Luke was hammering in the study when Tess let herself back into the flat after walking Oscar to school the next day. She put her head round the door to wish him a brief good morning, unwilling to admit to herself how pleased she was to have somebody else in the flat.

It had been another disturbed night. She hadn't dreamed again, as she had half-expected that she would, but the scrabbling in the wall came and went until she had to put a pillow over her head to block out the sound. Then there was the phone that rang at odd times in the evening after Oscar had gone to bed, only for Tess to get the dialling tone when she answered, or that horrible steady breathing.

'Please stop calling me,' she had said, hating the way her voice had teetered on the edge of angry tears, but in the end she had had to unplug the phone altogether.

'That's awful,' sympathized Richard when she rang him. 'You do sometimes get cold calls at odd hours, but if it's bothering you, of course I don't mind at all if you disconnect the landline. Everybody who matters has got my number here anyway. Presumably you've got a mobile you can use?'

Tess wished she could reassure herself as easily as she reassured Richard. The idea that Martin had tracked her down already was disturbing, but if it *was* him ringing from London, then unplugging the phone ought to put a stop to it. He would surely have a harder time tracking down her new mobile number.

'Richard, did you ever notice anything odd about the back bedroom?' she asked him.

'I can't say I ever spent any time in it. I used to put guests in there.'

'And they never said anything about a noise or anything like that?'

'A *noise?* What sort of noise?'

'A scrabbling, or sometimes a banging, but it's very faint. Like there's something in the wall.' Her shoulders twitched at the memory of it. 'I think it might be rats.'

'Oh, my dear, how ghastly!' Richard was horrified.

'I'm sure it's nothing,' said Tess. 'I just wondered if anyone had ever mentioned anything to you.'

'No, not that I remember. I'd have called the council at once if I thought there were rats around. You must get something done about it.'

'I will.' Tess wanted to ask Richard about the way the air pulsed sometimes, about the way the flat seemed to be waiting for something, but she didn't know how. Richard was an eminent historian. He had written magisterial tomes on the social history of the Elizabethan period. He pored over documents and analysed the evidence. He wasn't interested in feelings or atmospheres. He wanted facts.

'It's a great flat,' she said instead. 'Do you know anything about the history of it?'

'Only in as much as it relates to Stonegate. As far as I know, there's no documentary evidence about the house itself before the late seventeenth century.' Richard wasn't interested in anything more recent. 'Why do you ask?'

'No reason,' she said. 'Just interest.'

'How are things going otherwise? Has Luke started work on my shelves yet?'

'He has. He's here right now, in fact.'

Tess thought her voice was perfectly neutral, but Richard picked up on it straight away. 'It's not a problem him being there, is it? He seemed nice enough when I met him, and he came highly recommended.'

'No, no, not at all. He's fine.' Hastily, Tess changed the subject. 'I'm enjoying working on the records. I came across a case of suicide yesterday.'

'Really?' She could hear him sitting up in interest. 'That's unusual.'

'I think the folio has been bound in with the others by mistake. It's in a different hand, but the same date. I don't know anything about suicides in that period,' she went on, hoping she sounded suitably casual. 'What would have happened to the body? It is true it would have been buried in unconsecrated ground?'

'Absolutely.' Unconsciously, Richard shifted into lecture mode. 'There was very little compassion for people desperate enough to take their own lives in the sixteenth century. They were considered to have committed a sin, an act of violence against themselves, and they were commonly believed to haunt the site of their suicide. So there was a macabre ritual of driving a stake through the heart of a corpse before it was buried. It's quite well documented. It's an interesting link with later popular mythologies of vampires, isn't it?'

'Very interesting,' said Tess faintly. She hesitated. 'Did you ever do a lecture about burial rituals or anything like that when I was an undergraduate?'

Richard thought for a bit. 'I honestly don't remember. I might have done. I've always had an interest in death. As an academic subject, of course.'

So she might have heard about the burial of suicides from him. Or read about it in some obscure journal. Tess was feeling better by the time she put the phone down. She had read so many books and articles for her dissertation, there was a whole mass of information stored away, ready to be plucked out of her subconscious and woven into a dream for reasons best known to a psychiatrist.

It was called recovered memory. She definitely remembered reading about *that*. The brain simply couldn't deal with all the information it absorbed every day, so it filed it all away where it wouldn't cause the mind to overload. So everything she had ever read or seen or heard about the Elizabethan period could have contributed to the texture of those two dreams.

As for Nell and Tom and that scene by the riverbank, well, it wouldn't be a huge stretch to interpret that as sexual frustration somehow brought on by seeing Luke again. Their relationship might have been doomed from the start and they had had virtually nothing in common, but she had never been able to deny the physical attraction between them.

She could hear him moving around in the study, where he was dismantling all of Richard's old bookcases, and warmth tingled deep in her belly. The trouble was that her memories of him were all muddled up with those of Tom now.

Except she didn't *remember* Tom. She had imagined him, that was all.

So now those weirdly vivid hallucinations were explained, she could get on and sort out everything else that was bothering her. She had promised Richard that she would deal with the rat problem straight away, so she looked up pest control on the council website and arranged for an inspection. She would have to pay for it, but after two broken nights' sleep she would do anything to stop that awful noise.

But when the pest control officer came, he couldn't hear anything. There was no sign of rats anywhere in the flat, he said. 'You've got no droppings, which is usually your first indication, and as far as I can see there aren't no holes in the wall either.'

'But I can hear them!' Tess protested.

He shook his head. 'There's not much I can do. If you've got a little boy, you want to be careful about putting poison down unnecessarily,' he warned. 'Besides, you've got a cat.' He bent to stroke Ashrafar who was preening herself on the bed. 'She'll deal with them for free if they do get in. If they're contained in the wall, they'll move on after a while.'

Tess was frustrated. She'd had just as little success with the solicitor when she had asked if there was anything that could be done about Martin harassing her with phone calls.

'Can't I get a restraining order or something?'

'Has he actually threatened you?'

'No, but I'm sure it's him who's been ringing.'

Her solicitor looked dubious. 'Have you got any proof of that?'

'No.' She should have thought to dial 1471 and get the number, Tess realized. 'No. I just know,' she finished lamely.

The solicitor was no more encouraging when it came to setting divorce proceedings in motion. 'I'm obliged to suggest that you and your husband try mediation first,' she said. 'You should both be thinking about your child.'

Tess thought about the way Oscar had stiffened his thin shoulders whenever he heard Martin's car crunching over the gravel drive. 'I *am* thinking about him! Martin isn't interested in him at all.'

'Nonetheless, he's entitled to contact with his child.'

Tess had been appalled to discover that Martin could compel access. If Oscar was reluctant, the meeting could be arranged under the supervision of social services, but as things stood, there was no way she could stop Martin seeing his son.

Her only hope now was that he would lose interest in them both. She had unplugged the landline and was just using her mobile, so unless he actually came up to York, he would find it harder to harass her.

If he *had* been harassing her.

At least the weather had improved, Tess thought as she let herself in a couple of days later. She had been to the supermarket on the way back from dropping Oscar at school, and had stupidly bought more than she could easily carry. The temperature had soared and the sun had been pleasantly warm on her back, but it had made for a hot walk with frequent stops to rest her arms from the heavy carrier bags.

Vanessa would say it served her right for living somewhere without parking.

The door open, Tess flexed her fingers as she bent to pick the bags up again. It was odd how often her hands felt sore now. They would throb as if they were torn and bruised, but whenever she turned them over they looked perfectly normal. She hoped she wasn't getting arthritis already.

'Want a hand with those?' Luke appeared in the doorway of the study, which was just opposite the door to the flat.

He was wearing a faded T-shirt and jeans that were ripped at the knee. There was a curl of sawdust in his hair, a saw in his hand, and Tess was dismayed at the treacherous kick of her pulse.

That was Nell's fault. If it hadn't been for that explicit, arousing dream, there would be no jolt of blood to her head, no sly stirring of heat in her belly.

There had been no more dreams of Nell, but the memory of that throb of pleasure unsettled Tess and made her brittle and tense whenever Luke was around.

Still, there was no point in turning down his offer. 'Thank you,' she said stiffly. 'That would be a help.'

He bent and gathered all the bags up in one fluid movement and she followed, half grateful, half resentful, as he carried them into the kitchen and set them on the worktop.

'Thank you,' she said again.

His presence seemed to suck the oxygen out of the confined space and the silence jangled between them. 'Would you like a coffee?' she asked after a moment, not looking at him, concentrating on unpacking the bags. She wished he would leave so that she could breathe properly.

'Coffee sounds good,' he said laconically. 'Black, two sugars. But maybe you remember that too?'

She did, of course, but Tess was too flustered to respond to his smile.

'Give me five minutes and I'll bring it in,' was all she said.

Tess was waiting for the kettle to boil when the phone in her pocket started to ring. Vanessa. Pulling it out of her jeans, she switched it on. 'Hi,' she said, without checking the call display.

Vanessa was the only person she had given the number to. 'Vanessa?' she said after a few seconds. Sometimes it took a little while for the connection to be made.

When there was still no reply, she took the phone from her ear and looked at the caller display, and everything in her stilled. It wasn't Vanessa calling at all. Whoever it was, they had blocked their number.

Slowly, she switched off the phone and stood by the kettle, biting her knuckle worriedly. How could Martin possibly have got the number? It had to be a mistake. Keying in the wrong digit was easily done. Of course it was just a mistake.

But there was still a pucker between her brows when she took Luke his coffee.

The study was still in a state of organized chaos. Richard's books sat in lumpy piles under dustsheets, while the old bookcases had been dismantled and were propped against the wall. Luke had set up a saw horse by the open window and the smell of cut wood on the warm air hit Tess as soon as she stepped in.

The closet.

The kist.

She faltered under the onslaught of memories so vivid that for one awful moment the floor tilted perilously beneath her feet.

'Hey.' Luke reached her as she tried to fumble the mug onto a surface. He took it from her and set it down before guiding her over to a pile of books. 'Sit here for a second. Put your head between your knees.'

He kept his hand on the back of her neck as she

hung her head and drew in some ragged breaths. The warmth of his palm was disturbingly reassuring.

Slowly, the hollow sense of falling faded and Tess's head cleared enough for her to be able to sit up. 'Thank you,' she said to Luke, who was hunkered down beside her, ferocious brows drawn together in concern. 'I'm all right now.'

'You look like shit,' he said brutally.

'Same old silver-tongued devil,' said Tess, but it was an effort.

He straightened, frowning down at her paper-white face. 'I'm serious. You don't look well.'

'I'm just tired,' she managed. 'I'm not sleeping very well.'

'Tough time?'

Her eyes slid away from his. 'I've had worse,' she said. 'I'm fine now. Really.'

She summoned a smile, but it clearly didn't convince Luke, who stood studying her with a worried expression that sat a little oddly on his stern features. She must look as bad as she felt, Tess decided with an inner grimace.

'Here, have some coffee,' he said after a moment. 'The sugar will do you good.' He handed her the mug she had made for him and she wrapped her hands round it, glad of the warmth. She still felt jarred and queasy. Her teeth clattered against the rim of the mug when she took a tentative sip and she saw Luke shoot her a penetrating glance. He'd perched on a pile of dictionaries, obviously close enough to catch her if she toppled over. Tess wasn't sure whether to be touched or irritated by his concern.

She didn't want Luke to think of her as needy and pathetic. She'd had enough of being treated as someone incapable of making her own decisions, a fragile flower who had to be looked after by a man. But if she was determined to show that she could manage on her own, she wasn't going about it the right way by practically passing out at Luke's feet, was she? She really had to pull herself together and stop being so feeble.

Taking another sip of coffee, she steadied herself and tried a smile. 'Thanks, that's better.' She offered him the mug. 'Would you like your coffee back?'

'You have it,' he said. 'Your need is greater than mine.' He leant forward, resting his elbows on his knees, his eyes on her face, and Tess squirmed a little under his scrutiny. She wanted to meet his gaze calmly, but her eyes couldn't quite do it. They kept glancing off the angle of his jaw, skittering from the line of his cheek to the cool set of his mouth and back again.

'Have you been ill, Tess?' he asked abruptly.

'No!' Ruffled, she put down the mug and hugged her arms together in an unconsciously defensive gesture. 'There's nothing wrong with me!'

'You're really pale, and you're too thin ... I hardly recognized you at first. And what the hell happened to your hair?'

'I had it cut.'

'It was beautiful hair.' He scowled. 'I always liked it long.'

So had Martin. Sitting in the hairdresser's, hearing the snip, snip of the scissors had felt like an act of liberation. Tess was still light-headed with the defiance of it. Every time she caught a glimpse of herself in a mirror, she was startled and thrilled by her own daring. She looked so different. Older, sharper. More like the person she wanted to be.

She lifted her chin, touched a hand to her hair. The hair that was left. '*I* like it like this,' she said, and this time she was able to meet Luke's eyes directly.

His expression flickered in appreciation, and the corner of his mouth lifted in a crooked smile. 'Fair enough,' he said. He looked down at his hands, and then back up at her with those disconcertingly pale eyes – how could she have forgotten how they could look right through you? – and his voice changed.

'What the hell happened to *you*, Tess?' he asked quietly.

Tess pushed herself to her feet. 'Nothing,' she insisted. What did he want, the whole sad, sordid story? 'I'm not ill. I'm *fine*.' Arms wrapped around herself, she glared down at him with compressed lips. 'I know I'm not looking my best, but I've told you, it's just because I haven't slept well since I moved in here. I think it's just being in a new place, a new bed. Worrying about stuff. And the noise – it's awful.'

Luke's eyes rested on her face for a long moment, before he nodded and to Tess's relief looked away. 'I suppose the centre of the city isn't the quietest of locations,' he said as he got to his feet.

'I don't mind the pubs. I don't hear them at the

back anyway.' Grateful to him for accepting the change of subject, Tess let her shoulders drop. 'It's the rats that bother me.'

Luke bent to retrieve the discarded coffee, but paused at that and his brows shot up. '*Rats?*'

'Or something. Mice maybe.' Tess wished he hadn't stood up. He was too big, too close. He took up too much air.

Edgily, she moved away, pretending to peer under the dustsheets. 'I had a pest controller round a couple of days ago. He said there's nothing there, but there *is*. I can hear it! It sounds as if something is trying to get out of the wall. It's driving me mad!'

The mere thought of it made her voice rise in frustration, and Luke lifted his hands in an infuriatingly calming gesture. 'Would you like me to take a look?'

He was humouring her. Tess's lips pressed together so tightly they almost disappeared. She wasn't going to let Luke Hutton write her off as a hysterical woman. She wasn't going to be written off as anything.

She remembered the first time he had taken her on the back of his bike. They'd gone to the beach, lain in the sand dunes out of the wind.

I wish I could be like you, she had said. *You're so cool, so confident. You don't care what anyone else thinks*. While Tess was awkward and shy, hiding her insecurities and her grief for her father behind an aloof mask that only Luke seemed undaunted by.

Luke had turned his head to look at her. Tess could still see the curve of his mouth, the seriousness in his eyes, still feel the beat of her heart.

I care what you think, he had said. *I don't want you to be cool. I want you to be yourself.*

Tess wanted to be herself again, and the Tess she wanted to be wasn't going to rely on anyone else ever again.

She took a breath, forced calmness into her voice. 'That's kind of you, Luke,' she said, 'but there's really no need. I was just trying to explain why I look such a wreck.'

'If you're sure…'

Tess's phone started to ring before he could finish. She could feel it vibrating in her pocket, and she saw Luke looking around in case it was his. Tess was suddenly certain that it wouldn't be Vanessa calling. It would be that silent breathing again and weariness sloshed through her. She didn't want to answer, didn't want to think about who was calling and why.

She was doing her best to be herself, but she hadn't counted on anonymous phone calls and sleepless nights, on a world that kept slipping out of kilter or a sense of inexplicable dread that slithered at the edges of her mind.

Having checked that it wasn't his own phone ringing, Luke turned and raised his brows in a mute query. Reluctantly, Tess drew the phone from her pocket as if it might spit at her and made herself look at the call display. Please let it be Vanessa, she prayed.

Number blocked.

'Do you want to take that?' Luke made a gesture suggesting that he should leave, but Tess shook her head.

'No.' Making up her mind abruptly, she dropped the phone onto the dustsheet. 'Actually, would you mind looking at the wall after all?' She flashed Luke a brief, meaningless smile. 'I'll let that go to voicemail.'

Had the ringtone always had that awful jeering quality? Tess did her best to ignore the sound of the phone ringing in the study as she led the way along the corridor to her bedroom. Luke made no comment, but it was a relief when the noise cut off at last, although it only served to intensify the silence in the room.

Tess looked around, trying to see it through Luke's eyes. The bed. The chest of drawers pushed into the fireplace. The books that had looked so cheerful and inviting when she first saw them but that now seemed to watch her slyly. Would Luke notice? Would he sense the subtle malevolence in the room, the foreboding that trembled at the edge of her consciousness?

The air felt cold and congealed, and the morning sunshine had yet to make its way round to the window. Tess was very conscious of Luke's presence in the room. He was wonderfully solid, wonderfully *real*, and she had to fight the urge to move closer to him.

'It's a bit gloomy in here, isn't it?' he said.

Tess moistened her lips. 'It is a bit.'

Luke reached up and tapped the lampshade, setting the light swinging around the room. 'Nothing that a decent light and a radiator wouldn't cure.'

The swaying light was making Tess feel giddy, and she blinked hard, flinching as the silence was broken by the anguished rasp and scrabble behind the walls.

'So, where do you think this noise is coming from?' he asked.

Her face lit up. She hadn't wanted to face the fact that she might have been imagining the noise. 'You mean you can hear it too?'

'No.' He glanced at her, his eyes narrowing at the way her face crumpled with disappointment. 'Can you?'

Scrape. Scratch. Scrabble. SCRAPE. SCRAPE. SCRAPE.

It was all she could do not to cover her ears. Tess's eyes slid away from his. 'No,' she said. 'Not now.'

'I suppose it *could* be rats.' After another searching glance, Luke walked over to the wall and tapped on it. 'This would have been an internal wall. It might not be solid.'

A roaring filled Tess's ears, and she took a step back, groping for the edge of the bed, as the light fractured and the room wavered in front of her eyes. For a moment nothing was solid, and then the high-pitched whine of a drill started on the other side of the wall and, as if at a signal, everything slotted back into place.

'Christ, what a bloody racket,' said Luke. 'No wonder you can't sleep if you've got that going on.'

Tess was breathing very carefully, short, shallow breaths. The room seemed steady now.

'They're refurbishing the shop next door. They don't work at night.' The words felt odd in her mouth. She had to move her tongue around them carefully, as if they were stones, but Luke didn't seem to notice anything amiss.

'Maybe they've disturbed something. Let's go and have a look.'

A skip piled high with rubble stood outside, blocking half the street, and the shop window was clouded with swirls of white paint. A notice was taped to the open door. *Hiring now. Chef. Bar Staff (experience necessary). Also part-time waiting staff.*

'Looks like it's going to be a restaurant of some kind,' Luke commented, rapping his knuckles against the glass and walking in without waiting for a reply. 'Richard won't like that.'

Tess didn't answer. She had never been inside the shop before – she was sure she hadn't – but a sense of familiarity was crowding in on her, pressing towards her like the poor outside the Monk Bar barbican. Her throat was dry and clogged with a suffocating conviction that there was something she ought to do, something she ought to *know*.

'Hello?' Luke called.

A local radio station was playing at full blast upstairs, but not quite loud enough to drown out someone talking about a fight with his girlfriend. 'So I'm like, "You're a fucking crazy bitch," and she starts fucking going at me,' he complained, his surly account punctuated by hammering and the rhythmic buzz of a drill.

Luke took a few steps up the narrow metal stairs. 'Hello?' he said again. He glanced over his shoulder at Tess. 'Coming?'

Chapter Six

'I don't think...' Her voice was thin, squeezed out of her chest by the weight of recognition. She knew this place. This was the Maskewes' hall, and when she got to the top she would see the walls panelled with wainscot, the tapestry hangings, the turned armchair over by the fireplace.

She wanted to call Luke back, but he was already disappearing round the bend in the staircase.

Tess's eyes darted around her. The empty shop looked insubstantial, a transparency overlaying the house she had known. Here had been the draper's shop with the great, gleaming bolts of velvet and scarlet, of Holland cloth and lawn and cambric, leaning against the wall or rippling across the counter in swathes of colour. She could see the draper pulling the cloth from the bolt, rubbing the lustrous silk between his square, stubby fingers...

'No,' she whispered, and put out a hand to the wall to steady herself against the pull of memory. 'No, not now.'

Upstairs, she could hear Luke trying to make himself heard over the noise, and then a bellow to someone to turn the radio off.

'Tess?' Luke called.

There was nothing here. It was an empty shop, that was all. Tess took a breath and put one foot on the bottom stair, then the other on the next. Another step, and another. Any moment now would come the raucous creak of the ill-fitting board.

Except that these stairs were made of metal. There was no board, no creak. Of course there wasn't.

You imagine things.

Tess made herself climb the stairs, bracing herself for what she would see at the top. Luke was standing talking to the foreman, and as she hauled herself up the last steps, she made herself look round.

It was bigger and brighter than she had expected. The ceiling had been stripped away to expose the old roof timbers, and the sunlight so absent from her bedroom next door was striping through two dormer windows in what had once been another storey.

The wainscot had gone, the hangings with it. The walls were being stripped right back to uncover grimy grey beams, and the air was spangly with dust which lay thick on the floor where rush matting had once protected the boards. In the place of the turned chair stood a sawhorse, a plank of new wood balanced across it, and the smell rammed at her senses, just as it had done in Richard's study earlier.

Tess balled her hands into fists and struggled to focus on the present.

Luke was explaining about the noise, and the other men shook their heads. 'We haven't seen any sign of rats. You can see, we've stripped the wall right back.'

'Is there anything else it could be? Something in the wiring?'

Tess turned slowly, studying the room with half-narrowed eyes. It wasn't exactly as it had been. Walls had been moved, windows punched in, and the fireplace had been blocked off at some point, but it was the Maskewe hall. She could feel it in her bones. Against the wall directly opposite her was where the turned chair had stood. The stairs had been behind her, and there, where there was now a wall between this building and the flat, had been the door to Mr Maskewe's closet. Her bedroom.

She could hear music. The beat of a drum and the catchy whistle of the pipes. And laughter. Uncertainly, Tess looked around to see where it was coming from. Had the radio been switched on again? She glanced at Luke, wanting to hold on to his solid presence, but all at once he was blurred and the floor was tipping away from her while the music grew louder and louder and the room shuddered and span around her, faster and faster and faster...

'Faster, faster!' Nell was dancing with Peter, her youngest brother, and her favourite. He was eight now, a tow-headed boy with a snub nose and a merry disposition. Quick and restless, he reminded Nell of herself when she was younger. When he walked, he seemed forever on the point of breaking into a run. Nell thought of Peter whenever she watched steam lift the lid of a pot. It was as if there was too much of him to be contained in one boy.

And he danced with an energy that left her breathless. They spun each other round until they were shrieking with laughter, in the middle of the crowded hall.

Outside, winter had the city in a bitter grip. The iron cold had ridged the streets with ice, but inside the Maskewe house the hall was ablaze with candles and hot with the press of bodies. A great fire spat and crackled, and the men stood round it, their furred gowns hitched around their hips, their faces ruddy from the wine and the heat of the flames. They were dealing the way those men always did. Several times Nell had seen them spit on their palms and shake to seal a bargain. They were merchants, even at Christmas.

Their wives had gathered at the other end of the hall, their hoods bobbing and swaying, their voices raised shrill above the sound of the music and stamping feet. The tables had been cleared so the young people could dance, and the waits were crammed into a corner, blowing and drumming and strumming.

To Nell, swinging with Peter in the middle of the floor, the room was a blur of colour and noise. Round and round they went, until she was dizzy with it, and then there was a strange, still moment when everything jarred to a halt. The company spun away and she was alone in the empty hall. Peter had gone; Mr Maskewe's rich hangings had gone. There were no cushions, no candles. No fire in the hearth, no pewter goblets gleaming in the firelight. The room was bare, silent, leached of colour and warmth and life, and Nell stumbled in shock.

Then Peter was hauling her around once more and the hall slotted back into its rightful place.

Nell blinked, but the image had vanished. Everything was as it should be.

'What ails you?' Peter shouted over the music, frowning at the expression on her face, and Nell shook the memory of that empty hall aside and pinned her smile back in place. It was Yuletide. It was a time to be cheerful, not indulge in strange fancies.

'Naught,' she says as the danced ended with a great bang of the drum. Breathless, the company laughed and clapped and called for more. 'I am well.'

'Then let us dance again!' Peter grabbed her hand, but she hung back.

'Later,' she said. 'I want to dance with Tom.' Absently she twisted the garnet ring on her finger as her eyes searched the hall for him. Tom had been on edge all day, which was not like him. She needed to touch him and make him smile.

'Dance with Tom next time,' said Peter. 'Come, or we will lose our place!'

But another voice cut across him before Nell could reply. 'Dance with me.' An order, not an invitation.

It was Ralph Maskewe, resplendent in a red velvet doublet, intricately embroidered, and slashed breeches. His nether stockings were immaculate, and tied precisely at the knee with silk garters. His ruff was crisp and white and puffed rigidly around his neck. Oh, he was by far the comeliest man there. There was no denying that.

Ralph was always polite, always attentive, but something in those pebbly eyes still repelled Nell. She didn't like the way he looked at her, as if he would pin her down, a butterfly under a cat's gleaming claw.

He held out a hand. 'Dance with me,' he said again as Peter slipped away with a grimace behind his back.

Nell was supposed to curtsey and thank Ralph courteously. She was supposed to put her hand in his and smile as he led her out onto the floor, but something in her rebelled. She couldn't shake the conviction that Ralph only asked her to dance because he knew that she didn't want to touch him.

'I thank you, but I am waiting for Tom,' she said, her hands spread flat against her stiff skirts.

'Tom is with his master,' Ralph pointed out. His voice was smooth, but somehow sticky, like the slimy trails snails left on stones early in the morning. It always made Nell want to wash her face.

He gestured towards the fire, to where Tom could indeed be seen next to Mr Todd. In deference to the feast, Tom was wearing his best doublet and hose. He wore them stiffly, as if he would much rather be in breeches and a leather jerkin, and premonition, feather-light, touched Nell between her shoulder blades. Something was wrong. Not the clothes so much as the hunch of his shoulders and the muscle jumping in his jaw. It was not like Tom to look so sober.

'Come, Nell.' A smile played around Ralph's mouth. He was enjoying her reluctance. 'You will have to find a better excuse than that.'

She couldn't think of one. Nell put up her chin. 'I am Eleanor now,' she said instead. 'I am not a child any longer.'

'My brother calls you Nell.'

'That is different.'

'How so?'

'Tom and I are betrothed.'

Ralph shook his head pityingly. 'I think not,' he said. 'Tom has spoken to our father, and to yours. They are agreed. Tom is an apprentice still. He cannot afford a wife, and when he can, he will need one who can bring him honour.'

'Tom told me this,' Nell said. 'I am hurly-burly, the hoyden daughter of an impoverished merchant, and no fit match for a Maskewe, your father thinks.' The sting of it curdled her voice.

'Can you deny it?'

She curled her fingers into her skirts. 'I would be a good wife for Tom,' she said stoutly. 'I *will* be. We knew they would not let us marry immediately,' she told Ralph. 'It matters not. I will not marry anyone else and nor will Tom. We are promised to each other. He gave me a ring – see?' She held up her hand so the garnet on her finger glimmered in the candlelight. 'And I gave him a knife. We made the vow in front of witnesses. It is done.'

'Done?' Ralph's smile slid into a sneer. 'You know nothing of done, *Eleanor*. It takes more than a trumpery ring and a knife to make a betrothal. I do not advise you to take on my father as your enemy,' he added, his voice silky, and she took a step back, sensing a threat.

'I don't want an enemy,' she said valiantly. 'I only want to marry Tom.'

'Have you not yet learnt that we cannot always have what we want?' said Ralph. 'Now come, lower your chin and let us dance.' He lifted his hand to her again, imperative. 'You should be kind to me, Eleanor,' he said. 'If you are wise, you will try to get me on your side.'

He was right, Nell knew. She should be cleverer than she was. But still the thought of putting her hand in his made her skin shrink. She had no choice, though, she knew that. Tom was half turned away, nodding at something his master was saying. He could not come and rescue her, and why would he? Ralph was his brother. Ralph's father was godfather to her brother. She had no reason not to dance with him.

Setting her mouth in a smile, she laid her fingers against his cool palm. It wasn't clammy, it wasn't rank with sweat or dirt, but she couldn't stop the tiny flinch of revulsion, and Ralph knew it. He smiled as he led her into the dance.

'You look very fine tonight, Eleanor,' he said after a moment, his voice a caress that made her skin crawl more than his sneer.

'I thought I was a hoyden?'

'A beautiful hoyden.'

She didn't want Ralph to think she was beautiful. She had dressed for Tom, and she was pleased when she and Alice had finished lacing each other up. Her bodice was embroidered, her skirts sat stiffly over the padded roll at her hips and swished satisfyingly when she danced. In honour of Yule, a red ribbon was threaded around the edge of her smock and she had ruffs at her wrists and at her collar.

'You look beautiful,' Alice had said, twitching her skirts into place.

Nell liked it when Alice said she was beautiful, but in Ralph's mouth the word was tinged with something slimy and unpleasant.

She wished she was dancing with Peter again. The dance was slower, more stately, but the other dancers soon turned it into a romp. Not Nell and Ralph. They circled, bowed, pressed their palms together as they turned, and Nell looked everywhere but at Ralph.

The music played, the dancers turned. In a gap through heads and shoulders, Nell caught a glimpse of Tom. Mr Todd had turned to Mr Maskewe and Tom was watching the dancing now. Watching for her. His expression was set, determined.

The dance moved Nell round, and she craned her neck to catch Tom's eye. This time he saw her, and as always when they saw each other there was a little jump in the air, a sense of everything slotting into place, the way a good joiner slid a joist into a beam so that it fitted perfectly. And as always, they smiled. They couldn't help themselves.

The next moment, the smile was wiped from Nell's face and she gasped as Ralph's fingers closed around hers in a vicious grip. It only lasted an instant, long enough for him to turn her round in the dance, and then he dropped it again.

'I beg your pardon,' he said, smiling at her expression. 'Did I hold you too tight?'

Nell moistened her lips. Her hand was throbbing, and disquiet stirred in her belly at the queer gleam behind Ralph's smile. He was angry, she realized. 'It is nothing,' she said after a moment but she was careful not to look at Tom again.

The music seemed to last forever but at last the waits put down their instruments as ale was carried over to them. Nell curtseyed to Ralph, her eyes lowered.

'I thank you for the dance,' she said.

'Nell!' Tom grabbed her hand as she murmured an excuse and hurried away from Ralph, not knowing where she was going, only that she had to get away from him.

'Oh, Tom!' She clutched him gratefully. 'Where were you? I have had to dance with your brother.'

'I saw. You didn't look as if you were enjoying it much.'

'He makes me uneasy,' Nell confessed.

'He's a cold fish, but there is no harm to him,' said Tom, the way he always did. The truth was that he didn't know his brother well, and he didn't understand why Nell disliked him so much. She had never told him of her conviction that it was Ralph who shut her in the chest that day, and she didn't tell him now about that savage twist of his fingers around hers. Even if he believed her, what could Tom do?

All at once the hall seemed stifling. The heat and the noise were beating at her.

'It's so hot in here,' she said. 'Let's go outside.'

They slipped down to the yard, ignoring the couple hard at work in the shadows below the stairs, their muffled gasps and grunts and the rustle of skirts hauled to the waist not quite silenced by the sound of the feast spilling down the staircase.

Outside, the frost riming the roof tiles glittered

in the star light, and the air was blade sharp and so cold it set Nell's teeth on edge.

Tom stamped his feet. 'Should have brought a cloak,' he said.

'I don't mind the cold,' said Nell, although it was biting her face and stinging her eyes. Their breath puffed out and hung in frozen clouds of vapour between them. 'I haven't seen you all evening.'

'I know.' Tom drew a breath, then let it out. 'I am to go back to Hamburg in the spring,' he said abruptly. 'Mr Todd spoke to my father today. It is agreed.'

The numbness in Nell's toes crept higher, towards her heart. 'For how long?'

'A year or two, maybe longer.'

'Two years!' she said, stricken.

'It is part of my apprenticeship. You know how it is, Nell.'

Yes, she knew. She had always known. Tom had been learning to merchant. Now he was to manage his master's business overseas and complete his training. Not all young men were as lucky. She should be glad for him.

'We knew it would happen,' Tom ploughed on doggedly. He had been avoiding Nell until he had found the courage to tell her.

'I know. It's just...' Nell couldn't finish. It was all very well knowing that something would happen, but now that it was there, the news clanged through her like a tolling bell.

She was not a fool. Neither she nor Tom had the means to marry, but while they could steal away for a few hours every now and then, or snatch a kiss in a hidden alleyway, Nell had refused to look to the future. They had been as careful as they could, and in truth had done their share of field work and wall work. Nell had slipped out to old Mother Dent, the wise woman who lived on the common. She was not the first maid who had been to her, and she would not be the last. In exchange for a penny and a lump of cheese, Mother Dent showed her where to find the square stalks of hoarhound, with its rough crumpled leaves; how to mix the juice with honey or dry the leaves to make a concoction. She and Tom were careful, and they were lucky, but it was not a secret. Everyone knew she and Tom were sweethearts.

'How will I bear it without you?' she said.

Tom reached for her then. He didn't say anything, but he pressed his face into her hair as he held her tightly against him. His hands gripped her, nearly as tight as Ralph had squeezed her earlier, but this time Nell welcomed the hurt of it. When Tom's fingers dug through her bodice she couldn't feel her heart cracking. She clung to his waist with the same desperation, careless of who might see them now. The knowledge that Tom would go had been bobbing at the back of her mind ever since that day by the Foss. She had done her best to push it down and out of sight, but now it was back on the surface and she couldn't ignore it any more.

'I will miss you,' Tom said, muffled against her hair. Her velvet cap had slid to the back of her head and was in danger of slithering off her hair altogether.

'I will wait for you,' Nell promised desperately. 'You are my betrothed, whatever our fathers may say.' Pulling slightly away, she showed him the ring on her finger, although he put it there himself. 'This was your gift to me,' she said with a fierce look. 'I know what it means. There will be no one else,' she said. 'I have promised.'

She pressed herself back into the solid warmth of him. 'Perhaps it will not be so bad.' She was trying to make the best of it but her voice lacked conviction. 'At least when it is over, you will be free. Your father will support you, and when you are a merchant yourself you will be able to do as you please. We will be married then. We always knew that we would have to wait.'

Her feet were numb with cold, but she couldn't bear to move from Tom's arms. She could feel his heart beating through his padded doublet. He didn't want to leave her, she believed that, but she knew that he was excited too. He longed to be gone, to brace his feet on a plunging deck and lean into the wind, to feel the spray on his face and taste the sea on his lips. He would like being in Hamburg. Perhaps he would have to sit at his master's accounts, but he would also be able to plunge his hands into sacks of cloves, and unwrap bales of ginger. He would hold jugs up to the light to check for cracks and smooth his hand over furs. He would listen to the creak and groan of the ships and the curses of the mariners and he would be part of a wider world.

And she would stay in York.

Nell seethed at the unfairness of it. Yes, it would be hard for Tom, but how much harder for her.

She had nothing to do but wait.

But so it had ever been for women, she reminded herself, and she made herself tip her head back and show Tom a smiling face.

'Let's not be too sad too soon,' she said. 'It is not spring yet. We should make the most of the time we have.'

So they tried, but the knowledge that it would soon be gone was always there. Nell clutched every moment that she had with Tom now. In the past, she had grumbled about winter. She didn't like waking in an icy chamber, or having to blow on her hands to warm them when she was in the market. She hated the rain that fell day after day, turning the streets to a quagmire, and spilling out of blocked gutters. In the past, she had longed for spring to come, when she could escape out to Paynley's Crofts. She had always liked it outside the walls best, where there was space and she didn't feel so shut in. She liked to help old Dick tend the vegetables in the Harrisons' garden: onions, turnips, radishes, lettuce. They grew herbs too, in rows of rosemary and lavender, sorrel and thyme, tansy, rue and valerian. When spring came, Nell would kneel and press her knuckles into the warm earth, clearing the weeds away so the green shoots could grow. Alice couldn't understand it, but for Nell spring meant escape from the narrow streets and clustered houses. She could take her basket and gather wildflowers to dry for the still room, and there was always a chance of meeting Tom too.

Spring was her favourite time, but that year she dreaded its arrival. The winter passed too fast. It was Epiphany and then it was Lady Day and all at once it was Easter, and Tom's master went to Hull to arrange his passage to Hamburg, leaving Tom to say his farewells.

'It will be soon,' Tom told Nell. His gear was already packed in a canvas bag he could sling over his shoulder. 'They will send word when the keelboat is ready to leave and I will come and say goodbye.'

Almost, now, Nell wished the moment would come. She had been dreading it for so long. Inside she was rigid, braced against the time when she would have to let him go. Conversation, once so easy between them, had dried into a lumpy gruel as the time of his departure approached. There was too much to say, and not enough. The sooner Tom went, Nell told herself, the sooner he would return.

She thought that she was ready, but when the moment came it struck her like a blow to the stomach. It was a bright April day with a chill wind that made Nell's eyes sting as she beat the carpets in the Harrison's yard. There was still no word from the staithe, which meant another night to wait and wonder if this would be the last time she would see him, the last time she would touch him, for two long years.

The dust swirled in the air and she was coughing and spluttering when a small boy came running into the yard. 'You're to come now,' he told Nell breathlessly. 'Master Tom, he's bout to get on't boat. He told me to tell you to hurry.'

Nell didn't wait to take off her apron. She didn't ask permission of Mistress Harrison. She dropped the carpet beater, picked up her skirts and ran along Ousegate, careless of the pursed lips of the goodwives sitting at their doors, heedless of the catcalls from apprentices. Dodging the piles of horse dung, jumping over the gutter, she narrowly avoided a collision with Henry Judd, who was setting out his stall. He shook his fist after her, but Nell didn't wait to apologize. She was gripped by a terrible conviction that she would be too late, and panic pushed her on, stumbling over the cobbles until she reached the staithe, where she stopped to heave in a breath, a hand pressed to her waist.

'Tom!'

They were loading the last bales of cloth onto the keelboat and Tom's canvas bag was already stowed in the prow.

The sail was snapping and cracking in the wind, and the mariner's man was hauling it up the mast, the mariner himself shouting on the quayside, impatient to get everyone on board, to catch the tide.

'Nell!' Tom pulled her behind a stack of barrels. 'I thought I'd have to go without seeing you! Ralph has kept me here all morning, and then he decided we'd have to catch the tide...' Desperately, he kissed her, and she clung to him. She had meant to be brave, to smile at him as he left, but she was overwhelmed by the knowledge that the time had come and any minute now he would be gone.

'I love you,' she said unsteadily, pressing frantic kisses along his jaw, against his mouth. 'I love you.'

She couldn't believe that this was the last time that she would touch him for two years. The last time she would be able to press her face into his neck and smell his dear, familiar smell.

'It is not so long,' Tom tried to comfort her. 'It is not so far. The same moon will shine down on both of us, Nell, and when I am away, wherever I am, I will look up at it and think of you.'

It was a comforting idea and Nell seized on it. 'And you will know that I am looking up too, and dreaming of you and waiting for you to come home.'

Tom nodded, tried to smile. 'The moon will be our messenger. Every time you look at it, it will remind you that I love you, that I will come back, that I have not forgotten you.'

Nell's answering smile wobbled, but it was there. 'I will look,' she said. 'Every night when I go to bed, I will look for a message from you.'

'You will stand by your promise?' he asked, suddenly urgent.

'I will be torn apart by wild horses before I break my vow,' she said fiercely. 'I will be true.'

'The tide is on the turn,' shouted the mariner. 'If you don't come now, I'll go without you.'

'Go.' Nell pushed Tom from her, her throat closing on a painful rasp. He had to go. There would be no future for him until he completed his apprenticeship, and learning his master's business overseas was part of that. 'Go.'

So he did. He let her hand slip from his and he took a despairing step back before forcing himself to turn and run for the keelboat, where the mariner was already pulling up the gangplank.

He leapt aboard as the sailors started to push away from the quay with their long poles.

Dry-eyed, Nell stood, her arms wrapped around herself, while a lead weight settled inside her. The wind snatched at her cap and stung her cheeks with tiny slaps, but she barely noticed. She was watching the second sail flutter and then fill as the men hauled it up. They were away from the shore now.

She wanted to cry out to Tom, to make them stop and come back. She needed to tell him that she couldn't bear it, but already the boat was moving out into the current and Tom was getting smaller and smaller as it headed steadily away. It dipped, lurched to one side in a gust of wind, then recovered, before sailing on and on until it curved around the gentle bend and was lost out of sight.

He was gone.

Moving stiffly as if she were an old woman, Nell turned and found Ralph Maskewe watching her, an unsettling gleam in his pale eyes, and even through her numbness, something in her jerked at the sight of him.

'I will take you back to your mistress,' he said.

Nell shook her head dumbly. The last thing she wanted at that moment was company, and Ralph's least of all, but Ralph insisted. He made her take his arm, and in the end she did, because what did it matter? What did anything matter now Tom had gone?

She looked over her shoulder to the place where Tom had been, as if he might miraculously reappear, but he didn't, of course, and Ralph urged her on, up the lane, back to the world where there was no Tom any more.

'You should be careful of walking alone in these streets,' Ralph said. 'It is not safe nowadays. Have you not heard? There was another body found yesterday morning. A rogue is responsible, no doubt, but he is prowling in search of young girls like you.'

Nell was thinking about Tom, sailing away, away from her. With an effort, she roused herself to speech. 'Not like me,' she said tonelessly. 'I thought the dead girls were all vagrants.'

'So I believe, but there is no telling when this monster's tastes may change, and we all know that you are reckless, Nell.'

Her name in his mouth sounded faintly unpleasant. She imagined it being pushed forward by his tongue, bumping against his teeth.

'Eleanor,' she reminded him clearly. She was only Nell for Tom and for herself. 'I am Eleanor now. And I thank you for your concern, but you need not trouble yourself about me. I will stay safely at home now.'

The slaps of the breeze were getting harder and harder. No, not the wind, she realized. Someone was patting her face.

'Tess? Come on, Tess, wake up.'

'Is she okay? Should I call an ambulance?'

'I think she just fainted – ah, she's coming round ... Tess? Can you hear me?'

She didn't recognize the voices. 'Tom?' She groped for his hand, and the fingers that clasped hers were calloused like Tom's, and reassuringly steady and warm.

'It's all right. Just stay there a moment.'

Her lids fluttered open, and she looked uncomprehendingly into a strange face with keen grey eyes, shaggy hair and a rogue's prickle of stubble. Snatching her hand back, she scrambled away in fright. What if Ralph was right, and this was the rogue who preyed on the unprotected girls of the city? How had she fallen into his clutches?

'Tom?' Her voice was thin with fear as she looked wildly around for him, but she was in a bare, dusty room with a cluster of men watching her with odd expressions.

'It's Luke,' said the rogue.

Memory slammed through her, rushing into her head, swirling around like a wave that was sucked out again, leaving her sick and dizzy.

'Luke...' Tess pushed shaky hands through her hair. Yes, she remembered now. She had come with Luke to speak to the builders. She remembered climbing the stairs, waiting for the step that creaked. Remembered that frightening sense of familiarity, how she had stared around the empty hall.

'Sorry, I ... what happened?'

'You were just standing there when you keeled over. You gave us a hell of a fright!' Luke helped her up when she made to struggle to her feet. 'Are you sure you should be getting up yet?'

She had to cling to his arm to stop her legs buckling beneath her. 'How ... how long was I out?'

'A couple of minutes, maybe. Long enough for me to be really worried about you anyway.'

A couple of minutes. Yet as Nell she had lived through a whole winter. Pain jabbed behind her eyes and her throat burned with unshed tears.

'I ... see,' she managed with difficulty, but she didn't see at all. She didn't understand anything. Recovered memory had seemed the obvious answer to her dreams of Nell, but how could dreams feel that real, that *true?*

One of the builders produced a stool. 'Sure you don't want to sit down, love?' The others were eyeing her warily, as if afraid that she was going to be sick, or burst into tears. Tess didn't blame them. She felt like doing both, but she mustered a smile.

'I'm fine, really. Sorry for the fuss.'

Luke was still scowling with concern. 'I think I should take you to hospital.'

'No!' Tess's response was instinctive. At hospital they would want to examine her. They would want to know what happened, and what could she tell them? *Oh, I was just off in the sixteenth century for a while?*

If Martin got wind of it... Ice pooled at the base of Tess's spine at the thought. 'I mean, no, I'll be fine,' she said more moderately. 'Really. I just need to go and sit down for a while.'

She had managed to let go of Luke at last, but her hands were shaking, and they throbbed agonizingly. She saw Luke's gaze drop to them, and she dug her fingers into the pockets of her jeans.

'I'll go with you,' he said. 'We'd better leave the rat problem for another day.'

Tess wanted to insist that she could manage on

her own, but in the end she was glad of his support. Clearly unconvinced by her protestations that she was fine, Luke helped her back down to the street and then up the stairs next door to the door of her flat. Steering her into the front room, he settled her onto a sofa and brought her a glass of water. 'Here,' he said, proffering it brusquely.

Her throat was hot and raw and the water was soothing. 'Thank you.'

Luke pulled out one of the chairs from the table, swung it round and sat on it facing her. 'Are you sure you shouldn't see a doctor? That's twice you've gone faint on me today.'

'It's nothing,' said Tess, holding tightly on to the water. 'Nothing medical.'

His eyes narrowed. 'Then what? Something's wrong, Tess. I know. Tell me what the hell is going on.'

Chapter Seven

There was a long silence. Luke just sat there, waiting for an answer. She had forgotten how patient he could be, how stubborn. He was going to insist on an answer, and he wouldn't go until he had one. Tess could feel her strength sagging, but what could she tell him?

In the end, she opted for the truth. 'I don't really know,' she said.

'Who's Tom?' Luke leant forward. 'Is he your husband?'

'No.'

'Your lover?' His voice took on a harsh edge, and to Tess's horror, her eyes filled with tears.

Tom. Oh, Tom. 'No.'

She fumbled the glass onto a side table, but she had hesitated just a little too long, and Luke had seen the sheen of tears. Tess could practically see his defences going back up as he sat back.

'It's none of my business anyway.'

'I don't have a lover! It's nothing like that. Tom ... oh, I can't explain,' she said wretchedly. She put a hand to her head where the pain still jabbed behind her eye. 'Something weird is going on and I don't know what to do.'

Luke's expression sharpened. 'Weird?'

The words teetered on the edge of Tess's tongue. *I keep slipping back to another time. I'm living another life. I'm a girl who died over four hundred years ago.*

Part her of her longed to tell him, longed to share her fear, and her fascination. She wanted to trust him, but how could she dare? The old Luke would have listened, but what did she know about him now, this man with the intent gaze and the inflexible mouth? He was tougher now, sterner, harder to read.

Tess would like to think that he had put their past behind him, but they had parted so bitterly all those years ago, and she sensed a wariness in him now that was probably equal to her own. True, he had been kind earlier, and there had even been a moment when that awful stilted politeness had evaporated and she had let herself wonder if it might be possible to be friends again, but how would he react if she told him exactly what was happening to her? Tess couldn't bear the thought of confiding in him, only to be written off as a middle-class hysteric: spoilt, neurotic, attention-seeking. It was what Martin would say, after all.

Luke was watching her face with those unnervingly keen eyes. 'I'm worried about you, Tess,' he said.

Tess hesitated, gnawing on her knuckle. The temptation to confide in him was very strong, but she couldn't bear to see his expression change. She couldn't bear it if that cool mouth twisted with contempt, if he said what Martin would say. If he made her feel what Martin always made her feel.

No, she couldn't risk it.

Besides, how could she tell him what was happening if she didn't know herself? Something was wrong – there was no getting round that. She couldn't fall asleep without warning in the middle of the day, but if she wasn't asleep, she wasn't dreaming. And if she wasn't dreaming, she was ... what? Travelling through time? *Really?*

It couldn't be true. Everything in Tess rebelled at the very idea. She didn't want to accept it. She *wouldn't* accept it. There must be another explanation. But nothing else made sense.

And until she found one that she could believe, she would have to deal with this alone. Whatever *this* was. Wearily, Tess rubbed her hands over her face.

'Forget it,' she said. 'I'm just tired.'

'Come on, Tess–' Luke had started to protest when the phone in the study began its shrill, insistent ringing.

Tess's stomach flipped at the sound. She wanted to ignore it again, but the alternative was to stay there and try and convince Luke that she wasn't crazy, and she wasn't sure that she had the strength for that. Besides, it might be about Oscar.

She levered herself unsteadily to her feet. 'Excuse me. I'd better get that.'

Her legs were so wobbly still that she had to hold onto the wall, but she made it to the study, followed by an obviously concerned Luke.

Tess was thinking more clearly now. She was glad she hadn't succumbed to the temptation to blurt out her fear and confusion. If their positions were reversed, she wouldn't hesitate to recommend that he see a doctor, and she knew Luke would do the same. She couldn't risk him frogmarching her to a GP for Prozac or arranging for her to be carted off to a psychiatric ward at Bootham Park. Not until she had ensured that Martin would never get custody of Oscar.

Turning her shoulder on Luke, she picked up the phone without looking at the caller display. 'Sorry, I need to take this,' she said. 'Hello?' she said into the phone as she walked out of the study, leaving Luke behind, and she wasn't even surprised when the only response was the hiss of static in her ear.

'You haven't given my mobile number to anyone, have you?'

Tess turned her phone edgily in her hands.

'Of course not,' said Vanessa in surprise. 'Why?'

Tess told her about the calls she had been getting. 'Only you, Mum and the school have this number.'

'It's probably a mistake.' Vanessa had been running and was wearing tight Lycra shorts and a top with complicated straps. Her hair was twisted up in its usual scrunchie, and her feet shifted restlessly in her trainers. 'Graham's always ringing me and not saying anything, and when I ask him about it later it turns out he had the phone in his pocket and pressed my number by mistake.' She laughed merrily. 'Goodness knows who else he rings by accident!'

'But why would it keep on happening? Nobody else should have the number in their phone.'

'Perhaps whoever it is put your number in by mistake. It's really easy to mix up digits and input the wrong number.'

'Perhaps.' Tess was unconvinced, but Vanessa clearly didn't think there was anything to be concerned about.

Chewing her cheek, Tess watched Oscar running around the playground, his sweatshirt trailing behind him in the dust. He was laughing, and her heart clenched at the sight of him absorbed in his game. He was such a solemn little boy. He had quickly learnt to make himself quiet and still when Martin was around. This was what he had needed: other children to run around with, a normal school, silly games.

She had done the right thing bringing him to York, Tess told herself. She couldn't let silent phone calls or bizarre dreams knock her off course. She had to stay steady for Oscar.

'Is everything all right?' Vanessa was passing the

time doing a few bends and stretches. 'You look a bit peaky.'

Anyone would look peaky next to her glowing fitness, Tess thought with a touch of sourness. Luke's insistence on how dreadful she looked was still rankling.

'I'm just a bit tired. I haven't been sleeping well.'

Luke hadn't believed her, but Vanessa accepted the explanation without a blink 'I'm not surprised in that horrible flat!'

'It's not that.'

Tess drew a breath. Ever since the incident with Luke, she had been thinking about how much she wanted to talk to someone about what was happening. It was stupid not to, she had decided in the end. Whatever she had told Luke, she hadn't been doing a good job of coping with it by herself, had she?

She half-regretted not telling Luke now, but the opportunity had passed and he had withdrawn like a snail shrinking into its shell. If she hadn't known better, she would have wondered if he had been hurt by her refusal to confide in him.

Anyway, wouldn't it make more sense to talk to Vanessa? It was Vanessa who had befriended Tess when her parents had first moved to York, and they had been inseparable all through school, hanging around in each other's bedrooms or in the Museum Gardens until they were old enough to spend Saturday nights in Ziggy's or Harry's Bar in Micklegate.

Vanessa had been her closest friend. Until Luke. And though they had lost touch once Tess moved to London, the moment Tess had come back, Vanessa had been there to help. Perhaps Vanessa could be a bit bossy, and there were times when Tess had to grit her teeth at her smug certainty about everything, but she was kind and she was generous, and they had known each other a long time. If she couldn't tell Vanessa, she couldn't tell anyone.

'I've been having these dreams,' she said.

'Dreams?' Vanessa took her elbow and pushed it behind her ear. 'What sort of dreams? Nightmares?'

'No, well, not exactly. They're just so vivid, Van. I'm this girl in Elizabethan York. I know it sounds mad, but it's like I'm her. It's like I'm *there*.' Tess flexed her sore fingers impotently, trying to explain. 'In the dreams, I have memories. I know how the street smells. I know how tight my bodice is laced. I can taste the food.' She ran her tongue over her teeth, remembering the congealed sauces with their spicy edge, the heavy pastry, the tantalizing aroma of roasting meat. 'Do you ever have dreams like that?'

'Never.' Vanessa's ponytail bounced emphatically when she shook her head. 'I hardly ever dream. If you ask me, Tess, you're not tired enough. You should take some exercise. Come for a run with me and I promise you, you'll have no problem sleeping.'

'So you don't think there's any chance those dreams might be ... real?'

'Real?'

'Like I might be somehow reliving the life of someone in the past.'

'Of course not.' Vanessa laughed, then stopped

when she saw Tess's expression. '*You* don't, surely?'

'No ... at least ... is it so unthinkable?'

'Tess! You're not serious?'

Of course she wasn't serious. How could she be?

'No ... it's just that Mum was reminding me the other day about things I used to see when I was a kid. Things there was no good explanation for.'

'It doesn't sound like your mother to encourage you in that!'

'She didn't. She said I was just overimaginative.'

'Well, you *were* a bit of a drama queen at times,' said Vanessa, and although she smiled, Tess could hear an undercurrent of something – amusement? contempt? – in her voice.

'I *was?*' She didn't remember that. When she thought about growing up in York, she thought about how desperately self-conscious she had been about her weight. And how much she had missed her father. She didn't remember making scenes.

'Oh, yeah. Remember that school trip to Margaret Clitherow's house?'

Tess shifted uneasily. 'No.' That headache was back, jabbing insistently at her mind.

'Yes, you do,' Vanessa insisted. 'It wasn't much of a trip as it was only to see the shrine in the Shambles, but they brought us in on a bus. Jeanette had a huge bag of marshmallows, and we had a race to finish them by the time we got off the bus...' She trailed off when Tess still looked blank. 'You must remember that!'

'I don't.'

'We were all feeling sick when we got to the Shambles, but of course you had to be sicker than anyone else.' Vanessa smiled again but the glance that went with it was pin sharp. 'The rest of us just felt queasy, but you made a huge performance out of it. You started panting and groaning and carrying on, and then you reeled out of the house and threw up all over the Shambles. It was gross!' She looked hard at Tess. 'Oh, come on, I can't believe you don't remember that!'

It was coming back. The dim room, the horror lurking in the air. She hadn't wanted to go inside – Tess did remember that now. There had been a dreadful pressure on her chest, a huge weight pressing her down, down, down, so that she couldn't breathe. She didn't remember getting herself outside, just a roaring sound in her ears. She had been sick, yes, but there was something wrong with Vanessa's story...

'I didn't eat any marshmallows,' she said slowly.

'Yes, you did,' Vanessa corrected her. 'That's why you were so sick.'

'But I never liked them.'

'I can see why you wouldn't like them now. Being sick like that would be enough to put anyone off. I'm not surprised you haven't touched one since. I'm not mad about them myself.'

'No, I meant–' Tess stopped. There was no point in arguing with Vanessa. She was so sure of herself that Tess would never convince her that she wasn't right.

But she had always loathed marshmallows. Her father had taken her on a memorable camping trip when she was six. Their campfire meal had ended with toasted marshmallows, and was followed that night by a bout of food poisoning that had inextricably linked the two in Tess's mind. There was no way she would have stuffed herself with marshmallows on a school trip when she was thirteen. Something else had made her sick in that house in the Shambles.

Vanessa might be sure Tess had been dramatizing herself, but Tess remembered only the horror, the sensation of being crushed, as Margaret Clitherow had been. They had known about Margaret's fate, of course. That was the point of the trip. Margaret Clitherow was a butcher's wife who had been pressed to death between two doors for refusing to renounce the Catholic faith, and who was later canonized. The house where she had lived in the Shambles was now a shrine. So it was always possible that Tess had been so involved in the story that she had a physical reaction to it. Overreacted, Vanessa – and no doubt her mother – would say.

But that wasn't how Tess remembered it.

Why were so many of her memories out of kilter with everyone else's?

'I wouldn't worry about it anyway,' said Vanessa briskly. 'It sounds to me as if you're just overtired. Your marriage has broken down, you've moved house ... it's no wonder you're stressed.'

'Yes.' Tess looked away. 'Yes, I'm sure you're right.'

Oscar was still engrossed in his game. It was time to change the subject.

'Hey, you'll never guess who's making Richard's shelves.'

Vanessa paused in mid-stretch. 'Who?'

'Luke Hutton.'

She had wanted it to sound a funny coincidence, no big deal, but Vanessa was appalled.

'You're kidding! Oh, Tess, you poor thing. How awful for you!'

Tess was taken aback. She had known Vanessa hadn't cared much for Luke but she hadn't thought she disliked him that much.

'It's okay, really. I don't mind.'

'He was such a bastard to you,' said Vanessa with such venom that Tess found herself driven to defend Luke, something she had never expected to be doing.

'He wasn't *that* bad.'

'He was!' Vanessa's mouth was set as she moved on to the other elbow. 'I always thought he was using you.'

'Using me?' Tess let out a little huff of amusement. Either her memory was completely wrong, or Vanessa's was. 'How on earth do you work that out? I was just a fat lump, too shy to talk to anyone. I couldn't believe he wanted to go out with me at all.'

'You come from a nice family.'

Tess stared at her friend, wondering if she was joking, but Vanessa seemed perfectly serious.

'Oh, come on, Van! That's the last thing someone like Luke would care about.'

'You think so?' Vanessa sniffed. 'You know his father spent some time in prison, don't you?'

Annoyance bubbled in Tess's throat. 'Yes, I did know,' she said evenly. 'Luke told me. Not that it's got anything to do with Luke. If he wanted to cash in on my connections – although God knows what they were! – he went the wrong way about I when he dumped me, didn't he?'

'Only because he could see you were moving on to better things.'

Better things? Tess thought about her life with Martin and said nothing.

'I just don't want you to get hurt again,' said Vanessa, misreading her silence. 'You were devastated when Luke dropped you like that. I never trusted him,' she said. 'And how right I was! You just be careful around him, Tess.'

Tess sat at the table in the bay window, but she couldn't concentrate on the records. The scrawled writing kept blurring on the screen and her eyes were drawn again and again to the blue sky that beckoned above the rooftops opposite. The flat felt stale, the air oppressive.

Nothing to do with the fact that Luke wasn't there.

Strange how much safer she felt when he was around. Not that she had been having much to do with him. He didn't work on the shelves every day, and when he did turn up, he was often gruff. Once or twice Tess had caught him giving her searching looks, but their conversations were limited to whether or not he wanted a coffee.

Once or twice Tess had caught herself wishing that he would look at her with the same concern again, that he would sit her down and make her tell him what was bothering her, but each time she pushed the thought aside. She didn't need Luke Hutton to make things easier for her. If she wanted to talk to him, she could talk to him, she reminded herself.

Her choice. Her way.

It had been two weeks since Tom had left. Since she had *dreamt* about Tom leaving, Tess corrected herself quickly. At odd moments she had found herself thinking about Nell. When the moon hung over the rooftops, she would look up at it and remember the promise she had made.

No, the promise she had *dreamt* making.

The memory was still extraordinarily vivid but Tess had begun to think that Vanessa was right, and it was just a bizarre episode brought on by the stress of leaving her marriage. It had been frightening in its intensity, but fascinating at the same time. There was a little bit of Tess that wished she could return and find out what happened to Nell, but whenever she caught herself thinking that, she would clamp firmly down on the thought to stop it going any further.

Recovered memory was the only reasonable explanation, and that meant Nell had no story. She was just a figment of Tess's imagination, just like the faces which sometimes jumped into her head as she worked on the records, making her mind stumble in the startling detail with which she could picture them: Ambrose Cook with his mournful mouth and spindly legs; Michael Mudd, gap-toothed, bulbous-nosed, his butcher's hands rimed with dried, brown blood; the widow Barker, her hands knotty, her back buckled; Cuthbert Dawson, with eyes that turned down at the corners and made him oddly attractive in spite of the stained doublet straining over his substantial stomach.

Tess told herself it didn't mean anything. They were just echoes of characters in a film she had seen once, or figments of her imagination. They weren't real.

There had been no more dreams, and she told herself she was glad.

Still, she always preferred it when Luke was around. The sound of him banging and hammering in the study was strangely reassuring. In spite of the restlessness she sensed in him, in spite of the occasional surliness, there was something steadying about his presence. Once, years earlier, Tess had been wretchedly seasick on a cross-Channel ferry. Her father had told her to concentrate on the horizon. 'Keep your eyes on a fixed point,' he had said. 'It'll settle your stomach.' Now, whenever time and reality threatened to slip and slide, Tess thought of Luke as her horizon, her fixed point. It seemed to work.

Her hands still felt raw; sometimes the pain was so great she would have to stop typing. But just when she decided that there was no choice but to go to the doctor, the ache would subside, and she would put it off for another day.

She was still sleeping badly too. More than once Tess had given up and slept on the sofa rather than listen to the anguished scrabbling in the wall. She'd had the pest controllers back, and twice been back to the builders next door to ask if they would look in the wall, but they had obviously written her off as a crazy lady. There was nothing in the wall, they said. No rats, no noise, no nothing.

At odd times of the day and night, her phone would ring. Tess always checked the display now, and if it said 'blocked number', she would let it ring until voicemail kicked in. There was never any message. She'd debated getting a new phone, but if it was Martin and he'd tracked down her number, there was nothing to stop him finding the new one. She would wait him out, Tess decided. As long as she didn't answer, it was an irritant, no more. But still she jumped every time the phone rang, and she had taken to turning it off as soon as she had picked up Oscar, much to her mother and Vanessa's annoyance.

Tess set her teeth against their complaints, against it all. Oscar was happy and that was all that mattered. He liked school, he loved to go and play with Vanessa's children, Sam and Rosie, and he rushed home every day to see Ashrafar. He was wary of Luke, and avoided him as much as possible, but he had Bink, he had his mother and he was allowed to watch television. In Oscar's world, all was well. Tess intended to keep it that way.

From Martin there was no word. Rather than be reassured, Tess grew more and more tense, waiting for him to make a move. Once or twice she thought she caught a glimpse of him in the street and her heart would jerk, but when she followed, determined to force a showdown, it always turned out to be a perfect stranger.

You're highly strung. You imagine things.

Anyone would say the same.

With a sigh, Tess pushed her laptop away. It was hopeless trying to work when she was this tired and the sky over the red-tiled roofs opposite was a high, soft blue. She would go out for a walk and clear her head.

It was good to wear sandals again and be able to walk out without a coat, to feel the sun warm on her face. The trees lining the riverbanks were in full, lush leaf, and dazzlingly green. Tess walked briskly, down to the new bridge built for the millennium and then back along the south bank. Perhaps Vanessa was right about this too: perhaps all she needed was to take some exercise.

On Ouse Bridge, she stopped for a while to watch a solitary rower who was also making the most of the weather. His oars dipped delicately into the river – in, out, in, out – and as they lifted, the sunlight caught the glitter of water dropping like diamonds. Something about the steady rhythm reminded Tess of standing on the staithe below, watching the keelboat bear Tom remorselessly away.

Desolation flooded her, and Tess jerked her head back. That wasn't her memory. It was Nell who had stood there, Nell whose gut had twisted with love and longing.

Nell who might be a figment of her imagination but who was questing, probing, trying to find a way back into Tess's head.

Just when she had thought it was over.

No. No, I won't let you.

Tess set her jaw, steeled her mind. She was not going to give in this time. She couldn't afford to drift between worlds, couldn't risk blanking out in the middle of the street. Oscar needed her sane and sensible. He needed her *there*. If anything happened to her, no court in the country would stop Martin from taking his son back. Tess couldn't let that happen.

Martin might never have laid a finger on him, but Oscar was afraid of his father, she knew. She had seen it in the flinch of his thin shoulders, in the instinctive jerk back of his head and the shuttering of his eyes. No child should look the way Oscar looked when his father came into the room. Tess was going to make sure he never looked like that again.

She put both hands flat on the stone parapet to feel it solid and sternly real. The bridge Nell knew had been demolished in the nineteenth century. It was safe. She lifted her face to the sky, and breathed in and out carefully as she watched a jet leave a wispy trail high overhead.

That was it. Concentrate on everything that belonged to the present. The rumble of traffic behind her. The hiss of air brakes. The smell of fumes. The flash of plate glass. The urgent beep of a mobile phone.

When she felt more connected, Tess let go of the bridge. She couldn't stay there all day. She had to go home. She would need to pick Oscar up from school.

Biting her lip, she began to walk, but she felt naked, exposed, raw. She didn't trust the street not to stay solid beneath her feet. She kept stopping to look down at her jeans, wondering why they seemed so peculiar. Several times in Coney Street she reached out to touch a wall for reassurance. At the bottom of Stonegate she stopped by a flower stall and focused fiercely on the bright colours, the sharply defined petals, until the stallholder came round and she had to fumble for her purse and buy a bunch of gerberas she didn't want.

She was nearly home. She just had to walk up Stonegate.

It was crowded as she turned into the street, and she had to pick her way along the mid part between the gutters where the cobbles lurched drunkenly in the mud. A needle-fine rain was stinging her face. It had been wet for days now and the sewers ran as fast as a goodwife's tongue. She fisted her hands in her skirts to lift their guards out of the mire.

She was thinking about Tom and whether it was raining in Hamburg. Every night in the attic chamber she shared with Alice she would peer out of the casement and hope to get a glimpse of the moon. The best nights were those when the sky was clear and the moon was full. Then she imagined herself throwing her longing for Tom up, up into the dark sky, bouncing it against the silver moon like a ball against a wall so that it would fall back to where he could catch it and know that she was thinking of him. That she loved him and missed him still.

That she was waiting for him.

'Well, now, if it isn't little Nell Appleby come home to see us.'

The voice with its blurry edge jerked her out of her thoughts, and she looked up to find John Harper leaning in the doorway of his shop under the shelter of his pentice, watching her from his hooded eyes. Through the shutters, Nell could hear the snip of shears as his apprentice laboured over a new doublet.

The man was a rogue and a Scot, her father always said, and indeed Harper had few friends amongst his neighbours. He pushed and needled the good men of the city until they snatched off their caps in frustration. Their wives thought differently. Say what you wanted about him, the man knew how to sew a gown, and those heavy lidded eyes could make a beldam blush. To Nell, it always seemed as if he were unpeeling her garments one by one in his mind. As if he were pulling the pins from her sleeves, one by one, until they slid down her arms, and then very slowly taking hold of the laces that held her bodice together, tugging them apart so that her smock billowed free and her breasts with them...

She swallowed. She had always been slightly repelled by John Harper – by his carnal mouth, the redness of his lips, the coarseness of the black hairs on the back of his hands – but there was something inexplicably attractive about him too. Whenever he looked at her, she could feel the blood pumping hot around her body, and her cheeks would burn.

Nell wanted to ignore him, but how could she? When all was said and done, he was a freeman and a neighbour.

'Good day to you, Mr Harper,' she said primly, very glad of the cloak that laced high on her throat and the modest ruff that hid her neck where she could feel blotches of heat.

'You still pining for young Tom Maskewe?' asked Harper. 'He'll be away a year or more, you know, and a lass like you will get lonesome. I'd be happy to keep you company until he comes home.' He leered and winked, and Nell's blush reached her cheeks.

'You are too kind, sir,' she said, without quite meeting his eyes. She wanted to sound cool and composed, but she was only eighteen. 'I fear I must refuse.'

John Harper only laughed – a laugh that made her think of tangled sheets and hot nights and the dark pulse of desire.

'You on your way to see your pa?' he asked. 'I heard he was sick.'

'Yes, I–' Nell broke off, suddenly confused. What was she saying? She wasn't going to see her father. Her father had been dead for years. She was going back to work in the flat.

Her heart was racing with a fear she didn't understand. She looked down at her feet and in place of her sturdy clogs saw a scant strip of leather and bare toes tipped with paint the colour of blood. Her breath jammed in her throat and her stomach tipped as if she had tripped over her feet, even though she was standing quite still. Desperately, she glanced up at John Harper, but he had gone and she was staring at a window made of a single pane of glass, with a great red banner slanted across it: SALE.

Another tip of her stomach and Tess jolted back to the present. Jarred and faintly sick, she put a hand to her pounding head.

How had Nell slid beneath her defences so easily? She had been determined to keep her out, to stay in the present, but it was as if Nell were already in her mind, waiting for the moment, for the place, for the tiny gesture that would let her pull Tess back into the past.

She had to face it, Tess realized starkly. Nell was no figment of her imagination. She was powerful and she was real and she was in Tess's head.

Somehow Tess was going to have to find a way to get rid of her. She wasn't sure how yet, but in the meantime she would have to be more careful and pay close attention to the wanderings of her mind. These past couple of weeks, Tess had let herself relax. She had let herself believe the danger was over. That had been a mistake. It wasn't one she would make again, she vowed.

Her hand was shaking so much it took several attempts before she could get the key in the lock. The first thing she heard when she let herself into the flat was the sound of sawing, and her heart leapt in relief. Luke was back. Without thinking, she went to the study to see him, to steady herself.

He glanced up when she appeared in the doorway. 'You shouldn't have,' he said.

'What?' She followed his gaze to the flowers in her hand. She had forgotten that she was still holding them. 'Oh. Oh, these,' she said, feeling stupid. Her mind was fuzzy and she couldn't think of a single excuse. 'They're just ... for me.'

Luke put down his saw. 'What's wrong?'

Tess opened her mouth only to close it again. How could she tell him without sounding like a crazy woman? She couldn't deal with a cross-examination just then. She just needed him to be there. Her fixed point.

'Nothing. A bit of a headache, that's all.' She

lifted the flowers helplessly. 'I'll ... er ... I'll just put these in some water.'

The kitchen felt strange. Tess noticed it as soon as she walked in, but she couldn't work out what it was. The flowers still clutched in one hand, she turned slowly, checking the room.

The fridge hummed noisily in the corner. The cooker was wedged in a gap between the units, brown blobs of fat encrusting the edges. The sink looked out at an unlovely view of a blank, brick wall. No, there was nothing wrong.

She put the flowers in a jug, slipped a pinny over her head and began to mindlessly clear up. Anything other than having to think about what was happening to her. The headache hadn't just been an excuse – she felt as if her brain were in a vice.

Wiping up the debris of cereal and toast crumbs. Scraping plates. Filling the washing-up bowl. Tasks she had done a thousand times before, but which that morning felt eerily different, as if she had never before seen a cornflake, never flipped the lid of a bin. The plastic bowl felt odd in her hands, its smooth density somehow repellent.

Fighting the disquiet that prickled over her shoulders, she stared down at it. She couldn't think what it was for.

'You okay?'

Luke's voice behind her made her jump and she turned. 'You gave me a fright!'

'Sorry.' He studied her with eyes that were too observant for Tess's comfort. 'What happened to the weather? It was a beautiful day when I got here.'

She moistened her lips and forced herself to concentrate. 'Yes, it's lovely out.'

'Why are you all wet then?'

'What?'

Following his gaze, she lifted a hand to her hair. It felt damp, and when she dropped her eyes, she saw that the bottom of her jeans were wet and her toes muddy. She clutched at the apron as the world tilted and slithered away.

Nell could hear the wind tearing at the roof tiles and rattling the pentices as she went to answer the knock at the door. Wiping the flour off her hands on her apron, she pulled it open and clicked her tongue as autumn leaves swirled busily into the house. 'Pappa!' A smile of surprise lit her face when she saw her father, holding his hat against the wind.

Strange how seeing him out of his usual context made him seem older, smaller than she thought of him normally. She was used to seeing him in the house in Stonegate where she was a child, and for a moment it was like looking at a stranger. She had never noticed before how worn his gown was, how patchy its fur lining. Had his hair always been that thin?

He looked ill at ease, and his eyes didn't quite meet hers. 'I saw William Harrison at Trinity Hall,' he said, raising his voice to stop the breeze whipping his words away. 'I asked him if I could come and speak to you here.'

'Is something wrong?' Nell stood back and held the door open. 'My stepmother?' Her voice sharpened in concern. 'The boys?'

'No, no, they are well.' He ran a finger under his limp ruff. 'There is ... something I have to tell you.'

'What is it?' Now she really was worried by his expression, and a thought struck her, stopping her heart. 'Is it Tom?'

'No ... well, yes, it is to do with Tom, but I have no news of him.'

Nell let herself breathe again. 'Then what? Come, Pappa,' she said, leading him into the hall and urging him down onto the settle. 'Sit here.' A window was set high in the wall and in the light his face looked grey and drawn. She frowned, wishing it were not too early to light the fire in the great stone fireplace. 'Shall I bring you some ale? Or a glass of wine?'

'No, I need nothing,' he said wretchedly.

'Then tell me.'

He took a breath. 'I have received an offer for you. An offer of marriage,' he added to make himself clear.

Chapter Eight

'Is that all?' Nell shook out her apron and lowered herself onto a stool beside him. 'Then you must thank the gentleman kindly and tell him I am already betrothed,' she said, smiling.

'Nell, you are not betrothed to Tom Maskewe. Henry Maskewe did not agree. No contracts were drawn up. Nothing is settled.'

'It is settled between Tom and me,' she said firmly. 'We are promised to each other.'

The truth was, she had felt easier since Tom's father died. He was adamant in his opposition to a match between them, although Nell didn't really understand why. Certainly, her father was not the most successful of mercers – little more than a chapman now, if truth be told – but he was a member of the guild and the Applebys had connections in York. It was not so bad a match for a younger son like Tom.

Tom ... the thought of him was like a spear in her heart still. Six months he had been gone, and she yearned for him as much as she ever did. The days were long without him, but Nell did her best. She showed the world a bright face. She scorned to droop and moan. She was stronger than that, truer than that. She was learning to be a good housewife for when they were wed. She struggled to cast accounts, it was true, but she could cook and sew and she had some skill in the still room. It would be enough for Tom, she knew.

She had allowed herself a little hope that he might come home when his father died, but he had his apprenticeship to complete, and besides, he was not needed here. Or not by anyone except her. Ralph had taken over the family business, and cut a fine figure these days in his fur-trimmed robe and velvet cap.

Her father's eyes slid away from hers. 'Nell, it cannot be.'

'What do you mean?'

'Ralph Maskewe has asked for you, and I have said yes.'

'Ralph?' Nell stared uncomprehendingly at her father. 'No!' She half-laughed, it was too absurd. 'You cannot mean it!'

He didn't answer. He just looked at the rush matting and his face worked.

'No,' she said again, surging to her feet as she realized that he *did* mean it. 'No!'

'Yes, Nell.'

'I refuse.' Everything in her recoiled at the idea of it. It could not be true! 'Tell him I am betrothed to Tom. I will not forsake him while breath is in my body! Ralph knows well there is an understanding between us.'

'He does know, and he will not allow it.'

'Not allow it? It is not up to him!'

'Nell, please!' Hugh Appleby's voice rose, cracking in desperation, so that she stopped and stared at him. 'You do not understand how it is,' he said after a moment.

His expression sent dread crawling up Nell's spine. 'What?' she said, twisting the apron between her hands. 'What is it? *Tell* me!'

'I ... I owed Henry Maskewe everything,' he said, stumbling over the words, forcing them out as if each one hurt his mouth. 'I lost it all on an unwise speculation soon after I married Anne. I went to Henry and begged him to help me. I said I would repay his loan, but the interest has grown greater and greater. Not even the house will clear it. And now Ralph has the books and he wishes to call in the loan. It is his right. I ... I begged him not to. I asked him to think about my sons, my wife.'

'Your daughter?' Nell asked, her voice not quite

steady. She could not quite believe this was happening.

He nodded. 'You too.' He swallowed. 'There is no dowry, Nell. Not any more.'

'Tom will not care for that,' she said stoutly.

'Nell,' he sighed heavily. 'This friendship you have with Tom, it is all very well for children, but you are a young woman now. You know sentiment has no place in marriage. It is time to put off childish things. Marriage with Tom Maskewe will never be. You must accept that.'

'No!' Nell backed away from her father, both hands clenched to her bodice. 'No, you do not understand…'

'It is *you* who do not understand,' he interrupted her, his face abruptly twisted into a stranger's. 'If you do not marry Ralph Maskewe, your stepmother and your brothers and I will lose everything. *Everything*. We will be beggars, living on the street and hoping for alms. Ralph has made the deal clear enough. He will forgive the debt, if you agree.' His voice rose again, this time in anger. 'Is that clear enough for you, Nell?'

Nell squeezed her eyes shut. Panic was darting around inside her, seeking a vulnerable spot so that it could seize her completely. She told herself that when she opened them again, she would find this was just a terrible dream. She would be in bed up in the attic, and Alice would be snoring beside her, the moonlight seeping in through the casement.

But when she lifted her lids, her father was still there, sitting defeated on the settle. She couldn't bear to look at him. She stared instead at the cupboards, at the pewter she had polished only that morning while Alice straightened the cushions. Nell had grumbled at the tedious task. Now she wished with all her heart that she could go back to rubbing the dishes with a cloth, back to the time before her father had knocked at the door and split her world asunder.

'Why me?' she whispered. 'Why does he want me if I have no dowry?'

'You are fair. More than fair.'

'I?' she said in astonishment.

'You have never had eyes for anyone except Tom Maskewe. You do not notice the way men look at you, Nell. Perhaps you are not as graceful as some, but there is something about you ... something that makes men feel more alive when they look at you.' He smiled faintly. 'Your mother was the same.'

'Even if it were true, Ralph Maskewe is not interested in my fairness,' she said flatly. She didn't know how, but she knew that it was true.

'Come, Nell, he is a fine man. He is sober and civil and prosperous, and he is comely, as your stepmother bids me remind you. What more do you want in a husband?'

Dark eyes. Warm laughter. Warm hands. A body that fitted into her own.

'I want Tom,' she said bleakly.

Her father sighed. 'It cannot be.' And then, 'I am sorry.'

It seemed there was no more to say. They looked at each other in silence, her father slumped on the settle, Nell on her feet, her hands fisted to her breast as if to keep her pummelling heart from bursting through her ribs.

'This deal he makes with you,' she said in a low voice at last. 'It is wicked.'

'I know,' he said heavily.

'How can he want a wife who goes to him under such a threat to her family?'

Hugh Appleby just shook his head.

'He is willing to hurt you for me.'

'If it were just me,' he said, 'I would say him nay. Of course I would.' Weariness deepened the lines in his face. 'But there is your stepmother, and your brothers.'

Aye, her brothers. What would happen to them if she said no to Ralph Maskewe? Nell dropped her hands to her apron in defeat.

They were dear to her, those boys. Harry was a quiet lad, gentle, a dreamer, while Peter was merry and rough, but they were close all the same. Harry was the elder, at twelve, already four years older than Tom had been when he went into service – but Harry was not Tom. Tom would take whatever came at him and if he was floored by a blow, he would get back up again, fists raised. Harry, Nell feared, would just lie there, stunned and unmoving.

Her father had done nothing to get them into service. How would they manage if they had to beg for charity?

'Would it be so bad?' her father asked after a while.

Nell wound the apron tighter and tighter, twisting it around her fingers until they hurt. How could she explain to him about Ralph's teeth? About the light in his eyes that made her stomach curdle? About the wrongness she sensed in him?

'I have lain with Tom,' she said, a last desperate bid for escape from this terrible thing her father asked of her.

'He knows.' Hugh would not meet her eyes. 'He does not regard it. He says he loves you.'

'Fine love, to be bought with blackmail!'

Nell's mind was scurrying like a little wood creature, frantic for a hole to hide in. But if she hid, what would happen to her brothers? She thought about Harry's gentle smile, about the mischief in Peter's eyes as he came in from some devilry. How could she abandon them to beggary and blows? And her father and stepmother, they too deserved her loyalty.

She closed her eyes again, tried to see things from her father's point of view. If there wasn't Tom, she wouldn't think twice about a marriage such as this.

But there *was* Tom, everything in her cried. There was. There always would be Tom.

'Nell?'

A rock was lodged in her throat. She could hardly swallow past it. 'May I at least think about it?' she managed, and her father nodded and placed his hands on his thighs as he got heavily to his feet.

'Think about it,' he agreed, 'but not too long. Ralph is waiting for an answer.'

After he had gone, Nell stood in the middle of the hall, turning Tom's ring round and round and round on her finger while the wind knocked at the window. Somewhere a shutter was bang,

bang, banging but in the hall it was utterly still, as if time itself had stopped. A single shaft of sunlight pierced the gloom and she stared blindly at the dust motes trapped there. They hung in the light, unmoving, as weightless and insubstantial as she felt.

Reaching out, she made a fist in the beam. She imagined her fingers closing around those tiny specks, crushing them the way her dreams had been crushed.

Oh, she had been a fool! A fool living in a fool's paradise, she understood that now. No one was free to wed where they may. Everyone had to think about money and connections, and the value each partner brought to the marriage. Why should she and Tom have thought it should be any different for them?

And all at once the truth plummeted through her: she would not marry Tom. She would not be able to wait until he came home. She would never hold him again.

She would marry Ralph.

The horror of it made her double over, her arms wrapped around her stomach. It was like being back in that chest. The panic was suffocating her, pressing over her mouth and nose, cracking her ribs even as she struggled for breath.

'Nell? What are you doing down there?' Dimly she was aware of Alice peering down the stairs. 'Do you not hear Mrs Harrison calling for you?' Alice broke off as she saw Nell's distress, and she hurried down the last steps. 'God's bodkin, what has happened? Are you ill?'

'No.' With an effort Nell straightened and

sucked in a reedy breath. 'No, but I have to get out. I have to, Alice.'

She was already halfway to the door when Alice grabbed her arm. 'Wait! I'll tell her you've gone to the orchard to pick up apples, but you can't wander around the streets like that! Take off your apron, and I'll find you a gown.'

What did it matter? Nell thought wildly. What did any of it matter compared to this weight that had dropped on her without warning? But she untied her apron strings with clumsy fingers and let Alice help her into a brown gown trimmed with black velvet, standing like a child as Alice fastened it, clucking under her breath.

'And take this.' Alice thrust a basket at her. 'You might as well get some apples while you're at it.'

'Thank you,' Nell roused herself to say. Alice was right: she needed a job to do. 'I...' But she couldn't put into words what she wanted to say. 'Thank you, Alice,' was all she said in the end.

The wind grabbed at her as soon as Nell stepped outside, and she had to put up a hand to keep her cap in place. Above the stalls the pentices rattled and the shop signs creaked and groaned. Folk walked with their heads down, leaning forward into the gusty air or back to stop themselves being bowled along the street. William Buckbarrow's apprentice was running after some ribbons that had blown off the stall and Cuthbert Vause cursed as he gathered up the teetering pile of pails that had blown over.

Once, Nell would have stopped to help, but that day she just pulled her gown closer around her against the cold and hurried by.

Towering clouds raced across the sky. The sun kept plunging behind them, only to burst out again a few moments later in a dazzle of brightness that made Nell screw up her eyes. The constant shift from brilliant light to shade gave the air a jagged, fractured feel that mirrored her mood.

The Harrisons had an orchard next to the garden in Paynley's Crofts. Nell slipped through the vagabonds, carts and countrymen that clustered outside Monk Bar, unable or unwilling to pay the market tolls. No one clutched at her today. It was as if she were invisible, wrapped in a cloak of misery.

But Nell saw them. She saw the poor with their gaunt faces and sharp, feral eyes; saw the boniness of their shoulders and the way they shivered as the wind cut through their threadbare garments.

She saw them but she couldn't meet their eyes for fear they would be too familiar. How many of the men there were once like her father? How many of those hard-faced women squatting with their children once had houses to call their own like her stepmother?

If she refused Ralph, he would see that Harry and Peter ended up out there, their skin grimy, their sores untended.

I will stand true, she had promised Tom. *I will be torn apart by horses before I break my vow.*

She had no need for horses to tear her apart. She was torn already. There was a rawness inside her, like a shriek of pain, and she had to clench every muscle in her body to stop herself being ripped open.

Head down, she cut across St Maurice's churchyard and over the stile to one of the paths that criss-crossed the crofts. She walked to the Harrison's orchard; she unlatched the gate. The wind shook the apples from the trees even as she gathered them. She worked dry-eyed, unthinking. She couldn't bear to think. She couldn't bear to *feel*.

Desolation was a huge fist squeezing her tighter and tighter inside until there was just a pebble where her heart once was, just a small stone lodged cold and heavy where giddy joy used to dance and twirl.

Because she knew what she must do.

She would marry Ralph Maskewe. She would learn not to shudder when he bared those big teeth.

She would do as her father said and put aside her childish dreams. She would grow up and be sensible. She wouldn't let herself remember how a single glance from Tom could heat her blood, how the touch of his hands set her skin afire.

How her heart swelled at the sight of him. How her senses sang when he was near. How peace settled over her as she lay in his arms.

She would forget it all.

Instead she would remember that Ralph was a wealthy man. That fine house in Stonegate was his now, and she would be mistress of it. Ralph was a good catch, better by far than Tom, the new cold-hearted Nell tried to tell herself. Many maids would be glad to have him.

And what, after all, did she know of him to

object to? An expression she caught in his eyes sometimes? A feeling? Perhaps she had just imagined it, as she imagined the book being placed on the chest where she hid so long ago. She was a child, with a child's fancies, and she had panicked, just as her stepmother had said. Ralph had simply been the easy person to blame, and she had held it against him ever since.

Nobody else had aught but good to say of Ralph Maskewe. She could not sacrifice her brothers because she didn't like the teeth everyone else admired so much.

Or because he was the kind of man who would force his wife into marriage with such a threat.

Nell's basket was full. She closed the orchard gate behind her and walked back into the city through Monk Bar. She stopped at her father's house in Stonegate. She told him and her stepmother that she had made up her mind, that they were safe, and then she carried the apples back to the Harrisons' house in Ousegate where she boiled them and mashed them with ginger and cinnamon and stirred in the yolks of two eggs, because life went on and the household still needed to be fed – and as long as she didn't let herself feel she would be all right.

That night, she undressed methodically, letting Alice's chatter and exclamations wash over her without hearing them. She hung her apron on its hook and unbuckled her shoes to that she could pull off her stockings. She unpinned her sleeves, and laid them one after the other in the chest, and then, as if it were something she did every night, she tugged Tom's ring from her finger and dropped it into the chest where it slipped down the side past the sleeves and out of sight.

Nell closed the lid. She unfastened her petticoat, then her bodice, and laid them on top of the chest. She stood in her smock while she unbound her hair and brushed it. She rubbed her teeth. She stripped off her smock, pulled on her nightgown and got into bed next to Alice, and not once did she look up through the casement at the moon. She tugged her share of the coverlet from Alice and pulled it up to her chin. Moonlight poured mockingly into the little room, but that night Nell whispered no message to Tom. There was nothing she could say. She just pummelled the bolster into shape and turned her face away.

Darkness roared in her head, so loud that she knew she would never sleep. She tried keeping her eyes closed and pretending, but when she gave in and opened them, the moon beams had vanished and it was daylight. Her first thought was that none of it had been real, and her heart leapt.

Oh summer's day, it was a dream!

Limp with relief, she blinked slowly, and then again as she realized that the attic room had vanished along with the moonlight. There was no offer from Ralph Maskewe, but there was no bed either. No bolster; no kirtles laid across the kist in the corner; no shoes abandoned where Alice had kicked them off before she jumped into bed.

No Alice.

Instead there was a narrow room and a man with fierce brows and a jutting nose. 'Jesus, Tess,' he said as she focused on his face, 'what is it?'

The blood drained from her head and she put out a hand to steady herself, just as her phone started to ring and ring and ring. The noise drilled into her control, a tiny fissure at first that raced across her rigid composure until the strain of it simply snapped and she wrenched the phone from her pocket.

'Shut up! Shut up! Shut *up!*' She threw it down and it cracked on the tiles but the phone just kept on ringing. She stamped on it, kicked it across the room, watched it skid across the floor, still ringing, and she couldn't stand it any more.

At the expression on her face, Luke put up his hands and took a hasty step back. Ignoring him, Tess swept an arm along the counter and pushed. Tea bags, cereal packets, a jar of coffee and some biscuits went tumbling to the floor, but that wasn't enough. The contents of the fruit bowl went next. Flour and sugar exploded onto the tiles. She was grabbing at anything that was to hand, venting the muddled rage and frustration and fear in her head. Her jaw was clenched, the tendons in her neck rigid, her eyes stark.

It wasn't until she reached for a plate and smashed it on the floor that Luke intervened.

'Okay,' he said calmly, stepping through the debris to where she stood panting and wild-eyed. 'That's enough now.'

Tess didn't resist as he took her by the elbow and steered her into the front room, and down onto the sofa. Her expression was utterly blank. She heard him say, 'Stay there,' but her limbs were locked in place and she couldn't have moved even if she had wanted to.

With a strange detached part of her brain she watched him rootle around in Richard's sideboard, muttering to himself. 'Aha!' he said, pulling out a bottle of Courvoisier. 'I thought a bloke like Richard would have some booze lying around.'

Sloshing some of the brandy into a glass, Luke put it in Tess's hand and folded her fingers around it. His were firm and warm against her cold flesh.

'Drink that,' he said, standing over her until Tess had obediently raised the glass to her mouth and taken a sip that had her coughing as the brandy burned her throat.

Luke waited until she had drunk half of it before he dropped into the chair opposite and rubbed a hand over his face. 'What in Christ's name was all that about?'

Tess looked down into the glass. 'I'm sorry about that,' she muttered, embarrassed at how utterly she had lost control. 'I don't usually give in to hysterics.'

'Maybe you should,' said Luke. He leant back and studied her speculatively. 'It can't be good to keep all that bottled up inside you. I've done a lot of travelling over the last few years and seen a lot of crazy people, but I don't think I've ever seen anyone lose it as completely as you just did.' To Tess's surprise, he sounded interested rather than judgemental. 'You were a woman possessed.'

If only he knew. Tess wanted to laugh but she was afraid it would sound as if she were succumbing to hysteria again. She took another slug of brandy instead. Perhaps it was the Courvoisier, or perhaps it was the cathartic effects of her tantrum, but she was feeling rather strange, emptied out but oddly calm.

'I've been under a bit of strain,' she started to excuse herself, only to stop and glare when she caught the disconcerting smile that hovered around Luke's mouth.

'I gathered that.'

'Do you want me to explain or not?'

His smile glimmered stronger. 'It's good to hear you sounding tart again, Tess,' he said, but then his expression sobered. 'Yes, tell me.'

Tess tipped her head back against the sofa. It was a relief to be able to talk about this at least. 'My husband's been ringing me for two weeks,' she said, keeping her eyes on the ceiling. 'He'll ring repeatedly, but say nothing if I answer, and as soon as I switch off, he rings again. Or he'll leave it, and then call at odd hours of the night.

'I can't prove it's him,' she said, nodding as if Luke had objected. 'I just know that it is. It's driving me crazy.' She smiled crookedly at the ceiling. 'Wrong: it *drove* me crazy just now. I was hoping he'd get tired of the game and give up,' she added with a sigh. She slid both her hands behind her head and stretched her neck with a grimace. 'I should have known better,' she said. 'Martin doesn't give up. Ever.'

She felt rather than saw Luke stiffen. Felt his eyes on her face as she tilted her head from side to side to try and loosen the knots in her neck.

'I didn't realize,' he said slowly.

'Why should you?'

'No, I thought ... I assumed your husband had left you and that you'd come back to York with your tail between your legs,' said Luke. 'I thought that's why you were so uptight and snotty.'

Ruffled, Tess let her hands drop and straightened her back. 'I wasn't *snotty!*' she objected. Luke was a fine one to talk about being snotty!

'Okay, maybe snotty is too strong a word, but you were very stiff.'

'So were you!'

'Only because you were.' Luke stopped as he caught her eye, and his mouth twisted down in a rueful grin. 'Well, okay, maybe I wasn't very mature,' he conceded. 'I bumped into your mother soon after I came back to York last year,' he told Tess. 'You can imagine what a pleasure that was for both of us.'

A little mollified, Tess settled back into the cushions once more. 'Not the cosiest of chats, I gather?'

'No.' Luke leant forward and rested his elbows on his knees. 'She was at pains to impress on me what a wonderful life you had in London. How rich and successful your husband was. What a big house you lived in. How deliriously happy you were and so on.'

'Ah.' Tess buried her face in her glass once more, cringing inwardly as she pictured the scene all too easily. She could just hear her mother boasting, and see Luke sneering in response. The two of them had always rubbed each other up the wrong way. Her mother was a snob, Luke prickly and defensive.

And very quick to think the worst of her, she realized with a stupid stab of hurt.

'You thought I had turned into my mother, in fact?' she said as lightly as she could.

Luke hunched a shoulder. 'I might have made a few assumptions about you having turned into a yummy mummy,' he admitted grudgingly.

'Thanks a lot!'

'When Richard told me you were going to live in his flat, I thought your husband had kicked you out or something.' He paused, rubbed a hand over the back of his neck. 'I guess when your mum told me about your wealthy husband and perfect life, it made me feel ... well, jealous. Or inadequate. Or something. It was like you'd moved on, left me and York behind, and I was just a second-rate photographer making ends meet with a bit of joinery.'

Jealous? Inadequate? *Luke?* Tess blinked, uncertain of how to react.

'Anyway,' he said after an awkward moment, 'that's why I was so quick to jump to conclusions. The honest truth is that there was a bit of me that was pleased when I heard your oh-so-wonderful marriage had broken up, and I'm not proud of it.' He met her gaze straightly. 'I'm sorry it didn't work out for you, Tess.'

She looked back at him, conscious of a warmth stealing through her veins. How long was it since someone had looked at her directly and said that they were sorry?

'I'm sorry if I seemed snotty,' she offered.

They smiled at each other, tentatively at first, and then more easily, but the smile lingered a little too long until neither of them knew what to do with it any more. Tess felt the warmth spreading, tingling up her throat and into her cheeks, and she made herself look away just as Luke jerked his own gaze down to his hands and cleared his throat.

'Yes, well, I'm sure I was a dick too.'

'Let's just say you were very intimidating.'

Luke lifted his head. 'Come on, Tess, I never intimidated you! It was one of the reasons I always liked you.'

'Of course I was intimidated.' It was good to be able to tease him, to feel the stiffness between them evaporate. 'I was petrified, in fact. You were always so fierce, all snarling and surly.'

'Not with you,' said Luke. 'Don't rewrite history! We used to talk and laugh all the time, do you remember?'

'Yes.' Tess smiled a little sadly, thinking about how little she had been able to talk to Martin about anything. Her job had been to listen to her husband and to agree. She had never laughed with him the way she had with Luke. Even now, it was amazingly comfortable to sit across from Luke and talk. Almost as if they had never been apart.

He seemed to read her mind. 'Did you ever think about what it would have been like if we'd stayed together?'

She thought about lying, decided against it. 'Sometimes,' she said. 'Then I'd remember how hurt I was when you left,' she added with a look.

'Hey, you were the one who went to London,' he said mildly.

'*You* went off to Ouagadougou or Timbuktu or wherever you were so determined to go!'

'Only after you'd made it clear that all you wanted to do was settle down. A good job. Marriage. Kids. You had it all worked out.'

Tess folded her lips in frustration. How could Luke remember things so differently? He had made it clear that his plans to travel the world taking photographs didn't include her, so of course she had pretended that she didn't want to go anyway. And she *had* wanted a career and a family. Was that so wrong?

Look where it had got her, hallucinating about a life in the past and having hysterics in the kitchen.

'Oh, what does it matter anyway?' she said, draining the last of the brandy. The warmth and ease she'd felt only a few moments ago had frayed on the jagged shards of memory. Perhaps it was just as well. 'It's all a long time ago.' She put down the glass. 'I'd better go and clear up that mess in the kitchen.'

'Tess,' Luke said quietly as she made to push herself up from the sofa.

'What?'

'Was it very bad, your marriage? I know it must have been,' he said as she sank back down. 'I know you'd never have left if it wasn't. And if I hadn't been so choked with my own sense of inadequacy, I'd have realized that it was more than wounded pride making you so brittle.'

Tess didn't answer at first. 'It was pretty bad,' she said at last. 'Oh, Martin wasn't violent,' she added quickly as she saw Luke's face change. 'I wasn't deprived. I was living in a beautiful house with no financial worries, just like Mum told you. I kept telling myself that I didn't really have anything to complain about.'

She picked at the piping on the sofa arm, needing to explain to Luke, but at the same time reluctant to spoil the fragile trust they seemed to have built up. She was ashamed, humiliated by what she had to tell him. For a few moments there she had let herself feel like the Tess Luke remembered, the girl who had loved and laughed and trusted, the girl who had defied her mother's snobbery and her friend's disapproval to climb on the back of his bike and believe in the restless, passionate boy she glimpsed beneath his brusque exterior.

She didn't want to tell Luke that that girl had vanished, but there would be relief, too, in telling the truth.

'It's hard to explain what Martin's like,' she began again after a while.

'He's older than you, I bet.'

Tess looked at Luke, surprised. 'How did you know?'

He shrugged. 'I always figured you were looking for someone to replace your father.'

The idea caught Tess on the raw. 'Martin's nothing like Dad,' she said sharply.

'I just meant...' Luke looked as if he was searching for the right words. 'I know how much you missed your dad after he died, that's all.'

'Yes, I did.' All these years later and the thought of her father could still make her eyes sting with tears. 'He was so...' Tess couldn't finish. There were no words to describe her father, or how safe and loved he had always made her feel.

Swallowing past the constriction in her throat, she made herself think about what Luke had said. 'Maybe you're right,' she told him. 'Maybe at some level I was looking for someone to look after me.'

Martin had made her feel cherished at first. He took her to restaurants with discreet lighting and chose wines she had never heard of. He helped her on and off with her coat, walked on her right to protect her from the traffic, and summoned taxis so that he could take her home. Tess had never been with anyone who knew how to attract a waiter's attention with just the lift of an eyebrow. He was assured and sophisticated and caring – everything Luke hadn't been.

I just want to look after you, darling, he would say whenever Tess offered to pay or to arrange an outing herself, and she had been charmed.

At first.

'I was lonely when I met him,' she said. She'd been missing Luke too, but she didn't tell him that. 'Wondering if I'd made the right decision going to London after all. I had a fantastic job working as a historical researcher for a film company, but working in libraries and archives all day meant that I never got to meet anybody. So when one of the producers tossed me an unwanted invitation to a gallery opening, I thought I would make the effort and go along on my own. Of course, it was awful. Nobody spoke to me. Except Martin.'

The gallery was full of tight little groups engaged in

vivacious conversations. Tess was clutching a glass of warm white wine and staring desperately at a vast canvas covered in splodges of colour when a warm voice spoke in her ear.

'I can't make head nor tail of it, can you?'

Startled, she turned to see Martin smiling at her. He was wearing a dark suit and his nearly blonde hair caught the gallery lights. The edges of his blue eyes crinkled engagingly, and Tess felt her heart stumble.

'He was so ... *perfect*,' she remembered bleakly. 'Attractive, intelligent, charming, articulate, funny... I was bowled over. Martin was so *interested* in me. We had dinner that night, and I was sensible enough not to give him my address, but I'd told him enough about what I did for him to track down my work address and send me two dozen red roses the next day. It should have been a warning, but I thought it was so romantic.'

'Red roses?' Luke shook his head. 'Jesus!'

'So of course I agreed to dinner the next night, and the next. Martin told me he'd never met anyone like me, and I was overwhelmed by being adored. I fell madly in love with him. Head over heels, upside down. He swept me off my feet. Pick your cliché.'

Now that she had started, she wanted to get it all out. Letting out a long sigh, she picked up her glass once more, only to find that it was empty, and without speaking Luke leant over and topped her up.

'If I'd had more friends in London, I might have been more cautious,' she said, watching the golden liquid sloshing into the glass, 'but I let him bowl me over. I was thrilled that he couldn't bear to be apart from me, that he was jealous if I spent any time with anyone else. I was a fool,' she said bitterly.

'You were young,' Luke offered, pouring brandy into his own glass, but Tess wasn't going to let herself off the hook that lightly.

'I was twenty-three. I'd done a degree and an MA. I had a good job. I should have known better, but it all happened so fast. It was like tumbling down a hill. I couldn't seem to stop and get my bearings.

'And then his mother died. Martin was distraught, and he couldn't bear for me to leave him. He needed me, he said, and when he asked me to marry him, of course I agreed. His grief for his mother seemed a reasonable excuse to keep our wedding just between the two of us. There was no York wedding, no hen party, no involving my old friends.'

'How did your mum take that?'

'She was nearly as bowled over by Martin as I was. She came to London once and as soon as she met him and saw what a beautiful house he had, she was sold. You know what a social climber Mum is. Martin went to public school, speaks in a cut-glass accent and had a trust fund to fall back on whenever he needed it.' Tess's smile was twisted. 'She's still lobbying for me to go back to him. She doesn't understand how I could possibly have left him.'

Luke picked up his glass and swirled the brandy absently. 'Sounds like your Martin is a classic narcissist.'

'He's a sociopath.' Tess nodded, kept her voice carefully neutral. 'I read up on it in the end. The only person who matters in Martin's world is Martin, but of course I didn't want to believe that at first. I loved him, and I wanted to believe that he loved me too. And he said he did. Why wouldn't I believe him?'

'No reason,' Luke said warily when she glared at him as if he had accused her of being the fool she knew she had been.

Realizing, Tess made a helpless gesture of apology and blew out a breath. 'Sorry. It's not your fault. I just hate remembering what an idiot I was. But Martin's got this way of making everything he wants seem utterly reasonable. Of course I told myself that he was only possessive because he adored me. The last thing I wanted was to accept that he didn't want a wife at all, he just wanted someone to control.'

She stared down at the brandy, not drinking, just turning the glass round and round between her fingers, remembering.

'I was like one of those frogs put in a pan and brought slowly to the boil. By the time I realized what was happening, it was too late to jump out.'

Chapter Nine

'At first it was just little things,' she said. 'Martin didn't like coming back to the house and finding me not there. We were just married and he was still in such a state about his mother that I didn't feel as if I could insist on keeping my job. How hard-hearted would that have been when he needed me so much? I wanted to be there for him. So I gave up my job. I gave up suggesting that we come to York for a weekend. I should have taken a stand, but it didn't seem worth up-setting him.'

She had been so passive. The memory sent a flush of humiliation creeping up Tess's throat and she took another slug of the brandy.

'And, of course, I kept thinking that I had nothing to complain about, not really. It's not as if Martin *hit* me. I used to tell myself that I was lucky, that it wasn't really abuse if a husband flies into rage or punishes you with silence if you don't hang the towels up with the edges properly aligned or if you don't close the flap on a box of cereal. I was middle class, educated … how could I be abused? I was just doing what I could to save my marriage. I was just being a good wife. And if I ever felt unhappy, I would convince myself I was stupid and selfish, just like Martin said. He worked hard all day to keep me in luxury. Was it too much to ask for him to come home to a tidy house? I had nothing else to do all day, after all.'

Tess's lips curled with self-loathing as she mimicked herself.

She had tried to be normal, to go out and make friends, but Martin hadn't liked that either. Wasn't he enough for her? He would ring every few minutes, or come home unexpectedly, and if she wasn't there, he would find a way to punish her. Sometimes he would be furiously angry, sometimes she would be subjected to an icy silence, or he would take out his displeasure on someone else – her mother if she rang, or some unfortunate person who happened to call at the door.

'The thing was, Martin could be lovely,' she tried to explain, risking a glance at Luke, wondering why she was blurting out her whole sorry story to him of all people. His brows were drawn together and his mouth was bracketed by two grim lines. Did he think she had been pathetic? Pitiful? Or just sad? Was he shaking his head inwardly at how easily the girl she had been had let herself be vanquished?

It shouldn't matter to her now, but it did.

Tess had never told anyone all this before. The words had been dammed up inside her, firmly under control. She had known that the slightest breach would let the whole humiliating story burst out in an unstoppable torrent, and so it had proved. Now that she'd started, she had to tell it all.

'Sometimes he'd come home with flowers, or insist on taking me out to dinner so that I didn't have to cook. He'd be charming and affectionate. He'd buy me presents and tell me how much he loved me, how much he needed me. Just when I'd decided I couldn't bear it any more, he would disarm me. It was as if he knew just how far he could push me before I'd break.

'I never had any idea what kind of mood he would be in when he came through the door, and he could switch so suddenly...'

She faltered, remembering how eggshell thin the atmosphere had been. The slightest lapse of attention was liable to fracture it. It had been exhausting having to concentrate so hard on not making a mistake. A careless word, a thoughtless gesture, could crush the surface calm like a boot crunching through a rime of ice on a winter puddle. Tess had learnt to move slowly, carefully.

'It sounds crap,' said Luke bluntly. 'Why didn't you leave him?'

How could someone like Luke understand? Tess took another sip and felt the alcohol burn her throat before it settled, warm and steadying, in her stomach.

'I told myself we just needed time to get used to being married. I thought it would be different when we had a family. I had a miscarriage quite early on and it took me a long time to get over that. I couldn't think about anything, let alone getting to grips with my marriage.

'When Oscar was born, I hoped things would get better, and for a while they did. But the baby took up too much of my attention, and toddlers and immaculate houses don't mix well. As soon as Martin realized Oscar wasn't one of those beautiful, smiley, *clean* babies you see on the ads, he lost interest. He expected me to have put

Oscar to bed and be waiting for him when he came home, looking perfectly groomed with a perfectly cooked meal simmering on the stove.'

Luke coughed in the middle of swallowing brandy. 'You're kidding?'

Flushing, Tess shook her head. 'No. I tried, but I couldn't do it. No one could. You can't just put a baby away when it's not convenient.'

'So how did Martin deal with that?' Luke said Martin's name as if it tasted unpleasant.

'He hired a nanny to take care of Oscar. He didn't even consult me.' Tess's lips thinned with remembered outrage. 'The woman just turned up on the doorstep one morning.

'It's the only time I ever stood up to Martin,' she said. 'I sent her away and I told him that I was going to look after my baby myself.'

'I don't suppose he liked *that* very much.'

'He was never closer to striking me. I could see in his face how much he wanted to, but then he did the kind of volte-face he specialized in. One moment his eyes were blank with rage; the next he was all smiles and telling me what a good mother I was, how he had only wanted me to have some help as he hated seeing me so tired and how much he loved me.'

Luke snorted, unimpressed.

'The worst thing is how *reasonable* he made everything sound. It was so easy to think that I was the one being selfish and silly for rejecting help when he was so understanding and generous.'

There was a pause. Tess rested the glass on the arm of the sofa and watched as she turned it slowly between her fingers. Afraid that she might read contempt in his face, she didn't look at Luke, but when he broke the silence she couldn't hear any judgement in his voice.

'So what made you leave in the end?'

'Oscar.' Her throat constricted again at the thought of her son. 'He was such a quiet little boy, so good. It was all wrong, but I kept letting it go. And then one day we were in the kitchen baking those little cakes with rice krispies and chocolate. Oscar liked to help me cook. He was standing on a chair, covered in chocolate, and we were laughing at something when we heard Martin's car in the drive. He'd said he was going to Birmingham for the day, but he used to try and catch me out like that. He'd come home at unexpected times, just to check that I was where I said I was.'

'Did he object to the mess?' asked Luke when she paused, and Tess shook her head.

'There was no mess. As soon as he heard the car, Oscar's face just went blank. He scrambled down from the chair, went over to sink and rubbed a cloth over his face and hands without being told, and then he ran up to his room. And I...' Tess faltered, swallowed. 'I didn't follow him,' she said. 'I hid the bowl and wiped the table and by the time Martin got in, the kitchen was immaculate.'

Her face burned, and she couldn't raise her eyes from the glass. 'I was so ashamed that I let that happen,' she said, her voice low and bitter. 'Ashamed that I'd let my little boy grow up afraid to laugh and be messy. And that's when I decided to leave.'

There. He'd heard the worst. Tess risked a

glance at Luke, who was still sitting with a set, stern face. She half-expected him to rise and point at her in disgust, to accuse her of being the worst of mothers, but he didn't. He just looked back at her with eyes that were warm with sympathy and concern.

'I'm sorry, Tess.'

Sorry? Was that it? Twisting her fingers in her lap, Tess stared at him in disbelief. Hadn't he been listening? Why wasn't he telling her how pathetic she had been, how useless? What a failure she was?

'It was my own fault,' she insisted in case he had misunderstood. 'I put Oscar through that because I was too much of a coward to stand up to Martin.'

'And you found the courage to leave.' Luke leant forward and covered her tangled fingers with one warm palm. 'You did your best in a difficult situation, and now you're doing better. None of us can do more than that.'

Tess swallowed hard. She had been so sure that he would despise her as much as she despised herself. But when she tested her feelings, cautiously at first, she realized that she didn't feel as bad as she usually did remembering that time. It was like the aftermath of a bad bout of food poisoning: she felt weak and a bit wobbly, but relieved to have got the turmoil and humiliation out of her system.

Very conscious of Luke's fingers covering hers, Tess tugged her hand free and Luke sat back. Her skin felt warm where his had touched it. She cleared her throat.

'I tried talking to Martin about a separation,

but he wouldn't discuss it, and in the end I just took Oscar and we got on a bus to York. I knew Martin would guess where we'd gone, but I had nowhere else to go, and I was hoping that once I left, he'd realize that I meant what I'd said.'

'But he hasn't?'

'No. He turned up at Mum's house, and in his mind, I think, he let us come to York on holiday. But he won't have liked it when I moved here and changed my phone and email address. I know I sound paranoid, but Martin has all sorts of shady contacts through his work, and I don't think it will have been hard for him to track me down. I keep waiting for him to appear, but he's playing some kind of cat-and-mouse game instead. I'm sure of it. That's what the phone calls are about. He wants me to know that *he* knows where I am, even though I've changed numbers.'

Luke scowled. 'That's harassment, Tess. Can't you go to the police?'

'I've got no way of proving that it's Martin.' She told Luke about the landline and how the calls had switched after a couple of days to her mobile. 'I don't know what to do about it. I could buy a new phone, but what's to stop him tracing it again?'

'Nothing, if the paperwork traces back to you.' Luke rubbed his chin thoughtfully. 'I've got an old phone you could have,' he said after a moment. 'It's very basic, but it works. Martin would have a harder time making that connection. Do you want to try it?'

'I ... I couldn't.'

'Why not? It's just sitting in a drawer.'

Tess looked at him properly for the first time. Really looked at him. Saw the lines edging his eyes, the tough mouth, the hard, exciting angles of his cheek and jaw. Saw the man he was, not the boy he had been, and her throat tightened at the dangerous stab of hope. Not that they could recreate what they had once had, but that she had found a friend again.

'It's ... hard for me when you're kind,' she tried to explain, but Luke was having none of it.

'It's hard for me when you're brave and insist on doing everything by yourself,' he countered.

'I need to manage on my own,' said Tess. 'I can't afford to rely on anyone else ever again.'

'No harm in getting a bit of help now and then, though, is there?'

Tess gave in and let go of a shaky laugh. 'No, I suppose not.' She swallowed. 'Okay, I'd like to give the phone a try. I think it might work. Thanks,' she said as she got to her feet. 'And Luke – thanks for listening.'

'Beats working,' said Luke, making it easy on her. He drained his glass and got up to follow her out into the passage. 'I'd better get on with Richard's shelves.'

Tess was grateful to him for bringing the conversation back to normal. 'How much longer do you think you'll be?'

'I reckon a couple more days should do it, and then a day to put the books back once the varnish is dry. I've got some more picture-desk jobs coming up and I'll have to fit round them, but I should be out of your hair soon.'

He peered over her shoulder as she paused in

the kitchen doorway. 'You made a hell of a mess in there. You sure you don't want help cleaning it up?'

'I'm sure.' Tess squared her shoulders as she regarded the kitchen. She had made the mess, she would put it right. 'This is something I have to do on my own.'

'Okay.' Luke turned away, then stopped. 'Tess, are you sure it was just the phone ringing that upset you? You looked as if you'd had bad news before it rang.'

The worst news. She was to be married to Ralph. The memory rolled queasily in her stomach. It had been awful remembering her life with Martin, but better than thinking about Nell's misery.

But she couldn't tell Luke about that, not now. He had listened enough, and besides, she was wrung out. She couldn't face another explanation.

'It was nothing.' Her eyes slid away from Luke's. 'Just ... a lot of stuff happening at once.'

'Hmm.' Luke leant against the door jamb. 'How long is it since you've had a break, Tess?'

'A break?' she echoed, as if she'd forgotten what the word meant.

'You know. Got away for a day. Done something different. Forgot about things for a while.'

'Oh. Yes.' Tess tried to think. It had been a very long time, since before she met Martin. 'Not for a while.'

'Come to Bridlington tomorrow.' Luke seemed almost as taken aback by the offer as Tess was. 'I'm taking pictures of some kitesurfing competition on the beach,' he said. 'I've got to go anyway. You could come along for the ride.'

'It's Saturday tomorrow. I'll have Oscar.'

'Bring him too. He likes the beach, doesn't he?'

'He's never been,' she had to admit. Martin didn't do beach holidays. They were too messy, too noisy, too crowded.

'Then it's time he went, don't you think? It's a boring drive on my own,' he coaxed when she hesitated still. 'I sold out and replaced the bike with a sensible car that can take all my gear, but it's no fun any more. I could do with the company.'

Tess thought about a wide, blowy beach, and damp sand between her toes. She had always loved how big the sky seemed on the Yorkshire coast. She and Luke had gone on his bike. She remembered the erotic thrill of it, the speed, the power and the danger of the machine between her thighs. Her arms clamped around Luke's waist, leaning with him into bends, looking for the first gleam of the sea in the distance. Climbing stiffly off the bike, she had pulled off her helmet and let the wind plaster her hair across her lips.

It had always been windy. They had a special place in the sand dunes where they would lie on a blanket, sheltered from the North Sea blast, and look up. Above them were only the tussocks of marram grass, bent almost horizontal over the rim of the dune, and beyond that just light and air and space. Tess had sworn that she could feel the earth turning beneath them until she was giddy with it.

She mustn't expect too much from Luke. It

would be a mistake to get too reliant on him ... but it was just a day, Tess reminded herself. She thought about how much Oscar would love it, about being away from this flat with its rasping walls and its atmosphere of crouching anticipation.

'I'd love to,' she said. 'If you really mean it?'

'Did you touch the cat flap when you came in?'

Luke looked up, his arms full of books. 'No. Why?'

'I just found Ashrafar yowling outside on the roof. She was locked out.'

'I haven't been in the kitchen,' said Luke, dumping the books on a shelf. 'Could you have done it without thinking?'

'I don't think so,' said Tess. 'I never lock it. Richard likes her to be free to come and go.'

'Maybe Oscar's been fiddling with it.'

'Maybe.'

Tess left him a mug of coffee and carried her own back to the front room. She needed to finish another year of records today, but instead of pulling up the documents, she sat and stared unseeingly ahead of her, gnawing absently at her knuckle. The cat flap was only the latest in a series of inexplicable incidents. They were all tiny in themselves – a roll of kitchen paper in the middle of her bed, a bar of soap by the laptop, a lamp left on when she was sure that she had turned it off – but Tess was beginning to get a bad feeling about them. Could they all really be down to absentmindedness? She had never been vague or ditzy, and the thought that she might be having memory lapses was a disturbing one.

Otherwise, life was much more under control. She had been using Luke's old phone, and had been careful to give the number to the school and Vanessa and, reluctantly, her mother, but no one else. Her relief now that the constant ringing had stopped was so great that it was only then that Tess realized how it had worn on her nerves. Luke had never referred to what she had told him, but it felt good to have cleared the air, and although they were not quite friends again yet, that dreadful formality between them had gone.

There had been no more hallucinations either. Perhaps they really had been due to strain, after all. Occasionally a memory of Nell would surface – of her hair damp with rain on a lovely summer day, or bare feet stained with mud from a paved street – but she pushed it away. There would be a rational explanation if she had the time to look for it. There had to be.

Just as there would be an explanation for the locked cat flap too. Tess was still puzzling over it as she walked to pick Oscar up from school. Vanessa was already at the gates. Dressed in her usual Lycra, she was bouncing from foot to foot, as if eager to be off. Her energy made Tess feel guilty for the way she strolled through the streets and out through the bar at such a leisurely pace.

It was impossible to walk to the school without thinking of Nell and how much she had loved the crofts, or how the tarmacked roads had once been rough tracks. Of course, it was well known that the area outside Monk Bar had been one of orchards and market gardens until the nineteenth century, Tess reminded herself. There was nothing strange about knowing that. It wasn't as if she *remembered* it.

Sometimes, it was true, the pavements felt precarious, the past very close. Then Tess would keep her eyes down. She didn't want to look up in case she saw that the streets had closed in, the houses leaning inwards with their overhanging jetties. A blink and the plate-glass windows of the modern shop could be replaced by stalls and shuttered workshops; by women spinning in doorways. Turn her head, and the delivery vans could become carts and wagons. Lose concentration for a moment, and she could find herself amidst the clutter and clamour of the Elizabethan street. Once or twice she had risked a glance up and it seemed that the faces she saw were disturbingly familiar.

But why wouldn't they be? Tess reasoned. She had grown up in York. It was a small city. She was likely to recognize all sorts of people.

Vanessa looked pointedly at her watch when Tess arrived. 'Sorry I'm late,' Tess said automatically, and then wondered why she was apologizing. There were other children in the playground with teachers to supervise them. She wasn't accountable to Vanessa.

'I suppose you've been buried in those records again,' said Vanessa, who for some reason disapproved of Tess earning money in such an unconventional way. In Vanessa's world, you worked in an office, or a school or – at a push – in a hospital until you got married and signed up to be a full-blown yummy mummy.

She was being a bitch, Tess scolded herself. Vanessa was kind and generous and she should remember that. Still, she turned with relief when Oscar spotted her across the playground and came galloping towards her.

'Mummy! Mummy!' His face was pink, his hair tousled, and his shirt had come loose from his trousers. Tess felt her chest tighten at the sight of him looking so messy, so normal. Martin would have made him stop and tuck in his shirt. He would have had to smooth down his hair and straighten his sweatshirt. Pick up the jacket that trailed along the ground behind him.

'Hello, pip,' she said, unable to resist pushing his hair back anyway. 'Have you had a good day?'

'I drawed you a picture.' He thrust the piece of paper at her, and Tess took it and made a show of inspecting it.

'That's the sea,' she guessed, looking at the blue scribble. 'And Ashrafar.' The cat was unmistakable: black, sling-backed, with a bushy tail and teeth like a shark. She pointed at the two stick figures. 'And is this you and me?'

Oscar shook his head. 'That's me and Luke.'

The trip to Bridlington had been an unqualified success. They had watched the kitesurfing while Luke took photographs, and afterwards they had had fish and chips on the promenade and paddled in the sea, and Oscar had been tense with excitement the whole day. His wariness of Luke had turned overnight into slavish admiration, and he rushed home every day if Tess told him that Luke was going to be at the flat, and slid into the study, Bink under his arm, to watch him work. He hung by the door at first, but gradually moved closer and closer, until Luke let him sort out screws or hold the end of the tape measure. As far as Tess could tell, they had no conversation, but the silence didn't seem to bother either of them. It was bittersweet for her to see her son forming a tentative bond with Luke, a bond he had never had with his own father.

He was going to miss Luke when the shelves were finished.

Tess was going to miss him too, but she was trying not to think about that. She had got used to having Luke around. She'd make coffee for them both and perch on the books while he finished planing a board or fitting an awkward corner. There was usually sawdust in his hair and his clothes were stained and shabby, but his fingers were deft and his movements easy and unhurried for a man who had once been so restless. Tess liked to watch him concentrate, liked the way he set his jaw and lined up his sight, the way he rolled his shoulders and relaxed when it was done.

Then he would hunker down beside her and take the coffee she offered and they would talk about nothing in particular. Sometimes she'd even make him laugh, and whenever those stern features lit up, something in Tess would twist and tighten dangerously. She was being careful not to rely on him – she was – but yes, she would miss him.

'Luke?' Vanessa didn't even pretend that she wasn't listening. 'Luke Hutton?' Her voice was blade sharp, and Tess felt a ridiculously guilty flush prickle up her throat.

'Yes. I told you he was making some bookshelves for Richard, didn't I?' Tess was carefully casual. She laid a hand on the top of Oscar's head. 'He took us to the seaside, didn't he, pip?'

Oscar nodded importantly. 'An' he lets me help.'

'I thought you weren't going to have any more to do with him?' Vanessa's mouth was pinched as she drew Tess aside.

'It was just a day out, Vanessa, and it was great,' said Tess with an edge of defiance. 'I needed to get away.'

'You could have asked me.'

'It was a spontaneous thing.' She shifted her bag to her other shoulder. 'Besides, you've done so much already.'

'You know I don't mind. I'm glad to have you back in York. But I thought we were friends,' said Vanessa with a hurt look. 'I can't believe you didn't tell me about Luke.'

The prickle of guilt crept higher. 'There's nothing to tell.'

And there wasn't. Oscar had been sound asleep by the time they got back from Bridlington, and Tess was woozy from the sun and wind as she carried him upstairs and put him straight into bed.

Luke had brought her bag up and waited by the stairs as she gently closed Oscar's door.

'Everything okay?'

She nodded. 'Thank you for today, Luke. Oscar loved it.'

'He's a nice kid.' The words were said so grudgingly that Tess couldn't help smiling. After a moment, a reluctant answering grin tugged at

Luke's lips.

'Thank you,' said Tess again, and then without warning their smiles were fading and the air began to thrum with something frighteningly new and yet achingly familiar.

He was going to kiss her, thought Tess, torn between panic and anticipation. She wasn't ready for it. She longed for it. Should she lean forward in invitation, or put some space between them? Her breath shortened.

She was still dithering when Luke stepped back. 'Well … bye then,' he said roughly, and he turned and left Tess alone at the stop of the stairs, not knowing whether to be glad or sorry that he had gone.

Nothing had happened.

'Really,' she told Vanessa. 'He's just … building shelves.'

'Well, I hope you know what you're doing,' Vanessa said. 'You're still married, you know.'

Tess took a step back before she could snap at her friend. 'I haven't forgotten,' she said.

Luke had gone by the time they got home. 'Never mind,' said Tess as Oscar's face fell and she tried not to notice the dip of her own heart. 'I'll make you a sandwich and you can watch TV with Bink for a bit if you like.'

Television was still a treat. Now there was no father coming home, no need to watch with one eye on the clock, one ear straining for the crunch of tyres on gravel. Oscar's face lit up. He ran down the corridor to his room while Tess got out bread and jam, but she was still only buttering when he was back, his bottom lip stuck out.

'I can't find Bink! He's gone!'

'Don't be silly, of course he's not gone,' said Tess, pausing with the knife in mid-smear.

'He has! He's not there!' Oscar wailed.

An unpleasant feeling twitched in Tess's belly, like a snake stirring its tail. She put down the knife. 'I'll come and find him for you.'

She had set Bink on Oscar's pillow that morning, the way she always did. Hadn't she? She was sure she remembered doing it.

But Oscar was right. There was nothing on his pillow.

'Where is he?' Her son's face crumpled.

Tess stretched her lips into a reassuring smile. 'He must be here somewhere. Perhaps he's gone on an adventure?' she suggested, looking under the bed, behind the headboard, on top of the small wardrobe.

No Bink.

Oscar perked up at the idea of his beloved toy adventuring away from the bed, and entered into the search with gusto, but Tess was feeling increasingly panicky. What had she done with Bink? Oscar might believe in an adventure, but he was only five. She was nearly thirty-one and she knew that stuffed monkeys didn't move themselves.

'Do you think he's gone outside, Mummy?' Oscar asked.

'I don't think so, pip. I think he's hiding in here somewhere.' Surely she would remember if she had carried him out of the room? Or would she? There was too much she didn't remember nowadays. A memory of Nell flitted into her mind.

There was also too much she did remember nowadays that she shouldn't.

Mindlessly, Tess pulled open the drawers of the chest, more to look as if she was searching than with any expectation of finding Bink.

'There he is!' Oscar gave a shriek of excitement. 'There's Bink!' Pushing past Tess, he grabbed the toy from where he had been stuffed in amongst his socks and underwear and hugged him to his face. 'Naughty Bink!' he said delightedly. 'You've been hiding.'

Tess stared down at the drawer. Had she really taken Bink and hidden him in the drawer? Why would she do such a thing? But if it wasn't her, then who? Her mind darted to Martin, but there was no sign of a break-in. How would he have got in? How would anyone have got in?

She didn't know what was worse – that someone had been in the flat without her realizing it, or that she had lost her memory and was randomly moving objects around.

Or perhaps she had just misplaced them. She had been making a point of learning to be untidy. Martin had insisted on a rigidly controlled environment at all times, but now she didn't have to have everything perfectly ordered any more she could leave a pile of books on the desk if she wanted, or a newspaper open on the sofa. Deliberately, Tess left her clothes tossed over the back of a chair. She left dirty mugs in the sink and cluttered the worktop in the kitchen with herbs and spices. She left books open on the sofa and took pleasure in shoving the cutlery back into the drawer any old how. In her new, happily muddled world, it wasn't surprising if not everything was where she expected it to be.

But the monkey's disappearance nagged at her. It seemed bound up with locked cat flaps and scrabbling walls and Nell and the whole strangeness of life in this flat. It was never so bad when Luke was around, but he would be finished soon, and she would be alone here all day, every day. The ache that always seemed to be lurking behind her eyes these days simmered into life, not bad enough to take an aspirin, but too insistent to ignore completely.

Perhaps she should think about moving, Tess thought, frowning, as she peeled potatoes. But where could she afford to go? Besides, she had promised Richard that she would look after Ashrafar for him, and she owed him too much to let him down.

Oscar's euphoria over finding Bink had evaporated by the time she called him in for supper, and he was in a petulant mood. Tess let him feed Ashrafar, and he carried the dish over, the cat weaving industriously between his ankles, to set it precisely down in the middle of the tile in front of the cat flap that was set into the wall. It led out onto a tiny terrace from where Ashrafar could jump down into the yard or prowl the red-tiled rooftops.

'Oscar, did you touch the cat flap this morning?' asked Tess, remembering the cat's outraged yowl at being stuck outside.

She wasn't surprised when Oscar shook his head, not even a flicker of guilt on his face. He clambered onto his stool at the tiny breakfast bar, but he was more interested in watching the cat than eating his own supper. Listlessly, he pushed slices of cucumber around his plate.

'Don't play with your food, Oscar,' Tess said. Her headache was getting worse and she put down her own fork, unable to eat herself.

'Mummy.' Oscar's voice seemed to be coming from a long way away. 'Mummy, look at Ashfer!'

The cat was crouched low by the dish, but she was not eating either. Her ears were flattened, her fur erect, and a low, somehow terrible growl was rumbling from her throat.

And her great yellow eyes were fixed on Tess.

'Ashrafar,' she whispered, her mouth dry, fear beating a frantic tattoo in her chest. She half-rose from her chair, thinking to reassure the cat about whatever was distressing her, but the moment she moved, Ashrafar abandoned her meal uneaten and shot outside, leaving the cat flap to bang back into place behind her with a sharp crack.

Bang! Bang! Bang! The feast had been cleared away, the tables put to one side. The waits had been tuning their instruments, and now there was a stir of anticipation as the drum was beaten to announce the dancing.

'Wife?' Ralph Maskewe's big teeth flashed as he smiled at Nell and held out a hand.

She couldn't refuse to take it, just as she was unable to refuse when he put his mouth on hers to seal their betrothal. There were witnesses, who had looked on approvingly. They knew that she and Tom were sweethearts, that she was betrothed to him, but they nodded anyway. Nell could not find it in her to forgive them that.

'Husband.' Nell dipped a curtsey and let Ralph lead her into the dance. She had a smile fixed to her lips, but every time he touched her, every time he looked at her with those eyes like pale pebbles, something in her shrank away.

And he knew it, she was sure. He knew it and he liked it.

A great weight had gathered in her chest, so heavy she could hardly hold herself upright, but she kept her chin lifted. She would not weep, she would not wail. She had made her choice and her kin were safe. She would not give Ralph the satisfaction of knowing the depths of her pain.

'I lay with your brother,' she told him clearly when her father had left them together. She would not lie. 'I do not come to you a maid.'

Something had shifted in his face at the mention of Tom, but the next moment the toothy smile was back. 'So be it,' he said. 'Tom is in no position to think of a wife in any case, and you, Eleanor, are in need of a husband. You are too beautiful to wither away in waiting for a boy like Tom who may never come home. You know what Tom is like. He has foolish dreams of setting sail and seeing the world. No, he won't be coming back, Eleanor.'

Tom wouldn't come back *now*, Nell knew. He wouldn't come back when he heard that she had wed his brother. She had taken his ring and hidden it in her purse. She would not wear it now, but she kept it as the only way she could be true to him still as she had promised.

Ralph was watching her face. 'Foolish Eleanor, did you really think he would?'

Oh, Tom! Nell hated the fact that a little bit of her wondered if Ralph might be right. Tom had always longed to see the world. Did he really want a wife to chain him to home?

But she would not let Ralph see her doubt. Tilting her chin at him, she answered his question with another.

'Why would you want to marry me, knowing that I love your brother? That I have lain with him? If I marry you, I will be breaking my troth to him. Do you really want that?'

'Ah, Eleanor, if you knew how I loved you, you would not ask that!' Ralph reached for her hand, and she had to force herself not to pull it away in disgust. 'I burn for you. I have always burned for you!'

'It is not love when you force me against my will.'

'Force? Who said aught of force?' His eyes glittered at the word. 'I will give you everything: fine clothes, a fine house, fine food to set on the table.' He gestured down at his embroidered doublet, at the slashed velvet breeches and expensive nether stockings. 'Aye, and a fine husband! What other maid would talk of force so? The choice is yours, Eleanor,' he reminded her.

A choice that was no choice. They both knew that. Nell looked back at him coldly. 'I ask only for security for my family,' she said. 'You will forgive my father's debt if I wed you?'

'Eleanor, Eleanor...' Ralph sighed. 'So crude!'

'Will you?'

'It shall be done.'

And now they were wed.

Chapter Ten

November was not a good time to be married. The city had been shrouded in fog all day. The damp gloom crept murkily, sneakily, into every corner, muffling sound and blocking out the sun, smothering the light and the air and the life in the city, and Nell didn't seem to be able to get enough breath. She was suffocating under the weight of the fog, under the knowledge that she was trapped as surely as she had been trapped in the chest so long ago. When she stood in the church porch with Ralph and made her vows, she could have sworn she still smelt the oppressive heat of that day and the wood of the kist.

She wanted to wait until spring, hoping for a reprieve, but Ralph was not to be put off. 'I cannot wait for you any longer,' he told her. So there were no flowers strewn in the street, and her maids shivered beneath their cloaks as they picked their way through the puddles to the church, the fog swallowing them up so the front of the procession could not be seen from the back.

After the marriage there was the nuptial mass in St Helen's, and cakes and wine, and then the wedding procession made its way back through the fog in Stonegate to the Maskewe house. The hall was richly decorated for the celebration, and there had been a feast fit to put before the Queen's Majesty herself. Capons, fowl and suckling pigs served with frummenty and fritters. Then pigeons and partridges, rabbit and roast beef, young herons and baked larks. Jellies, custards, comfits. Ralph insisted on putting a slice of everything on the dish that they shared. Nell watched his big teeth biting into a tiny roast sparrow and nausea rolled thick and clotty in her stomach.

Out of the corner of her eye she could see the door to the closet, closed now for the feast. Sometimes she could almost see her younger self, tiptoeing over, peering inside, spying the chest and the chance of somewhere clever to hide.

'No!' Nell wanted to shout. 'No, don't go in!' But then she would blink and the vision would be gone, leaving only a sense of impending dread looming over her shoulders and tickling the back of her neck.

Her wedding feast. It was not as she had once imagined it. People were laughing too loudly, eating too greedily. The wine was too spiced, the food too rich. The flickering candlelight sent shadows swooping over familiar faces that gleamed with such grease they looked like strangers. Beside her, Ralph's lips glistened with fat and he smiled as he methodically pulled the little birds apart piece by piece with his teeth and sucked every little bone clean.

But through it all Nell smiled. What else was there to do?

Behind the smile, she felt disconnected from it all. She picked at a fritter, but it might as well have been the rush matting on the floor, chopped onto her plate, for all that she tasted. She chewed and smiled, chewed and smiled. Sometimes she took a sip of wine. The sweetness of the honey tasted bitter in her mouth, but still she smiled.

Chew, sip, smile. Chew, sip, smile. Smile, smile, smile. Never had smiling been so hard. The muscles in her cheeks were aching with the effort.

'You are not eating.' Ralph took a partridge wing and held it out to her when she decided she had made enough of a show of enjoying the food. His fingers were slippery and slick and she pressed her lips together against another heave of revulsion.

Even then, she kept her smile in place. 'I thank you, but I have had enough.'

'Eat it,' he said, and though his mouth was stretched in an answering smile, there was an implacable note in his voice. At last Nell's own smile faltered. There were just the two of them, marooned in a pool of silence while the feast chortled around them. 'You want your father's debt paid, do you not?' said the devoted bridegroom.

Nell took the wing from him. Her gorge rose but managed a tiny bite and forced it down. The gamey texture of the flesh stuck to the roof of her mouth and sauce thickened with bread clung unpleasantly to her tongue. She tasted ginger, vinegar, despair.

'Eat it all,' said Ralph.

Somehow Nell made her way through it all. When she finally judged that she could lay the bones down, Ralph took them and sucked them between his teeth, on and on and on. The sound made sweat break out on her forehead.

I must not be sick. I must not be sick.

I must not think of Tom.

'You're so lucky,' Alice had sighed as she helped Nell dress earlier. 'I wish William would give me a kirtle like this!' She fingered the fine worsted enviously. Alice had done what no other maid could do. She had penned William Carter's wandering eye, she had pinned him down, and now they were betrothed. Nell thought privately that William himself was not quite sure how it had happened, but Alice was happy and she was glad for her friend.

Happy she might be, but Alice was hard-headed enough to know that lust alone was not enough to make a marriage. She knew how Nell felt about Tom, but she approved of her decision to marry Ralph instead. 'Ralph Maskewe is a fine-looking gentleman, and rich too. He is a man of substance and good reputation. William says he will be alderman long before anyone else his age.'

Nell smiled faintly, but only because she had heard a lot about what William said since Alice's betrothal. He seemed to have an opinion on every subject.

'And he dotes on you, Nell. You will have everything you want.'

Nell didn't answer. *Not everything*, she wanted to say. *I cannot have Tom, and if I cannot have Tom, I do not want anything.* But what would be the point?

It was the way of the world. *We cannot always have what we want*, Nell told herself. *We do what we must and we endure*. There was no point in telling everyone her heart was breaking. It would not make any difference, and it would just make them feel bad. Already her father's shame-faced gratitude was more than she could bear.

And now she was dancing with Ralph, his hands pressed against hers, his teeth glinting in the candlelight. Nell went through the motions, her smile still pinned to her face, while their guests put their heads to one side and smiled indulgently at the newly-weds. Couldn't they see? Nell marvelled. Couldn't they tell just how wrong this was?

She was dreading the night to come, so much so that now she was impatient to get it over with. At least she did not have to try and pretend that she was still a maid. She had been honest with Ralph. He couldn't accuse her of being untrue.

After Ralph, she danced every dance. Her bride-laces fluttered blue and green from her golden headdress and she could smell the posies of rosemary pinned to the hair that today fell loose down her back. The wild hair that Tom used to love to twine his hands in. *I see gold and bronze and copper ... I see flames, hot and red.* And then he would rub his face in it. *I smell gillyflowers.*

Nell kept smiling. Oh, she was the perfect bride. Let no one say she was not playing her part. But her eyes were blank and she didn't notice who she was dancing with except when she danced with her brother, gentle Harry, who minded his steps carefully and whose eyes were troubled.

'Nell,' he said. 'Will you be happy?'

He was the only one who had asked, the only one, it seemed, who cared.

For a moment, Nell could not answer him. She looked away, her throat too tight to speak, and then the dance separated them. She turned, clapped, smiled, and when they came back together again she was able to look into his face.

'I will try,' she said.

She had lost Tom, but she had saved Harry. That was something, and when the dance ended, she embraced him, this brother who was so dear to her heart.

For the first time it occurred to her that she might have children of her own. Ralph would never be Tom, but they might come to an understanding. Perhaps it would not be too bad.

Only it felt very bad when Ralph beckoned her. 'It is time for us to retire,' he said. 'Make yourself ready, my dear.'

Stifling giggles, Nell's maids led her to the great bedchamber overlooking the street. A tall bed draped in red damask nearly filled the room. In the light of the candles one of the maids set on a table, Nell could see the great curtains, embroidered with bees and flowers on the outside, pulled back and looped to the bedposts with twisted golden cords. There was a turned chair by the window, with a tasselled cushion, and a huge chest that made memories freeze like ice in her belly.

She averted her eyes from it as her maids helped her out of her gown. They took the posies of rosemary from her hair, rolled up the bridelaces and brushed out her hair, whispering advice and encouragement. Nell had already had an awkward conversation with her stepmother, who advised her to lie still and let her husband do what he wanted, and it would be soon over. For a second, she allowed herself to remember Tom and how easily they had moved together. She had never been able to lie still, had never wanted it to end.

But she couldn't think of Tom, not now.

She had been smiling so long, her face felt fixed in a grimace. Nell let them help her into the great bed. Tonight she would lie still; tonight she would wait for it to be over. She could smell rosemary on the sheets, in her hair from the posies.

Rosemary for fidelity. Rosemary for remembrance.

But she had not been faithful to Tom, and remembrance was the last thing she needed then.

Her maids left and for one blessed moment Nell was alone and could let the smile drop from her face like a stone. She lay and looked up at the canopy over the bed. She was used to sleeping with Alice in the little chamber in the Harrisons' attic. This bed on its own was almost as big as that chamber, but the heavy curtains made it seem close and dark in the guttering candlelight.

What if Ralph wanted to close them? A new dread swamped Nell, twisting her stomach and clogging her throat and ringing in her ears. They would be shut in the thick darkness and she would not be able to breathe. It would be like being closed in the chest again, but this time it would be worse.

Ralph would be with her.

Nell's breath raced to catch up with her accelerating heart. If he closed the curtains, if he closed them ... what would she do?

Perhaps he wouldn't. She latched onto the thought. The cords and tassels were very grand. Perhaps they were just for show. Perhaps Ralph, too, felt stifled when the heavy silk fell down and cut the bed off from the rest of the room. With an effort, Nell slowed her shallow breathing. She could endure this. She must.

She would have to be careful not to offend Ralph. He must not guess the terror that awaited her if he tried to close her in. So she would put her smile back and speak fair words and hope that he would want her enough to treat her kindly.

She had no more time to think in any case. There was boisterous laughter outside, then Ralph came in. Laughingly, he pushed out the men who pretended they would crowd into the chamber to help him. They left at last, jeering advice and encouragement.

Ralph and Nell were alone.

Nell's heart was thudding slowly and painfully in her chest, as if it would smash her ribs and burst out of her body. The beat of it was deafening in her ears, so loud that she was sure Ralph must hear it.

'So,' Ralph said. He began to unbutton his doublet, his eyes on Nell, his expression unreadable. She wondered if he expected her to get up and help him undress, but it felt false to her so she stayed where she was. No doubt he would tell her what he wanted.

In the hall along the passage, their guests were still drinking, and dancing had begun again after the bride and groom had been delivered to their wedding bed. The waits spent the break making the most of the liberal supplies of spiced wine, and now the music was getting more raucous, but in the chamber there was only raw silence.

It went on so long that Nell lost her nerve. She cleared her throat. 'The feast seemed to go well enough,' she said at last.

'It did,' Ralph agreed pleasantly, 'had it not been for the fact that you acted the harlot.'

Nell thought she had misheard. 'Acted the what?'

'Do not act the innocent with me, mistress. We had an agreement. You are my wife now.'

'I am not like to forget it,' she said bitterly, forgetting that she had meant to give him soft words and smiles, to make him forget how the bed curtains could close around them like a shroud.

'I saw you.' He stripped off his doublet, his hose, until he was down to his linen undershirt. There was a tautness to him, like a pinner's wire stretched tighter and tighter and tighter until with a final twist it would snap. 'I saw you flirt with every man you danced with.'

Nell puffed out a laugh at the absurdity of it, but that was the wrong thing to do. His face darkened. 'It amuses you, to shame me in front of our guests?'

'I was not flirting,' she said honestly. 'I barely knew who I was dancing with.'

'So you do not know who you embrace?'

She was puzzled at first. 'You cannot mean Harry?' As far as she remembered, that was the only moment of affection in the whole day. Ralph just looked grimly at her, and she looked back in disbelief. 'Ralph, he is my brother!'

'And you kept all your embraces for him. Do you never do that to me again, wife,' Ralph said and the expression in his eyes made her shrink back onto the pillows. 'You are my wife now, do you understand me?'

'You're being absurd–' she began, but his hands lashed out without warning and grabbed her arms so hard that she cried out.

'Do not dare call me absurd,' he ground out savagely. 'You are *mine* now. You are not to embrace anyone but me. Do. You. Understand?' He shook her between each word, and his fingers bit agonizingly into her flesh.

'Yes,' she gasped. Anything to be free of the pain of his grip. 'Yes, I understand.'

He let her go so suddenly she toppled back against the pillows, shaken by this brush with violence. He hadn't touched the curtains, that was all she could think. She could cope with anything as long as she wasn't shut in the dark.

She hoped that would be end to his roughness, but it seemed Ralph was just beginning. He climbed over her, bigger than Tom, broader and heavier, and his expression was feral, glinting with such menace that Nell caught her breath.

'You ... do not need to force me,' she managed.

'Oh, but I do. I know you are thinking of him,' he snarled. 'You have been thinking of him all day, haven't you?'

Nell knew who he meant. 'No,' she said in a level voice. 'I cannot bear to think of him.'

'Do not lie to me!' He pinched her breast so hard that she yelped. Immediately, he clapped a hand over her mouth.

'Be quiet!'

'You're hurting me,' she gasped, struggling to free herself from his hand.

'You deserve to be hurt. Don't you?' he added, when she stared up at him, aghast at the man unravelling before her eyes. He pinched her again, and this time she managed not to cry out. 'Don't you? No sooner married than unfaithful in thought. Do you think to make a cuckold of me so easily? Do you? *Do you?*' He was twisting her flesh, hurting her, pinning her down with the brutal weight of his body as she tried to wriggle out from beneath him.

'Where do you think you're going?'

'In God's name, Ralph! You are *hurting* me!' she tried again, but he was panting, his eyes fevered with excitement, and he wouldn't let her go.

'I've dreamt of this, dreamt of you, and you're spoiling it,' he told her through clenched teeth, pulling her back by her hair until she whimpered with pain.

'That's better,' he said, his voice clotted with satisfaction, and she realized in a cold wash of horror that he wanted her to feel pain. He needed it.

'What is wrong with you?' she whispered.

'There is nothing wrong with me!' His face changed and he punched her with brutal efficiency under her ribs, and he kept on punching as she curled up protectively. 'Nothing! Nothing! It is you who are wrong, you little slut, lying with my own brother, fornicating in the hedges, like a common whore. Did you think I did not know every time you were busy at your stair work and your trunk work and your field work? Did you really think you needed to *tell* me?'

He kept hissing vile words in her ear as he turned her onto her front and forced himself into her, driven frantically on by the violence spewing out of him. To Nell, lost in a red mist of pain, the horror seemed to go on and on, but at last he cried out and slumped over her.

When he finally pulled away and crawled off her, she hauled herself to the side of the great bed and clung there, fighting down nausea and forcing herself to breathe through the pain. *At least he didn't close the curtains*, that was all she could think. *At least he didn't do that.*

All she could hear was the rasp of Ralph's breathing. 'I thought it would be better than that,' he said peevishly into the darkness at last. 'I've dreamed of bedding you for so long. Nell Appleby, a little nobody who only ever looked at me as if I were an earwig scuttling out from under a stone – I, Ralph Maskewe!'

He spat out a breath. 'I've watched you for years – watched the way you sway your hips, the way you smile at everyone but me – and I knew when you and that goatish fool-born brother of mine were at it out on the common. I could smell it on you both, and I wanted it to be me.' His voice was high, querulous. 'I thought of it all the time, having you beneath me, doing what I wanted with you, and now you have spoilt it.'

Dimly, Nell realized that he was waiting for her to apologize. She dragged in a shuddering breath. Nothing could make this worse.

'I am sorry,' she said dully.

It was the right thing to do. Ralph let out a long sigh of satisfaction. 'Well, you are new to the way things should be between man and woman,' he said, all understanding. 'I doubt not my cloddish brother knew nothing of pleasure. I will teach you,' he said. 'You have much to learn, but we may make a good wife of you yet.'

Nell lay awake all night, listening to Ralph sleep beside her. She throbbed all over where he had beaten and pinched her, but he had been careful not to mark her face, she realized. Her ribs might be tender, her belly bruised, her arms and breasts covered with pinches, but from the neck up she looked as she had always done. Short of stripping down to her shift, she would not be able to convince anyone that her husband had hurt her.

And what if he had? What could they do? She was Ralph's property now. She was his wife, and he could do what he liked with her.

'Mummy, is Ashfer frightened? Why won't she come in?'

There was a red mist in front of her eyes. She ached all over and her head throbbed with pain. She didn't want to wake up. She wanted to sink back into the merciful darkness of oblivion, but something about the voice tugged at her. She didn't recognize it, but it was important, she knew that. She had to pay attention.

She blinked slowly, and looked around, uncomprehending at first. The bed had gone, and so had the dark, oppressive curtains. Instead of the chamber, she was in a tiny narrow room lined with cupboards and strange shiny boxes. A small boy crouched by a hole in the wall, peering through it.

'Mummy,' he said, 'Ashfer won't come in.'

Oscar. Memory swung back and hit Tess like a wrecking ball. She just managed to catch her head in her hands before it crashed onto the breakfast bar. Dear God, how long had she been unaware?

How long had Oscar been here effectively on his own while she was being raped and tortured by her own husband?

'Mummy–' Oscar began again, only to stop at the scrape of Tess's chair across the tiles.

'Just a minute, Oscar.' Her legs barely held Tess up, and she just made it to the bathroom before throwing up.

'Are you sick, Mummy?'

Tess was curled in a foetal position on the floor, her arms wrapped round her. Shivering, she lifted her head to see Oscar in the doorway. Bink was tucked under his arm, and his eyes were huge and brown, his mouth wobbling with distress. 'What's happening?' he demanded in a thin voice that cracked Tess's heart.

Somehow she struggled up to a sitting position. 'I've just got a bit of a bug,' she told him and ventured a smile, although she guessed it must be a ghastly one. 'Why don't you and Bink watch a bit more television while I have a wash, and then I'll feel better?'

'What about Ashfer? She hasn't eaten her supper.'

Tess rubbed her hands over her face, struggling to remember who Ashfer was. The cat, yes. Ashrafar. The cat who had turned tail and bolted as Nell took Tess over.

'She'll come in when she's hungry, pip.' She hoped. 'You go and watch TV. I'll be in in a minute.'

''Kay.' Oscar hesitated then trailed off to the front room. Normally he would have been thrilled at the chance of extra television, but he could tell that something was very wrong.

Shakily, Tess got herself onto all fours, and then pulled herself upright. Imagination or not, she ached inside and out, and the memory of being brutalized made her gag still. She ran a bath as hot as she could bear and sat in it, scrubbing at herself until she was raw, desperate to get the feel of Ralph off her skin, but she couldn't get clean and she couldn't get warm.

Afterwards, she huddled into a towel and pressed the heels of her hands into her eyes. It was all in her mind, she made herself remember. As far as Oscar was concerned, she had been sitting in the kitchen with him all the time. She hadn't *actually* been raped, Tess told herself, but when she looked down, her arms and breasts and inner thighs were covered with bruises where Ralph had pinched and twisted her flesh.

'You must be boiling!' Vanessa looked at Tess in surprise when she saw her hugging a cardigan around her. 'Is that a long-sleeved T-shirt you're wearing too?' She herself was wearing a cut-off jogging top that showed her enviably flat stomach, and skintight Lycra shorts. Spreading her hands, she looked significantly up at the sky, its blueness barely feathered with a few high wisps of cloud. 'It's a gorgeous day, or didn't you notice?'

Tess bent to kiss Oscar goodbye and ruffled his hair. 'I've had one of those twenty-four hour bugs,' she said as she straightened to watch him run into the playground. 'I'm still feeling a bit yuck.'

'You should have said. I'd have come and got

Oscar for you.'

'I'm okay now. It's good to get out.'

It was. Somehow Tess had got through the routine of bath, book, bed with Oscar. Fortunately, Ashrafar reappeared when she was reading a story and curled up on Oscar's bed. Tess had reached out a tentative hand to stroke her, half-expecting her to take off once more with a yowl of fright, but Ashrafar only stretched and purred, which reassured her. It meant Nell had gone ... but for how long?

Unable to settle, Tess had tried to watch television, but the pictures on the screen were of a reality she couldn't connect to any more. She flicked through the channels, but every programme seemed to involve flashing lights or complicated computer graphics. The images changed so fast, her brain couldn't keep up, and she began to feel dizzy and nauseous. It was as if she were wired to a different world now and she gazed uncomprehendingly at adverts for cars and broadband, for yoghurts and dating agencies, and none of it made sense.

She watched a happy family eating cereal together, smiling brightly, and shuddered as she fingered her bruises. The father looked a bit like Ralph. Behind that handsome, smiling face, was there another vicious brute? How could you tell? When she had looked at Martin, she had seen an attractive, charming, caring man, the sort of man she expected to end up having jolly family breakfasts with. There had been no way of knowing that before the cereal could be poured in a precise amount, the bowls had to be spotlessly clean, that the spoons had to be kept carefully aligned in the cutlery drawer.

Tess switched off the television. In spite of the wretchedness churning in her belly, she craved human company, but there was no one she could call. Vanessa would be with her husband, her mother didn't like to be disturbed after nine, and Luke... She could hardly call Luke and ask him to come over, could she?

She had wandered over to the window instead and looked down into the street where at least there were ordinary people, out enjoying the soft summer evening. Even at this time of night, Stonegate had its share of tourists admiring the old houses and the view of the illuminated Minster at the end of the street.

But as she watched, the world wavered and she was looking into a narrower, more cluttered street. It was early evening, and her neighbours were taking in goods from their stalls, closing up their shutters, and sweeping the debris of the day from their doors into their gutters. John Bean's apprentice was labouring in and out with scuttles full of refuse which he was piling up ready for the scavengers the next morning.

'You're too early!' Goodwife Carter shook her broom at him. 'Not till seven of the clock! Your master knows that well enough!'

She leant further out of the window. There was Elizabeth, maid to the Bowes, setting down the heavy pails she was carrying and flexing her fingers before stooping to pick them up once more and trudge on up the mid causey towards the Minster. There was John Harper, leaning against his door. She saw him exchange a lascivious look with Margery Dixon, and she raised her brows. Margery's husband must be away again.

With a wistful sigh, she turned away from the window, only to be brought up short at the sight of strange, softly cushioned chairs and an uncannily gleaming black box where the great bed should be standing.

A blink, a jolt, and Tess remembered who she was. Her pulse pounded and she had to breathe deeply in and out before the roaring would subside. Her limbs felt strange, weightless, as if she might float away, and she held onto the table to anchor herself.

So this was where Ralph Maskewe had raped his wife. Why hadn't she realized that before? Tess wondered. She should have guessed from the configuration of rooms with the hall that was now part of the house next door. She had already worked out that her bedroom had been the closet. Of course this had been the great chamber.

Down in the street she could hear voices, laughter. From the present or from the past? Steeling herself, Tess turned back to the window and looked down. John Harper had gone but in his place stood another man, looking straight up at her in the window.

It was Martin.

The instinctive dart of panic had her jerking back out of sight, a hand to the hammering pulse at the base of her throat. She had been so shocked by her experience at Ralph's hands that she had forgotten about Martin.

Why was he just standing there? What did he want?

Heart thudding, Tess edged forward, very cautiously, until she could peer into the street without being seen. Martin was walking away, looking casually around him.

She bit her lip. He didn't look so familiar from behind. Perhaps it hadn't been Martin at all? It was difficult to tell now. She had been so sure it was him, but how could she be sure about anything at the moment?

And Martin wouldn't be hanging around in the street, she tried to reassure herself. He would have rung the bell, surely? Demanded that she pack her things. Waited inexorably until she did as she was told.

She must have imagined it.

Still, Tess had lain awake into the small hours, afraid to fall asleep and find herself back in that great bed with Ralph. It reminded her of the nights she had lain rigidly next to Martin, afraid to fidget in case she irritated him. But Martin had never beaten her the way Ralph had beaten Nell. He hadn't wanted her to cry out in pain. Martin liked her to lie still and silent. He had a horror of spontaneity and the mess of sex disgusted him. They had never had sex anywhere but in bed, where Martin liked her to wear the long silk nightdresses he bought for her.

'I like a woman to look like a woman,' he was fond of saying. He insisted that Tess kept her hair long, that she wore skirts and pretty dresses, lacy bras and high heels, and she, God help her, had gone along with it – at first because she was so desperate to please him and then because it was easier to put on stockings and a suspender belt than to make a scene.

In the early days of their marriage, Tess tried to initiate lovemaking. Hoping to excite him, she surreptitiously read a book on how to spice up a sex life, but Martin was appalled when she suggested some new positions they could try. He took it as a slur on his virility, and punished her with silence for a week.

Compared to Ralph, was that so bad?

Eventually she had slept, though, exhausted by her ordeal, and it was a huge relief to wake to a bright morning. Only the rawness inside and the bruises on her flesh remained to convince her the whole thing hadn't been a terrible nightmare.

Now she shifted as Vanessa studied her, evidently taking in her drawn features and the bruised look around her eyes. 'You really don't look well, Tess. Why don't you come back with me and have a coffee?'

'I thought you were going straight to the gym?'

'I can go a bit later. Come on. I'll even find you some biscuits!'

Tess hesitated. She longed for someone to talk to, but she knew how her friend would react if she pulled up her sleeves and showed her the bruises on her arms. Vanessa would take charge immediately. Even if she believed that Tess hadn't made the marks herself, which was doubtful, she would insist on driving her straight to a doctor. Then there would be probing questions and an examination, and who knew where it would end? Tess could just imagine the reaction if she told the doctor what was happening to her. There would be whispered consultation with Vanessa, talk of stress and breakdowns and whether she should be in charge of a child... No, Tess wasn't having that. She had to stay strong and well for Oscar.

She managed a strained smile. 'Actually, I think I'll go back, Van. Thanks anyway. I've got to catch up on the records. I didn't get much done yesterday.'

'All right. If you're sure. Why don't I pick Oscar up tonight, and he can come and play with Sam and Rosie? That would give you a bit of a break.'

It would be churlish to refuse. 'That would be great. Thanks, Van. You're a good friend.'

She watched Vanessa stretch her legs and then set off for the gym at a brisk jog, her ponytail swinging from side to side with self-satisfaction. The bottoms of her trainers were bright pink, and they flashed up and down against the grey pavement. Tess couldn't imagine having enough energy to lift her feet that high. It was all she could do to stand upright today.

Perhaps she should have taken Vanessa up on her offer? She couldn't deal with this by herself, that was for sure, and what if next time she was out for longer than a few seconds? And there would be a next time, Tess was sure. Nell would not let her go that easily. She wasn't going to rest until Tess knew her story, of that Tess was certain.

There was her mother, of course, but Tess couldn't imagine trying to explain her experience to her. Her mother would simply tell her that she needed to go back to Martin and stop being so silly.

The church? Tess turned the idea over in her mind. She had never been a churchgoer, finding more wonder in evidence than blind faith, but weren't priests always called in to exorcise the Devil in horror movies? Nell wasn't the Devil, but she was dead and somehow she was using Tess to live again. Tess faced the idea squarely at last. She could no longer pretend that Nell was just a trick of the imagination, some forgotten memory embellished into a dream, not after Ralph's rape. Not with the bruises livid on her flesh and the raw ache inside her. It had been real. It had happened, and she needed to make sure that it didn't happen again. It wasn't safe for Oscar or for her.

Chapter Eleven

Tess's eyes rested on the great central tower of the Minster thrusting over the rooftops in the distance. If she could find a priest, a vicar, someone who believed in life after death, and talk about what was happening to her, surely they would help? They could perform some sort of ceremony and make Ralph leave her alone.

Make *Nell* leave her alone, Tess corrected herself.

She needed help. She couldn't go on drifting in and out of time in the middle of the day. Once the vividness of the experience had been intriguing, but she was frightened now. Nell's hold on her was becoming too strong, and her pain

too real.

The Minster was right there, but the thought of its soaring glory was intimidating. Its power was unmistakable, but Tess couldn't imagine shuffling in with all the tourists and demanding to be exorcised. She needed an ordinary workaday church and a vicar who wouldn't send her straight to her GP.

An elderly woman walking a wheezy pug gave her directions to a church which she said wasn't far from the school. Screwing up her eyes against the jagged light, Tess wished that she had thought to bring some sunglasses. Vanessa had been right about it being a beautiful day, but the sun was peculiarly intense, turning the Victorian terraces into blocks of raw and unfamiliar angles.

Another headache thudded behind her eyes, and she averted her gaze from the passers-by, all of whom seemed garishly dressed or half-naked, somehow menacing with their uncovered heads and hair shamefully cropped as if for the pillory, until she stopped and shook herself back to the present with an effort.

Her hands were throbbing again.

Tess set her teeth and walked on.

St Chad's turned out to be an uninspiring brick building set back from a suburban street. And it was shut. Wincing at the jab of pain in her fingers, Tess tried the handle, and was shaken by the jumble of relief and despair when she found the door locked.

Well, what had she expected? That the vicar would hang around by the altar just in case someone dropped in wanting a ghost exorcised?

'Can I help you?'

Tess turned to see an attractive woman of forty or so watching her. She had a helmet of dark, glossy hair and was wearing a black suit that made Tess feel crumpled and scruffy in her cotton skirt and T-shirt and battered pumps.

She hugged her thin cardigan around her in an unconsciously defensive gesture. 'I was looking for the vicar.'

'You've found her.' The woman smiled. 'I'm Pat French.'

Tess's jaw sagged. '*You're* the vicar?' Too late she heard the incredulity in her own voice and she blushed furiously. 'I mean, I'm not surprised to find that the vicar is a woman,' she tried to explain. 'It's just I hadn't expected someone quite so glamorous.'

Pat's laugh held genuine amusement. 'That's very kind of you. I used to be an investment banker, so I still have my old wardrobe, but you're right: this isn't normally a glamorous profession.' She paused and looked more closely at Tess.

'Did you want to see inside the church?'

'No ... no.' Tess hesitated. Her knowledge about regression or reincarnation or possession was gleaned from magazine articles and the occasional horror film; from half-remembered stories told in the pub or on sleepovers when she was a girl.

Ghosts felt uncomfortable in a church, right? Or was she thinking of vampires? Tess chewed her lip. She couldn't ask Pat French. She seemed too sensible, too practical, too in control. Now that she was here, she couldn't imagine telling her about Nell.

But if Nell *was* a ghost, perhaps she would be able to tell if she went into a church.

Pain pulsed warningly in her hands, and she flexed her fingers.

'Actually, I would like to go in, if it's not too much trouble,' she said to Pat, abruptly changing her mind. Doing *something* felt better than just standing there not knowing what to do. She should feel something in a church, surely?

But when Pat unlocked the door and let her inside, there was nothing but the smell of musty hymn books and the charged silence so peculiar to churches.

'Do you have a connection with St Chad's?' Pat asked after a moment.

Tess shook her head. 'No, not really.' Deliberately, she walked towards the altar, testing Nell to react in some way. 'When was the church built?'

'Oh, not until the late nineteenth century. Until then, there were very few people living out here. This was York's market garden area.'

It was on the tip of Tess's tongue to say 'I know', but she swallowed the words. She didn't want to get into a discussion with Pat French about what she knew of York's history, or how she knew it.

'You seem troubled,' said Pat after a moment. 'Would you like to talk?'

No! The voice rang so loudly in Tess's mind that she actually took a step back. So Nell was there after all.

Her mouth was dry and it was an effort to swallow. The sensation of Nell in her head was so strong that she had to fight to remember where she was, and all at once the pain in her hands was agonizing.

'I'm...' She stopped. Inside her head Nell was shouting *No! No! No!* And she was right, Tess realized. This felt all wrong.

'That's kind of you, but I'm fine. Really,' she added when Pat looked unconvinced. She made a show of looking at her watch. 'I should be going. I ... I need to get to work.' She couldn't wait to get away from the church and from Pat French's shrewd gaze.

'All right,' said Pat slowly. She dug in her pocket and pulled out a business card. 'Call me at any time if you change your mind. You're always welcome here.'

'Thank you,' Tess managed over the noise of Nell chanting *No! No! No!* in her brain. Gritting her teeth against it, she took the card and resisted Nell's impulse to throw it away. She stuffed it in her bag instead as she backed away towards the door. 'Thank you,' she said again. 'I'd ... better go.'

It felt like an escape and she practically ran down the street. Only when she had turned the corner did Nell loosen the grip on her mind and fade away as suddenly and completely as she had arrived. Tess sagged against a wall, so drained that her legs wouldn't support her. The pain in her hands had gone.

Now what was she going to do?

The Minster shimmered in the distance, challenging her. Perhaps it had been a mistake to try a little church, Tess thought, still shaken by how completely Nell had seized control of her.

Perhaps she would only be matched by the power of a great cathedral.

Or perhaps she should leave well alone.

Was that her thinking or Nell? Tess was no longer sure. She began walking again, heading slowly back into the city through Monk Bar. It was a route she had walked so often she barely noticed her surroundings most of the time, but today the buildings roared at her with their unfamiliarity and the tarmac pavements felt strange beneath her feet. The light hurt her eyes and the air seemed to scrape against her tender flesh. It was as if an outer layer of her had been ripped off, leaving her raw and vulnerable.

The drilling ache in her fingertips started up again as Tess hesitated outside the Minster. Tourists milled around and she stood with them, comforted by the babble of voices, by the ordinariness of cameras pointed and smiling poses. Nobody else seemed overpowered by the sheer size of the cathedral looming above them, a threatening mass of stone and glass that made Tess's head spin as she looked up. It commanded and repelled her at the same time, pinioning her with dread and startled awe.

Had the Minster always been that enormous? Had it always been that powerful? Tess wanted to go in, but she didn't dare move. She felt tiny, precariously situated in time and space, and the world around her was wavering. The slightest ripple in the air might pitch her back to the sixteenth century. Back to Ralph. Every muscle tensed to keep her in place.

'Hey, Tess ... *Tess!*'

It took Tess a moment to realize that it was her name being called. Very cautiously she turned her head without moving the rest of her body.

'Oh ... Luke,' she said, letting out a ragged breath as she saw him lower his camera. He was lean and dark and unshaven, wearing a battered leather jacket, but the sight of him was unaccountably steadying.

'You were in another world,' he said, hoisting the camera bag on his shoulder and coming over to her.

Tess smiled weakly. *You have no idea.*

'I got some good shots of you dreaming in front of the Minster.' He scrolled through the pictures on the camera screen, frowning slightly. 'That one, I think.' He showed it to Tess. 'Like it?'

Tess studied her image. He'd caught her as she stood alone, gazing up at the cathedral. Her arms were tight around her, and the tendons in her neck stood out, but there was something ethereal about her profile against the massive stone, something about the angles of her face and the contrast of lights and textures that made the picture beautiful and oddly powerful.

'I don't look very happy,' she said.

'No.' Luke took the camera back, looked at the image again with a frown. 'You look lonely.' He glanced up at her, his grey eyes uncomfortably keen.

In spite of herself, Tess flushed. Why did loneliness always feel so humiliating?

'What are you doing here?' she asked, avoiding his unspoken question.

He patted his camera. 'I've got a job later.

Taking pictures of some civic party at the Guildhall. I've only got a few more books to put back in Richard's study, but I'll do that tomorrow. I'm just killing time for now. This is the morning Dad's carers come, and he likes to grumble to them about me, so I clear out whether I've got a job or not... Something's wrong, isn't it?'

Caught unawares by his abrupt question, Tess opened her mouth to tell him that he was talking nonsense and that she was absolutely fine. She meant to say that. She was quite sure that she was going to say that, that the words were already formed on her tongue, but instead she heard herself say, 'I'm scared.'

Luke didn't tell her that she was being silly, or chivvy her into cheering up the way Vanessa would have done. His eyes were fixed on her face. 'What of?' he asked.

'Something's happening to me.' Tess couldn't look at him. She kept her gaze fixed on the carved stonework behind his shoulder. Part of her was appalled that she had admitted her fear, but it was a relief to be able to tell someone the truth, and Luke felt safe. He had listened before, and he would listen again. 'Something I don't understand and I don't seem to be able to control. I don't know what to do. I'm scared,' she said again.

'Let's go and have a coffee,' said Luke, touching her arm. 'There's a quiet place just round the corner. You can tell me about it there.'

'All right.' Anything was better than going back to the flat where Nell – or Ralph – might be waiting for her.

'We'll go upstairs,' Luke said when they got to

the coffee shop in Goodramgate. 'It'll be quieter up there.'

Tess climbed the narrow stairs, already regretting that she had told Luke as much as she had. What if he thought she was crazy? But she could hardly turn round and run out. He really would think she was crazy then.

She sat at a table and reached for the menu to disguise her discomfort, sucking in a sharp breath at the white-hot searing sensation in her fingers as they closed around the laminated sheet. Luke swung his camera bag to the floor and pulled out the chair opposite. 'I often come here,' he said. 'The coffee's good and they do great bacon butties.'

An oppressive sense of familiarity was beginning to nag at Tess's senses. 'I've been here before,' she said.

'Really? I don't remember what was here before. I don't think it was a cafe.'

'It was a parlour,' Tess said and it felt as if the words were being dragged out of her mouth. 'Elizabeth Hutchinson's parlour.'

Luke pursed his lips. 'Elizabeth Hutchinson? I don't remember her.'

'It was panelled.' Without realizing it, Tess's voice had dropped to a whisper. 'There are new painted cloths on the wall. Elizabeth is very proud of them. Ralph imported them from Italy, no less, and made the Hutchinsons a gift of them. Elizabeth thinks Ralph is so generous.'

She saw Elizabeth looking at her taffeta doublet and her slashed sleeves. A roll at her hips set her skirts fashionably wide. Her rebato ruff was dyed blue and sat stiffly up from her collar, while a purse of red silk and a crystal looking glass hung from her girdle. A necklace glimmered at her throat and jewels trembled in her ears.

'She thinks I am the luckiest woman in York.'

'Who does?'

The voice was unfamiliar, distant. She didn't answer. She was looking beyond him now, at the embroidered cushions on the window seat, at the little table, at the carpet on the wainscot chest ... oh, sweet Jesù, the chest! It was not as big as the chest in the great chamber she shared with Ralph, but terror crouched inside it anyway.

She jerked her eyes away but it was too late. Ralph had seen her notice the chest. His gaze flicked between it and her face, and he smiled, showing his teeth. Elizabeth looked on enviously. She wished her husband would treat her the way Ralph Maskewe treated Nell.

It did not take Ralph long to discover what Nell feared the most. He had found the perfect punishment for her, and it pleased him. In public he was the most doting of husbands. He showered Nell with jewels and gifts, and boasted of her beauty. In private he corrected her for the slightest transgression. Sometimes she smiled too widely; sometimes not widely enough. Sometimes he chastised her for turning her head away so that she didn't have to meet his eyes; sometimes for staring at him. The slightest hesitation could provoke him to a fury. Choosing to wear one of the presents he had given her rather than another could make his eyes blank with rage.

Four months she had been married, and

already Nell was expert in the signs that she had done something wrong. There was always something wrong, because if there wasn't, Ralph would not be able to punish her in the great bed at night, and if he couldn't punish her, he couldn't get hard enough to get his satisfaction with her.

In the chamber was a long chest, heavily carved, bigger even than the one in the closet. Ralph opened it one night barely a week after they were wed, and without thinking, Nell flinched.

Immediately, he was alert to the possibilities. She corrected herself straight away and stood perfectly still, but Ralph was like a cat at a mouse hole, scenting its victim, gleaming with anticipation.

'What is it?' he asked her.

'Nothing.'

But he was looking between her and the chest and the bone-white teeth showed in a smile of pure understanding. 'You are frightened of being shut in the chest,' he said, nodding, pleased to have a riddle solved so easily. 'That day you climbed in as a child, that has marked you.'

'No,' said Nell, knowing she must not show him any weakness, but he knew anyway. He sensed it. He had a gift for it.

'Prove it,' he said.

'There is no need.' Nell moved away, pretending disinterest. She picked up her hairbrush and began brushing out her hair, hoping that he could not see how her hands were shaking.

Ralph wasn't fooled by her nonchalance. 'If you are not afraid, get in the chest.'

Her heart was ramming into her throat. The jabs, the slaps, the pinches, the blows ... she could bear those if she had to. But this she could not bear. To lie in the stifling darkness; to feel the blackness press down on her. She would not be able to breathe. She would die, and wretched as her life was with him, Nell was not ready to die.

'It was you that day, wasn't it?' The words were out of her mouth before she realized. She lowered the brush, turned to face him.

He didn't even try to pretend that he didn't know what she was talking about. He laughed. 'You were such a reckless little thing. You had no right to go in the closet and you knew it, didn't you? I watched you tiptoe in. I could not resist. The ledger was there, just heavy enough to stop you getting out. I imagined you in there, realizing too late what a mistake you had made.' He chuckled, as if remembering the antics of a puppy. 'Such a pretty little thing you were, but you only ever had eyes for Tom.'

His face changed at the mention of Tom. 'It was always Tom, wasn't it?' he said savagely.

'Tom would not have trapped me in a box,' she said, her voice quavering in spite of her efforts to keep it steady.

'That is because Tom has no imagination. He has no idea of how exquisitely we feel when we are at the edge of our capabilities. Can you tell me you do not appreciate the pleasure more when the pain is past?'

'You were not in the box,' she pointed out. 'I was frightened. I couldn't breathe.'

'That is the whole point!' he cried. 'Was not that

first lungful of air the sweetest breath you ever drew?'

Nell was backing away from him. 'I was a *child*,' she said even as she wondered why she was trying to reason with him.

He laughed, a high titter that made her skin prickle with disgust. 'You were old enough to know that you didn't like me. You didn't even *try* to like me.' His voice was pettish now. 'You deserved to be punished. So sweet you were, insisting on taking Tom's punishment for him! Your little hand outstretched ... how those lashes must have stung!'

'They did,' said Nell, hoping that she could distract him from the chest now. She was edging her way towards the door. If he tried to make her get in the chest, she would run. She would scream for the servants. Janet slept above. She would come and help her mistress.

'Get in the chest.' Ralph's voice was silky smooth. He was watching her, coming at the door from the other side of the chamber. He knows, she thought. He knows. 'Show me that you are not afraid.'

'Ralph – husband – do not make me do this.' To her dismay, Nell heard her voice tremble.

'You lied to me, didn't you?'

'No!'

'Yes, you lied. You *are* afraid. I told you before not to lie to me, Nell.'

Nell dropped the brush and whirled for the door. The latch was in her hand when Ralph dragged her back and knocked her with the back of his hand clear across the room. She banged her head against the floor as she landed, and she lay, stunned and helpless, as he stood over her and dragged her up.

'No...' she moaned. 'No, please no...'

'You lied to me and I won't have it,' he said, twisting her hair in his hand until she sobbed with the pain of it. With his other hand, he scooped the clothes out of the chest to make room for her.

Nell struggled then. She opened her mouth to scream and shout, but he banged her head again on the edge of the chest until it rang. Then he was bundling her into the chest and slamming down the lid, trapping her in the blackness where terror licked its greedy lips and reached for her.

Nell screamed and screamed as she hammered frantically on the lid. Ralph must be sitting on it. There was no air. She had to have air!

'If you scream, I will not let you out,' Ralph said conversationally, and at the same time she heard the sound of knocking on the chamber door. 'Master? Mistress? Are you all right? We heard shouting.'

'Go back to bed,' Ralph shouted. 'Your mistress was having a nightmare.'

'Help me!' Nell gasped but she was weakening, and they did not hear. The blackness was swallowing her, chomping at her like a vagrant on a snatched pie, and the chest had turned into an abyss. She was falling into it, twisting and turning in the terror, and just when she was about to smash into the bottom of it, the lid was wrenched open, and Ralph was staring down at her with affection in his eyes.

'Poor little Nell,' he said as she sucked air into

her raw throat, too rigid with fear to even move. 'You don't like it, do you?'

'No.' Her voice was hoarse.

'Then you must never lie to me again. Come.' Almost tenderly, he lifted her out of the chest and laid her on the floor, pushing up her shift so he could have his way with her. He pumped briskly, elated by his victory, and Nell lay, legs splayed, utterly defeated, the tears running silently down her cheeks.

After that, Ralph only had to look at the chest to make her do whatever he wanted. She was bruised and battered the next day, and he insisted she lie abed. He had forgotten himself so far as to hit her face and a great yellowy black bruise blossomed on her cheek. She told Janet that she fell and hit her face on the chest, and Janet seemed to believe her. Why should she do otherwise? Ralph was hovering attentively, making sure that wine and delicacies were brought to tempt her appetite. He was always charming with the servants, who blushed and fluttered whenever he teased them. They thought he adored her.

So when Janet exclaimed at her bruise, all Ralph had to do was flick a glance at the chest, and Nell looked at Janet. 'I hope I did not disturb you last night, Janet,' she said obediently. 'Such a foolish dream I had.'

And that was that.

The Hutchinsons' chest was all it took to bring back the bitter memory. Nell could feel Ralph's smile like a smear. In spite of herself, she glanced back at the chest, but there was something odd about it. It was rippling, and she blinked at it again, certain she must be imagining it. But no, it was shifting, changing shape, and now it was a round table with two strange straight-backed chairs on either side. What was happening? She looked at the others to see if they had noticed, but Elizabeth had gone. John Hutchinson had gone too, and so had Ralph. In their place was a hatless man with keen eyes narrowed thoughtfully.

'Who is Ralph?' he asked.

'Ralph is my husband,' she whispered fearfully. She felt disconnected from everything, as if she were floating above the room, looking down at herself, except it wasn't her. It was an older woman with cropped dark hair and peculiar clothes. She wore no cap, no gown, and her face was haunted.

'Tess?' said the man.

Tess? *Tess*. She was Tess. Tess slammed back into her body and she jerked back in the chair, her eyes wide and shocked, her hands flat on the table to steady herself.

'It's OK,' said Luke. 'Just breathe.'

Breathe. A good idea. Tess drew in a breath, let it out slowly. In, out, in, out, while her racing pulse slowed. A waitress was standing by the table and Luke was talking to her, but Tess just kept her eyes on her throbbing hands and concentrated on making each breath slower and deeper than the last.

'I've ordered you a latte,' said Luke when the waitress had gone. He leant forward and covered her hands with his own. His touch was warm and incredibly comforting. 'Are you okay?'

He knew. Tess nodded and moistened her lips. 'How long was I ... like that?'

'Not long. A few moments. You were looking round the room and you started to talk about Ralph. It was as if you were there, but not there at the same time.' His smile was a little crooked. 'I don't mind telling you, the hairs went up on the back of my neck! What happened?'

'You won't believe me.'

'Why wouldn't I?' he asked reasonably.

'Because I hardly know whether I believe it myself. Everything I've ever studied tells me that it's impossible, that I *don't* believe it, but it's real – it's happening.' In spite of the pain, she twisted her hands together on the tabletop and looked at Luke. 'But if it's not real, I'm losing my mind, and that scares me even more.'

'Tell me,' he said.

So she did. She told him everything, from that first memory of hiding in the chest in Mr Maskewe's closet to making love with Tom by the Foss, and her eyes slid away from his then as she remembered how she and Luke had also made love with the same awkwardness and exhilaration and giddy pleasure.

Luke didn't interrupt her. He didn't gasp or shake his head or try to tell her that she was talking nonsense. He just listened until the waitress brought their coffee. He waited until she'd gone, and Tess had wrapped her hands around her cup for comfort.

'What's wrong with your hands?' he said, noticing her involuntary wince.

'I don't know.' Tess wasn't sorry to be diverted

from her story. She took one hand away from the cup to turn it over and look at it. 'My fingers are sore. It comes and goes. I think it must be some kind of rheumatism. I can't see anything wrong with them.'

Luke nodded. 'Go on then,' he said quietly. 'Tell me it all.'

She told him about saying goodbye to Tom. About Ralph and the way he had used her father's obligation to him. About the wedding and the chest, and the hatred and fear of Ralph that now settled like a stone in her gut.

And when she had finished, her face was burning with shame at how easily Ralph had vanquished her spirit.

'Tess, it wasn't you,' said Luke.

'It feels as if it was me,' she said. 'Listen to me. I started off talking about Nell because I wanted to make her something separate from me, but I ended up talking about what *I* did and what *I* feel.'

She sounded crazy. Maybe she was crazy. But she had proof, didn't she?

The cup rattled against the saucer as she put it down, eager to show Luke that she wasn't making the whole thing up. 'I've still got the bruises from last night,' she said, pulling her sleeve up her arm to show him where Ralph had pinched and twisted her tender flesh. Only that morning her breasts and the inside of her arms had been covered with livid purple bruises, but now she stared in disbelief at her smooth skin.

'I don't understand...' Frantically, she pulled up her other sleeve, but that arm was as unblemished as the other. 'They've gone,' she said blankly. 'They were there this morning, and now they've gone.'

Slowly, she raised her eyes to Luke. 'What's happening to me?'

He looked back at her thoughtfully. 'What do *you* think is happening?'

'I think I'm regressing. I think I'm possessed and that Nell is taking over my mind.' There, she had said it. Tess was simultaneously relieved and terrified, and a tide of colour rose in her face.

'Why are you blushing?'

'Because I can't believe I just said that!' Tess dropped her head into her hands and dragged her fingers through her hair, biting back another wince. *Her* hair. She had had it cut when she left Martin, and now it bounced choppily around her face. Nell's hair fell to her waist, and it was a rippling brown, while hers was dark. They were completely different.

'It's embarrassing,' she muttered after a moment. 'Trained historical researchers don't run around seeing ghosts or talking about travelling through time. It's crazy. *I'm* crazy.'

'What other explanation is there?' asked Luke, so reasonably that she was taken aback. She would have thought it was obvious.

'My mother would tell me that I was hysterical or making it all up for attention.'

'Supportive of her.' His lip curled.

'You remember what she was like.' Tess sighed. 'But what if she's right? What if I'm having some kind of breakdown?' Twisted in her hair, her fingers dug into her scalp. 'What if I'm losing my mind? That's what a doctor would say, I know. They'd chuck me into Bootham Park Hospital and then what would happen to Oscar?'

'Now you *are* sounding hysterical.' Luke's brusqueness cut across her rising voice. 'Wouldn't it be better to work on the assumption that Nell is real, and deal with that?'

Tess lifted her head to gape at him. 'You believe me?'

He lifted his shoulders, non-committal. 'I can't see any reason *not* to believe you,' he said. 'That's twice now I've seen you come round from an episode – or whatever you want to call it – and it's been clear that for a few moments you're just not there. There's someone else behind your eyes and your voice is different ... it's creepy, if you want to know the truth.'

'But ... but it's not possible,' she stuttered. 'You don't believe in ghosts!'

'I don't know what I believe,' admitted Luke, 'but if there's one thing I've learnt over the last few years, it's to keep an open mind. I've seen people possessed by spirits in voodoo ceremonies in Haiti, and a perfectly healthy man in Africa turn his face to the wall and die because he believed he was cursed. I've spoken to sane, sensible people in Canada who've said they've seen Big Foot, and a woman in Spain with stigmata on her hands. There are a lot of things out there that can't be explained.' He shrugged. 'You could say that rationalism is just another belief.'

Tess stared at him, still grappling with the idea that he had accepted so easily. Luke kept surprising her. He had been so restless when he was younger, so eager to go out and take on the world – like Tom, she realized with a pang – and now she couldn't get used to how steady and thoughtful he had become. True, the resentment she remembered still surfaced on occasion, but his patience and tolerance were apt to catch her unawares.

'Maybe,' she said, 'but aren't most of those cases of people simply seeing what they want to see? I've never believed in any of that stuff – I don't *want* to believe in it! My whole career has been about examining the evidence, not wild flights of fantasy. I'm the last person to start regressing!'

'Are you? My mum always said you were fey.'

Her hands dropped from her head. 'What?'

'Don't you remember? You never made a big deal of it. It was just that sometimes you'd make a comment about someone sitting in a corner, and then cover it up quickly when it was obvious that none of the rest of us had seen anything.'

She'd forgotten. Just like she'd forgotten the monks at Rievaulx Abbey and the rotting heads on Micklegate Bar until her mother had reminded her. How had she been able to block those memories so successfully?

'*My* mum thought I was attention seeking if I said anything when I was a child,' she said slowly. 'I guess I learnt not to mention it after a while.'

'There you go. That's probably why you studied history,' said Luke. 'It was the perfect way to deny that side of your personality.'

Tess chewed the inside of her cheek. It was possible. 'Okay, say that's true ... but why would it all start up again now? Nothing like this ever happened to me in London.'

'I don't know. Maybe it's something to do with being in the flat? From what you've told me, it's definitely connected in some way. Or maybe you're particularly vulnerable at the moment. It's a stressful time, leaving a marriage, starting a new life. Could be your mental defences are down.'

'Maybe.' The rigid muscles in Tess's back were starting to unclench, and she sat back in her chair. It was extraordinarily comforting to hear Luke talk as if being possessed was something understandable, even normal. To be able to talk to him without having to convince him that she wasn't having a breakdown or making it all up in a wild bid for attention.

'Lots of people would love to be in your position, you know,' he said. 'They'd do anything to be able to go back and see what it was really like in the past.'

Tess thought about Ralph, about the vicious satisfaction on his face as he raped her. 'They're welcome to it,' she said bleakly.

'Okay, I was sort of fascinated at first,' she went on after a moment, considering. 'Nell was such a courageous, curious little girl. I wish I'd been more like her when I was a child. I don't know how to describe it. When I'm her, I feel ... a zest for life that I can't imagine in this one. Everything then is rougher, and harder I suppose, but it's more vibrant too, and there's an energy in the air. It feels foreign now, that appetite for extremes. Doing an appallingly filthy job one day, and feasting and carousing the next. Horrible cruelty, right next to laughter and kindness.'

Remembering, she looked around the cafe, comparing the wooden tables and tasteful whitewashed walls with Elizabeth Hutchinson's parlour.

'We're all so moderate now,' she said. 'Everything's more muted.'

'Really?' Luke leant forward, interested. 'I always imagined life was all sober and black and white after the Reformation.'

Tess pursed her lips and tilted her head to one side while she considered the matter. 'Nell's world is much more colourful than this one, or maybe it's just that she appreciates colour more...' she said. 'Her gowns are blue and red and green, and they're embroidered with flowers and insects.' She looked down, as if she could see the gloves on her hands. 'The walls are hung with tapestries or painted cloths, and the cushions and bed clothes are brightly coloured.'

She smiled faintly, looking around at the plain walls and unvarnished tables and chairs. 'Nell wouldn't think much of this decor.'

'You're making it sound like a good time to live.'

'I was happy,' said Tess after a moment, not noticing that she had slipped back into talking as if she were Nell. 'It was all I knew. And when I was with Tom...' She stopped, swallowed hard. 'Well, anyway. Yes, it's true, there were times when I've wished I could be back there, but Tom's gone now, and I'm married to Ralph. He can do what he likes to me. He's my husband, and I'm his property.' Fear fisted in her belly at the thought of him.

'Nell,' said Luke.

'What?'

'*Nell* was his property, not you.'

'Yes.' She drew a breath, settled her breathing, steadied her hands. 'Yes, you're right. It's not me. At least I could leave my husband. Nell can't run away. She's got nowhere to go and no one to help her, poor cow. She belongs to Ralph.'

The horror of the wedding night hit her anew, and she covered her face with her hands. 'I don't want to go back now,' she said, muffled. 'I don't want him to put me back in that chest.' When she looked up again, her eyes were stark. 'I'm frightened.'

Chapter Twelve

Luke nodded. 'I think you should be,' he said seriously. 'This is dangerous stuff. If Ralph can hurt you in the past and you can wake with bruises in the present, what else could he do? Shit, I'm sorry,' he said when Tess blanched. 'I didn't want to frighten you any more. I just think you should talk to someone who knows a bit more about what you're dealing with.'

'What, you mean there are people out there who know about being trapped in the past with a sadistic husband?' Tess's laugh held a wild edge.

'There are people who know about regression,' said Luke, unfazed. 'I had a job in Lincoln last year, taking pictures for a story in the *Express*. It was a piece about regression, and they'd hyped it up with stories about housewives believing that they'd lived again as Cleopatra and so on. There was this guy who hypnotized them, who was made to sound like a real charlatan by the reporter, but I got to meet him when he agreed for some shots to be taken of him with a client during a session.'

'A session?' she echoed in disbelief. 'People do this voluntarily?'

'Apparently.' His eyes crinkled at the corners. 'I turned up, all ready to be amused, but it wasn't anything like I was expecting. Ambrose wasn't the flamboyant character the reporter had made him out to be. I was...' Luke paused, searching for the right word. 'Impressed,' he decided. 'I didn't see any evidence of anything bogus. It felt surprisingly normal.'

Tess considered that. 'What does he do, exactly?' she asked, still suspicious.

'In the session I photographed, he put the client in a hypnotic trance, and asked her some questions. Her experience was nothing like as vivid as yours, but she said when I asked her afterwards that she had found it really helpful, and that the experience had helped her understand some of her fears.' Luke spread his hands. 'It could be mumbo-jumbo psychology, but Ambrose seemed to know what he was talking about. I think he'd be really interested to meet you, and maybe he could help you find an explanation about what's happening to you.'

He glanced at Tess, who had gone back to chewing her cheek. Her expression was wary.

'Do you want me to see if I can find his number? I could call him, set up a meeting if you wanted.'

'I don't know...' Tess was torn. She had always hated the idea of being hypnotized but it would be a relief to talk to someone who wouldn't necessarily ship her straight off to a psychiatrist.

Her hands, she realized, had stopped aching, and she turned them palm up to study the lines and creases as if she had never seen them before. Her fingers were slender, completely unmarked. She remembered the searing pain at the church, the clamour of reluctance in her head. Would she fare any better with Luke's hypnotist? Instinctively, she was resisting the idea of hypnosis. Perhaps it would be better to try talking to Pat French again?

The instant jab in her fingertips made her hands jerk, and Tess folded them back in her lap.

'Maybe,' she said slowly. 'I'll think about it.'

She walked back to the flat feeling steadier than she had for days. Perhaps that was all she had needed, she thought hopefully. To talk to someone about what was happening and to not be dismissed as hysterical or overimaginative.

You live in a world of your own, Theresa. You make things up.

Firmly, Tess pushed the memory of Martin away. She *hadn't* made Nell up. Luke believed her. Tess held on to that thought. She should have talked to Luke before, the way she had talked to him about Martin. It had been a mistake to think that she could deal with Nell on her own. She should have trusted him.

But then, she had made so many mistakes, she hardly knew how to trust herself.

At least Luke hadn't urged her to see a doctor. Tess feared that more than anything. His suggestion of a deliberate regression was interesting, she thought as she set up her laptops for work, but the idea of hypnosis made her uneasy. It felt too much like putting herself into someone else's control, just as she had done when she married Martin. Tess didn't want to be controlled by anyone, ever again.

She switched on both laptops and watched the screens blink into life. If things got worse again, she would consider talking to this Ambrose, she decided. For now, as long as she didn't look in the corner where the chest had been, or at the wall where the great bed had once stood, she was fine.

The flat hummed quietly. The air was calm, and Tess even managed to get some work done. Her eyes were beginning to glaze over when she leant back and stretched her arms above her head to release the tension in her shoulders. She was hungry.

Barefoot, she padded through to the kitchen, enjoying its clutter. Enjoying being normal.

It was working, not thinking about Nell or Ralph. All she needed was to be normal like this. She didn't need to be hypnotized or exorcised or analysed. She would just think about putting on the kettle, making a sandwich, ordinary tasks that anchored her in the present. The bread was sitting on the work-top, twisted and sealed with an old clothes peg. The butter and the jam were still out from breakfast, and the flap on Oscar's cereal box was open where she had forgotten to close it neatly. Martin always insisted that everything was tidied away and the worktops were kept immaculately clear. It gave Tess a small stab of satisfaction every time she left things out simply because she could.

She was still smiling at her untidiness when she pulled open the cutlery drawer to find a knife and her sense of wellbeing juddered to a shocked halt.

The cutlery she had taken such pleasure in tossing carelessly together was now immaculately neat. The forks lay tucked together on their sides; the knife blades were all pointing in the right direction; every spoon was precisely aligned so they slotted neatly into each other.

Exactly as Martin liked them.

Tess felt as if a cold hand had closed around her throat, and it was a moment before she could breathe. Shock and fear jostled together and then, shoving them aside, surging rage. This was Martin's doing, it had to be. Just when she had started to relax. Just when Oscar was beginning not to jump at the sound of a door banging. Without thinking, she reached in and jumbled knives, forks and spoons together in a kind of frenzy.

How had he got in? And what else had he done? The thought drove her upright and out of the kitchen to check the rest of the flat in a fury, but there was nothing else out of place.

Tess went back to the cutlery drawer. It was a mess again, the way she had left it that morning. Now it was hard to remember how chillingly neat it had been when she opened the drawer. Why had she let that moment of anger ruin her evidence? But evidence of what?

Luke might believe her, but surely even he might start to question her reliability after a while? Certainly nobody else would listen. She imagined showing the drawer to Vanessa, telling her about Martin's obsession with order, trying to convince her that he had been in the flat.

Perhaps you imagined it, Vanessa would say soothingly. *Or perhaps you arranged it yourself out of habit and you just don't remember doing it. You've been under a lot of strain, Tess. There's no sign of Martin breaking in, is there? Are you sure you couldn't have done it?*

Tess *wasn't* sure, that was the problem. She had been imagining so much lately she was no longer sure what was real and what had been no more than a dream.

Suddenly defeated, she slumped against the worktop and dragged her hands down her face.

Her first impulse – to ring Martin and confront him – was evaporating. He would take her contacting him as a sign of encouragement, and then he would have her phone number.

Besides, what would she say to him? *I know you were in the flat? I know you rearranged the spoons?* She would sound hysterical and neurotic, and Martin would use that. He would claim that she was ill or depressed, that she couldn't look after Oscar properly. It would be best for everyone if she went home, he would say, and her mother, Vanessa, any GP hearing wild stories of cutlery that magically arranged itself would agree.

And that was before anyone got wind of the fact that she had been experiencing life in the sixteenth century.

Shameful self-pity sloshed through Tess and she pressed the heels of her hands to her eyes to stop herself giving in to tears. Wasn't it enough that she had to deal with a vicious husband who had been dead for more than four hundred and fifty years without one playing games with her mind in the present too?

Now you are *sounding hysterical.*

Luke's cool words sliced through her rising panic and stayed in her mind like a knife stuck in cheese. As before, the thought of him was something fixed, something steady for her to hold onto. Tess drew a quavery breath and set her jaw. She was not going to give in. Not now. Not now she had just found the strength to leave Martin and start again.

Stony faced, she closed the cutlery drawer and went back to work. She had lost her appetite. A vicious headache was building behind her eyes but she would not give in to that either. She wiggled the mouse so that the screen leapt to life. Oscar needed her. She had to stay strong.

She had to stay strong. Under the cover of the table, Nell laid a hand on her stomach. *Sweet Jesù, let it be true. Let there be some hope.*

'The keelboats came in today.' Across the table Ralph was brimming with self-satisfaction. 'I have my merchandise from Hamburg at last.'

Hamburg. Where the moon still shone on Tom. The thought of him was like a skewer through her heart still and Nell's ears rushed with the effort of not showing it to her husband.

Sometimes when she thought about Tom, it was like remembering another life, a life that had belonged to someone else altogether. Had she really been that girl, smothering giggles on All Hallows Eve as Tom smeared honey on a door, or hunkering down on a step with him to share gingerbread hot from the pan? Could that maid who had tumbled so joyously in the long grass with him really have been her?

If she let it, her life would narrow to a joyless sliver, so Nell was learning to take pleasure in moments: licking a finger to press it on a crumb of sugar crumbled from the loaf, letting the sweetness burst on her tongue; folding the linen, crisp and clean from the laundresses in St George's Close; listening to a bee bumbling drowsily through the lavender. Since Tom's mother had died, the garden behind the Maskewe house had been neglected, but Nell was bringing it back to life. She planted herbs for her still room – sweet basil, bay, borage, camomile, mint, hyssop and purslane – and flowers for her pleasure. She grew daisies and goldenrods, and marigolds and poppies, and she pruned back the old roses so that they flowered. She set a bench amongst them so that she could smell their fragrance.

She spun out each moment like a spider its web, stringing herself from day to day, not letting herself think about the night. The more pain she suffered, the more Ralph liked it, and Nell had learnt to scream and whimper straight away, so that he got his business over and done with quickly.

After that first time in the chest, he was careful not to mark her face. For a man with such unnatural appetites, Ralph cared deeply for his reputation. It mattered to him that his fellow citizens considered him a fine man. He liked it when they nodded and bowed and whispered behind their hands about his wealth and importance. He was generous with his gifts, generous with his hospitality, and Nell was decked out in the finest silks and furs. Gold glowed at her throat and glinted on her fingers. She was the treasure chest Ralph threw open to display his wealth. It pleased him to watch their neighbours ogle her with envy. No one must doubt that she was the most fortunate of women.

But what was their envy if he was not there to bask in it? He didn't like Nell to go out on her own. He wanted her at home, where he could see her. Where he could watch her for the slightest, transgression.

Nell had learnt to be careful. If Ralph knew how much it meant to her to escape the house, he would forbid it altogether. So she told him that she needed to go to the market like a good housewife.

Ralph scowled when she first raised the subject. 'Send one of the maids,' he had said. 'That is what they are for.'

'I need to teach her how to look out for short measures,' said Nell, feeling her way carefully. His reputation was his vanity, the one weak spot she would exploit whenever she could. 'You would not want it said that your wife does not know how to keep a house, would you? We must have the

best of everything to set before your guests. I will not be fobbed off with anything less the way a maid would be.'

So now she was allowed out to shop with a maid – but not too often – and sometimes she could take Mary or Eliza and show them which plants to gather from the hedgerows outside the city. Those were the best times. Nell would look up at the sky and gulp in the sight of it. She wished she could preserve it like the leaves and seeds she dried, or make a decoction of sky and light that she could unstopper and breathe in when she was back in the grand Stonegate house with its ostentatiously glazed windows and the wainscot walls that seemed to press in on her.

And sometimes, God forgive her, she looked at the hemlock that grew in cloudy swathes out on the common and she remembered how dangerous it could be, how easily its root could be disguised as a parsnip, and she thought how much easier her life would be if Ralph would die.

But she couldn't think of a way to make sure he was the only one to suffer, and when she caught herself pondering the problem seriously, she caught herself up. What was she thinking? She could not kill Ralph. It would be a mortal sin and she would hang for it. No, she would tend her garden and she would endure. She would not allow Ralph to break her spirit.

Nell was surprised at first when Ralph gave her permission to attend a lying-in when one of her neighbours was in child-bed. She had thought he would fear what she might tell the other women of the way he treated her, but, of course, there

was little she could say. He still held the debt over her father's head, and he would not hesitate to punish her family if she stepped out of her role as a dutiful wife.

Besides, she soon discovered that there was little that shocked the other women. The first time she attended a neighbour in childbed, she was reassured by the women gathered around in the chamber. They talked frankly about their husbands and the problems they had with their servants and children, but when Nell hinted that her husband was rough with her at times, they only laughed comfortably.

'Oh, they all like to show how big and strong they are at times,' they said. Nell was aghast to realize how many of them took a beating as a matter of course. It was nothing new to see women in the market place with a black eye or a swollen lip, but her own neighbours? Marriage, it seemed, gave her access to a whole hidden world she had never suspected, and sometimes doubt niggled. Would Tom have beaten her if she had married him, just because he could or because he felt like it?

Ralph told her what he did to her at night was normal. That he was a normal man with normal appetites, while she was the frigid, unnatural one.

If Nell hadn't known Tom, she might have accepted it without question, but she remembered how glorious love between a man and a woman could be. It was not glorious with Ralph. It was shameful and humiliating and it sickened her every night to lie with him. Once or twice she had dared to complain, but it wasn't worth it, for

she was simply punished for not appreciating how lucky she was to be married to him. Everyone knew how much he loved her; how could she possibly complain at her fortune?

She was allowed to church, of course, but Ralph stayed firmly beside her and she knew to keep her eyes demurely downcast. When he invited guests to the house to impress them with his lavish hospitality, it was the same. As his wife, Nell must sit modestly and display his wealth. She was not to laugh or smile or talk too deeply with anyone, especially not any man. And Nell did as she was instructed, because it was not worth the pain of defying him.

It was not long before she had acquired a reputation for aloofness. Her old friends thought that marriage to a wealthy merchant like Ralph Maskewe had gone to her head and that she considered herself above them now. Her neighbours were similarly aggrieved to find their overtures rebuffed. Who was Eleanor Maskewe after all? Just the jumped-up daughter of an unsuccessful mercer. She was no one to hold her nose so high. Hoity-toity, they thought her.

Her family, too, were distant now, puzzled by her coldness. She hardly saw them any more and when she did, she had to be so careful not to show them affection. Ralph was jealous of the least look, the briefest touch. He would not hesitate to take out his rage on her brothers if he chose, so the best Nell could do for them was to keep them at arm's length. But when she saw Harry and Peter grow stiff and formal with her, it broke the little piece of her heart that remained after Tom left.

Nell had long since abandoned the dream that Tom would find out what had happened and come and rescue her. She had not dared to send him word herself, knowing there would be no limit to Ralph's rage if he found out, but it seemed that Ralph himself had written. He would have enjoyed writing that letter, Nell thought afterwards.

They were dining alone in the parlour. The servants in the Maskewe house were banished to the kitchen now for their meals. It was the new way of doing things, Ralph insisted. It was for Nell to sit in her chamber and let the maids do the work, instead of working beside them the way her mistress had always done. It was seemly for her to keep some distance, he said, and Nell acquiesced for the meals, but she could not keep house sitting in her chamber. When Ralph went out, she pulled on her apron and went down to the kitchen so that she could direct the maids, Mary and Eliza, and Janet who had been servant in the house since little Joan had killed herself, more than ten years since. There was little Nell could teach Janet, but it was her duty to teach Eliza and Mary how to keep house, just as Mistress Harrison had taught her.

Were it not for the servants, Nell would have no companionship, but now, God willing, there might be a babe, a child she could love. Surely that would not be denied her? Nell yearned for it, but knew better than to let her husband glimpse the depth of her longing.

'I trust the goods arrived to your satisfaction,' she said to Ralph, careful not to make eye contact.

She never corrected him. She never committed herself to a thought or an idea. She made herself as bland and smooth as she could be so that nothing would snag his attention. It was like a game between them, she sealing herself like nut, he needling, prodding, poking in search of the woman he knew was hidden away inside her. Nell paid for it. If he failed to rouse her, her resistance would infuriate him and he would devise a special punishment for that night, but still, it was a point of pride for her not to give in.

'Indeed. I have some fine silks and tapestries to sell.' Ralph paused to crack the leg off a roast chicken and Nell repressed her instinctive flinch as he gnawed at it with his teeth.

'Oh, and I had news of my brother.'

Nell went very still. She wasn't sure how he wanted her to react to this news, and there was such a clamour of longing in her heart that she could scarcely breathe.

'Oh?' she managed, her voice a reedy whisper and Ralph looked at her, his glance pin sharp with malice.

'Are you unwell, my dear? You seem upset.'

'I am quite well, I thank you.'

'Yes, it seems Tom has abandoned Mr Todd,' Ralph went on, sleek with satisfaction at his news.

'I ... I had thought he would be wise to continue his apprenticeship. He had not long to serve.'

'Quite. It is most foolish of him. But Tom always was a fool,' said Ralph.

Nell wasn't going to give him the satisfaction of asking why Tom had left. She already knew. Tom had heard of her marriage and he would not come back to York to see her wed to his brother.

It was madness to continue the conversation, but now that Tom's name had been mentioned out loud, she craved news of him. She had to know. She forced disinterest into her voice. It wouldn't fool Ralph, but her pride demanded it. 'Does he find other employment in Hamburg?'

'Nothing so sensible. He has gone adventuring, it seems. He has joined a ship to the New World and will be little better than a pirate. Mr Todd is most disappointed in him,' Ralph told Nell, his eyes fixed on her face, avid for a reaction. 'As am I, of course. He brings dishonour to our name.'

Dishonour! Nell thought in contempt. *Pretty good from a man who must hurt his wife before he can mount her!* But she kept her expression smooth as silk.

Her mind churned. She needed to be alone to understand how she felt. Tom had thrown away his chance to come back to York, but how would she have been able to bear it if he had?

And how would she bear it now that she knew he never would?

Tom had yearned so for the sea. Nell remembered how he had talked of his dreams of sailing out to the horizon and then beyond, to the New World where sugar grew and the sun beat hard and hot. Of bracing his feet on a deck as the ship pitched and reared on the waves. Now the sea spray would sting his face, and he would be happy.

But she would never know where he was. She would never know if he was safe. She would never see him again. *Never.*

Only then did the truth hit Nell and she put a hand to her stomach which was pitching as if it too were at sea.

She would have to endure this life without Tom, and without the hope of him. It would be too much to bear were it not for the fact that it was two months since her flowers had come down. She had started to wonder if the nausea she felt was less due to Ralph and more to a child growing inside her. The thought filled her with wonder.

And with hope. She might not have Tom, but perhaps she might have a child to light her life. Surely Ralph would not treat her so when it might hurt the unborn babe? But if she told him too soon, and she was wrong, she would suffer for misleading him.

Aware of his eyes devouring her for the least sign of weakness, Nell decided to risk it. He wanted her to moan and cry at the thought of Tom, but there would be chance enough for that. For now, there was another day and night to get through.

'I am sorry for your disappointment,' she said to Ralph, 'but perhaps I can give you better news, sir.'

Ralph wasn't expecting that. He frowned. 'Better news?'

'I have reason to believe I may be with child,' she said carefully.

'A child!' She could see his mind going round, trying to work out the advantages and disadvantages. 'A child,' he said again, tasting the word in his mouth. 'A son.'

'If God wills,' said Nell and she added, 'and if we are careful.'

'Careful?'

'It may damage the babe if you are too rough with me,' she said bluntly.

His face worked. It was clear that he was puffed up at the thought of a son of his own, but the prospect of months without being able to beat her the way he liked was less pleasing.

Nell bowed her head. 'It will be as you desire, of course, husband.'

She had said enough. It would be wise to leave the choice to him.

Tess came round to find herself staring at the screen saver spiralling endlessly in mesmerizing patterns. She had a hand on her stomach, and she was trembling with longing.

Please let me have the baby. Please, God. Please, please, please.

Hope. It was extraordinary how uplifting it could be. Tess wasn't even dismayed by the fact that Nell had taken control of her again so soon. She simmered with an odd exhilaration. Nell might have a baby, a baby that might change everything.

And perhaps, then, she might leave Tess to her own child.

Oscar. She had her son, Tess reminded herself. She had a job; she had somewhere to live. Her mind flickered to Luke. She had someone who believed her. She would not let herself be derailed by a cutlery drawer. She was strong enough to cope with anything Martin might do.

Hope was better than sleep. The tiredness and distress of the night before were forgotten, and she worked on the records all afternoon, barely stumbling over the familiarity of some names. Her step was light and newly energized as she headed out to Vanessa's house soon after five.

'Thank you so much for picking Oscar up, Van.' Tess breezed past Vanessa when she opened the door, not registering the set face or tight lips. 'I got so much done with that extra hour or so. I feel a million times better!'

'Oscar's outside with Rosie and Sam.'

'I hope he's been behaving himself.' Tess followed Vanessa into the kitchen. French windows at the back opened onto a garden where Oscar and Rosie were shrieking and running round in circles, their arms spread wide like aeroplanes. Oscar's face was pink, his hair rumpled, and the back of his shirt was flapping free of his trousers.

Tess warmed at the sight of him. Her baby. Only a few weeks ago, when she had first brought him to York, Oscar had been pale and withdrawn, prone to obsessing over details and struggling to make friendships.

If Nell had a baby to love as much as she loved Oscar, she would be happy, Tess was certain of it.

She turned back to Vanessa with a smile. 'It's been so good for Oscar to spend time with Rosie and Sam. It's been wonderful for him to have them as friends.'

Vanessa didn't say anything. She was stacking the dishwasher in a very tense way. The kitchen was huge compared to the cramped space in the flat and always looked to Tess as if it was posing for an advert for kitchen design. There was an island with willow baskets underneath, a gleaming hood over the high-tech hob and a retro larder fridge.

She had had a kitchen like this in London, stocked with every gadget she could possibly desire so that she could produce immaculate, soulless dinner parties for Martin's acquaintances. It had always felt like a prison to Tess.

Vanessa and Martin were alike in some ways. The thought flickered through her mind before Tess could stop it, and she pushed it away uncomfortably.

Perhaps Vanessa could be a little bossy sometimes, but she meant well. The last thing Tess wanted was to alienate her. Oscar would be devastated if he could no longer come and play with Rosie and Sam. Vanessa was kind, and she was helpful.

Like Martin could be kind and helpful? Tess pushed that thought aside too. Oscar was happy here, that was what mattered.

Her smile faltered a little in the face of Vanessa's silence. 'I'm really grateful to you, Vanessa,' she added after a moment, belatedly noticing the frigid atmosphere, and doing her best to warm it.

It was clearly the wrong thing to say.

'Grateful?' Vanessa snapped off the word. *'Really?'*

If anything, the temperature had dropped even further. Tess frowned. 'What's the matter, Van? You seem upset.'

'Upset? What would I possibly have to be upset about?' Vanessa shoved plates into the dishwasher racks with such savage force that Tess was afraid that she was going to break them.

'I don't know. That's why I'm asking.'

Slamming the dishwasher closed, Vanessa wiped her hands on her Lycra gym shorts and smacked the kettle on. 'Cup of tea?' she asked in a brittle voice. 'Oh, no, you prefer coffee, don't you?'

This was said so viciously that Tess could only stare blankly at her. 'Coffee?'

'You remember Sally Beckwith?'

Thrown by the abrupt change of subject, Tess searched her memory. Sally Beckwith ... hadn't she been one of the cool girls when she was at school in York? 'Vaguely,' she said.

'She's at the same gym as me.'

'Right...' said Tess carefully. She had no idea where Vanessa was going with this conversation.

'I saw her this morning. She was a bit late getting to the gym because she'd been in town. She had to pick up something in Goodramgate.'

'Okay,' said Tess, none the wiser.

'And guess who she saw there? None other than my best friend going into a coffee shop with Luke Hutton!' Vanessa clattered mugs together as she pulled them from a cupboard. 'You should have remembered that you're back in York, Tess. Somebody's always going to see you, wherever you are.'

Irritation flicked at Tess. In the anonymity of London, the smallness and nosiness of York, the sense that everybody knew your business, had been a charming memory. She had indeed forgotten that it had also been the reason she couldn't wait to get away.

'Having coffee isn't against the law yet, is it?'

Vanessa pressed her lips together as she threw teabags into the mugs. 'You didn't have to lie to me!' she burst out, and Tess stared at her in exasperation.

'I didn't *lie* to you!'

'I asked if you wanted coffee this morning, and you said you needed to get on with some work! If you had a date with Luke, you just had to say.' Her voice trembled with emotion. She seemed so upset that Tess had to bite back a sharp retort.

'It wasn't a date,' she said. 'I bumped into him outside the Minster.'

'And suddenly decided that you had time for coffee after all?'

'I was worried about something. He seemed like a good person to talk to.'

'You could have talked to me! I asked you if you were all right, and you said that you were.'

Vanessa poured boiling water into the mugs and began jabbing at the teabags, while Tess pinched the bridge of her nose. She wasn't sure what was going on. If she didn't know better, she would have said that Vanessa was jealous, but what reason did she have to be jealous of Tess, whose life was a mess?

'I'm sorry, Van,' she said in a conciliatory tone. 'It's just ... things have been very strange recently.'

Vanessa seemed to relax at her apology. She handed Tess a mug of tea. 'I'm sorry too,' she said with a lightning-quick change of mood that reminded Tess disquietingly of Martin once more. 'I've been snappy myself. I told you my sister's having another baby? Her third!'

Baby. The word set up a warning reverberation deep inside Tess. Tightening her fingers around her mug, she did her best to ignore it as she smiled back at Vanessa, relieved to see her restored to good humour.

'Julie? No! I can't believe she's got two already. That's great news!'

'I think it's really irresponsible of her, to tell you the truth,' said Vanessa, purse-lipped. 'They can't afford another child at the moment. She'll have to go back to work, and who's going to look after it? She thinks because I don't have a job I can drop everything and pick up the pieces every time anything goes wrong.'

Baby. The air itself was shimmering with the word. Tess forced herself to focus.

'They say there's never a good time to ha–' Tess broke off with a gasp as an abyss seemed to yawn in front of her without warning. There was a rushing in her ears and she threw up her hands to ward off the past, but it was too late. She saw Vanessa's mouth drop open in shock, saw the tea spraying through the air in slow motion, and then she was falling too, down, down, down, like the mug as it smashed onto the floor.

Chapter Thirteen

The latch clattered, and a gust of wet wind blustered into the kitchen. Janet came in with it, stamping the wet from her clogs. 'Ee, it's dreich out there,' she grumbled.

'Shut the door, Janet!' said Nell sharply as the other maids set up a chorus of complaint. The kitchen was the warmest place in the house these days and Nell spent as much time in there as possible. Autumn had been long and grey, day after day of rain runnelling against the windows and turning the streets to a quagmire.

Janet huffed and rolled her eyes, but she kicked the door to and set her basket on the table, swinging the two rabbits that hung from her other hand down beside it so that she could shake the rain from her cloak.

'What news from the market?' Nell asked as she picked out leeks, turnips, a pat of butter, a wedge of cheese. There was a tired-looking cabbage too. She inspected it without enthusiasm. Ever since she had been carrying a child, she had been craving the tartness of strawberries, but it would be a long time before they were in the market again. She was sick of winter vegetables, sick of salt fish and salt meat and the constant dampness that clung to her clothes and spangled her skin and made the air smell mouldy and stale. They put up their shutters when the wind drove the rain down the streets, whipping it on like a furious carter, hurling it against the houses and thrusting it through the fissures in the walls. The wet pooled under the doors and between the cracks in the windows. It dripped from the roofs and dug out the cobbles and turned her garden to mud.

Yet Nell was content. In the months since she had told Ralph she was with child, he had not touched her once. His frustration was clear, but Nell kept her eyes downcast and concealed her jubilation as best she could. At night, Ralph turned away from her in the great bed, his expression surly. If he couldn't hurt her, it seemed he did not want her at all. Nell suspected some whore was suffering in her place, and she was sorry for it, but she would not risk her babe by encouraging his blows.

Janet hung up her cloak and held out her hands to the kitchen fire where a savoury broth simmered. 'They say there's another harlot found dead in't river,' she said.

Nell looked up, startled by the way Janet seemed to have picked up on her thoughts. 'Another?' she said, dismayed.

'Three since Michaelmas,' Janet confirmed.

'And still no one cares what is happening!' Nell dropped the cabbage back in the basket. 'Anyone would think they were no better than dogs, to be beaten and left to die in the street!'

'They're not much better than dogs,' said Janet, unimpressed. 'Rogues and vagabonds. Nowt but trouble.' Just in time she remembered that Nell didn't like her to spit on the floor. 'One whore less to spread her legs against a wall is no loss to us.'

Janet was not alone in thinking thus, but it left Nell feeling uneasy. From all accounts, the dead girls were all vagrants, all young. She guessed that they had little choice but to lurk in the back alleys behind the ale houses and pull up their skirts for a farthing. It seemed they were all beaten too, so battered and bruised when they were found that no one would have recognized them even if anyone had cared to look for them. Nell knew what it felt like to have a fist slam under her ribs, to have her arm twisted until she whimpered, to have her wrists tied to the bedpost and her back lashed until it bled; to feel her husband's big teeth biting into her breast. All that saved her from the dead girls' fate was Ralph's care for his reputation. He never touched her face. The marks of his desire lay hidden beneath her shift, tucked away by the starched ruffs at her wrists and at her collar.

She was better off than the vagrant girls at least. Her husband took pleasure from hurting her, but he wouldn't kill her. Where else would he find a woman he could beat with impunity, and without paying a farthing?

As if her thoughts had summoned him, there came the sound of Ralph shouting for wine to be brought to him in his closet.

Instinctively, Nell flinched but Janet turned from hanging up her cloak, her face alight. 'Shall I go, Mistress?' she asked eagerly.

Nell had been glad of Janet's experience when she was first mistress of the great house in Stonegate. Already thirty, Janet knew what needed to be done, and she was capable and loyal. Nell often wondered why she had not married. She was whey-faced and sandy-featured, with a thin, questing nose like a vole and pale lashes, but she was not so old or so plain that she wouldn't make some man a good wife. Eliza and Mary teased her about John Scott, the glazier, who came to the door sometimes to mumble inarticulately and take Janet for a walk, but Janet seemed content with her place in the Maskewe house. She considered Ralph the best of masters, and couldn't understand why Nell was not dizzy with the pleasure of being his wife. Nell had seen the way Janet stroked Nell's gowns when she brushed them, the way she glowed at the most careless word of thanks from Ralph.

If only she knew.

'Thank you, Janet,' she said. 'There is warm wine by the fire. Take two cups in case he has someone with him.'

She felt guilty for letting Janet serve him. If she were braver, she would go herself. A good wife would warm his wine with her own hands. She would carry it up to him, fetch his gown and make sure the fire was stoked. And if she were not with child, Ralph would expect her there. He knew well how much she hated the closet. He called her in whenever he could and made her stand next to the chest. He didn't say anything, but he looked at the chest and he looked at her, and his teeth showed bone white in a smile. He liked it when she was afraid.

It was his favourite thing.

But no more. Nell spread her hand on her

stomach which jutted proudly, high and round. Definitely a boy, the goodwives said, inspecting her with experienced eyes. She had let out her laces. She was doing everything she could for her son. Every morning she drank a good draught of sage ale. She rubbed powdered tansy on her belly. She kept an eagle stone in the purse that hung from her girdle.

And she prayed.

She prayed that the babe would hold. That Ralph would not beat her while there was a chance she might bear his son. Nell longed to hold the baby in her arms, but at the same time she wished she could be with child forever.

But Ralph was in a sour mood that night. She could tell the moment they sat down to eat in the parlour. He put on a smiling show for Janet when she served them, but Nell saw the muscle ticking under his right eye, and apprehension uncoiled within her. Something had triggered a fury of frustration in him, that much was clear. He would want to vent it and she prayed it would not be on her. She prayed that he would go out after supper, but her prayers were in vain. When he came to bed, she knew by the way he closed the door to their chamber that his abstention was at an end. The best she could hope for was that he would be less rough.

'It is time you resumed your wifely duties,' Ralph said, coldly stripping off his clothes. 'No man can be expected to abstain until a child is born.'

'As you wish, husband,' said Nell. 'But take care not to harm the babe.'

'What am I, a monster?' he snarled as he climbed on top of her.

Nell didn't answer. She opened her legs and turned her face to the wall but it was not enough for Ralph. He heaved and grunted on top of her, but his yard would not rise and he cursed her for it. She knew better than to speak, but much good it did her.

'This is your fault, you witch,' he said savagely. 'You have unmanned me! Can you do no better than to lie there like a sack of turnips? I would get as much pleasure from it!'

Nell moistened her lips. 'I do not want to hurt the babe,' she said carefully, but of course that was the wrong thing to say too.

'The babe! The babe!' His voice rose in fury. 'I am sick of hearing about the babe. If you showed a fraction of that care for your husband, it would be a fine thing indeed! But, no, you just lie there mocking me. I can tell.'

'No.' She shook her head, her mind scrabbling frantically for a way out of this.

'*Yes*,' he contradicted her. 'Do you think I do not see the way you laugh behind your hand at me?' He yanked her up onto her knees. 'I'll wipe the smirk from your face!'

Frantically, Nell shoved both her hands at his chest. 'Don't!'

There was a moment of stillness as her voice rang around the chamber.

'Don't?' Ralph echoed incredulously, but there was delight there too. At last he had his excuse and he savoured it. '*Don't?* You dare say nay to your husband?'

'Ralph, I beg of you–' she began, but it was much too late. There was a blankness in his eyes she recognized all too well as he raised his hand and cuffed her so hard across the head that she fell back across the bed and tumbled to the floor.

For a moment she lay there, dazed, and then he was standing over her, naked, his mouth peeled back like a dog's. He dragged her to her feet so that he could knock her down again. 'Do you try to master your husband? I'll teach you to say "don't" to me!'

Whimpering, Nell tried to curl up into a ball, but Ralph was having none of it. He kicked her in her side until she could get herself to her knees, retching in pain, and then he dragged her by the hair to push her against the bed. He was panting, excited by her stifled moans. She lay half on, half off the bed, her face crammed into the coverlet. Her head was ringing and she could hardly breathe.

Now he was hard. *Now* he could take her the way he wanted to. He bucked into her, finishing with a cry of triumph, and then he took his wife and dropped her to the floor in disgust.

The pain was agonizing. Nell wrapped her arms around her stomach and rocked herself backwards and forwards on the cold boards. Tears trickled silently down her cheeks, as silently as the blood already seeping between her thighs.

'Oh my God!' Vanessa dropped to her knees beside Tess, who had crumpled to the kitchen floor and was curled up in a foetal position in a pool of tea and broken china. 'Tess! What happened?'

'My baby...'

'*Baby?* You're pregnant?' Vanessa scrambled back to her feet. 'Oh my God, I have to call an ambulance!'

'No!' Desperately Tess hauled herself back to the present. 'No ambulance!'

'But Tess–'

'Please, Vanessa.' With an effort, she struggled to a sitting position and put her head between her knees. 'I don't need an ambulance.'

'Tess, you passed out! One minute you were standing there and the next you went absolutely white and pitched onto the floor! And if you're pregnant…'

'I'm not.'

'You were talking about your baby,' said Vanessa, still agitated.

Leaden with misery, Tess shook her head against her knees. 'There's no baby.'

'At least let me run you to the walk-in centre–'

'I'll be fine.' Tess summoned a smile, and pulled herself shakily to her feet to prove it. 'I'm sorry I gave you such a fright.' She looked down at the mess on the floor. Her skirt had a dirty brown stain spreading up from the hem. Pointlessly, she brushed at it. 'Sorry about the mug too.'

'Heavens, don't worry about *that!* Sit down and I'll make you another cup of tea. You'd better have some sugar.'

Vanessa was at her best when she had something to do. She bustled around, clearing up the broken mug, wiping the floor, taking juice out to the children in the garden. Tess was glad to sit for a bit while the pounding in her head subsided and the wrenching ache of loss began to ease.

'Now.' Vanessa pulled out the chair across the table from Tess and sat down at last. She had on her firm-but-kind face. 'I'm worried about you, Tess. What's all this about a baby?'

'It's nothing.' Tess knuckled the last of the tears from under her eyes.

'I had no idea you might be pregnant!' Vanessa allowed hurt to creep into her voice. 'I do think you might have told me.'

'I'm not pregnant, Van. There's no question of it.' Tess stirred her tea, watching the liquid swirl round and round without really seeing it. There was nothing for it. She was going to have to tell Vanessa what had happened. She had told Luke, hadn't she? That had been okay. Maybe Vanessa would be able to help too.

Straightening, she tapped the teaspoon on the rim of the mug to get rid of the drops and laid it carefully on the table. 'Do you remember I told you about those vivid dreams I had when I first moved into the flat?'

Vanessa nodded to her to go on, but Tess could see a guarded look dropping into her eyes already.

'I've been having them regularly,' Tess went on, picking her way cautiously. 'I'm the same person every time, but I get older… It's so *real*, Van. I know you think it's crazy, but I really don't think these are dreams. I think for some reason I'm slipping back in time to live Nell's life in the past.'

'Oh, Tess, come on…'

'Just now, when you mentioned a baby, that was enough to tip me back,' Tess ploughed on without letting Vanessa finish. 'I was here, but I was in Elizabethan York. I was ... I was pregnant then but my husband beat me and I lost the baby and then I came round on your kitchen floor,' she finished lamely, knowing how unconvincing she must sound. 'I can't explain it, Van, but that's what happened.'

Vanessa's silence was eloquent. 'Now I really am worried,' she said at last. 'I can't believe you haven't been to a doctor about this, Tess.'

'I don't *need* a doctor! I'm not ill!'

'You might not think you're ill, but you're not behaving rationally,' said Vanessa in a soothing voice that scratched Tess's nerves raw. 'You're talking about time travel and babies that don't exist... I really think you need some help.' Reaching across, she laid her hand over Tess's. 'The person having a breakdown is often the last to realize what's happening.'

Tess snatched her hand away. 'I. Am. Not. Having. A. Breakdown!'

Vanessa smiled sadly. 'And how many people do you think are going to believe you about that?'

'Luke does.'

Wrong thing to say. Vanessa's expression shuttered and she sat back.

'Luke would. It's typical of him to encourage you in this nonsense. He's always been irresponsible that way. I mean, has he thought about Oscar? Have *you* thought about Oscar?'

'Of course I have,' said Tess coldly. 'Oscar's my priority. He's fine.'

'Is he? What if you passed out like this when you were alone with him? He'd be terrified!'

'He didn't even notice the one time it happened.' Too late, Tess heard the defensive note in her voice, and, spotting a sore spot, Vanessa was quick to follow up.

'So you've already had one of these ... lapses ... when you were alone with Oscar? Oh, Tess, that's dangerous! Have you told your mother about this? I *really* think it's time you saw someone who could help.'

'Vanessa, please...'

'It's not like the GP will send you straight off to a psychiatric hospital, if that's what you're worrying about.' Vanessa leant forward once more, determinedly supportive. 'I think it's more likely he'll refer you for counselling. Maybe Martin could come too.'

'Martin?' Tess reeled back, aghast at the idea, but Vanessa wasn't ready to let it go.

'It sounds to me as if these "dreams" of yours are a bizarre way of working through some of the difficulties in your relationship with him. Really, he needs to be here, so you can talk it through together, and he can be there for Oscar too. This could be just what you need to put your family back together.'

'No.' Tess felt cold. She pushed back her chair. 'I should probably think about getting Oscar home. I know you're trying to help, Vanessa, but no. I'm sorry I told you anything.'

Vanessa was determined not to be pushed away. 'I'm very glad you did.' She was smiling with determined patience. 'It's not easy being on your own and you need someone to watch out for you. You need help, Tess, and I won't let you down, I promise.'

It sounded to Tess like a threat. She called Luke on her mobile when she and Oscar were walking home. He wasn't answering so she left a message.

'I'd like to see that guy you told me about, the one who knows about regression. Can you ring him for me? As soon as possible.'

Hunched forward over the wheel as he peered at house numbers, Luke drove slowly along the street. 'I think ... yes, this is it.' He pulled in to the drive and stopped the car in front of an unassuming semi.

'*This* is where he lives?'

'What were you expecting? A haunted house?'

'I don't know. Nothing this...' Tess studied the house through the windscreen. It had a neat front garden, with standard roses lining the path up to a blue front door. The windows were criss-crossed with mock-Tudor panes and discreetly screened with lacy net curtains. 'Nothing this ordinary,' she said at last.

'Ambrose seems very ordinary when you meet him. His name's the weirdest thing about him, I reckon.' Luke glanced at Tess. 'You've been very quiet for the last few miles. Nervous?'

'A bit.' She wound down the window to let in some air. It was hot in the car but she wasn't ready to get out just yet and put herself in the hands of Ambrose Pennington.

She'd liked the drive across the flat Lincolnshire fenland. The sky was wider than in York and the sense of space liberating. For miles, it seemed, they had been able to see Lincoln's cathedral perched atop a ridge that jutted into the horizon. For Tess, it had been a time of limbo, and she had felt curiously weightless sitting next to Luke as the old car rattled along. In motion, there was nothing she could do, but the closer they got to the city, the faster her reservations came crowding back.

'I haven't – what should I call it? – slipped ... for two weeks now.' It had been an enormous relief to be able to reassure Vanessa, who had taken to studying her with an anxious frown, that she was fine.

And she was. She thought she was anyway. There had been no disturbing phone calls, no glimpses of men who might or might not have been Martin in the summer holiday crowds. Once or twice, the doorbell had rung, and she had answered the intercom to find that nobody was there, but it was an easy mistake to press the wrong button, after all.

There had been no Nell either. Tess still ached for the baby she had lost. That *Nell* had lost, she had to keep reminding herself. She held onto Oscar so tightly now that he wriggled to get away.

The desperate scraping and scratching in the wall still rasped into her dreams, but Tess was almost used to it now, just as she was used to the pain in her fingers that came and went without warning. She wanted to relax, but she didn't quite dare.

It had taken Luke some time to set up the meeting with Ambrose Pennington. Several times Tess had picked up the phone to ask Luke to cancel it, only to change her mind at the last minute. That very morning when she and Luke dropped Oscar off with her disapproving mother, she had been tempted to suggest they forget the whole thing and go to the coast instead, but in the end she had decided to go through with it.

'I'd like to think it means Nell has finished with me, but I can feel she's still there,' she told Luke. 'She's waiting for something, and she's ... frustrated with me. I wish I could see some kind of pattern and then I could understand it better, but I can't. I don't know why I should slip three times in one day, and then not at all for a whole week. It doesn't make sense.'

'Maybe it depends on you being in a certain place, or a certain mood,' said Luke. 'Maybe that makes you more vulnerable to her.'

Tess made a face. 'It's possible. But then why didn't I slip when Vanessa started talking about calling Martin and I was beginning to panic?'

'Maybe you're stronger than you think you are,' said Luke.

A tiny silence fell. Tess looked through the windscreen at the house and sighed. She was very conscious of Luke beside her. 'I wish ... things could just be normal,' she said. Whatever normal was. She could hardly remember any more. 'I want to be in Lincoln to look at the castle and the cathedral, not talk to some oddly named man I've never met about regression.'

'We can go into the city if you want. You don't have to see Ambrose. He said he'd understand if you decided against it at the last minute.'

'No, I need to.' Tess sucked in a breath. 'This has been going on long enough. I need to take control. I need to deal with Nell, and then I need to deal with Martin. This Ambrose seems to be my best bet.'

'Okay.' Luke pulled the key out of the ignition. 'But if you change your mind at any point, you just need to say, and we'll go.'

Tess started to get out, then turned back, one hand on the door handle. 'I'm glad you're going to be with me, Luke.' She hesitated. 'You won't let him do anything funny, will you?'

Luke's mouth set in a grim line. 'No, I won't do that. Don't worry, I'll stay with you,' he said gruffly, and then, as if against his will, he reached out and grazed a knuckle down the side of her cheek with a twisted smile. 'I won't let anything happen to you,' he said. 'You can count on it.'

Ambrose Pennington was a short, very dapper man in his sixties. He wore beige slacks and a blue jumper over a checked shirt and a tie. His hands were small and he had a soft, unassuming voice. Shaking his hand, Tess was unimpressed. *This* was her best hope of dealing with the situation? She had expected someone with a bit more presence.

She exchanged a glance with Luke as Ambrose led them into the living room. It had been extended into a small conservatory at the back of the house. Beyond it Tess could see a small, well-tended garden.

Gingerly, she sat on the edge of a beige armchair which was part of a matching suite. Like everything else about the house and its owner, it was inoffensive, but there was nothing to inspire confidence either.

'You're having some doubts,' Ambrose said in a mild voice as he took a seat opposite her. 'About me or about what you're doing here?'

Tess hesitated. She didn't want to be rude.

He smiled. 'Be honest!'

'All right.' She drew a breath, slowly let it out. 'Both, I think.'

'I'm not here to persuade you to believe anything you don't already believe,' said Ambrose. 'But I can't help you unless you trust me.'

She could see that. After all, what did she have to lose? If Ambrose was a fake, nothing would happen. And if he wasn't... She shot a glance at Luke, who had taken a seat near the conservatory, the usual ferocious look on his face, and she remembered what he had said. *I won't let anything happen to you.* Her cheek prickled with heat still where he had touched it.

Deliberately, she made her shoulders relax.

'What exactly are you going to do?' she asked Ambrose.

'Nothing you don't want to do, I promise you,' he said. 'Why don't you start by telling me about Nell? Luke's already told me something of your story, but it would be good to hear it in your own words.'

'From the beginning?'

He smiled faintly. 'From whenever you think it began.'

Tess began, haltingly at first, and then more fluently. Like Luke, Ambrose didn't interrupt other than to ask an occasional question to make sure that he was following. He steepled his fingers under his bottom lip and rubbed them slowly from side to side as he listened. It ought to have been annoying, but his gaze was steady and Tess was insensibly reassured.

'Remarkable,' he said when she had finished. 'It's rare to come across a past life experienced so coherently.'

'Do ... do you think Nell is real? Or is she just some part of my subconscious?'

Ambrose didn't answer immediately. His palms were still pressed together and he rested his mouth on the tips of his fingers.

'Does it matter?' he asked. 'Nell is real to *you*, and it's clear that she is a powerful force.'

'What does she want from me?'

'I think you're in a better position to answer that than I am.'

'She wants me to relive her life,' Tess said slowly.

Ambrose nodded. 'I think that is clear. Perhaps she wants you not to make the mistakes that she made, but, of course, you can't do that. You are bound on her path, and you can't change it.'

'But what if that path ends badly?' Luke put in.

'Indeed. If Nell is so set on reliving her experience, I think it's safe to assume that it *did* end badly. This could be very dangerous for you, Tess. You've told me that you woke with bruises once, that you have had pain that lasts into the present. What if Nell is more badly hurt? What if she dies? I'm not trying to alarm you, but you need to understand how serious a situation you may be dealing with.'

Tess swallowed. 'What can I do?'

'If you will allow me to hypnotize you, I think the best thing would be for me to try and make contact with Nell. Whether she is a ghost or whether she exists deep in your subconscious, it doesn't matter. If we can find out what she is searching for, maybe then we can decide what to do.'

'I've never been hypnotized.' Tess bit her lip. 'I'm not sure I'll be able to relax enough.'

'Let's just try, shall we?'

She shifted uneasily in the armchair. 'What should I do? Lie down and close my eyes?'

'You can lie down if you think you'd be more comfortable, otherwise stay where you are.'

'I'll stay here,' she decided after a moment. She shuffled back against the cushions and laid her arms along the rests as she closed her eyes.

'OK,' she said.

'Good.' She strained to hear if Ambrose was moving, but the only sound was the tick of a clock on the mantelpiece. 'Are you comfortable, Tess?'

'Yes,' she said determinedly.

'In that case I want you to keep your eyes closed and think about a time you were really happy.'

Tess's face puckered with effort. She wanted to relax, but her mind kept jumping feverishly between being swung up in her father's arms to lying in the sand dunes with Luke, and then to Oscar. The first time she had held him in her arms. No, later, when he was a toddler, learning to walk. She remembered how he had let go of the chair, how he had wavered for a moment before staggering into her outstretched hands.

But then the door had opened and Martin had come in.

Her eyes snapped open. 'It's not working!'

'Let's not force it.' Ambrose was unfazed. 'Luke,

would you mind making some tea? A warm drink can help relaxation.'

'I think I should stay with Tess.'

'It's okay, Luke.' Tess forced a smile. 'I'll be fine.'

Ambrose turned back to Tess as Luke left the room reluctantly, and his eyes followed hers to the mirror above the mantelpiece. It had an ornately carved wooden frame. 'I see you're looking at my mirror,' he said casually. 'It's unusual, isn't it?'

'Mmm,' said Tess, but she couldn't focus on the frame properly. Her eyes were screwed up as if the light bouncing off the mirror was too bright.

'Is the light bothering you?'

'No, it's fine,' she said, and it was. All of a sudden the glare had gone and instead the mirror seemed to give off a beckoning luminosity.

Ambrose kept his voice quiet and easy. 'Can you see what's in the mirror?'

'Ye-es,' she said slowly. She could, but the image was indistinct, as if the surface was dull and smudged. She peered closer.

'What do you see?'

'I see my face,' she said, unaware of her voice thickening and broadening. She was puzzled by the question. What else would she see when she looked in a glass?

'How do you look?'

'I look tired. I look hot.' She wiped her cheeks with her fingers. Her face was shiny with sweat. It had been a long, hot summer, and beneath her cap, her hair was sticking to her scalp.

She hadn't slept for what felt like weeks. Nell lowered the glass with a sigh and dropped it onto the coverlet beside her. What use in looking at her

reflection? It would not change her puffy eyes or the ankles swollen like two bolsters. Those days she was like some lardy sow weighed down by her dugs.

But it was worth it. Nell laid her hands over her belly. It was high and tight as a drum, and she smiled and winced as she felt the babe kick. It was as restless as she was these long days. Part of her longed to have the baby and be rid of this great weight that pinned her to the bed and made the simplest of tasks an effort, but part of her dreaded it too. Not for the pain, though she knew it would be great, but because once the child was born, there would be nothing to keep Ralph away from her again.

This time when she told Ralph she was with child, she didn't say anything about being careful, but it seemed that he remembered how she lost the earlier babe and he had managed to keep his fists to himself. Thus far anyway. He slept in his closet, and Nell was glad of it.

The prospect of a child had made her strong, and she moved around the house with a new confidence. She saw Ralph's jaw working in frustration when he looked at her sometimes, but his desire for a son was great and he stayed away from her. Nell didn't know where he went at night, and she didn't want to know. He would be inflicting his warped desires on some woman, she doubted not, and, like the last time, she was sorry for it, but she had to keep her baby safe.

It could not be long now. Grimacing at another vigorous kick, Nell hauled herself up against the bolsters. She had been resting as Janet told her

she must, and as Ralph insisted, and for once she was not sorry to do as he said. But now she was bored and restless. Fine as it was, her linen smock itched and stuck to her skin and she had to relieve herself *again*.

Once getting out of bed was easy. She didn't even have to think about pushing back the coverlet and swinging her legs to the floor. Now she had to roll herself awkwardly over to the edge and struggle to sit upright before sliding to the floor. She used the chamber pot and once more dragged herself to her feet.

Unaware of the open window only a few inches away, a fly was trapped against the casement, bumping and buzzing frantically as it attempted to beat its way through the glass. Taking pity on its wretchedness, Nell cupped her hands around it and edged it towards the air. It vibrated unpleasantly against her palms and she wrinkled her nose, glad to let it go as soon as it caught the scent of freedom.

The fly disappeared into the heat, leaving a turgid silence behind it. Nell brushed the feel of it from her fingers and pushed the window as far as it would go in the hope of catching some air, but there was no breeze to be found. Below in the street, work went on; the shutters were open, but folk walked slowly as if it were an effort to push themselves through the thick air. It was too hot for conversation. Even the bells ringing the hour sounded muffled. It reminded Nell of the day she had played hide-and-seek with Tom.

Every now and then, like now, the memory of him slipped past the guard she had put on her

memory and stabbed her, dagger quick, dagger sharp, and she flinched away from it.

She turned away from the casement. Enough. She had a babe to think of now. There had been too much resting, too much time to think. She needed a simple task to keep her mind occupied.

When she went down to the kitchen, the maids Mary and Eliza were sitting in the yard, fanning themselves, eyes closed. Their heads were tilted back, their throats slick with sweat. Their legs were splayed and they had hoisted their skirts to their knees. She should reprove them, Nell knew, but how could she when she and Alice had done the same on hot days? She didn't have the heart to make them go back inside into the stifling kitchen.

The linen was back from the laundresses who worked in St George's Close. The baskets were full and still sitting near the kitchen door. She would fold the linen and put it away, Nell decided. It would be a nice restful job. She would ask Janet to carry the baskets up to the parlour and pull the cloth up since Nell could no longer bend to reach it. They would do it together. Janet wasn't giddy like the two maids. Her stolid competence was soothing.

Where *was* Janet? Nell stood at the bottom of the stairs, pressing her hands to her aching back.

And that was when she heard it.

Chapter Fourteen

'What do you hear?'

Oddly, the voice breaking into her head did not startle her.

She didn't recognize it, but it seemed natural to answer as she looked up the stairs towards the hall.

'A noise,' she said.

'What sort of noise?'

A stifled grunting. A gasping, quickly smothered. Disquiet tickled the base of her spine. 'It's the kind of noise I make when Ralph wants me to be quiet. The noise he makes when he is rutting.'

'What do you want to do?'

'I want to pretend that I haven't heard it. I want to turn away and go and sit with Eliza and Mary out in the yard. But I can't.'

The stairs had never seemed as steep or as long. Without meaning to, Nell found herself moving softly, silently.

Step by step, she pulled herself up and memory came slicing again, swift as a knife: fisting her skirts and running up the stairs, while Tom counted to a hundred in the yard. She couldn't imagine now being able to run at all, let alone that quickly or that easily. Before, she had jumped over the step that creaked. This time, there was no way to avoid it. Her weight bore down on it and the silence was fractured with a great groan of straining wood.

When she was on the next step, Nell paused. Listened.

Nothing.

Had she imagined those noises?

Still, she crept on, up to the top where she stood in the dim hall and looked around, just as she had done that day. The wainscot was smooth and polished now. Instead of new wood, Nell could smell the herbs she had directed Mary to strew on the floor only that morning: fleabane and wormwood, lavender and pennyroyal, lady's bedstraw and wild thyme. She had dried the herbs herself, and kept them in great jars in her still room.

Nell was thinking about herbs because she didn't want to think about what was in the closet. Once the door had stood ajar, beckoning her in, but today it was firmly closed.

Very quietly, she moved across the hall, and put her ear to the door. Inside, she could hear grunting and slapping, sharp cries of pain quickly stifled.

The cries it was her duty to make as Ralph's wife. In Janet's voice.

Nell put a hand to her mouth, smothering her own gasp of shock and shame. She should open the door. She should put a stop to what was happening. Her husband was in there, forcing Janet, subjecting her to his dark and twisted desire, because Nell was untouchable for now. So stolid, stoical Janet must stand in her stead.

Nell's stomach roiled. She had been so happy to be free of him, but deep down she had known that he would look elsewhere, that some other woman would have to suffer in her place.

Janet was her servant. Her expression might be hard to read at times, and her humour not the lightest, but she was part of the household. If she could not be safe there, she was safe nowhere.

Nell stepped back from the door. She should go in. The knowledge hammered in her chest. She should stop Ralph. But inside her the babe kicked a warning. Nell didn't need to imagine how Ralph would punish her if she thwarted him right then. The red mist would descend over his eyes, and he would have no mercy. She wrapped her arms protectively around her belly as if his boot were already aimed there. She had to keep the baby safe. She couldn't lose it, not now.

So she backed further away, quietly, ashamed. She went to her chamber and she lay back down on the bed, sick at heart.

Two days later, when Ralph was out, Nell summoned Janet. She could hardly meet her eyes for shame. Certain that Janet must despise her for putting her in this position, Nell looked away after a fleeting glance. Janet looked as impassive as ever, but then so did she look composed after Ralph had been at her. Sometimes the only way to survive was to retreat into a place where everything was still and calm and no one could touch you. Nell knew this well.

She cleared her throat. 'I have found you another position,' she told Janet.

'Mistress?' Janet gaped at her, astounded.

'I ... I fear this has not been a happy household for you,' said Nell with difficulty. 'I am sorry for it. You've been a good servant to me, and I didn't expect that... I didn't want for you to suffer for me.'

There was a pause. 'I don't understand,' said Janet at last.

Nell drew a breath and made herself look into her servant's face. 'I know what my husband has been making you do,' she said directly. 'I am sorry.'

The colour rose in Janet's cheeks, and this time it was she who looked away, but she said nothing.

'So ... so I thought you might prefer to go to another house,' Nell floundered on. 'My step-mother needs help with my brothers. It is not such a fine house as this, perhaps, but they will be kind to you. Or I will find you some money so you may marry if you wish,' she said when Janet still said nothing. It would be more difficult, as Ralph controlled the purse but she could make the housekeeping stretch further if she had to. 'I cannot get it immediately, but if you can wait, I will see what I can do.'

She wanted to ask if Janet was still walking out with John Scott, but it didn't seem appropriate. Some money would help them marry, but would it erase the memories from Janet's head? Nell didn't think so.

She waited patiently while Janet wrestled with her thoughts. In the end, Janet said that she didn't want to go to a new household and be with strangers. 'In that case, I will get you some money,' Nell promised. 'You can go back to your family until you decide what you wish to do. I will give you a good character if anyone asks.'

Ralph's face went ominously blank when he heard that Janet had gone. Nell did not dare tell him the truth about why she had sent her away. 'She was idle,' she lied instead, not meeting his eyes. 'And insolent. I will have Eliza as my maid now and I will find a new girl to work with Mary.'

There were several families eager to send their daughters into service with the Maskewes. Nell would take the plainest, and keep her well out of Ralph's way.

'I see.' The blank look faded from Ralph's eyes and he dabbed at his mouth with his napkin before pushing back his chair. 'Yes, I see, my dear,' he said, all affability. 'You must, of course, do as you think best. If you are certain.'

The smile that went with this was wide and white, but it told Nell that he was not fooled. He knew exactly what she had done, and why. He would wait until the child was born, and then she would pay for it.

'I am certain.'

Nell kept her expression steady until the door closed behind him. Only then did the calmness slip from her face, and her fingers twist in her skirts.

'It is the right thing to do,' she whispered. 'I cannot regret it.'

'Yes, you have done the right thing,' the voice said. 'You have saved Janet from Ralph. But now I want you to wake up, Nell.'

Nell frowned. Wake up? What did he mean? She was not asleep! But even as she thought it, there was a rushing sensation in her ears and she was sitting in a strangely stuffed chair in a strange room with two strangely dressed men studying her with creased brows. Sucking in a breath, she clapped a hand to her throat where she could feel her heart pounding in fright, while her eyes darted around the room, widening at the unfamiliarity of it all. Where was she? What had happened?

And then her mind jolted without warning, and she was Tess again. Her hand dropped from her throat to her stomach, but it was flat beneath her jeans. The babe was gone.

'Tess, are you all right?'

Ambrose Pennington's expression held an undercurrent of panic. Her own must be ghastly, Tess realized.

She summoned a smile. 'Yes ... yes, I'm OK,' she said, but she wasn't, not really. It was as if she had lost the baby all over again, and grief lodged like a rock in her throat. She swallowed hard. 'I'm fine,' she said. 'What ... what did you see?'

'We didn't see anything,' said Luke. He looked edgy, uneasy. He was rubbing the knuckles of one hand into the palm of the other, his mouth tight. 'It was just you sitting there, but you were describing what was happening. It was eerie. Your voice ... it changed. You sounded really different. The Yorkshire accent was broader, but softer at the same time. Like it was mixed up with a bit of Dorset and a bit of Scotland.'

He glanced at Ambrose who nodded. 'Those rounded r's were very distinctive. Rrralph...' He tried to imitate the way she had sounded, and Tess shuddered at the name.

'I hate him,' she said in a low voice. 'I hate how powerless I am to stop him.'

'Yes, that came across very clearly.' Ambrose's voice was comfortingly prosaic, as if talking about your feelings for a man who had been dead four centuries was perfectly normal. 'I've never come across such a vivid regression,' he said. 'Many people experience snatches of a past life, or there's a certain blurriness to what they remember, but it's so clear for you ... quite remarkable,' he said. 'You are really very fortunate.'

Tess thought about Ralph's big teeth and the marks they made on her skin. She thought about his fists and the pain and the degradation she felt when he pushed roughly inside her. She thought about the blood puddling on the floor between her thighs and the baby killed by its own father.

'I don't feel very fortunate,' she said.

'No.' Ambrose sobered. 'That was tactless of me. You have suffered as Nell. It's just to spend your life with people ridiculing the idea of past life regression, and then to come across such a spectacularly vivid example…'

'I understand,' said Tess.

'How do you feel now?'

'A bit shaky. Okay.' To her horror, her eyes filled with tears. 'I want my baby.'

'Do you want to try again?' Ambrose asked. 'Nell was responding before. I could try and ask her what she wants from you this time?'

Luke shifted in his chair, ground his fist harder into his hand. 'Do you think that's a good idea? Tess has already had an unpleasant experience this morning. What if it gets dangerous?'

'Nell has a powerful hold on Tess,' Ambrose said. 'I think it will be more dangerous if we're not able to make a connection with her through Tess. It's always better to know what you're dealing with.'

'I don't like it,' Luke said stubbornly, and Tess

reached out to lay a hand on his arm.

'It's all right, Luke. I *want* to do it. Nell seems to be reliving the key times in her life, so surely the next important moment will be the birth of her child... I want to know if the baby survived or not.'

She *needed* to know if the babe was healthy. It felt all wrong now to have been wrenched out of a state of pregnancy. If there was a chance she could go back and feel the baby kicking inside her again ... oh, how could she explain that to Luke?

'I think Ambrose is right,' she said instead. 'I'd feel better if he could establish some kind of connection with Nell to ask her what she wants from me.'

Luke's mouth was still set in a mulish line. 'That's all very well, but what if the baby *didn't* survive? What if *Nell* didn't survive? Childbirth was a dangerous time in those days. Mothers and babies *died.*' He swung round to Ambrose. 'What happens if Tess starts haemorrhaging? She's been bruised before. What's to stop her bleeding while she gives birth to a baby who doesn't exist? Are you qualified to deal with that?'

'Luke.' Tess drew a breath. She knew he was making good points, but she couldn't think of anything beyond the clamour of need in her body. She had to have her baby back. What mother wouldn't risk everything for that? 'I know you're worried, but it will be fine.'

Scowling, Luke pulled his arm away from her hand. 'You asked me not to let anything happen to you, Tess,' he reminded her. 'I promised I'd stay with you.'

'And you are staying with me. Nothing is going to happen.' She moistened her lips. She had forgotten her earlier fears. All she wanted now was to go back to her baby. 'Ambrose could talk to me in the past before,' she reminded him. 'He told me to wake up and I did, remember? So if things get difficult, he can just wake me up again. Please, let me do it.'

'You don't need my permission,' he snapped. 'If you're determined, I can't stop you.'

'But you won't go away?'

Luke didn't answer immediately. She knew he wanted to argue more, but in the end his shoulders slumped and he looked straight into her face with an expression that squeezed her heart. 'No,' he sighed, 'I won't go away.'

'Thank you,' she said softly, and, reassured that he would watch over her, she settled herself back in the chair and closed her eyes.

'A girl?' Ralph was disgusted when he was told, but Nell was euphoric. After the pain of the marriage bed, the pain of childbirth felt pure and true, and when she held her daughter in her arms, she was happy for the first time since Tom.

She called the baby Meg after Margaret the midwife. Ralph didn't care. He wanted a son. He would be back in her bedchamber soon enough, Nell knew, but first she could enjoy her lying-in. Ever mindful of his reputation, Ralph let the neighbouring women come and sit around the bed to admire the baby. Nell had wondered if her coldness would keep them away, but they were curious, and they came anyway. Besides, there was wine and there were sweetmeats, and there was the chance to look around the fine Maskewe house, to nudge each other and look significantly at the luxurious hangings, or to surreptitiously finger the coverlet.

Cocooned in the warmth of the women around her, Nell relaxed for the first time in her marriage. The others exchanged bawdy stories and grumbled about men in general and their husbands in particular, but they didn't sound too bad to Nell. She would have liked a husband who fell asleep over his dinner, or fretted endlessly about his health. She wouldn't have minded so much if he was mean or snored or was foolish. She didn't say anything about Ralph. There was no point. None of these women could help her. They couldn't undo her marriage, more was the pity. They couldn't change Ralph.

No, Ralph wouldn't change, but she could. Meg had altered everything. When she held the warm weight of her baby in her arms, Nell's heart constricted painfully. Her love for her daughter was so powerful, Ralph mattered little in comparison. If she had to submit to his blows to make sure that her daughter was fed and clothed and safe, so be it. She could endure for Meg's sake.

As for Tom ... Meg had changed that too. Tom had nothing to do with Meg. Nell had locked him away in a secret chamber of her mind. Compared to her daughter, he couldn't matter.

She smiled down at Meg, who had fallen asleep at her breast, a bubble of milky foam between her lips. Her hand was curled around Nell's little finger, and Nell marvelled anew at how tiny she was, how perfect.

Nell? Nell? Tell me what you want.

Nell looked up, a frown touching her eyes. Until she was churched, the chamber was for women. The voice was male, and there was an urgency to it that she didn't understand. She had heard this voice before in her head. It ought to seem stranger than it did. For there was no man there, only her stepmother, Anne, straightening the linen in the cradle.

'I want my child to be safe,' she said. It was impossible to imagine wanting anything more than that right then.

'Aye, that is all any mother wants.' Anne thought that she was talking to her. She turned from the cradle, smoothing down the small blanket over her arm. The maids were busy downstairs, the neighbours had gone, and for now there was just the two of them together.

Anne hesitated. 'Do you think you can be happy now in this marriage, Eleanor?'

'Happy?' Nell considered the question as she looked down at her sleeping baby. Once she would have said 'no' instantly, but now there was Meg. 'I can be happy with my daughter,' she said.

'It is easier when you have a child.' Anne settled on a stool by the bed, still absently stroking the blanket.

It was the first time they had talked like this. Is this what motherhood does? Nell wondered. Did having a child of her own make her a member of a secret guild of women? She was one of them now. She knew how it felt to carry a babe inside her. She knew the wrenching, tearing pain and the wonder of giving birth. She knew what only another mother could know.

It was the first time, too, that Nell had wondered what it was like for Anne to be married to her father.

Anne kept her eyes on the blanket. 'I have seen the light go out of your face since you were married, Eleanor. I had hoped that you would deal well with Ralph, but I fear it is not so.'

'There is a darkness to him,' Nell said in a low voice. 'A viciousness that no one would ever guess. He shows a courteous face to the world, but when we are alone...'

'I am sorry for it,' said Anne, still without looking up. 'I urged the marriage. Your father ... he hates to see you so unhappy. I was the one who said you must agree. I was wild with worry about what would happen to Harry and Peter. They were so young. I did not know what would have become of us if Ralph called in the loan. For myself or your father, I could have borne it, but not for my boys.'

'*Nell.*' It was that voice again. '*Nell, tell me what you fear.*' It held an edge of impatience this time, and Nell frowned it away. She was talking to Anne. This was women's time. She didn't want to stop and answer to a man's voice.

She stroked Meg's downy hair. 'Mother,' she said. 'May I ask you something?'

'If you wish.'

'If I had been your child, and not just my father's daughter, would you still have pushed me into marriage with Ralph?'

'How can I know? I knew you disliked him, but

I didn't understand why. I thought it would be a good marriage for you. It is only since I have seen the shadows in your eyes that I have wondered...' Anne lifted her shoulders and let them collapse in defeat. 'Well, it is a woman's lot to be handed over to a man who may treat her as he wills. We all know this.

'But I am sorry for your unhappiness, Nell,' she added with difficulty after a moment. 'You had such spirit as a child. I hate to see you crushed.'

'I am not crushed.' Nell's chin went up, and she pushed aside the voice nagging in her head, demanding that she go somewhere else, be someone else. No, this time she would not do as she was bid! The voice was urgent, and somewhere she knew that it was important to listen, but her stepmother's words had stung.

'I am not crushed,' she said again. 'I endure. I *will* endure. I have Meg to think of now.'

'*Nell! Tess, can you hear me? I'm going to count to three, and when you hear "three", you will wake up and you will feel relaxed and happy. One, two...*'

Nell ignored the voice. She was thinking about Meg. She was thinking about being strong. She was thinking about how much she could endure if she had to.

There was an odd light shining through her eyelids. She stirred and mumbled a protest, turning her head aside from the light. Her neck was stiff and she hunched a shoulder as she tried moving it tentatively from side to side. 'Ouch!' The jab of pain brought her abruptly awake, and she squinted through still blurry eyes to see Luke jumping to his feet.

'Tess! Thank God! *Ambrose!* She's awake.'

Ambrose came hurrying back into the room, wiping his hands on a tea towel. 'I'm very relieved to see you awake,' he told Tess. He leant over and peered anxiously into her eyes, one after the other. 'How do you feel now?'

'Okay, I think.' Tess rubbed her sore neck. She must have been sleeping with her head at unnatural angle. 'What happened?'

'It was fine at first,' said Ambrose, standing back in relief. 'You were talking about how happy you were with your baby, but when I tried to contact Nell directly, she just closed down. I've got to admit I panicked a bit, and did my best to wake you up, but you wouldn't respond, and after a while it seemed as if you'd fallen asleep for real.

'I don't mind telling you we had a few anxious moments, but you were breathing and you didn't seem distressed, so we thought we'd better leave you. I had to forcibly restrain Luke from shaking you awake. Being wrenched from one plane to another before you're ready puts a terrific strain on the heart.'

'I don't remember falling asleep.' Tess pushed herself upright in the chair. 'But I've got an impression of ignoring a voice in my head...' She looked at Ambrose. 'That was you?'

'I'm afraid Luke was quite right to say "I told you so",' he admitted. 'Nell is a very strong presence. I couldn't get past her and through to you at all. But this time, you don't seem as disorientated as you were before.'

'No, I know exactly where I am.' Still rubbing

her neck, Tess looked around her. 'I think perhaps I fell asleep in the past so there wasn't that sudden transition coming back to the present.'

'Do you remember anything that happened after Meg was born?'

'Of course,' said Tess, surprised. 'Meg's six now.'

'Six! Have you made such a big jump in time before?'

Tess tried to think. 'Not quite so long, perhaps, but it's not as if that time is blank. I remember all of it.' She smiled. 'I have a son now too. Hugh, named after my father.'

'Nell's father,' said Luke and Tess blinked, taken aback by the sharpness of his tone.

'Yes, I mean Nell's father, of course.'

Ambrose shot Luke a warning glance. 'How old is Hugh?'

'Three.' Tess's face softened. 'He is very dear to me. Such a sunny-natured child. He has a smile that lights up a room. Everybody loves Hugh.'

'Even Ralph?'

Her expression hardened. 'Ralph is glad to have a son. That is all that matters to him. But he does not know his children. He does not know how quick Meg is with her fingers or how she loves to dance. He does not recognize Hugh's laugh. His children are to be shut away until he is ready to barter them for gold or service.'

'And what of you?' Ambrose asked carefully with another warning look at Luke. 'Does Ralph beat you still?'

'Sometimes.' Tess shrugged. 'But I have found a way to survive. I submit without protest. I let him do what he wants with me, and I have ceased caring. It is just one more thing to endure. And because I do not hate it any more, it is no pleasure for him. Even the chest has lost its horror,' she told Ambrose. 'One night when he dragged me by my hair towards it, I didn't even struggle, and he threw me aside in disgust.'

She smiled grimly. 'I deny Ralph hate and fear and pain, and it unmans him. He takes his fists to me sometimes just because he can. He might come to my bed and pinch and slap me until he is aroused, but I can blank my mind off, so most of the time he takes his pleasure elsewhere. I have closed my mind to where he goes and what he does. I cannot think of that. I can only look to my children and keep them away from him as much as possible.'

'So you are happy?'

Tess considered the question. 'I am content,' she decided eventually. 'My children are safe and well fed. That is enough for me.' She frowned and shook her head, and when she looked at Luke, her eyes were clear once more. 'Sorry, that was Nell ... but it's so strange, I remember all of it.'

Luke was still looking grim and she tried a coaxing smile to lighten the mood. 'You see, I was fine! I didn't die in childbirth after all.'

'Nell died sometime, though, didn't she?'

Darkness breathed on the nape of Tess's neck, and slithered down her spine.

'Yes, of course, but ... yes, I know what you mean, but for now, when I'm her, she's okay. You heard what I – she – said. She's content, and maybe that's enough. Maybe that's it. She's told her story and she can leave me in peace.'

'Do you really believe that?' asked Luke with a sceptical look.

No, of course she didn't. Tess chose not to answer. She looked at her watch instead.

'Oh my God! It's nearly four o'clock! How long was I asleep?'

'A couple of hours.'

'I need to get back.' Tess jumped to her feet. 'I left Oscar with Mum–' Oscar! She broke off and clapped a hand to her mouth, aghast to realize that she had been so involved with Meg and Hugh that she had forgotten her own son.

The colour rushed into her face, and the eyes that met Luke's were stricken.

'I rang your mother,' he said brusquely. 'I told her that you'd had a touch of food poisoning and were lying down, so you'd be a bit late to pick Oscar up.'

Tess slumped in relief. It wouldn't be too hard to pretend that she had been ill. In spite of her eagerness to be with her children in the past, she was shaken by how powerful Nell's hold on her was. In the space of an afternoon she had given birth twice. No wonder her insides felt jumbled and knotted, her emotions stretched raw and brittle. She felt sick and empty, exhilarated and guilty, all at the same time. Convincing her mother that she had picked up some bug wouldn't be difficult. She couldn't tell her the truth, anyway, that was for sure.

She tried to thank Luke, but he brushed her aside. 'We'd better get back if you're feeling up to it.'

He was monosyllabic in the car and after a

while Tess gave up trying to make conversation. Her fingers were aching, and flashes of scarlet pain were shooting up her arm and behind her eyes without warning. She held her hands curled upright in her lap, as if making an offering. She was glad she didn't have to drive, but when she tried to say as much to Luke, he snarled at her and told her he was trying to concentrate.

They were on the A1, one in a long queue of cars passing a truck. His jaw was tense, his hands rigid on the wheel, and he cursed as a car cut in front of him without indication.

'Fucking BMWs.'

'You're angry,' said Tess.

'I should never have taken you there.'

'I'm glad you did. Now I can think of Nell as happy with her children.' A smile tugged at the corners of Tess's mouth as she remembered the warm weight of Hugh on her lap, brushing the tangles out of Meg's hair. How could she regret precious memories like those?

Except they weren't her memories, were they? Her smile faded, and Luke noticed.

'Exactly,' he said, savagely changing gear. 'I thought Ambrose would be able to help you, but as far as I can see, he's just made things worse. Nell's hold on you is even stronger now.'

Tess swallowed. 'Perhaps, but Ambrose still helped. You were right. It was good to talk to someone who didn't immediately assume that I was crazy. Ambrose made me feel normal.'

'You think it's normal to forget about your own son? I know you did. I could see it your face.'

Forget Hugh? Never! As if she could. Tess was

outraged before the realization hit her like a blow. He meant Oscar.

She had forgotten Oscar.

The queue of red tail lights ahead blurred before her eyes. *Oscar, forgive me.*

'No,' she said in a low voice. 'No, of course I don't.'

'What do you think it was like for me to watch you lying there?' Luke demanded. 'Christ, Tess, you were ... *gone*. You were nothing, and instead there was this dead woman in your body, using your mouth, smiling your smile...' The gears scraped as he shoved at them again. 'We couldn't get you back. I thought we'd have to leave you stuck in the sixteenth century, and how would I have explained *that* to Oscar? *Sorry, Mummy's busy with some other babies that have been dead for four hundred years?*'

'I'm sorry.' Tess pressed her fingers to her temples and then regretted it as pain jabbed through the guilt churning inside her. 'I didn't think.'

Helplessly, she dropped her hands back in her lap. Luke had been so understanding up to now. She didn't like him being angry with her. She wanted him to understand this too. 'You haven't had a child, Luke. Maybe only another mother would understand. It was just so *strong*, the need to get to my baby. It was like I didn't have a choice.'

'Oh, don't pull that you-can't-possibly-understand-if-you're-not-a-woman crap,' said Luke. They had laboured past the truck and he jerked the car into the inside lane behind a lumbering tanker so that the car behind could flash past in a blur of sleek lines and bright headlights. 'You'd rather be with some dead kid than your own.'

'What's it to you anyway?' Guilt soured Tess's voice, made her lash out. 'You're not Oscar's father.'

'No, right, I'm just the joiner.' Swearing under his breath, Luke moved out again to pass the tanker. 'All right, all right.' He gestured in the mirror to the car that was powering up behind him, headlights blazing. 'God, I miss my bike,' he muttered as he pulled in again. 'This car's a heap of shit. That's what you get for trying to grow up and do the right thing.'

Tess made herself take a breath. She was baffled and hurt by his reaction, and it made for an unpleasant mix with the guilt and shame curdling in her stomach.

'Look, I'm sorry,' she said in a different voice, turning in her seat to face him. 'Really. I've been so consumed by Nell, and so desperate to try to hold things together that I haven't thought about what any of this has been like for anyone else, and that's not fair. I don't know what I would have done without you, Luke. You've kept me sane and tried to help, and driven me all the way to Lincoln and stayed with me, and I've just taken it all for granted. I'm sorry,' she said honestly.

Luke took a hand off the wheel and dragged it through his hair as he blew out a breath. 'No, I'm sorry,' he said. 'I shouldn't have said anything. You've got a kid, a harassing husband, a critical mother and a ghost intent on sucking you back into the past to deal with at the moment. That's more than enough for anyone.'

Relieved to see the tension slip from his face, Tess swivelled back in her seat. 'You're one of the reasons I've been able to deal with any of it,' she said. 'I'd forgotten what it was like to have a good friend,' she added in a low voice. 'I'd forgotten how to *be* a good friend. It shouldn't be one-sided. You've done everything for me, and I've done nothing for you.'

'For God's sake, Tess, don't start beating yourself up,' said Luke with an alarmed glance at her profile. 'Forget I said anything.'

'I can't do that. You were angry with me.'

'Only because... I was frightened, all right?' It was Luke's turn to sound defensive. 'You were out of Ambrose's control, and I felt responsible, and powerless to help you. And yes, if you must have the truth, I was jealous too. You were so absorbed in the past when you came round, so happy with your babies, it was like you had nothing left for anyone in the present – not for Oscar, and certainly not for me.'

Chapter Fifteen

'You don't need to say anything,' he said gruffly as Tess opened her mouth. 'I know it's mad. There's no way you can think about me at the moment. You're married, you're possessed by a ghost ... it's not exactly great timing, is it?'

'Could be better,' said Tess, but a treacherous

glow was uncoiling deep inside her, curling through her distress and her guilt, warming her.

'I'm just telling you why I was angry.' He held the wheel at arm's length, concentrating fiercely on the road. 'I wanted some of your attention, that's all. I'm not proud of it.'

Tess moistened her lips while she tried to get her jumbled thoughts in order. It was difficult to know how she felt exactly. Reassured, definitely. She hadn't realized how much she had come to rely on Luke until his anger had made her think about how self-absorbed she had been. There was guilt, too, and pleasure, and a little throb of anticipation. It was so long since she had felt wanted, desired.

But mixed up with it all was fear and frustration and a touch of exasperation. Luke was right: his timing was appalling. There was so much going on in her head. She had Oscar to think about, and Martin, not to mention a whole other life in the past that was clamouring at the back of her mind. How could she give Luke the attention he deserved too?

Her hands throbbed as she looked down at them. That was something else she needed to do something about. If the pain got any worse, she would have to go to the doctor.

'Luke–'

He held up a hand, like a traffic cop. 'No. Please don't try and explain. I understand.'

'Then you know more than I do,' said Tess tartly. 'I don't understand anything at the moment – that's the truth. But I do know that I'm really glad to have you as a friend again, and I know I'm really sorry that I hurt you.'

Luke made a face, slid a glance at her. 'We're not going to have a let's-just-be-friends conversation, are we?'

'We are,' she said, but her smile softened the words before she sobered. 'I've got things to be scared of at the moment, Luke, but the thing that scares me most is that I might end up using you.'

She looked down at her hands where they lay in her lap, cool and undamaged on the surface, pulsing and flinching with pain inside. 'I'm afraid of being needy, of letting myself depend on you. I really need to prove that I can manage on my own. I never want to be the way I was with Martin again. I need to be strong, and I'm afraid you might tempt me to be weak.'

'Weak?' Luke shot her a look, shook his head and turned his eyes back to the road ahead. 'You? You're the strongest woman I know, Tess.'

Tess stared at him. 'What are you talking about? I'm pathetic. If I was strong, I would never have let Martin walk all over me for so many years.'

'You were strong enough to leave.'

'I don't feel strong,' she said. 'I feel scared. I'm overwhelmed by everything and I don't know how I'm going to cope with any of it.'

'But you *are* coping with it,' Luke pointed out. 'All these awful things are happening to you, and you haven't fallen apart once.'

'Apart from smashing plates and throwing cereal all over the kitchen.'

'Okay, once.'

'And time travelling back to Elizabethan England and forgetting my own child.'

'Has it occurred to you, Tess, that anyone else would have been having the screaming abdabs if they did the same? They'd have been running off to their doctor in a panic, but not you. You won't risk Oscar, so you're just gritting your teeth and sticking to your plan, just like you always did.'

Puzzled, Tess shifted round with a frown. 'What do you mean by that?'

'You always had a plan.'

'No, I didn't!' She gaped at him, amazed that he could remember things so differently. 'I was always a follower. Look how I always tagged along after Vanessa at school.' She swung back to look through the windscreen. 'I was lucky she was so kind to me, or I'd have been really lonely.'

Luke snorted. 'Vanessa wasn't kind. She needed you much more than you needed her.'

'What are you talking about? Vanessa didn't need *me*. She was always pretty and popular.'

'Was she?'

'Of course she was. She had loads of friends.'

'I don't think so. Oh, she had the boys after her, but you were her only girlfriend.'

Tess opened her mouth to protest, only to shut it again. She had never thought of it before, but Luke was right about that. 'It was still kind of her to take me under her wing,' she said finally. 'I was so gawky and too shy to talk to anyone else.'

'And what better foil for pretty Vanessa?'

'Perhaps you might like to try that again?' Tess suggested, sweetness tinged with acid. 'Here's a suggestion: of course you weren't gawky, Tess?'

Luke laughed. 'You weren't, but you would never believe it. You were awkward and aloof, but you were interesting. I liked that about you. And you knew you wanted more than just to stay in York being safe. I liked that too, even if your plans didn't involve me.'

Tess was silent. She looked at the cars ahead, unseeing, trying to remember the girl she had been, the dreams she had had. 'I don't remember having a plan,' she said at last. 'I thought I was being a good girl, doing what was expected of me. Go to university, get a job, get married. That's not much of a plan, is it?'

'You said that was what you wanted,' said Luke. 'You were very clear about it.'

'Only because you made it clear that your plans didn't include me,' Tess said. She remembered *that*. 'You were always talking about going off and travelling on your own. There wasn't much scope for archival research bumming around the world with you, even if you had wanted me, so of course I pretended that I wanted something different.'

Luke's mouth twisted. 'I only made such a thing about travelling because you were so set on a life that had no place for me. The truth is that I didn't *know* what I wanted. I just knew that it wasn't to stay in York without you.'

Tess wished that she had known. She wondered how different her life would have been if she had, if she hadn't been hurt and lonely when she met Martin, if she and Luke had talked, found some way to compromise. But what was the point of regretting? The past was past. She had made her choice and she had to live with the consequences.

But maybe, just maybe, they would have another chance. Tess slid a glance at Luke, at his beaky profile; let her gaze linger on the cool curl of his mouth. His hair was too long and standing every which way where he had dragged his hands through it. His jaw was dark and rough with stubble, and the urge to lay her palm against his cheek, to feel its prickle and anchor her swirling emotions in the physical reality of him, rose in her on a flood of heat so powerful that her hand twitched with it.

She could do it. She could tell him to pull over, into a layby, onto the hard shoulder. She wouldn't care. She could clamber all over him the way she had used to. She could burrow into his lean, hard body. She could forget Martin and Nell, forget the pain in her fingers, forget *herself*. Blot out the turmoil and the fear and the uncertainty and the shame and the regret in the feel of him, the taste of him.

But that would be using him, and she didn't want to do that.

Luke glanced at her and Tess jerked her gaze away. 'Your colour's back,' he said. 'That's something.'

She had enough to deal with, Tess reminded herself. As Luke had pointed out, being regressed by Ambrose only appeared to have made Nell stronger, but Tess was running out of options. She still had Pat French's card in her bag, but just thinking about contacting her made her fingers jump as pain and panic slashed across their tips like a knife. In the end they had agreed that Ambrose would do more research on safeguards and that he would try to regress Tess again in a couple of weeks. Luke wasn't happy about it, but Tess didn't know what else to do.

She wasn't going anywhere near a doctor. Doctors would talk about drugs and psychiatric evaluations. Doctors put records on computers. Tess didn't trust Martin not to find them, and use them against her.

She had told Luke about the cutlery drawer on the drive down to Lincoln, and his response had been instant.

'Change the locks,' he said.

'I might be wrong. I could have tidied it up without thinking.'

'Change them anyway,' said Luke.

'But how could Martin have got into the flat? There was no sign of a break-in.'

'You told me yourself that he's got money and contacts,' Luke had said. 'You can get pretty much anywhere you want if you've got enough cash, and a flat like Richard's would be a cinch. I could probably get in myself if I put my mind to it. Get some new locks,' he had said, 'and be very careful about who you give spares to.'

Tess locked up with special care that night. Oscar had been tired and whiny by the time they picked him up from her mother's and it was some time before she could get him to bed. Feeling guilty still over how easily Nell had been able to push him from her mind, she had allowed him extra time watching television and gave in to his demands for two more stories, but at last he was asleep and, worn out by the emotional turmoil of the day, Tess was ready for bed too.

Change the locks. Luke's words rang in her head as she checked that the door was firmly closed. It seemed secure enough. He had promised to come and do the locks himself the next day.

'I'll be fine,' Tess had said when he left. 'Nobody's going to come into the flat while I'm there.' She was perfectly safe, but on an impulse she hooked the chain across the door.

Her fingers still resting on the door handle, she stood and listened. For Nell or for Martin? Tess wasn't sure which.

The flat was quiet. She could hear the faint hum of the fridge in the kitchen, the muted sound of the television in the front room, and, louder than both, the roar of her own pulse in her ears.

No sinister creaks, no creepy footsteps.

Still, there was *something*. She had been aware of it all evening. As if the air had been disturbed and was still settling.

Tess let her hand fall. She was getting paranoid. She switched on both computers in the front room, and got out the transcript she had printed out so far to check, but she couldn't concentrate. She kept thinking about the flat, about that sense that something didn't belong.

Deliberately, she turned and studied the room. There was nothing out of place here, she was sure of it.

She checked the kitchen. The cat flap was open as it should be. Ashrafar was out patrolling the rooftops, but she could get in whenever she wanted. Bink was squashed under Oscar's arm, tail flopping over the duvet, while Oscar breathed deep and slow. Tess stood looking down at him for a long time, watching the dark sweep of his lashes on his cheek, the way he lay sprawled as if he had taken a knockout blow to the chin.

Hugh had slept like that too.

'No,' she whispered, curling her fingers into defiant fists and deliberately forcing Meg and Hugh from her head. 'No, *this* is my son.'

The bathroom was undisturbed.

In the doorway to her bedroom, she paused, braced for the icy wave of horror and panic that would roll over her without warning sometimes when she walked into the room. It was muted today, like a ripple lapping at her shore rather than a breaking roller. Tess stepped past it and stood in the centre of the room, turning very slowly.

Silence. Not even the desperate scrabbling that still woke her sometimes in the night.

Tess's eyes moved from her bed to the chest and onto the wardrobe, before jerking back to the chest. Frowning, she went over and laid her hand on the top. Her favourite picture of Oscar as a toddler was there, along with a china dish where she kept the few pieces of jewellery she had brought with her. She touched them one by one. Everything Martin had bought her, she had left in the house in London, but she had her grandmother's pearl necklace and a pendant that had been her father's last gift to her, and a pair of earrings Luke had given her the last Christmas they were together. They were tiny silver squares and Martin had hated them.

'They make you look butch,' he had said dismissively. 'Wear those pretty pearl drops I gave you.'

And, God help her, she had done. She had

given away her worn jeans and leggings. She had thrown out her comfortable bras and knickers and worn silk and lace instead. Every morning now when she pulled on jeans and a T-shirt it felt a like dangerous act of defiance.

Nothing was missing, nothing was wrong. It was all fine. She was just spooking herself.

Tess didn't know what made her do it. Perhaps the drawers had been too carefully closed. Perhaps there was some other sliver of wrongness that tugged at her subconscious, but before she had even thought about it, she had jerked open the top drawer, where she kept the plain bras and knickers she had bought since leaving London, shoved in anyhow where she could grab at them the way she had that morning.

Inside, beautifully rolled in neat lines, lay an array of lingerie. Lacy bras. Wispy thongs. Silky camisoles and French knickers. Suspenders and gossamer stockings. Everything that Martin had insisted that she wore. Everything she had left behind in London.

Sick at heart, Tess stared down into the drawer. How was Martin doing this? Why was he doing it? Her blood felt thick and sluggish with fear until an unfamiliar sensation began to throb through her veins. It was so long since she had felt it that it took her some time to recognize what it was.

Rage.

She was angry.

Angry with Martin; angry with herself for ever having loved him. Angry with Ralph, and with Tom for leaving her to endure alone. Fury surged through her. It filled her up, pouring into every cell, shimmering to the ends of every nerve, making her bigger, taller, stronger, like a new leaf unfurling in the sun. It felt better than guilt, better than shame, better than fear.

Slamming the drawer shut, she fetched her phone.

'How dare you come into my flat?' Her voice shook with rage when Martin answered. 'How *dare* you?'

'Theresa?' He drew a breath of satisfaction. 'I've been waiting for you to call.'

'You had no right to come in here!'

A tiny pause. 'I don't know what you're talking about.'

'I know it's you. I know you've been here.'

'Darling, calm down and tell me what the problem is.'

'*You're* the problem! I don't want you in here, Martin. This is my home.'

'Theresa, Theresa,' said Martin soothingly. 'You're overwrought, darling. And no wonder, trying to manage everything by yourself. Isn't it time you stopped this silliness and came home so that I can look after you?'

Too late, Tess realized her mistake. What a stupid thing to do! Now Martin would see her getting in touch as weakness on her part. Her solicitor would be cross with her. She had specifically told Tess to avoid all contact with Martin, but Tess had been too angry to think clearly. Martin would be recording the call, she was sure. 'Look,' he would say, waving his phone records at the judge, 'she said she didn't want to hear from me, but she was the one who rang *me*.'

Fool. Fool, fool, *fool.*

Should she end the call now, or try and retrieve something from the conversation? Tess swallowed her anger and strove to sound reasonable. If they could have a rational conversation, perhaps all might not be lost.

'I'm not going back to London, Martin,' she said. 'This is my home now.'

'That poky little flat!'

Tess refused to rise to his contempt. 'How do you know it's poky?' she asked, hoping that he might incriminate himself and wishing that she had thought to record the conversation herself.

'Your mother told me.'

'Mum?' Her fingers throbbed painfully as they tightened around the phone.

'She's very worried about you, Theresa, and so am I. She says you're very tired and very tense, and that you're not sleeping well. That's not good when someone's as highly strung as you are.'

'I am not highly strung!' So much for her resolve to stay calm and reasonable.

'It's not *me* that says that – it's your own mother. She knows what an overactive imagination you have. You've blown everything out of proportion.'

'Am I imagining the fact that you made Oscar sit in his room when you came home every night?'

'Theresa, I'm very tired at the end of the day. I work really hard to keep you and Oscar in the lap of luxury, and I don't think a little peace and quiet is too much to ask in return, do you?'

'Oscar's *five*. He's too young to be shut in his room.'

'Five's old enough to understand discipline. Oscar needs to learn to consider others.' Martin's voice thinned. 'You overindulge him, Theresa. If you treat him like a baby, he'll act like one, and he'll turn into a mummy's boy. I'm not having anyone say that about my son. If you persist in this ridiculous charade of asking for a divorce, I will sue for custody of Oscar and bring him up myself.'

Impotent rage and frustration dropped over Tess so heavily her legs almost buckled. 'Do not you dare take him from me, Ralph,' she said stonily.

There was a silence. 'Ralph?' said Martin.

Aghast at the slip of the tongue, Tess clapped her free hand over her mouth. What had she done?

'Stay away from us, Martin,' she said, hoping to recover, but of course Martin wasn't going to let something like that go. 'Ralph?' he said again in a glacial voice. 'Who is Ralph?'

'No one,' she said desperately.

'*No one?* And how is this "no one" part of your life and the life of my son?'

'He isn't! He isn't anyone.'

'He's an imaginary person?' Martin's words dripped with disbelief and Tess struck the heel of her hand against her temple in frustration. What had she been thinking?

'It was just a mistake.' She drew a breath, tried to move on. 'Look, Martin, this isn't getting us anywhere. Oscar and I are happy here. You don't want to live with a small boy. You said yourself that you need peace and quiet. Please, just sign the divorce papers and let me go.'

'Let you go?' Martin echoed blankly. '*Let you go?*' A polite laugh, as if she had tried a feeble joke. 'No, Theresa,' he said pleasantly. 'You're my wife. The sooner you accept that you belong here with me, the better it'll be for you – and for Oscar.'

'What's this about you having food poisoning?'

Vanessa had rung that morning, suggesting that they take the children to the Museum Gardens. 'Let them run around somewhere different,' she had said breezily, sounding so much her old self that Tess almost wondered if she had imagined the tension between them the last time they had met.

'I've got a hidden motive, I have to confess,' Vanessa said.

'Oh?'

'I don't get a chance to run when the kids are on holidays. I wondered if you'd mind watching Sam and Rosie for me while I get some exercise. I won't go far, just along to the Millennium Bridge and back.'

Of course.' Tess had said, relieved to have restored her relationship with Vanessa. 'It's a brilliant idea.'

Getting out of the flat was just what she and Oscar had needed. Oscar had been whiny all morning, and Tess herself on edge all week. It had been raining on and off since the school holidays started, and trapped inside the flat in Stonegate, she and Oscar had grown increasingly fretful. It was too gloomy to be inside all day. The air was dark, damp and disquietingly taut. Luke had changed the locks, but Tess was still alert to the slightest sound, jumping at every noise from the street below in case it meant Martin was at the door, and whirling at shadows, terrified that Nell would drag her back and make her forget Oscar again.

Luke had finished the shelves, and Richard's books were stacked in order. Tess missed Luke's fierce presence more than she wanted to admit. He was busy on other jobs now, and although he had dropped round once or twice to see Oscar, who was always asking for him, Tess had been skittish, wanting him to stay, wanting him to go before she forgot how determined she was to stand on her own two feet. She wanted to be friends, but she wanted to be more than friends too, and the arguments for and against circled endlessly in her head until she was worn out and ready to decide that it was easier not to see him at all. She was still on edge, waiting for Martin, waiting for Nell, never knowing when either might appear. Casual friendship or passionate affair, it was crazy to even think about embarking on a relationship of any kind until things were resolved.

When she'd tried to explain that to Luke, he hadn't argued. He had just looked at her for an uncomfortably long moment before shrugging. 'If that's what you want,' he'd said. 'It's up to you, Tess. I'm not going to make you do anything you don't want to do. You've got my number. Call me if you need me.'

So then, of course, she couldn't call without sounding needy.

All in all, she had been glad when Vanessa had rung. After the last few dreary days, the sun had finally come out and the gardens were crowded with people sprawled on the grass or strolling along the paths, feeding the squirrels or playing Frisbee, or dutifully admiring the ruins of St Mary's Abbey. Surrounded, Tess let herself relax. There was safety in crowds, surely, from both Martin and Nell.

Once Vanessa had jogged off, Tess was happy to sit with her book, keeping an eye on Oscar as he chased pigeons with Sam and Rosie. She refereed the occasional dispute, but they were absorbed in some game, the rules of which she didn't try to understand, and in the end she was too lazy even to read and she leant back on her hands to watch the city expanding in the sunshine around her.

But now Vanessa was back, pink with exertion. She dropped onto the grass beside Tess and began doing a complicated series of stretches, bending low over her knee to hold first one ankle then another.

'Food poisoning?' Tess was caught unawares by Vanessa's question.

'Your mother said you'd been sick when you were out with Luke the other day.'

'I didn't realize you talked to Mum.'

Vanessa lay back and stretched one leg above her. 'Hard as it is to believe, Tess, we're both worried about you. Or have you forgotten that you passed out in my kitchen?'

'You didn't tell Mum about that, did you?'

'Of course I did. You'd want to know if Oscar had passed out, wouldn't you?'

What else had Vanessa told her mother? If her mother knew about Nell... Tess felt sick. It would be just the incentive her mother needed to call Martin. But if Vanessa had carried through her threat to contact him herself, surely she would have said something? And Martin would have been here already.

'I just had a bad piece of fish or something. I was vilely sick.'

'What were you doing with Luke anyway?' Vanessa had her leg up by her ear now. Tess couldn't imagine ever being that flexible. She hunched a shoulder, feeling clumsy and tense and defensive, just as she had at fifteen.

'We went to Lincoln,' she half-lied.

'*Lincoln?* What on earth for?'

'It's an interesting city. The cathedral's lovely. It was nice,' Tess added defiantly.

Up went the other leg. 'Your mum thinks Luke's a bad influence on you.'

'I know.'

Her mother had been frigidly disapproving when Tess eventually turned up with Luke on their way back from Lincoln the previous week-end. 'She never liked him.'

'Mothers usually know what's best for their children,' said Vanessa, then she held up her hands in mock surrender at Tess's glare. 'Just saying. I think it's a very bad idea for you to get involved with him again.'

Her words flicked on the raw indecision festering inside Tess. She didn't want Vanessa to tell her what to do about Luke.

She didn't want Vanessa to be right.

'I'm not *involved* with Luke, Vanessa,' she said tightly. 'As you pointed out the other day, I still haven't been able to extricate myself from my marriage and the last thing I want to think about right now is another relationship.' All true, so why did she feel so leaden? 'Luke and I are just friends.' She got to her feet to end the discussion. 'I'm going to get an ice cream. Would Sam and Rosie like one?'

'I don't usually encourage them,' Vanessa began, but the children had already seen Tess get up, and some sixth sense had them running over, clamouring for the treat. 'You can come and choose,' Tess said to them, laughing. 'Van, do you want one?'

'Oh, go on then, since you all are. No extra chocolate, though. It's unhealthy enough as it is.'

The children chattered as they queued at the van, and Tess smiled down at them, enjoying their delight in such a simple pleasure. She loved seeing Oscar animated like this. He would never have jumped up and down and tugged at her hand impatiently in London. Whatever it took, she would make sure he never went back to the timid child he had been.

She handed down the ice creams once each of them had made their agonizing choice, and Oscar ran off with Rosie and Sam. Tess followed more slowly, licking her own cone and enjoying the warmth of the sun on her back.

'Here you go.' She passed the ice cream down to Vanessa and then froze, still half stooped, as her eye snagged on the little boy standing in the shade of a tree behind. He had a cap tied over his fair hair and was wearing a linen smock and as she stared at him, he lifted his arms towards her.

Tess's heart stopped. 'Hugh,' she whispered.

'What? Who's Hugh?' Vanessa looked up and her expression changed as she looked over her shoulder to where Tess was staring. 'Tess, you're creeping me out. There's no one there.'

Tess didn't hear her. 'Hugh.' She sank to her knees, the ice cream falling unnoticed from her hand. 'Sweeting.'

'Hush now, sweeting,' Nell crooned, trying to keep her voice steady. Gently, she wiped a cloth over Hugh's face. He tossed restlessly in the bed as the fever burned him up. Sweat slicked his skin and plastered his hair to his head.

Her sweet boy was dying.

The sickness had sliced viciously through the city without warning. At least it's not the pestilence, folk told each other, but what difference did it make? Nell wondered bitterly. Hugh was still going to die.

He was only three.

One of the maids fell sick first, but she recovered, so when Hugh turned pale and listless, Nell told herself he would get better too. But he was not getting better. His small body, once so sturdy, was wasted and the fever shook him like a dog with a rat. He no longer even had the strength to cry, although he must have been hurting.

Nell cursed her own helplessness. All her skill in the still room counted for nought now. She had tried every remedy she could think of. Even prayer, though her heart surged with resentment against a God who could visit such suffering on a small child.

Ralph had a horror of sickness and hadn't been

near his son, although he was impressing the neighbours by the amount of time he spent on his knees in church. When he did come home, he was irritable. He took Hugh's sickness as a personal affront. He did not love the boy; he loved the idea of a son. And he objected to the way the child was consuming Nell's attention.

He took out his frustration on Meg, snapping and criticizing her, and when she dropped a jug, he erupted into a furious temper. Hearing him, Nell had to leave Hugh with the maid, Eliza, and hurry down to the hall. She got there just in time to see Ralph raise an arm to buffet a quailing Meg on the ear. 'Stop!'

Nell might have learnt to endure Ralph's fist, but to see her daughter suffer the same way... No, she would not have it. She squared up to him, pushing in front of Meg, her chin thrust forward and her eyes narrowed.

Ralph was furious. 'Stand aside, wife. Am I not allowed to discipline my own child?'

'Meg, go to the kitchen,' said Nell calmly. She would have sent her to be with Hugh, but she didn't want her to catch the sickness. She would face Ralph on her own.

Meg didn't need to be told twice. She slipped away and left Nell facing Ralph.

'So, wife, you think you can tell me what I must and must not do?'

'I will protect my children,' said Nell. 'Whatever it takes.'

She could see the savagery surging in his eyes, and spoke briskly before he could raise his hand to her.

'Your son lies sick upstairs,' she told him. 'You can beat me if you must, but it will have to wait. For now, I need to be with Hugh.'

'Go then,' he snarled.

'Do you leave Meg be,' she warned as she turned to go. She loved her children more than she was afraid of Ralph, and that made her stronger. 'She is nothing to do with you.'

'She is my daughter.'

'Then you treat her as such.'

Rage roiled in her belly as she climbed the stairs back to where Hugh lay in the grip of the sickness. She couldn't let herself be consumed by hatred of Ralph, not now. She needed all her energies for her son.

'How is he?' she asked Eliza, who shook her head.

'Oh, Mistress,' she said brokenly.

Nell's heart cracked but she set her jaw. She would not give up her boy to this sickness that was like a monster panting over the bed, its tongue lolling, its eyes red and glistening. She'd faced down Ralph at his worst; she would face down this.

'Hugh, little one, open your eyes for Mamma,' she urged, but he couldn't hear her. He just whimpered as he tossed his head from side to side.

Eliza was weeping. Nell took the cloth from her and wrung it out, then set to bathing Hugh's small body. His skin was afire with fever. She had to get him cool. It was all she could think of to do. The barber surgeon had been to cup him the day before, but Hugh screamed so desperately when the heated cups were placed on his chest that Nell had to cover her ears, and she told the surgeon not to come again. But perhaps she was wrong. What if only cupping could save him?

She had made a posset, mixing ale with lettuce, spinach and purslane, and a decoction of camomile, well sweetened with treacle. She had bathed him with the water of onions stewed in a close pot, and dripped sugar mixed with sweet almond oil into his mouth. She had strewn rose and rue on his pillow, lavender and sage on the floor. She had sent to the apothecary for a piece of unicorn's horn.

Mary had taken some hair from Hugh's head to the wise woman who lived on the common and gave her a whole shilling for a spell to ward off the sickness.

But none of it was working. None of it.

'There, there, my little heart,' Nell whispered, wringing out the cloth and starting again, refusing to see that he had stopped even whimpering now and that his breath was barely a thread. 'Mamma is here. Mamma will make you well.'

Her chest was so tight with fear she had to breathe in short, shallow gulps. The worst of nights with Ralph were not as bad as this. Not even being shut in the chest.

She thought of Hugh's wrinkled face when he was born. Her first thought was relief that she could tell Ralph that he had a son at last, but the moment they put him to her breast, her heart swelled, just as it had done when Meg was born, and she was lost in the wonder of him.

Hugh. Her little boykin. Her shining star.

'Please, Hugh,' she begged him. 'Please get better.'

But Hugh didn't get better. Nell's bones ached with the knowledge that he wasn't going to. She clung to every memory as if it would hold him to this world. Pressing her face to the back of his neck and breathing in the sweet baby smell of him. The dimples on his fat hands. The way he squealed with laughter when she tickled him.

When was the last time she had heard him laugh? Had it only been two days earlier?

When she accepted that Hugh would never laugh again, Nell dropped the cloth to the floor. She gathered the small, limp body into her arms and cradled him to her breast, and she sang to him, the lullabies he loved, and her heart splintered and ripped apart. The sound of it tearing was so loud in her ears that she didn't hear the moment when the last breath leaked out of him and was not drawn in again. But she felt the stillness in him, the absence of him.

She was still singing in a cracked voice, still rocking him, when Eliza touched her arm. 'Shall I fetch the minister, Mistress?' she asked, her eyes red with weeping.

Nell was closed up tight, her shutters sparred. She couldn't let herself feel.

'It is too late for a priest,' she said. Although she had been singing, her voice sounded rusty and unused, as if the words were coming out of another mouth altogether. 'He is dead.'

She should have known the moment he stopped breathing, Nell thought. The world should have cleaved open with grief. But outside the window the city was going about its business, uncaring. In the street below Christopher Willoughby was cursing a drayman whose cart had struck the edge of his stall. Two goodwives were having a raucous conversation outside the tailor's shop across the road. One of them was Marjorie Hodgson. Nell recognized her laugh. She honked like a goose.

And Hugh lay lifeless on her lap, his absence a dead weight in her arms.

Eliza buried her face in her apron. 'Oh, Mistress, he were such a sweet boy!'

Moving stiffly, Nell got to her feet and lay Hugh on the bed. She stroked the still damp hair from his forehead and kissed his little mouth one last time.

Then she went to tell her husband.

Chapter Sixteen

'Dead?' echoed Ralph. 'He cannot be dead.'

'I am sorry,' said Nell, stony faced, stony hearted. 'It is God's will.'

Ralph did not believe in God's will any more than she did, but he sat with her to watch over Hugh all night. Nell washed her son and wound him in a sheet with flowers and herbs from her garden, and then she laid him in the great hall, where she and Ralph sat side by side, dully watching the candle flames leaping and lurching until dawn.

Ralph's face was buckled with grief as he carried Hugh to church the next day in his arms. Nell and Meg walked behind, and they were followed by their servants and neighbours and the poor who had gathered at the door when they heard the bell tolling the night before, all carrying the sprigs of rosemary that a weeping Eliza had handed out.

Nell looked down at hers uncomprehendingly as the minister met them at the stile and led them over to the tiny grave. What was she doing, standing there with this rosemary in her hand? It was as if she had never seen rosemary before. Its narrow green leaves were faintly speckled with grey and the flowers had lost their blue bloom, but when she rubbed it between her fingers the familiar scent filled her nose and mingled with the smell of the earth that lay in a pitiful pile by the grave.

The toll of the bell thudded in Nell's head as the sun poured mockingly down around them. Ralph was sobbing, and beside her, Meg stood with tears running unheeded down her face, as the minister intoned the words Nell supposed were meant to comfort. 'Earth to earth, ashes to ashes, dust to dust,' he declared. 'In sure and certain hope of resurrection to eternal life.' They made no sense to Nell. She cared nothing for ashes or dust, nothing for eternal life. She cared only that Hugh was not there to tug at her skirts and beg to be lifted up in her arms and swung round and round and round until he was giddy with laughter.

But when the minister nodded gravely at her, she stepped forward obediently. She looked down into the grave and saw the crumpled sheet. That could not be Hugh down there.

'The rosemary, Mamma.' Meg leant closer and Nell nodded slowly. She lifted the sprig to her nose one last time and then she dropped it into the grave on top of her dead son and turned away.

Afterwards, they served wine boiled with sugar and cinnamon for the mourners. Nell didn't drink hers. Her throat was too tight to swallow and she was still holding her cup when everyone else had gone and she was left alone with Ralph. His grief had taken her by surprise. She hadn't known that he cared so much for his son.

'I am sorry for your grief, husband,' she said, wondering if it was possible that they could at least share this, but Ralph's ravaged expression held no warmth as he turned on her.

'Sorry? And so you should be! This is your fault, wife,' he snarled at her. God had punished her by taking his son, he told Nell. If she had been a better wife, a better mother, Hugh would not have died.

So Ralph said and Nell did not even try to turn her face away as he lifted his arm. The back of his hand smacked into her cheek and the blow lifted her off her feet. It was as if she were outside herself, watching as she fell in slow motion, and when her head struck the floor she welcomed the darkness that rushed to meet her like an old friend.

'Mummy! Mummy!' There was an insistent tugging, a voice wobbling with fear. 'Wake up, Mummy!'

'Oscar, leave Mummy a moment.' Another voice, brisk and capable. 'This man's like a doctor. He's going to have a look at her. Let him have some room.'

'No!' A small body threw himself across her with a wail, and she coughed at the impact.

'Oh, thank God! She's coming round.'

'Mummy!'

She opened her eyes to see a small boy staring at her, his face crumpled with the effort of not crying. When he saw that she was awake, he latched his arms around her neck and buried his head against her chest.

This wasn't Hugh. For one awful moment, Tess wanted to push the boy away, but even as she stiffened, her memory slotted back into place with jarring impact.

'Oh, God, *Oscar...*' Her arms went round him and she held him tightly even as grief for Hugh still choked her.

'Come along, Oscar.' Vanessa moved forward, taking charge. 'You can see Mummy's all right now. Let this nice man have a look at her.'

For the first time Tess became aware that she was lying on the grass and that there were people gathered around, all staring at her curiously. With difficulty, she struggled up, Oscar still clamped onto her, and put one hand to her head.

'What happened?'

'You collapsed again.' Vanessa wrenched Oscar off her at last. 'Fortunately, someone said they'd seen a paramedic pushing his bike past, so they rushed after him, and Nick here came back to have a look at you.'

Nick, dressed in cycling shorts and a neon yellow top, smiled encouragingly. 'I'm with the Cycle Response Unit,' he said. 'I'm glad to see you're awake. Why don't I give you a quick check over since I'm here?'

'I'm all right now,' said Tess, but it seemed easier to let him take her pulse and check her pupils while Vanessa shooed the onlookers away and made Rosie hold Oscar's hand.

Over Nick's shoulder, Tess saw her son press his lips together in a fierce line to stop them wobbling, and her heart cracked all over again.

'It's all right,' she mouthed at him.

Nick sat back on his heels. 'Well, all seems to be normal. How long is it since you last ate?'

'I had some fruit for breakfast.'

'And last night?'

She hadn't been hungry the night before. 'I had a yoghurt, I think.'

'Hmm, well, maybe your blood sugars are low. That ice cream would have been a good idea,' he said, looking down to where the cone lay forlornly in a puddle of melted ice cream.

There was no point in telling him that it was the sight of Hugh that had made her collapse. Tess smiled weakly. 'I'll go and eat something,' she promised. She wanted them all to go away. Her head was pounding. She wanted to be alone so that she could cry her heart out for Hugh, her dearest boykin. She felt wretched, speared by grief, and ripped between Hugh and Oscar, who was already running around with Sam, his panic at the sight of his mother collapsed on the grass forgotten.

'Thanks,' she said to Nick, who was getting to his feet. 'I'm fine now. I'm sorry to have troubled you.'

'No trouble,' he said. He eyed her critically.

'Are you sure you feel okay? You look very pale.'
'Really,' she said. 'I just need to sit quietly for a bit.'
'Well, take it easy,' he advised.
'Who's Hugh?' Vanessa asked when he had gone.
Tess drew up her knees and rested her head on them. 'It doesn't matter.'
'This is your "ghost" again, isn't it?'
'I saw him,' said Tess into her knees, muffled. 'He was there.'
'*Who* was?' Vanessa's voice held an edge of impatience.
'Hugh,' said Tess. 'My son.'
A long silence. Tess kept her face hidden but she could practically hear Vanessa marshalling her arguments. She was already regretting saying anything. Vanessa wouldn't believe her. Suddenly, fiercely, she wanted Luke. He would understand. He would make Vanessa go away, say something to keep her quiet. He would hold Tess and he wouldn't try to persuade her that she was imagining things and she wouldn't feel so alone, so afraid.
Her hands were agony, on fire, but she welcomed the pain. It helped her focus and distracted her from thoughts of Hugh.
'Tess, this has gone on long enough.' Vanessa was carefully kind, carefully patient. 'I really think it's time you saw a doctor. Whatever you saw just now, it wasn't a ghost. Maybe there was a little boy there, but he ran off when you stared at him like that. I don't blame him! I was totally freaked out.'
There was no point in arguing with her. 'Yes,

that must have been it,' said Tess dully.

'I know, why don't you and Oscar come back with me and the kids, and I'll make us all some lunch? Nick said you needed to eat something. Then you can make an appointment with your GP. I'll drop you off if you like, and take the kids swimming – or maybe you'd like your mum to go with you?'

'I don't need to see a doctor, Vanessa. Please don't mention this to Mum.'

'Tess, you must see that we're concerned!' Vanessa shook her head worriedly. 'I hate to see you like this.'

Tess lifted her head. 'Like what?'

'You know like what. Passing out, claiming to have babies who don't exist, little boys nobody else can see...' She laid a soothing hand on Tess's shoulder. 'I just think the strain of moving into that flat on your own has got too much for you. There's no shame in admitting you need some help.'

'I'm not having a breakdown!' Tess shook off Vanessa's hand angrily and Vanessa clicked her tongue.

'You're not yourself, Tess. You must see that.'

Rubbing her temples, Tess made herself take a steadying breath. 'I know how it looks, Van, but I promise you, going to see a doctor isn't going to help.'

'But you can't just ignore these episodes!' Vanessa protested.

'I'm not ignoring them.' Oh, God, why hadn't she kept her mouth shut? She should never have told Vanessa about the baby that day, but her misery had been so overwhelming that she hadn't been thinking clearly. And now, with Hugh dying ... grief struck her anew, a blow to the heart that would have had her buckling if she hadn't been sitting down. She wanted to lie down, to curl on the grass and howl and howl.

Nell hadn't been able to do that. Nell had had to carry, and she would too. The thought made Tess straighten. With an effort, she pushed her hair back from her face and forced herself to concentrate. Vanessa would keep badgering her, on and on, unless she said that she was doing something. 'As it happens, I've been to see a therapist, but I'd rather you didn't tell Mum that.'

Vanessa was instantly suspicious. 'What kind of therapist?'

'One who specializes in regression.' She didn't want to lie outright. 'That's what I was doing when I went to Lincoln with Luke.'

'I might have known Luke would be involved!' said Vanessa in disgust. 'Trust him to take you off to some quack. How do you know this guy isn't a charlatan?'

'I liked him,' said Tess defiantly. She began to struggle to her feet, anxious to put an end to the conversation, and Vanessa leapt up in one lithe movement to help her. 'It's sweet of you to worry, but there's no need.' She removed her arm from Vanessa's firm grip. 'Honestly.'

Vanessa was still looking worried. 'I don't like it,' she said with a sigh, 'but you've always been stubborn.' It was news to Tess for whom Vanessa had always had a far stronger will. 'I know there's no point in arguing once you've got an idea in your head.'

She started to gather up the children's discarded jackets. 'Come and have some lunch anyway.'

Tess couldn't wait to get away. Vanessa's concern was smothering and she was finding it hard to breathe. 'It's kind of you, but I think I just need to lie down for a bit.'

Vanessa looked at her narrowly, noting her pale face and the shadows under her eyes. 'Tell you what,' she said. 'I'll take Oscar back with me. I can bring him home later and check that you're all right at the same time. I've got the new key you gave me.'

Tess looked around for Oscar. Instinct told her that she should keep him with her, but he was racing around, his earlier fright forgotten, and having such a good time with Sam and Rosie that it seemed cruel to drag him back to the flat. Besides, there was a tight band of misery still behind her eyes, and her limbs were leaden with exhaustion. She needed to sleep, and she couldn't do that and watch Oscar at the same time. And perhaps it would keep Vanessa quiet for now. She didn't have the energy to argue any more.

'All right,' she said. 'Thanks. If you could keep an eye on Oscar this afternoon, I'd be really grateful. But don't bring him back. I'll come and get him. The walk will do me good.' She summoned a smile, aware that she was being less than gracious. Vanessa was only trying to help. 'You're a good friend, Vanessa. I don't know what I'd do without you.'

Vanessa patted the jackets over her arm complacently. 'That's one thing you'll never need to find out,' she said. 'You can rely on me, Tess.'

A vicious headache raked Tess's brain as she stood in St Helen's Square looking at the church. This was where she had worshipped. Where she had buried Hugh. She turned slowly, not seeing the shoppers or the tourists or the patient queue outside Betty's Tea Rooms. She blanked out the flower stall and the cycle racks, the buskers and the municipal planters, the shops and the bank. In their place was the churchyard, its stocks and its stile – and the pile of earth they were going to shovel over Hugh.

Grief clawed at her anew. She wanted to drop to the ground, to scrabble away at the paving, and her fingers stung as if she were frantically ripping up slabs, tearing through the earth with her hands to get to her boy. Was he still there, far below, or had he rotted with the rosemary and the winding sheet long ago?

Earth to earth. Tess could still hear the minister's sonorous voice.

Her vision blurred and her hands burned as she turned away to stumble up Stonegate and by the time she reached the door to Richard's building, she could barely see. She was fumbling to fit the key in the lock when a voice spoke behind her.

'Ah, so there you are, Theresa.'

The words sliced through her wooziness, through her grief and her pain, a cleaver falling sharp and true to the heart of her fear.

Martin.

The key dropped from Tess's nerveless fingers, and she span round, her heart thudding.

There he was: her good-looking husband, clean-shaven, expensively dressed in a blazer and open-necked white shirt. His fair hair was neatly brushed. His smile was charming.

'You look surprised to see me,' he said.

Tess's mouth was dry. 'What are you doing here?' she managed, hating the waver in her voice.

'I've come to take you home, of course.' Martin stepped closer, bent to pick up the key, and it was all Tess could do not to flinch. 'As soon as you rang, I knew it meant you were ready for me to come and get you.'

'No.' Tess retreated until her back was against the door. 'I'm not going back to London, Martin.'

'Darling, don't you think you're being a little childish? You know how important my work is and that I have to be in London. I can't possibly move to York.'

'I don't want you to.' Her heart rate had accelerated and her pulse was booming in her ears. 'I want a divorce. And I'd like my key, please.' She held out her hand, keeping it steady with an effort and, after a moment, Martin dropped the key into her palm.

'You're angry with me.' His face changed, puckered with concern. 'I don't understand, Theresa. What have I done?' A hangdog look under his lashes, a penitent smile. 'Is it because I left it so long to come and get you?'

'No.' Tess moistened her lips and her eyes flickered around her. The street was full of tourists, but none of them sensed that anything was wrong. She was trapped in a bubble, where there was just her and Martin smiling at her. Already she could feel his implacable will closing like a fist around her, squeezing her, crushing her. She forced herself to straighten, lift her chin. Nell flickered into her mind. She hadn't let Ralph break her spirit. Tess wouldn't succumb to Martin either.

'No,' she said again. 'I'm not playing games, Martin. I want you to go.'

'Darling, why are you being like this?' Martin looked genuinely puzzled. 'Perhaps I should have come before but I wanted you to miss me as much as I missed you. Oh, perhaps I wanted to punish you just a teeny bit for leaving me without a word, but I think we've both learnt a lesson, haven't we? And I'm here now. You've got what you wanted.'

'I didn't want you to come,' Tess said steadily. She had been afraid of this meeting for so long, but after the initial shock of seeing him, she was calmer than she had expected. 'I don't want to be married to you any more.'

'Theresa, this is crazy!' His face worked with distress before he got hold of himself. 'Look, why don't we talk about this inside? I can see you're pale. Aren't you feeling well?' He leant forward, all tender concern. 'Your mother says you've been under a strain.'

Thanks, Mum. Just what I needed.

He looked so contrite, so anxious to please. A model for a loving husband come to woo his wife again. Of course they should go inside and talk in privacy. Then Tess thought about her cutlery drawer. She thought about the lingerie laid out in neat rows.

'No,' she said. 'I don't want you inside.'

'Is it because I was short with you on the phone

the other day? Surely you knew that was only because I've been so upset? I don't think you understand how much you hurt me by walking out like that, Theresa,' he said plaintively. 'I was gutted. I could hardly eat or sleep. I've been a mess.'

In the past, Tess would have responded with automatic guilt but now she could look at him and think that he didn't look a mess. He looked fit and as fastidiously neat as ever, and a wave of tiredness engulfed Tess. Resisting Martin's will was exhausting. His presence sucked greedily at her energy until it she was too feeble not to give in, but she wasn't going to do that this time. She had to be stronger than him. She had to be strong like Nell.

'I don't want you in my home,' she said, pleased with how calm she sounded.

Something unpleasant stirred in Martin's eyes, and was quickly veiled. He heaved a long-suffering sigh. 'Then can we at least go and have a coffee or something? We can't discuss our marriage in the street.

'Please,' he begged when Tess hesitated. 'I know I've made mistakes, but all I want is for us to be together. A family again. I love you, Theresa. Please let's at least talk. You can tell me what the problem is, and we'll sort it all out, I promise.'

Oh, he could be so convincing when he tried! Even when she was on guard and determined to resist, Tess felt the tug of his words. To be a family again. To be loved. To talk. How could she refuse something so simple?

Surely it would be possible to have a rational

conversation now? She wanted to be civilized. She would make Martin understand that their marriage was over. She could reassure him that she didn't want anything from him. No alimony, no child support. It would be better than antagonizing him. And what could he do to her in a cafe? If the worst came to the worst, she could get up and walk away.

'All right,' she said. 'A coffee.'

There was a tea room on the first floor of the china shop opposite. It was popular and they had to queue on the stairs for five minutes before they were shown to a table by a window looking down on Stonegate. Martin didn't like to be kept waiting. His smile grew strained, and Tess could see the warning pulse throbbing in his neck. Her stomach tightened but she bit back the urge to apologize the way she would have done before. She didn't need to placate him, she reminded herself.

As soon as they had ordered, Tess pushed back her chair again. Instantly, Martin's hand shot out to clamp hers to the table.

'Where are you going?'

'To the loo,' she said evenly. 'I won't be long.'

'But we've just got here,' he protested, not letting go.

'And I've been out all morning. I'm not going anywhere, Martin. I've said I'll have a coffee with you and I will.'

Reluctantly, Martin released her hand. 'Hurry back,' he said with a smile that chilled her. 'I've missed you so much, I can't bear to be apart another minute.'

Tess felt his eyes on her back as she made her way to the cloakroom. Slumping back against the cubicle door, she fumbled for her phone.

Luke answered on the third ring. 'Tess.' He sounded brusque as always, but hearing his voice settled something inside her.

'I can't be long.' Quickly she told him about Martin.

He didn't waste time exclaiming. 'Do you want me to come along?'

She bit her lip. 'I don't know. I don't want to provoke him. I just want him to go away!'

'Look, have your coffee. He can't do anything to you in the middle of a cafe. I'll come over and wait outside your flat, so I'll be there if you need me.'

Tess felt better as she made her way back to the table. Martin was waiting for her with narrowed eyes but he relaxed when he saw her and he got to his feet to hold out her chair for her with an adoring smile. Tess saw two women on a neighbouring table look at Martin and exchange glances. It was obvious they thought he was an attractive man and were impressed by his chivalrous gesture.

'At last!' he said, reaching a hand across the table. 'Let me tell you how much I've missed you, my darling.'

Tess ignored his hand, kept her fingers linked in her lap to stop them trembling.

'Why are you being like this?' he demanded, hurt.

Seeing Tess return, the waitress brought over two coffees and smiled as she set them down. 'Can I get you anything else?'

Martin ignored her. His manners were for show and not to be wasted on mere waitresses.

'Thank you,' said Tess stiffly. 'We're fine.'

'Now,' said Martin, 'tell me what's the matter.'

Where could she begin? How could she possibly get through to him? Tess picked up her cup, holding it awkwardly between her throbbing fingers. Perhaps this had been a mistake.

'Theresa, I don't have a lot of time for this.' Martin sighed, carefully patient. 'I've got a number of important bids coming up and a government contract that has to be fulfilled ... but–' He held up his hand in a gesture of acknowledgement. 'I get it. I haven't been paying you enough attention. I'd have thought sitting down and talking would have been one option, but no, you had to make a big drama and run away as if I was some kind of monster!'

'I tried to talk to you about things,' Tess managed, setting her cup carefully in its saucer. 'You wouldn't listen.'

'I've been under a lot of pressure at work.' Martin again, his voice cool and calm. 'You know how demanding my job is, Theresa. When the government wants a contract fulfilled, I can hardly tell them to hold on, I need to go home and listen to my wife, who has nothing to do all day but spend the money I'm earning, can I?'

Temper boiled beneath Martin's surface, and it took all Tess had not to cower as she had done so often in the past. The next moment he slid a smile over it, a magician's hand smoothing over the turmoil so adroitly that she wondered if she had glimpsed it at all.

'But I'm here now,' he said with one of those lightning-quick changes of mood that had so often wrong-footed her in the past. 'And I've got something for you that will make it all better.'

A familiar, queasy sense of impotence gripped Tess as he pulled an envelope from his blazer pocket and pushed it across the table towards her.

'What is it?'

'Open it.'

'Martin–'

'Darling, *please*.' He smiled boyishly. 'It's for you – well, it's for *us*.' Leaning forward, he grasped her hands before she had a chance to pull them away. 'I know I haven't been as attentive as I should have been of late, but you know I adore you. I *need* you.' He tightened his grip as Tess made to tug her hands free. 'We were meant to be together – do you remember you said that on our honeymoon? You said nothing would ever keep us apart. Well, it won't. I won't let it.'

Tess felt sick. 'Martin,' she tried again, but he wouldn't let her finish.

'Open the envelope, darling,' he insisted.

She glanced around. The two women on the next table were eyeing her with open envy. Tess's stomach pitched nervously. She couldn't face the scene that Martin was more than capable of creating.

Reluctantly, she nodded, and he released her hands. She opened the envelope and drew out a piece of paper, bond, thick and classy. Unfolding it with a sinking heart, she scanned the type. It was an itinerary for a luxury trip to the Maldives. 'What's this?'

'A second honeymoon!' Martin laughed delightedly at her expression. 'Three weeks in a luxury resort. Our own villa. Just the two of us. Will that be enough attention for you?'

Tess raised her eyes from the paper to stare at him. His gaze was clear, bright, rinsed of understanding.

'What about Oscar?' she asked, numb with disbelief. It was all she could think of to say. Martin hadn't mentioned his son once.

He waved the issue of childcare aside. 'Your mother can look after him.'

He was serious, Tess thought in dawning horror. He really thought that she was playing games and holding out for him to spend money on her.

'Well?' Martin demanded, his face hardening at her lack of enthusiasm.

Tess dropped the itinerary on the table. Her hands ached savagely as she wrapped them around her coffee cup to raise it unsteadily to her lips while she tried to think of what she could say to convince him that she was never going anywhere with him ever again.

Nell raised the goblet to her lips and sipped the wine. It was well spiced and welcome on this cold spring day. Around her was the hum of women. The chamber was crowded with them and the air was stuffy and clogged with the scent of pomanders and wine and the faint milky smell of a new baby.

It was Cecily Fawcett's lying-in – her first. Cecily was nineteen, the same age Nell was when she had married Ralph. Her husband, George

Fawcett, was a draper nearly as wealthy as Ralph. His first wife had died a year since, and he had been quick to marry Cecily to be mother to his four children. Nell wondered what it was like for Cecily to be married to a man more than twenty years her senior. George was fat with a small pursed mouth and mean eyes, but Nell had to admit that Cecily didn't seem unhappy with her lot. She was sitting up in bed in a smock of the finest cambric, simpering at all the attention.

Well might she look pleased with herself. She had given birth to a fine baby boy, named for his father, who was being passed round the women, who held him up and clucked approvingly. Nell had had her turn. She had stroked little George's soft cheek with her finger and thought of Hugh, four years in his grave. He would have been seven by then. He would have been a sturdy, laughing boy.

Would Ralph have been kinder if his son had survived? Nell wondered that sometimes. Not that he had ever been an easy man, but since Hugh's death, the darkness in him had intensified. To their neighbours he was an important man, a godly man. They thought of him as sober and discreet. One day Ralph Maskewe would be Lord Mayor himself, they said, nodding knowledgeably. They didn't see the savagery in his eyes at times. They didn't feel the malevolence that shimmered in the air around him. They didn't sense the beast prowling beneath the surface.

But Nell did, and so did their daughter. Meg was eleven, a pretty child with Nell's coppery brown hair and blue eyes that reminded Nell heartbreakingly of Tom. She was afraid of her father.

Nell kept Meg out of Ralph's way as much as she could. There had been no more babes, or at least none that had lived. Two miscarriages, and a son stillborn. Each had torn at Nell's heart. Ralph blamed her for their deaths, and for the fact that Meg was the only child who had survived, and she a girl.

Ralph despised females, of that Nell was sure. And yet lately she had caught him looking at their daughter in a way that chilled her to the core. She didn't want to lose Meg, but she wondered if her daughter would be safer in service with another family.

But how could she be sure that Meg would be safe elsewhere? The face some folk showed to the world was not always the true one. Nell knew that better than anyone.

If Ralph touched Meg, she would kill him.

Nell had quite decided on that. She stood in her still room often now and thought about how it could be done. The surest way would be to hide ratsbane in Ralph's pottage if she could be sure no one else would eat it. She would hang, no doubt, but Meg would be safe. That would be enough.

Or perhaps she shouldn't wait. Perhaps she should kill him now? More and more often, Nell found herself considering the question quite seriously. She ought to have been horrified by how calmly she could contemplate a crime so heinous, but her sense of what was right had been beaten out of her by her years at Ralph's mercy. If anything happened to Nell, Meg would be powerless against her father. Ice spilled through Nell's veins at the thought. She could not risk it.

Ralph had to die.

But how?

Nell was prepared to die to save her daughter, but she would as soon not swing. Meg was only twelve. How could she trust anyone else to look after her?

Nell fretted at the problem as she sipped at her wine, only half-listening to the hum of conversation around her, until Margery Dixon leant forward beside her.

'What is this I hear of Mistress Clitherow?' she asked and her question dropped like a stone through the comfortable chatter of babies and servants and husbands.

There was a silence. The women looked at each other. Margaret Clitherow lived in the Shambles. It was not their neighbourhood, but they all knew of her now. She had reconciled to the old faith and she would not recant. She refused to go to divine service, no matter how many times they imprisoned her. She cared nothing for the law, it seemed. In the streets, they whispered that she concealed priests in her house, though none was ever found when it was searched. They found books and vestments and vessels used for Holy Mass, but of the priest there was no sign.

When Nell heard that, she thought about the closet in the Stonegate house, the one she had searched for that long-ago day. She wondered if it really existed, if it was ever used. Tom's mother had been a papist. Nell remembered that everybody knew, but nobody spoke of it. For the most part, folk kept their thoughts to themselves. It was wiser that way. Nell herself went to divine service with Ralph, but since Hugh's death, her faith had been a feeble thing, and just for show. She admired Margaret Clitherow for her bravery, for her refusal to do as she was bid, but she knew better than to say so to Ralph. Nell herself would not risk so much for the God that took her small son.

Jane Harrison spoke at last. 'They are saying she has refused to let her children be called to the court,' she said, and beside her Isabel Dickinson nodded.

'She will not make them give evidence against her.'

'I heard she was to be pressed,' another said and a hush fell on the room.

Pressed. Nell's hand went to her mouth. So it was true. Ralph had told her the same thing. His eyes had lit up when he described for her what would happen.

They would strip Mistress Clitherow naked. They would make her lie on a stone and they would place a door over her, and then they would put rock after rock on the door until her ribs cracked and her heart burst.

Nell's throat closed. She thought of how it was whenever Ralph had shut her in the chest, how the darkness and the horror had pressed down on her, how she couldn't breathe.

For Margaret it would be real. That weight would not be fear. She would be trapped under the door and even if she changed her mind, how would she be able to speak? She would not be able to move or speak or cry.

She would die for her faith.

They said there was a child in her womb. That would die too.

Nell was thinking about Margaret Clitherow as she walked back along Stonegate. She would put her child before her faith. She couldn't imagine choosing to die. Even in the darkest hours – her wedding night, Hugh's death – there had been a light inside her that refused to go out.

She was prepared to hang for Meg, yes. But to choose to be pressed ... Nell couldn't conceive of it. To know that her chest would heave uselessly against the dark, and the horror would crowd her head and suck the last breath from her lungs...

She would rather hang.

But even as she thought it, she shivered. A goose walking over her grave.

Or perhaps it was just the wind. It was a bright day, but it was only March and the breeze still nipped with the memory of winter. The air was sharp that day, slicing the street into blocks of sunshine and shadow.

The sun was in Nell's eyes as she stepped from the dimness of the passage into the yard, and she screwed them up against the dazzle. At first she couldn't see. She could only sense that there were two figures outside the door, figures who had turned to look at her, and she hesitated at the entrance of the passage, one hand shading her brow, waiting for her eyes to adjust.

'Ah, wife.' It was Ralph's voice, with an undercurrent that made Nell tense even as she squinted into the light. 'See who has come back to York to see us. Fresh off the boat.'

Blinking, Nell took a step forward, and then her

vision cleared like a sword falling and her heart stopped for a long moment before bounding into her throat. She clapped a hand there, afraid that it would burst out of her body and reach for the man standing next to Ralph by the door.

It was the last person she had expected to see.

It was Tom.

Chapter Seventeen

Nell's body reacted before her mind did. After all these years, still it was as if every part of her was dancing and twirling with joy at the sight of him. There was a ringing in her head, a buzzing in her ears. For one terrible moment she was afraid she might faint.

He was older, of course, and he had a trim beard, but it was unmistakably Tom. He was taller, tougher, and his mouth was hard now. He was burnt brown by the sun and there were lines at the corners of his eyes, but the blue, blue eyes were the same, alert and alive and able to reach right inside her and squeeze her heart.

It was *Tom*.

Nell's toes flexed; her heel lifted. The muscles in her thigh bunched. Instinct was about to send her running across the yard to him, but at the last moment before she launched herself forward, her eyes flickered to Ralph.

He was watching them both, his gaze flicking between them almost hungrily. He was enjoying this, she realized. He liked the idea that this meeting would be painful for her. He wanted her to lose control and give him an excuse to punish her in front of Tom.

So she lowered her heel and lifted her chin. She could do nothing about the fierce joy surging through her, but she disguised it behind a cool smile as she walked towards Tom to offer a kiss of welcome.

'Welcome home, Tom,' she said, amazed at the steadiness of her voice. For a fleeting moment, her eyes looked into his, but it was enough. The heat in his expression seared her, and when his mouth touched hers in the accustomed kiss, everything in her leapt and trembled and her heart soared.

'Nell,' was all he said, but nothing more was needed. He knew and she knew. It was the way it always had been between them.

Ralph was disappointed that she didn't appear more shaken, Nell could tell. His expression was peevish as he turned to Tom.

'You should have sent word that you were coming, brother. We would have had a more seemly welcome for you.'

'I hadn't planned to come,' said Tom. 'But I was in Hull and I got talking to the keelboat captain who said he was coming here on the tide, and I found myself thinking of you all. I jumped on before I had a chance to change my mind.' He smiled easily. 'I was ever one to look before I leap, as you know.'

'Indeed,' said Ralph with a thin smile. 'But why have you stayed away so long?' he asked, clapping Tom on the shoulder, although he must have known why. 'We have felt you had quite forgotten us.'

'Forgotten you?' Tom's gaze rested on Nell's face. 'Never.'

Nell was trembling inside with the reaction she could not afford to let Ralph see. She hid her hands in her skirts and forced a smile.

'Why are we standing outside in the cold? I am a poor hostess. You will be hungry if you have come straight from the staithe,' she said to Tom, as she would to a stranger. 'Husband, do you take your brother inside, and I will bring wine and cakes.'

The bones in her legs had turned to wool. It was all Nell could do to walk towards the kitchen as Ralph and Tom headed up the stairs, and when the door closed behind her, she slumped back against it, pressing her palms to her cheeks which were burning with reaction.

'Mistress?' Eliza looked up from the table where she was shredding a cabbage. 'What ails you?'

'Nought.' Nell straightened, took a breath. She must stay calm, she chided herself, but it was hard when her mind was topsy-turvy. Inside all was confusion apart from the one thought that shone steady and diamond bright: *Tom is here*.

She warmed the wine herself while Eliza set out cakes on a plate, and together they carried them up to the hall. The murmur of voices told them that Ralph and Tom were in the closet.

Perhaps it was warmer in the smaller room.

Or perhaps Ralph had chosen it deliberately because he knew how much Nell hated the closet. She couldn't step through the door without feeling her throat close. The chest was still there. It didn't look so big now, but to Nell there was something malevolent about the way it squatted there like a toad against the wall.

The two men were standing squarely in front of the fireplace. Both had their legs apart as if braced against the world, but there the resemblance between the brothers ended. Ralph toyed with the tasselled purse that hung from his belt. His fur-lined robe and velvet cap were expensive, but next to Tom, he looked grey and shrunken.

Tom needed no furs or fine cloths. His Venetians were narrow, his doublet plain, the buckles on his shoes unadorned, but he filled the room with his presence. It was as if he had brought in the wind, the salt-sting of the air, the restless surge of the sea that Nell had never seen.

He took the wine Nell offered and lifted the goblet to her and then, as an afterthought, Ralph. 'It is good to be home again,' he said.

As if sensing that standing next to Tom did him no favours, Ralph threw himself into the turned chair.

'So, brother, tell us what you have been doing with yourself since you abandoned your master. Sit, my dearest,' he added to Nell, who was still holding the jug of wine. 'I am sure you would like to hear what Tom has to say too.'

He wanted her to struggle to contain her feelings. He wanted her to be hurt. He wanted her to feel that Tom had abandoned her.

Nell smoothed her expression and sank onto a stool. If only Ralph had known that it would have been much harder for her to have left. Right now, it was enough to drink in the sight of Tom. She had not realized until this moment how much she had yearned for him over the years. She had not let herself wonder if he was alive or dead, but now he was there she was raw with longing for him.

What did Tom see when he looked at her? Was he shocked by how much she had changed since he left? Could he see anything of the loving, laughing girl she used to be? She had grown thinner, she knew. Her gown might be made of the finest scarlet, her kirtle might be satin and trimmed with velvet, her sleeves slashed to show her embroidered smock, but she had lost her bonny glow. Her eyes were guarded now, her body braced for the lift of Ralph's hand.

'I have sailed around the world with Captain Drake,' said Tom, as if it were no more than riding out to the white stone cross on Heworth Moor, but his eyes lit with an achingly familiar gleam at the memory of where he had been. 'Sir Francis, I should say,' he remembered. 'The Queen's Majesty dined aboard our plucky *Golden Hind*, and she knighted him. Little enough in return for the riches he brought her!'

'Drake? That upstart!' Ralph's mouth twisted into a sneer. 'They say he is little better than a pirate.'

'The Spaniards certainly think so,' said Tom. 'He is a man of great daring, that is for sure.'

'So you have been to the New World?' Nell said wistfully.

'I have been further than that, Nell. I have sailed through waves as tall as houses, and across an ocean so wide we thought there was no end to it. But then we came to the Spice Islands and we filled the ship with cloves.' His laughter bounced off the wainscot and warmed the room. 'I can smell them still! But we had to jettison most when we ran aground. We stood on the deck and poured sack after sack of them into the sea. Aye, it hurt but it had to be done. We would still be fixed on that reef else, but we trusted the Captain to bring us home safe, and so he did.'

'And how long do you plan on staying?' Ralph was regarding his brother with dislike.

'Well now, brother, that depends.'

'If you have come in the hope of money, I will have to disappoint you,' said Ralph. 'It was your choice not to finish your apprenticeship.'

'And I hate to disappoint *you*,' said Tom, 'but I have made my fortune with the Captain. There has been plunder aplenty.'

'I see.' It was obvious this was unwelcome news to Ralph.

'Perhaps I will buy a house in York,' Tom went on, Nell suspected deliberately to provoke her husband. 'I may settle down and establish myself as a fine gentleman.'

'But then,' said Ralph silkily, 'you would need a wife, would you not?'

There was the tiniest of pauses. Nell hurried to fill it.

'You would be bored before the week was out,' she said. 'You are used to the open seas now, Tom. I fear York would be too tame for you.'

'Sail across an ocean on a small ship and you soon learn a new meaning to bored,' said Tom.

'But if there is one thing I have learnt on my travels, it is that there is interest and excitement to be found everywhere.' His eyes rested on her face. 'Even in York.'

Ralph took his time with Nell that night, excited by the thought of Tom lying in the back chamber. He strapped her wrists to the bed post and he lashed at her with a switch until she bled. 'You are mine,' he grunted as he thrust into her at last. 'Mine.'

Nell just turned her face away. She could bear the pain. Tom was alive and Tom was there. For now, that was all that mattered.

'For God's sake, Theresa, what's wrong with you?'

Tess was jolted back to the present by Martin waving an irritable hand in front of her face. Her eyes snapped into focus, and she put down the cup with shaky hands.

'I'm sorry,' she said, moistening her lips. 'What were you saying?'

'What was I *saying?*' Martin echoed incredulously, looking injured as only he knew how. 'I'm doing my best to make amends here,' he said. 'I'm doing everything I can to save our marriage. I've arranged an extremely expensive second honeymoon which would have most women squealing with delight, but *you*, you can't even be bothered to pay attention!' His face crumpled. 'I'm disappointed in you, Theresa. I really am.'

Tess set her hands flat on the table. They burned and throbbed as if ripped raw. 'We're not having a honeymoon,' she said as calmly as she could. 'I've left you. I want a divorce.'

At that his expression changed, and his hand shot out to grab her wrist, and Tess couldn't help flinching. 'Is there someone else?' he demanded, low and cold. 'Is that it? Have you been fucking around? Who is it? Is it that Ralph you talked about on the phone?'

She jerked back at the name in spite of herself, and Martin's grip tightened. 'It is, isn't it?'

'No.' Tess had a wild desire to laugh. If only Martin knew!

'Then who?'

She ran her tongue over dry lips. 'There's no one.'

'In sickness and in health, Theresa, that's what you promised. For better, for worse. Remember? *I* am your husband. Remember *that?*'

'There's no one,' she said again.

'You wouldn't lie to me, would you, Theresa?'

Her wrist was hurting, but she wouldn't give him the satisfaction of trying to pull her hand free. Her mind flickered to Luke, and then away. 'I'm not lying.'

'Good.' A final cruel squeeze of her wrist and he sat back, satisfied, smiling, once more an ordinary husband having tea with his ordinary wife. 'Then the sooner we get back to normal, the better, hmm? We'll go and get your things right away.'

A headache was jabbing behind Tess's eyes. How was she going to get out of this? The conversation was taking on a nightmarish quality. 'I need to go and get Oscar, Martin,' she temporized. 'He's with Vanessa.'

'Your friend in the flash four-wheel drive?' he said knowledgeably and she stiffened.

'You *have* been watching me!'

'Darling, of course I have. At least, I've had someone watch you for me. You should have expected that,' he said, raising his brows at her expression. 'You're my *wife*. I needed to know no one was taking advantage of you, like that sweaty joiner who's always going in and out.' His eyes sharpened. 'That's not Ralph, is it?'

She had to be very careful. 'No. His name's Luke, and he's been building some shelves for the owner of the flat.'

'Yes, that was my information too,' Martin acknowledged as if disappointed not to have caught her out. 'At least I could sleep easier knowing that you were safe,' he said, and Tess felt the welcome anger seeping back.

'I haven't felt safe, Martin. I've been frightened. You've been breaking into my flat, messing with my things.'

He pouted. 'I just wanted you to know that I was there for you. You've been so stubborn, changing your phone, not answering my calls...' His face darkened. 'What was I supposed to do?'

'You were supposed to leave me alone.' Wearily, Tess rubbed at her temples, and he leant forward in concern.

'Darling, aren't you feeling well?'

'I've just got a headache.'

'I hope that's all it is.' Martin looked sombre. 'I hope you're mother's not right.'

'My mother?' Tess jerked back. 'What's she been saying?'

'Now, now, there's no need to be so touchy. She implied that you were under a lot of strain, and I can see that for myself. For a few moments just now, I watched you tune out. It was as if you weren't here.' He shook his head, his brow creased in concern. 'No wonder she's worried about you. She says you've been getting involved in a lot of hocus-pocus and she's afraid you're having some kind of nervous breakdown. I told her you were just being a bit naughty, but now I'm beginning to wonder if she was right all along.'

Tess's head whirled in panic. What did her mother know? What had she been telling Martin? She held onto the table to keep herself calm. 'I'm not having a breakdown,' she said clearly.

'I know you believe that, darling, but you've got to admit that you're behaving irrationally. You're losing the train of the conversation, you're spacing out... I've spoken to the builders doing up the bar next door to you, and they say you're always in there complaining about noises that no one else can hear. I don't want to accept it either, darling, but I'm glad I didn't wait any longer to come. You can't look after yourself when you're like this, let alone the boy.'

The boy. He couldn't have said anything better designed to clear Tess's head and give her strength. She wasn't going to put up with Martin's manipulation and bullying any more. 'The boy's name is Oscar,' she said very distinctly, 'and I can look after him fine.' She pushed back her chair and looked him straight in the eye. 'We're finished here, Martin. I want you to leave me, and Oscar, alone. My solicitor will be in touch with yours about a divorce.'

She had never stood up to him before. Never turned her back on him or walked out, and she didn't look back. Martin would have to find some money to throw on the table and it gave her a head start. A mixture of adrenalin, fury and frustration took her almost back to her flat before Martin caught up with her.

She had known he would but she didn't care. The boy. *The boy!* He didn't even care enough to call his own son by his name.

So when Martin grabbed her arm and swung her round to face him in the middle of Stonegate, she didn't even flinch.

'Let me go!'

Martin was so taken aback by the blaze of anger in her eyes that he dropped his hand. 'Theresa!' he said in astonishment.

'Tess,' she said clearly. 'My name is Tess.'

'What's happened to you?' Bewildered, he took a step back. 'You never used to be this hard. You're treating me as if I'm some kind of monster. All I want is my family back. Is that so wrong?'

She nearly relented. 'No, it's not wrong, but it's not going to happen, Martin. It's over. I don't want to be married to you any more. Please accept that. It's *over*.'

'No.' Martin pulled her back as she made to turn away. 'No, you can't do this to me, Theresa,' he said, very white about the mouth.

'Yes, I can.'

'I said *no!*' Careless of the curious looks they were starting to attract, he dragged her closer, his fingers digging viciously into her flesh. 'You can't walk away from me. I won't let you!'

Tess winced and tried to pull her arm away. 'Leave me alone, Martin!'

'Is there a problem here?'

Luke's easy voice broke in and Tess turned to him, dizzy with relief as the world miraculously steadied.

'Oh, Luke, thank God!'

'Who the fuck are you?' snarled Martin.

'I'm a friend of Tess's,' said Luke calmly. 'Let her go. You're hurting her.'

'Fuck off,' Martin said precisely. 'This is between me and my wife.'

'Tess, do you want me to fuck off, or do you want me to stay with you?'

'I want you to stay,' she whispered, dry-mouthed, and then sucked in a breath as Martin's grip tightened furiously.

'Then I will,' said Luke. He stepped up to Martin, until they were almost nose to nose.

'Let. Her. Go.' He spoke very quietly. He wasn't as tall as Martin, or as broad. Martin was proud of his physique, and liked to hint at his military training, while Luke was casual in his jeans and leather jacket, but there was something in his eyes that made Martin loosen his grip on Tess's arm.

Tess wrenched it free and scuttled gratefully behind Luke. 'Now *you* fuck off,' said Luke. 'Since we're keeping the tenor of the conversation so high.'

White-faced, Martin stared at him for a moment until something inside him collapsed, a balloon bursting, in the face of defeat. All at once he seemed smaller, pathetic, and when he peered round Luke to plead directly with Tess, his expression was beaten. 'Theresa,' he said brokenly. 'You can't mean this. You're my *wife*.'

'I do mean it,' said Tess, still braced for a backlash. She knew how quickly Martin's moods could change, but she had never seen him look like that before. 'I don't want to see you again.'

'*Theresa...*' His voice actually cracked.

Gathering her courage, she stepped out from behind Luke. 'I'm sorry, Martin,' she said. 'It's over.'

'But you *need* me!'

'No,' she said, and felt herself swell with the knowledge that it was true. 'No, I don't. I'm sorry,' she said again, 'but I'm not coming back.'

She was ready for him to lash out, to snap into a rage, but he surprised her. 'All right,' he said, shaking his head as if he wasn't quite sure what was happening. 'All right. I see.' His eyes flickered to Luke and he stepped back. 'Well, if that's how it is...'

In disbelief, Tess watched him turn and walk away, and the calmness and adrenalin that had kept her strong evaporated in a rush of reaction.

'Oh God... Oh God, Luke...' Without thinking, she turned and buried her face in his chest. She latched her hands around his waist and held on for dear life while the panic and fear she had been battling eddied around her.

'Hey.' Luke pulled her close, wrapped his arms about her. It was amazingly comforting. 'You're okay.'

How long had it been since she had felt as safe? Tess wanted to stay pressed tightly against him forever. Her racing heart slowed, and she let herself notice the smell of his freshly-washed T-shirt, of worn leather, of clean, male skin.

She fit so naturally into his solid body. If she lifted her face just a little, she would be able to press it against his throat. Tess thought about what that would feel like, and something shifted in her chest. The searing pain had vanished from her fingers and they itched instead with the temptation to sneak beneath his T-shirt and spread over his warm, smooth back.

What was she thinking? She caught herself up guiltily and made herself pull back out of his arms. She should be thinking about Martin, about Oscar, not how good it would feel to touch Luke again.

'Thanks,' she said with a smile that wavered just a little. 'Sorry about the hug. I couldn't help myself.'

'Any time,' said Luke lightly. He looked at her searchingly. 'All right now?'

She wasn't, not really, but she nodded and concentrated on letting them into the flat. 'I'm glad you were there,' she said as she double locked the door behind them. She told him what Martin had said, about the second honeymoon.

Luke prowled the front room, his fierce face even fiercer than usual. 'I don't like the sound of this. I think it's time you went to the police.'

Tess hesitated. 'Martin looked so ... defeated ... when he left. Maybe there's no need to go to the police now. Maybe it just needed you to stand up to him,' she said hopefully.

'Do you really believe that or do you just want to believe it?'

She rubbed her arm where her husband had dug his fingers into her flesh. Martin's moods were mercurial. He might be hurt and humiliated now, but she knew from bitter experience that he could change without warning. It was wishful thinking to imagine that he had given up completely.

She wasn't safe yet. 'I'd like to believe it, but no... I think he'll try again. He might go back to London and regroup, but he won't give up. I'm afraid he'll remember what he said about me having a nervous breakdown,' she said, still rubbing her arms, hugging them together to keep at bay the panic that threatened anew. 'I think he might try to get me sectioned and take Oscar from me.'

It was her worst fear.

'Martin's a bully,' said Luke. 'He can't get you sectioned just like that.'

'But what if he goes back to the builders, or finds out about Ambrose?'

'He's got no proof.' Luke cut across her voice as it started to rise, his own so level that the uncoiling panic began to subside. 'While you, on the other hand, have bruises on your arm and me as a witness that he held you against your will. I'm serious about this, Tess,' he said. 'I don't think you should trust Martin. He might seem crushed, but a guy like that is going to be humiliated, and it won't be long before he starts blaming you for it. You need to tell the police that he's threatened you, and see how you go about getting a restraining order.'

Tess nodded reluctantly. 'What about Oscar?'

'Where is he now?'

'With Vanessa. He'll be safe with her.' Martin had looked so pathetic as he walked away, Tess wished that she could believe he would accept that she had left, but she knew Luke was right. She didn't want to take Oscar to a police station to report his own father. 'I'll ring and ask her to keep him a bit longer. Let's go to the police now,' she said and it was only afterwards that she realized how she had taken it for granted that Luke would go with her.

The police station was out of town, on Fulford Road. Luke walked Tess to the car he'd managed to park behind the Minster – 'Contacts,' he said when Tess asked – and she rang Vanessa on her mobile as they ran into the usual queue on the inner ring road. She didn't want to talk about Martin. She told her she needed to report an incident she'd witnessed.

'I'm running out of battery, Vanessa,' she said when Vanessa wanted to know what had happened. 'I'm not sure how long it will take. Would you mind keeping Oscar until we come and pick him up?'

The police were wearily efficient. Luke said he'd wait outside and Tess found herself being interviewed by a female officer in a small windowless room. The furnishings were spartan, and the neon light flickered in her eyes while the nagging headache grew to monstrous proportions. The officer listened patiently enough, but Tess found herself stumbling and getting lost in the middle of sentences. Her palms were sweating and she was feeling guilty just sitting there. She wished she'd asked if Luke could sit in with her, and then felt guilty about *that* too.

It was hard trying to explain how much Martin had scared her. *My cutlery drawer was rearranged. The cat flap was closed. I suddenly acquired a lot of fancy underwear.* It didn't sound menacing when she put it into words.

The policewoman wore a badge with her name on it: Karen Davies. Her expression was carefully neutral but it flickered when Tess plunged into a stumbling account of how careful she had always been to keep the cat flap unlocked. Helplessly, she watched Karen make a note on the pad in front of her. Probably 'hysterical' or 'neurotic'.

Just the way Martin would want her to seem.

Closing her eyes, Tess took a steadying breath. She had to be careful.

She had to be careful. Nell longed to talk to Tom on his own, but marriage to Ralph had taught her patience. Ralph was waiting for her to betray herself. He was looking forward to punishing her for it. Nell could see the anticipation in his pebbly eyes; she saw him running his tongue over his lips with relish at the prospect.

She had to be very careful. And patient.

Ralph had insisted Tom stay for as long as he liked. He had calculated it would be more painful for Nell that way. He bedded his wife every night. Knowing that she would be thinking of Tom, so close but unable to help her, made it all the more exciting for him.

Besides, it enabled him to keep eye on Tom, whom he trusted not a scrap.

But business was business, and Nell knew that sooner or later Ralph would have to abandon his watch.

So she kept her eyes downcast and played the perfect wife while she waited. And sure enough, Ralph swaggered into the hall one morning in his best furred gown. His beard was newly trimmed and his ruff stood up proud around his chin.

While he drank his ale, his eyes stabbed around the room, looking for something to criticize, for a reason to hit her harder that night, but Nell kept house as profitably as any woman could. The cupboards were garnished with silver plate that gleamed in the meagre spring sunshine. The tapestries were beaten regularly, the floor swept every day. There was no dust on the overmantel and Nell made Eliza stand on a chair to clean the elaborate leaves and pendants that decorated the new plaster ceiling Ralph had had made. A spotless damask cloth covered the table where they were breaking their fast. Nell had soon learnt that her housekeeping must be beyond reproach.

Thwarted, Ralph lowered his ale and wiped his mouth with the back of his hand. 'I am called to a council meeting this morning,' he said importantly. 'What will you do, brother? Do you grow tired of us yet?'

'No,' said Tom, who was lounging at the end of the table. He wore no ruff, and his shirt beneath the battered leather jerkin was open at his throat. 'I am of a mind to revisit old haunts,' he said. 'I thought to see if the Foss flows as sluggishly as ever.'

He smiled lazily at Ralph, but Nell knew that

he was thinking of the first time they lay together. He didn't need to say anything. He didn't even need to look at her, but she knew, and her blood quickened and her face grew warm.

Ralph put on his velvet hat and adjusted it in the looking glass that hung on the wall. 'You should go with him, my dear,' he said to Nell, smoothing down the fur trimming on his gown. 'You two must have so many memories to share.' His back was to her, but Nell was not such a fool as to believe that he wasn't watching her in the glass.

'I fear Tom must do without me,' she said, her smile cool, perfectly judged. 'My stepmother is unwell. I must visit her and take some broth I have made. I am sure Tom can find his way without me.'

But when she looked at Tom, her eyes carried a different message. They said: *I will meet you there. Wait for me.*

And Tom understood. He was there, in their secret place, moodily throwing sticks into the river, when she pushed her way through the bushes later that morning. It was a fine day, with thin sunshine and air that smelt of damp earth and the promise of spring. There were tiny, tight buds on the hawthorns and green shoots poking tentatively out of the ground, but it was cool still and Nell had been glad of her cloak as she walked briskly along Monkgate with the basket that was her excuse should anyone wonder where she was going. There was always something to be gathered along the riverbank, even this early in the year.

Tom leapt to his feet when he saw her, and there was an odd moment when the world seemed to pause before Nell dropped her basket and they walked slowly, wordlessly, towards each other. The years they had been apart gathered behind them and pushed them together, like pieces of a lock sliding into place. The space between them narrowed until Nell closed the last tiny gap and leant into him and the distance, the absence, the missing him was over at last.

Tom's arms folded around her and she pressed her face into his neck with a shuddering breath.

'I'm sorry, I'm sorry,' Tom kept saying against her cap. 'I should have come back. I should have known what it would be like for you.'

'What could you do?' said Nell, clinging to him, caring only that he was there and she could hold him again. Their bodies remembered each other as if the years had dissolved, as if they had been made to fit together, from top to toe. 'You were a boy, and they sent you away. I thought you must have hated me when you heard.'

'Never,' said Tom vehemently and his arms tightened around her. 'I knew you would not have agreed unless you had been forced. I should have come back as I thought of doing to take you away, married or not.'

'I would have had to refuse. Ralph held that debt over my father until the day he died, and though it matters not so much now, I am no freer. My stepmother and my brothers are still alive, and now there is Meg,' she said simply. 'I have my daughter. It is enough.'

Tom held her away from him to look into her

face, the vivid blue eyes serious. 'He is my brother. I did not know what he was. I thought – I hoped – that he would be good to you, but when I came back... I have seen the way he looks at you. I have seen the way Meg cringes when he is near.' He shook his head, distressed. 'He sits and he watches like a cat toying with a mouse. If I had known it was like that for you, Nell, I would have come back for you, I swear it.'

'I know you would, Tom,' she said. She couldn't speak now of the long, lonely years when all hope of seeing him again had gone. 'Do not lash yourself with guilt. Life is as it is.' Digging in her purse, she drew out the garnet ring she had kept there since her marriage. 'See, I have this still. I dared not wear it, but whenever I touched it, I was true to you in my heart. This I promise you.'

'Ah, Nell, I have missed you so!' Heedless of the dampness of the grass, Tom drew her down, down into the delight of his warm touch. 'I could sail the world a thousand times and never find a woman who makes me feel the way you do.'

'Is it really so for you too?' she asked, breathless with pleasure already. She knew it was true, but she wanted to hear him say it. His words were balm on the tiny scars that crisscrossed her skin.

'When I saw you again, it was like sailing into home port,' said Tom, his hand searching for a way under her skirts, his palm burning through her stockings. 'I won't deny I fell into a railing frenzy when I first had word that you had married Ralph,' he said. 'That's why I ran away. I couldn't come home. I couldn't bear the thought of York without you ... but you came with me anyway,' he said, bending over to press his mouth to the side of her neck so that she shivered and her mind went dark with longing.

'I'd stand on the quayside and watch the spices being loaded onto the ship, and I'd remember how we dreamt of that as we lay here. I'd think how your eyes would shine if you could have been standing in the prow with me, feeling the wind in our faces; how good it would have felt if I had been able to hold you against me. You were a ghost always at my shoulder, Nell,' Tom told her, his voice so deep and so low and so close to her skin that it reverberated right through her. 'Sometimes, I'd sense you so strongly that I'd turn quickly, sure that I would catch you, but I never did.'

He smiled sadly. 'I tried to close my mind to the thought of you and Ralph. I couldn't stand to think of it. I was going to sign on for another voyage to the New World, and this time I told myself I might stay, but I couldn't go without seeing you one last time. When I found myself in London those few weeks ago, I knew that I couldn't stay away any longer. I had to see you.'

He lifted his head to look down into her eyes. 'I swear to you, Nell, if I had known that there would be this malice between you and Ralph, I would have come home sooner to take you away.'

'You are here now,' she said, closing her mind to her marriage. 'That is all that matters.'

The past unravelled as Tom drew her to him. He unwound it as he unwound her defences, his fingers busy beneath her shift, tracing tingling patterns of desire behind her knee, on the soft skin inside her thigh, while his mouth was hot on her breast. He loosened her bodice and she tugged at his shirt, frantic to feel him hard and hot against her.

Shameless, some would say, but for Nell there was no shame in it. Shame was in lying supine beneath her husband; shame was letting him beat and degrade her and not fighting back.

This was not shameful. She was gift and giver, a shrivelled flower opening and blooming gloriously beneath Tom's touch. Every hurt, every small shame that Ralph had inflicted on her evaporated in the heat that still burned between her and Tom. None of it mattered now. Nothing mattered but the race of her blood under her skin, the pounding of her heart and the need that drove them both to go further, harder, higher, more and more and more until the last memory was blotted out with the knowledge that this, *this* is how it should be between a man and a woman.

Afterwards, Nell let out a long, shuddering breath. 'Well,' she said shakily.

'Well,' Tom agreed, his own breathing ragged, and they both laughed softly.

Together they straightened their clothing as best they could. Deftly, Tom disentangled the laces of her bodice. He had ever been good with knots, Nell remembered, leaning back in the grass and watching the way his lashes lay against his cheek, her mouth curved with pleasure still.

'What now, Nell?' he said, looking up, and her smile faded. She sat up, hugging her knees.

'Now I look to my daughter. Tom, I am worried about her. Ralph ... there is a wrongness in him, a darkness that needs another to be in pain before he can be satisfied.'

His fingers stilled at her bodice. 'In pain?' he echoed blankly. It was clear that the idea anyone might take pleasure in pain had never occurred to him.

'He likes me to bleed,' said Nell matter-of-factly. 'Run your fingers over my back,' she said before he pulled up her gown. She felt his hand gentling over her skin. 'Can you feel the scars?'

'The Devil,' said Tom, shaken. 'God's wounds, Nell, how have you survived this for so long?'

She shrugged. 'I have learnt to endure, but Meg ... you are right, there is something not right in the way he looks at her.'

Tugging her shift back into place, she let Tom re-pin her sleeves. 'She is only eleven, Tom,' she said while his hands were busy. 'I can endure the slavery and subjection he metes out for myself, but not for Meg. If Ralph lifts a finger to her, I will kill him, I swear it.'

Her mouth hardened. 'I have thought how I would do it too. I would be subtle. I would take some ratsbane and put it in the bottom of a porringer and pour milk over it and watch him drink it, with a smile. Or I could lace sugar sops with poison.' Nell tilted her head to one side and considered the matter. 'Yes, that would be better. It is Ralph's favourite.'

'Nell, you cannot!' Tom looked at her in horror. 'They will hang you.'

'I would rather be hanged than see Ralph lay his hands on Meg.' She tucked her hair back under her coif. 'If I thought no one would guess, I would kill him anyway,' she said defiantly, thinking about

Janet and the doubtless many other women who had suffered at Ralph's hands while she was with child. 'I would.' Her chin jutted out. 'It would be a good thing to rid the world of him!'

Tom took her hands in a firm clasp and shook them. 'Nell, I have not come back to see you hang! It is too risky. Upon my life, I do not say he does not deserve it – I have felt the wounds on your back – but if he dies from poison, everyone will know that you did it, and you will hang, and what would happen to Meg then? And there would be no light left in this world for me.'

'What else can I do?' Nell cried, wrenching her hands away. 'I am in such a narrow strait, there is nowhere else for me to turn.'

'There is another way. We will go away.' Tom got to his feet and brushed down his breeches, ready to take action.

'Tom, we cannot.'

'Why not?'

'I cannot leave Meg.'

'That is easily remedied. We will take Meg with us.' He held down a hand to help Nell to her feet.

'It is not that easy,' she said. 'Ralph would never let me go.'

'We will not be asking his permission,' said Tom. 'We'll go to London. Who will know us there?'

'He would find us. I know it.' Nell bit her lip. She longed to let Tom sweep her away, but he didn't know what his brother was. 'He will never rest until he finds me and punishes me.'

Tom was not to be deflected. 'Then we will go to the New World. Even Ralph will not be able to find us there.'

Chapter Eighteen

'The New World!' Nell gaped at him. She had never imagined such a thing. 'Tom, it is full of savages!'

'Would a savage treat his wife worse than Ralph treats you?' asked Tom. 'I think not. The few that I have seen have been proud-looking men. It is a strange and wild place, to be sure. The Captain sailed us to Roanoke last year, and we brought the last of the colonists there home with us. They were in a bad way, I'll grant you, but already there is talk of setting up another colony. Raleigh plans to send another mission to Virginia next year.'

Tom's eyes were alight with the possibility. 'Why should we not go with them? It is to be a permanent settlement, Nell. There is a whole world for us there.'

'Tom, I don't know...'

'It would be hard,' he said. 'I do not deny that. And it is a strange place – stranger than we can imagine, perhaps – but there is such possibility too.' His eyes took on a faraway look. 'I wish I could tell you what it is like. It is wild and uncivilized, no doubt, but there you are not hemmed in by walls the way we are here. The sky is so big, you think you could walk forever and never get to the end of it. There are no rules there, Nell. No ordinances or neighbours or a governor always watching what you say and what you do. Who would be there to care if we are truly married or no? We could be ourselves. We could make a life together.'

His words called to Nell's reckless spirit, the one Ralph had done his best to break. She thought about a world wild and free, where she could be with Tom, and where Meg would be safe. She had never been anywhere but York. This quiet clearing down by the Foss was the wildest place she knew. Did she really dare to sail across an ocean and make her home amongst savages?

But what was the alternative? To watch and wait for Ralph to turn his vile interest to Meg? To kill him and then swing from the noose herself? To know that Tom was there on his own, across the seas, because she had not the courage to go with him?

Her brothers were grown men. They could look after their mother, and Ralph could not call in that old debt now. It was cancelled when Nell married him and she had more than paid on account. They would manage without her. York would carry on as it always did. Her disappearance would give the good-wives food for discussion for a while, but only until the next scandal. Ralph would be humiliated, Nell thought with satisfaction, but he would have his wealth to comfort him.

He would be so angry. If he found her, he would kill her. Of that Nell had no doubt.

But she couldn't bear to say goodbye to Tom again. She couldn't bear to lose hope again.

'How shall we manage it?' she asked him.

'Would you like a glass of water?' Tess opened her

eyes with a jarring sense of reconnection with the present. She was in a room, a characterless, airless room, facing a woman in uniform across a table.

A policewoman. Tess read the name on her badge again. Karen Davies. Yes, she remembered now. She was at the police station.

She moistened her lips. Karen Davies was appraising her with narrowed eyes. How long had she been in the past? What had she said? What had she *done?*

'Thank you,' she said, remembering the question at last. 'Some water would be good.'

There was a pause, and then Karen got to her feet. She left the room in search of water, and Tess took the opportunity to drop her forehead onto the table. She must keep her grip. If she let the police think that she wasn't completely in control, they would write her off as a neurotic, and Martin would exploit that with everything he had.

When Karen came back with a plastic cup of water, Tess mustered a smile. 'I'm sorry about that,' she said, sipping gratefully. 'I was just a little faint there for a moment.'

'Are you ready to continue?'

'Yes.' She cleared her throat. 'Yes. Yes, I'm fine. Where were we?'

'Does anyone else have a key to your flat?'

'My friend Vanessa has a spare key in case of emergencies. And Luke has one, of course.'

Karen's brows rose in polite interrogation. 'Luke?'

'Yes, he ... he's been building some shelves in the flat. But he wouldn't have had anything to do with this,' Tess added hastily. She didn't want Karen going off on the wrong track and suspecting Luke just because he was a man and had a key. She was supposed to be looking into Martin.

'How long have you known him?'

'Since I was at school! He's a friend!'

'Please don't upset yourself, Mrs Nicholson. I'm just trying to establish who has had access to your flat.'

'It's nothing to do with Luke.' Desperately, Tess tried to batten down on the shrillness she could hear creeping into her voice. 'I keep telling you, it's my husband. He got hold of a key somehow and he's been playing mind games, and now he's come to York and I don't know what to do. Can't you give me a restraining order or something?'

Karen straightened her notes. 'I'm sorry to say, Mrs Nicholson, that there's not much we can do for you at the moment. I've noted your complaint about your husband today, but there's no proof that he has been in your flat. By your own account, he hasn't been abusive or aggressive before bruising your arm today, but to be honest, if it's only happened once, you don't have much grounds for saying that you feel threatened by him.'

'Except that I *do* feel threatened,' said Tess. 'What do I have to do? Wait to be attacked by him?'

'My advice is to keep a detailed record of what's happening,' said Karen. 'Particularly any proof that he's attempted to harass you. If he rings you, note the time and how long the conversation lasted. Don't say anything. Even if the number is withheld, a judge will be able to see from the phone records that you were called frequently and that you ended the conversation as soon as you realized who it was. They're going to be less impressed if it seems that you had a long conversation, even if it was an argument.'

'Is that it?' said Luke, unimpressed, when Tess reported the conversation. 'Keep a record?'

'She said I should be vigilant. I got the feeling she was sympathetic, actually, but her hands are tied. Maybe Martin will give up,' Tess added without any great hope.

'He didn't strike me like the kind of guy who gives up,' said Luke, starting the car. He threw his arm along the back of her seat so that he could twist round and see where he was going as he reversed out, and Tess stared ahead, wishing she could just lean her head back against it and close her eyes. She wished he would slide his hand under her hair and rest it at the nape of her neck, pull her towards him. She wished she could forget about everything but this awareness of Luke that shimmered underneath her skin. She wished they were a normal couple out for a normal afternoon's drive, instead of leaving a police station, worrying about an implacable husband and a relentless ghost.

'No.' She knotted her aching fingers in her lap. 'No, he isn't.'

'Do you think you should go back to the flat?'

'I have to. Richard's relying on me to look after it. And then there's Ashrafar... Besides, why should I let Martin push me out of where I live?' she added with a flash of outrage.

'You shouldn't. I was just thinking about tonight.' He put the gear into neutral and hesitated, picking his words carefully. 'You and Oscar could come and stay with me and Dad, if you like. Martin wouldn't be able to find you there.'

He won't be able to find you.

Luke's voice was becoming muddled with Tom's in her head and the world seemed to blur and slide. In panic, Tess grabbed at the dashboard. Nell was back too soon. It was all happening too fast today. 'Luke–' she began, but she didn't hear his answer. There was a rushing in her ears and a tugging in her head and the car was dissolving around her.

'So, you have decided to leave us at last, brother?' A choppy little breeze stirred the fur on Ralph's gown as he stood in the yard to wish his brother God speed. He had been in a genial mood for the past few days, in public at least. At night Nell had been made to suffer even greater degradations than usual, but she set her teeth and endured it in silence. Only a few more days, she told herself, and she would never be subjected to Ralph again.

Tom's bag was packed and at his feet. 'I have,' he said. 'I find you are right, brother, and that there is nothing for me in York any more.' He slid a look at Nell as he said this, and she averted her gaze. She bit her lip, just a little, and when she said farewell, there was a tiny tremor in her voice.

This was what they had planned. Ralph had to think that she was heartbroken because Tom was leaving. He had to believe that all hope was ended for her and that she was resigned to her life as his wife.

But she was not resigned. Inside, Nell was jubilant. At last she could see a way out. They would call her a harlot or a graceless strumpet when she had gone; they would brand her an adulteress or worse. But Nell didn't care. Now that she had made the decision, she was wild to be gone. She laid her hand on the purse hanging from her belt as if she could feel Tom's ring pulsing with hope inside it.

Tom was making his farewells to Meg and the servants. Meg's lip was trembling. She admired her gallant uncle and told Nell that she wished he could stay. Nell hadn't told her the truth yet. Her daughter was young and every thought was writ large on her face. She had no talent for deception, while Nell was discovering an unexpected aptitude for it.

'God speed, Tom,' Nell said, a little catch in her voice, as Tom swung his pack over his shoulder. Meg moved comfortingly to her side.

'Do not cry, Mamma,' she whispered, alarmed by Nell's suppressed distress.

'I will come with you to the staithe,' Ralph decided.

He wanted to make sure that Tom really sailed. Let him, Nell thought. They had it all planned. Tom would board the keelboat, but get the mariners to let him off past Fulford. When it was dark, he would make his way back to Janet's house, and lay low there for a few days until the tide was right again. A friend of his, the captain of *The Margaret*, had promised to be there. Nell didn't know the whole story – some sense of obligation, some favour Tom had done in the past

– but Tom assured her that the ship would be ready to sail as soon as she and Meg could get there. 'I would trust Ned with my life,' he said.

It was Nell's idea for him to hide at Janet's house. Tom wasn't sure about it. He wanted to lurk in an ale house until the time to go.

'Someone would see you,' Nell said. 'This is not the waterfront at Hamburg. You forget how small York is.'

'But who is this Janet?'

'She was my servant once. She will help.'

Nell couldn't trust anyone else. Her stepmother would be horrified if she knew what Nell was planning. Since Nell's father died, Anne had become increasingly devout. She would not understand how Nell could imperil her soul by leaving her marriage. 'It is for God to put man and wife asunder,' she would say, and any of Nell's neighbours would say the same.

Janet was the only one who knew what Ralph was really like. The only one who would understand. And she owed Nell her loyalty. Nell didn't say as much when she visited Janet, but she didn't need to. There in the cottage the knowledge of how Nell gave her money to find a new place away from Ralph had hung in the air between them.

Janet's sandy brows lifted in surprise when Nell knocked on her door. Her husband, she said, had died Michaelmas past. She did well enough, she said when Nell asked. Nell wished *her* husband would die that conveniently. Then there would be no need to skulk away in the night and flee across the seas, but Ralph was sturdy and strong. He bloomed with health. He would not die to oblige Nell.

'And what may I do for you, Mistress?' Janet asked at last. Her eyes were sharp with curiosity.

Nell hesitated. 'You know what my husband is,' she said after a moment and Janet's gaze flickered oddly.

'Aye.'

'Once I stood your friend. Will you now stand mine?'

There was a pause. 'What is it you wish me to do?'

Janet's expression was curiously blank as she listened, and when Nell had finished she didn't say anything for a while. She looked at the wall behind Nell's shoulder and a curious little smile played around her mouth.

'This is your chance to pay my husband back for the vile way he treated you,' Nell said at last, and Janet nodded, tucking the smile away. For some reason, it made Nell uneasy, but she shook the feeling aside. If Janet was smiling at the prospect of helping to cuckold Ralph, who was Nell to blame her? If she couldn't trust Janet, who had suffered too at Ralph's hands, she couldn't trust anyone.

'I will help you,' Janet decided at last. 'As you helped me, Mistress.'

So it was decided, and all Nell had to do now was play out her part in the charade. She lifted a hand in farewell as Tom and Ralph left. At the entrance to the passage, Tom gestured to Ralph to go ahead, and he turned to exchange a last look with Nell. Her eyes were fierce in reply.

Soon, my heart, they told him. *Soon we will be together always*.

Tess sucked in a ragged breath as she found herself jolted back into the present. She was still holding on to the dashboard and Luke's gaze was flickering worriedly between her and the traffic.

'I'm back,' she said with an attempt at a smile.

He didn't smile back. 'This is happening too often, Tess.'

'I know.' Tess took her hands away from the dashboard and made herself sit back in her seat. 'It's as if Nell is speeding up somehow.' Worriedly, she fiddled with the seatbelt. 'I get the feeling I'm coming to the end of her story.'

She told Luke about Tom's return. 'It's good news, and she's so happy to see a way out of her dreadful marriage to Ralph, but I've got this awful sense of foreboding...' She trailed off, chewing her knuckle. 'Something's going to go wrong, I know it is. Well, it's obvious it's not going to go well, isn't it? Nell wouldn't be haunting me ... possessing me ... whatever she's doing to me ... if she'd lived happily ever after with Tom, would she?'

Luke shook his head. 'It would be nice to believe that but no, I don't think so. Do you think we should call Ambrose again?'

'Or the church?' Tess's eyes were fearful. 'Maybe it's time to see if a priest can help Nell rest? I've still got the vicar's number somewhere.' She dug around in her handbag until she pulled out the card Pat French had given her. Holding it between her fingers produced a strange mixture of yearning and revulsion in her head, and the cardboard seemed to sear her fingertips.

'Nell doesn't want me to call in a priest,' she said slowly. 'She doesn't want to rest yet. There's something else she wants me to know.'

'I could call,' said Luke, braking for a red light. He put on the handbrake and turned to Tess. 'Why don't you give me the card and I'll call for you?'

It was the obvious thing to do, but Tess's hand trembled under the dead weight of Nell's will. It was just a dog-eared business card, but it burned between her fingers. *No*, Nell said in her head. *No, no, no. Don't do this.*

When Luke reached out, she tightened her grip, and actually gasped as he tugged it free. Tucking it into his jacket pocket, he released the handbrake and put the car back into gear as the light turned green, while relief and desperation warred in Tess's head.

'Do you want me to call her now?' Luke asked.

'Yes ... no ... I don't know.' Tess hugged her arms together. Nell was very close. She could feel her, swirling in her head, pounding at her will. She wished she hadn't given Luke that card, and at the same time was relieved that he had it. Luke wasn't susceptible to Nell's power. It felt safer knowing that he was there and would know what to do. 'I think we'd better pick Oscar up first. Maybe you could come back to the flat with us and call from there?'

Luke looked as if he was about to argue, but in the end he just nodded. 'Okay,' he said. 'If that's what you want.'

Gradually, Tess let her rigid shoulders relax.

One thing at a time. She needed to get Oscar, then go home, and then she would worry about what to do about Martin. And Nell. Right now, Tess wasn't sure which of them was the bigger threat.

'I'll wait here,' said Luke as he drew up outside Vanessa's house. 'I know Vanessa isn't my biggest fan, and you've got enough to worry about right now without a scene.'

Tess tried to shake the feeling of foreboding as she walked up Vanessa's immaculate path to the front door. There were roses, perfectly trimmed, on either side. Everything would be fine, she told herself. Luke would call Pat French, Pat French would exorcise Nell, or do whatever she had to do to make her release her grip on Tess's mind. As for Martin, she would have to be careful for a while, but she would keep a record, just as the police had advised. It felt good to have made some decisions and be taking control.

But still, there was something unchancy in the air. The light seemed to be shifting around her, and she had to focus hard to press the bell.

Tess listened to the ding-dong echo inside. It reverberated inside her head, and she felt that sliding feeling that signalled a rush back to the past. *Not now, Nell!* she thought in panic, gritting her teeth against the sensation. *Please, not now!*

It was like standing on the edge of a sand dune, feeling the grains slide away beneath her heels, frantically trying to keep a grip. Tess put out a hand and pressed her palm against the brick until it hurt. She couldn't let Nell win this time. She had to get Oscar and go home.

'Tess!' Vanessa's expression of mingled surprise, guilt and dismay took a little while to penetrate.

'Hi.' With a massive effort, Tess pulled herself together. 'Sorry I've been a while, Vanessa. It's a long story, but I've been at the police station for what feels like hours. Is Oscar ready to go?'

'Didn't Martin tell you?'

There was a moment of frozen stillness, of utter clarity. To Tess, it was as if she was standing outside herself, thinking quite precisely: *Let Vanessa not have said that. Let it be a second earlier, to give her a chance to say something different. Let this not be the moment when everything,* everything *changes.*

Vanessa's words hung accusingly in the air.

'Martin?' Tess croaked.

'He said he would ring you on your mobile. I gave him the right number so I'm surprised he hasn't called you yet. I'm so pleased to hear that you're getting back together,' Vanessa rushed on, but the corner of one eye was twitching with guilt. 'He seems so nice.'

Tess clutched at the frayed edges of her control. 'Vanessa, what do you mean? Where's Oscar?'

'Why, Martin's taken him, of course.'

'*No...!*' Even though at some level she had known this was coming ever since Vanessa opened the door, Tess's knees buckled in despair. 'No, please, Van! Tell me you didn't let him take Oscar!'

'Tess, really, I think you're overreacting,' said Vanessa defensively. 'Martin's not going to do anything to Oscar. For heaven's sake, he's his father!'

Tess was backing away, shaking her head. 'I *told* you I didn't trust him. I *told* you I didn't want him near Oscar.'

'What's going on?' It was Luke, solid and steady beside her. Tess clutched at him.

'She's let Martin take Oscar! Oh God, Luke, what am I going to do!'

'Honestly!' Vanessa huffed. 'What a fuss! I'm not surprised Martin finds you difficult to deal with, Tess. I found him absolutely charming and reasonable. He said he'd had coffee with you and you'd talked, and how else would he have got my address? And I could hardly refuse to let him take his own son, could I?'

'Yes, you could have refused!' Tess's voice rose. 'Oh God, oh God...' She was stuck in panic, her wheels spinning uselessly, so horrified by the knowledge that Martin had Oscar that she couldn't think.

The anger, and the eerie calm she had felt confronting him face-to-face, had evaporated, leaving her to lash herself for her stupidity in believing even for a moment that Martin had accepted defeat. She should have known he would do something like this. He had told her he knew about Vanessa. She should have come straight to get Oscar instead of wasting time at the police station, wasting time deluding herself that Martin might have changed.

'If you ask me, it's a good thing Martin has come up to York,' said Vanessa defiantly. 'You've got to admit that you've been acting very strangely, Tess. We've all been worried about you: me, your mum *and* Martin. And Luke's been encouraging you,' she added, shooting him an unfriendly look.

'Martin's doing his best. He told me that he's

taking you off on a second honeymoon so you can relax and get over the strain of the last few weeks. He's so caring! I wish Graham thought about me the way Martin thinks about you. He obviously adores you, Tess, and quite frankly, I don't think you deserve him! I've been saying all along you need to talk about your problems instead of running away, and Oscar needs a father.'

Tess was barely listening to her. 'How was Oscar?' Her voice wobbled. 'Was he OK?'

For the first time Vanessa's certainty wavered. 'Well, he was a bit uncertain, but that's only to be expected. He hasn't seen his father in such a long time, he must seem practically a stranger. But he certainly didn't scream or make a fuss.'

Unlike you, was the unspoken addition.

Of course Oscar wouldn't have made a fuss. He would have done exactly as his father told him, but Tess knew that he would have been frightened. He would have made himself as small and as quiet as he could. Martin might have charmed Vanessa, but Oscar knew what his father was like.

She couldn't bear to think of him turning into that tense little boy again. 'Did Martin say where he was taking Oscar?' Luke asked when Tess covered her face.

'Back to the flat. He said you'd forgotten to give him the key, so I let him have the spare.' Vanessa seemed to take in Tess's distress for the first time and she wriggled her shoulders uneasily. 'It's not as if he's planning to whisk Oscar out of the country or anything. I really think it's time you accepted that you're the one with the problem. They'll be there when you get back. You can sit down and sort everything out. It'll be fine... Tess? *Tess?*'

But her voice was fading as Tess felt herself sliding once more, back into the darkness.

'Quietly,' Nell breathed in Meg's ear. 'Don't make a sound.'

Together they tiptoed down the stairs, stopping to help each other over the fifth tread from the bottom, the one that had cracked and groaned for as long as Nell could remember. It cost them precious time, but they couldn't afford to wake anyone with an unexpected noise.

How odd to think that she would never hear it again. Nell's mind kept fastening on to trivial details like that. She had tried to imagine life in the New World, but the idea was too huge, too unknown. She could only think about small things, like a creaking board, or whether anyone would remember to pot up the butter she had churned that day.

Nell worried about how the maids would fare once she had gone. Eliza and Mary were long married, but she had new servants in their place. Her dread was that Ralph would use them as he had used her, but Tom had quashed her idea of taking them with her as well. They had families to protect them, he had pointed out. 'You can't tell anyone, Nell. You must save your daughter, and yourself.'

So it was just the two of them creeping towards the front door.

Ralph was fast asleep, thanks to the draught she gave him in his wine. That had been Janet's idea.

She would go to the wise woman on the common, she whispered. Just a concoction to help him sleep while you get away. Nell could hardly believe it when he had drank it down unsuspecting. Even then he slumped in his closet. She had stood and listened to him snore before she went to wake Meg.

It was now or never.

If Nell had any doubts that she was doing the right thing, they were routed by the way Meg's face had lit up when Nell had roused her and told her that they were leaving. They had helped each other to dress warmly, fumbling with nerves, and Nell checked the purse hanging from her belt, which she had filled with as much money as she dared. Drawing out the garnet ring, on an impulse she slipped it back onto her finger where it belonged. The jewellery Ralph had showered on her she left in a box on the table. She wanted none of it.

The house slumbered, silent but for the familiar sound of old timber shifting and settling, and snoring from the servants' chambers. In the distance, a dog barked. Holding their skirts high, Nell and Meg made it to the bottom of the stairs. It was pitch-dark, but they knew the house so well there was no need of a candle.

They crept down the passage and paused by the door. Taking her bottom lip between her teeth, Nell turned the great key in the lock as carefully as she could. It fell into place with a clunk, and they both froze, but there was no shout of alarm. Shakily, Nell let out a breath. Now there was just the latch to lift, and the door to open. She mustn't hurry, or she would make it worse.

Only when they stepped out into the yard did she let herself breathe easily again. Now there was just the gate at the end of the passage to negotiate. Another clunk of the key, and this time the latch clattered under her hand. Immediately George Watson's dog next door set up such a barking that Nell's heart stopped.

'Quickly!' she muttered under her breath to Meg, and they walked as fast as they could along the mid part of the street. Nell had never been out in the streets this late before. Dark clouds had swallowed up the moon that shone earlier, but that was all to the good, she told herself. It was not far. Just down to the bottom of Stonegate and past St Helen's churchyard, where little Hugh was buried. Then along Coney Street and Ousegate and down to the staithe, and Tom would be there.

With an oddly detached part of her mind, she marvelled that this was really happening. They really were leaving. That was the last time she would ever walk down the stairs in the house, the last time she would hear that cursed dog bark. This was the last time she would walk down Stonegate. She would never pass John Harper's stall again, never feel his eyes pulling the laces free of her bodice, or sliding the sleeves down her shoulders.

She would be free.

The city was silent and yet not at the same time. There was a deadening quality to the darkness, but Nell's senses were so attuned she could hear the snorts and mumbles of her sleeping neighbours. A cough, a sigh, the grunts of bed work. The thin wail of a babe, quickly shushed. A drunken mumble and a sharp retort.

A breeze puffed down the street and set the shops signs swinging and creaking. All the better. They needed a wind to fill their sails. It was cold, though. Meg shivered and drew her cloak around her.

The sounds of the night were like no other. Nell could feel the streets breathing around her. It was a different city in the dark. It belonged to the cats slinking along the gutters, to the rats scuttling in the sewers.

To the evil spirits that slipped through the walls and danced in the dark.

Meg gasped and shrank away, and Nell grasped her arm, her blood hammering with fear. 'What is it?'

'I trod on something.' Meg's voice trembled. 'Something that moved.'

'Do not think of it,' said Nell in an urgent whisper. 'We are nearly there. Think about Tom waiting for us.'

They were not the only ones breaking the curfew. They passed a vagrant slumped in the entrance to a passageway, barely more than a bundle of rags. Two drunken sots reeled from one side of the street to the other, but Nell and Meg shrank into the deeper darkness of a doorway until they could slip past unnoticed.

Cautiously, they turned into Coney Street. The street was well paved and they could hurry, but another dog bayed as they passed. It woke another and another until it seemed every house had a dog barking out a warning that Nell and Meg were escaping, that they mustn't get away. Nell took Meg's hand and they started to run. Along Coney Street, dogs were sleepily cursed, but no one rose and unbolted their door. No one peered from their casements.

Still, Nell's heart was pounding as she practically dragged Meg down the slippery cobbles to the staithe. She was too desperate now to care about making a noise. All she wanted was to get on that boat and sail away.

She could smell the river, fresh and sour, and hear it lapping against the staithe. Where was Tom? Where was the boat? She peered through the blackness. The water was the faintest of gleams.

'Mistress!' The whisper made Nell whirl round, her hand to her throat.

'Oh ... Janet!' She could barely make out the other woman's shape in the darkness. 'What are you doing here?'

'I thought I'd best come and make sure everything went to plan.'

Nell swallowed. 'Where's Tom?'

'He's waiting out of sight in the master's warehouse.'

That was like Tom, Nell thought, laughing a little shakily. Only he would be reckless enough to hide in Ralph's own property.

'Come, I'll take you to him,' Janet murmured.

'Can't we wait on the boat?'

'Tom has agreed a password with the mariner. Best you go with him.'

'I suppose so.' Nell's pulse was still thumping from their run through the streets. She wished they could just get on the boat and be done, but she let Janet lead her into the warehouse. The heavy door clunked shut behind them.

At first Nell could see nothing. A candle was burning inside, its flame so bright in contrast to the darkness beyond the door that she had to screw up her eyes. Blinking against the candlelight, she could make out a figure over by the bales of white cloth.

'Tom?'

Beside her, Meg stiffened. Nell looked at her daughter, seeing an expression of such horror on her face that her own blood ran to ice and she clutched at her bodice. 'What? What is it?'

But already she was turning to follow Meg's gaze over to the bales, and although her eyes had adjusted fully to the light, she couldn't comprehend what she saw at first.

She didn't want to comprehend.

Tom was lying on the bales, staring up at the rafters. Why was he lying there? Nell wondered. Why didn't he leap up and greet them?

'Tom?' she said again, or maybe she didn't. Her mouth was moving, but no sound was coming out. Her body seemed to belong to someone else. Jerkily, it moved over to the bales.

The dark blue eyes were open as Tom looked up at her, but he didn't smile.

His ruff was red, his shirt too.

His head was tilted at an odd angle to his body. *It must be uncomfortable like that,* Nell thought.

It must be uncomfortable with that great slash under his chin.

There was a roaring in Nell's ears, and a dreadful keening filled the warehouse. Where was that terrible noise coming from, she wondered with that still detached part of her mind. Didn't they know they had to be quiet?

She turned to Meg who had moved stiffly beside her. She meant to shush her, but she couldn't speak, and it was only then that Nell realized the noise was coming from her own throat.

Vanessa took a step back as the howl erupted from Tess. 'Tess, for heaven's sake!' she said, but she looked shaken. 'Luke, what's the matter with her?'

'Tess.' Luke's voice was very gentle as he laid a hand on Tess's arm. 'Tess, can you hear me?'

Tess stared at him, her pupils dilated with horror. 'Tom,' she stuttered. 'Tom's dead... Tom's dead!'

'Oh my god!' Vanessa covered her mouth with her hands. 'Did she just say *dead?* Who's Tom? What's she talking about? Luke, what's going on?'

Luke didn't answer. He was too busy trying to deal with Tess who was bent over and sobbing, great retching, wrenching sobs that ripped up from deep in her belly. She flailed in distress as he gathered her to him as best he could. 'Shh,' he said. 'You're all right. It's all right.'

'It's not alright!' Vanessa's voice rose shrilly. 'Look at the state of her!'

'Tess, listen to me.' Luke took Tess's chin in one hand and made her look at him. 'Look at me. You're safe, okay? You're here.'

Her eyes were dazed still, but she was beginning to focus. 'Here,' she repeated.

'You have to focus now, Tess. You have to think

about Oscar.'

'Oscar?' Horror stirred anew in her eyes. 'I'm going to be sick,' she said, and turned away to throw up in Vanessa's freshly weeded rose bed.

Revolted, Vanessa turned away. 'Oh, for God's sake...'

'Vanessa, call the police,' snapped Luke.

'What?' Vanessa grimaced as Tess continued to heave over the roses. 'The *police?* Why?'

'Tell them Martin has taken Oscar against his mother's wishes.'

'I can't do that! Martin is Oscar's father. He hasn't done anything wrong.'

'Tess didn't want him to be alone with Oscar. You knew that.'

Vanessa flushed guiltily. 'Tess is overreacting – as usual. And you're encouraging her,' she added with a spiteful look. 'Tess was fine until she got involved with you again.'

'Oscar.' Tess wasn't even listening. She straightened on trembling legs and wiped her face with her hands. The thought of her son steadied her more than anything else could, and she forced the ghastly image of Tom's half-severed head from her mind. 'I have to find him.'

She had dropped her handbag on the ground when she had turned away to be sick. It started to buzz as she reached for it, and all three of them paused as if transfixed.

'My phone!'

Tess scrabbled inside for it. Unknown caller. She pressed answer anyway. 'Hello?'

'*There* you are.'

'Martin!' She threw a frantic glance at Luke

who spun his hand to indicate that she should keep talking as they hurried to his car, leaving Vanessa looking at them in outrage.

'What about this mess?' she called after them, eyeing the roses in disgust.

Tess ignored her.

'Where are you?' she asked Martin as she scrambled into the passenger seat and Luke ran round to the driver's side of the car.

'In your flat, of course.' Martin sounded surprised. 'I'm packing for you.' He chuckled. 'Seems like I have to do everything around here nowadays!'

As if they had never confronted each other in the middle of Stonegate. As if everything was normal. As if he had stepped gently over into insanity.

Trying not to think about Oscar alone with him, Tess covered the phone with her hand. 'Vanessa was right,' she told Luke. 'He's at my flat.'

'Call the police!' Luke yelled to Vanessa over the roof of the car. 'Tell them Martin is in Stonegate with Oscar. *Do it,* Vanessa!' he shouted when Vanessa started to object.

'Packing?' Tess said into the phone, trying desperately to control the tremble in her voice as she hauled the seat belt across her and snapped it into place one-handed.

'You won't want to take much with you.' She could hear him opening and closing drawers. 'Where are all the pretty bras I bought you? Everything else in here might as well go straight in the bin. You know I hate you wearing these awful T-shirts and things,' Martin clicked his tongue in distaste, and Tess pictured him grimacing as he held her tops out at arm's length.

Swallowing her disgust at the idea of his hands on her clothes, she took a breath and levelled the reediness from her voice.

'Is ... is Oscar there?'

Luke had shoved the car into gear and the tyres were screaming on the tarmac as they shot down the road to where the traffic was flowing out of the city in a seemingly unstoppable stream. Swearing, Luke slammed on the brakes, jolting Tess forward against her seat belt before shoving her back into her seat.

'Rush hour,' Luke muttered, edging out as far as he dared and ignoring the blaring of horns and irritable flashing of headlights. 'That's all we need.'

'Can't you think of anything but Oscar?' Martin sounded petulant. 'It's only ever Oscar, Oscar, Oscar with you.'

'I need to know if he's all right, Martin.'

There was an exaggerated sigh. 'Of course he's all right. For now,' he added almost as an after-thought.

Tess went cold. 'What do you mean?'

'Well, I think it's time for you to make a decision, don't you?'

Chapter Nineteen

'Decision?' she echoed numbly.

'I've been very patient, but things can't go on like this, I'm sure you'll agree?'

'Yes ... yes, I do.' *Keep him talking*, that was all Tess could think.

'So it's time to put things right,' said Martin. 'Isn't that right, Oscar?' he added and Tess flinched as she made out a whimpered agreement in the background.

Oscar. Oscar who had been running around so happily earlier would be shrunk into himself, confused and scared, and she gestured frantically to Luke to get going. He put his hand on the horn and shoved the car out across the traffic, making a van swerve and blast its horn in return. Tess was flung around in her seat and the phone slipped out of her grasp, but she managed to grab it between her knees and put it back to her ear.

'Are you still there, Theresa?' Martin sounded peevish.

'Yes, I'm still here.' She swallowed hard past the constriction in her throat. 'You ... you were saying?'

'Either we're a family together or we're not a family together.'

'Wh-what do you mean, Martin?'

'I mean it's your choice, Theresa.'

His voice was light, pleasant. Chilling. 'Let's

talk about this when I get there,' she managed as Luke accelerated.

'That's what I hoped you'd say,' Martin said. 'And this time we'll have a proper talk, hmm?'

'Whatever you want.'

'That's more like the Theresa I remember,' he said approvingly. 'But we don't want anyone else. This is just between us, isn't it? Don't even think about bringing that oik who interfered earlier with you.'

'I won't. I'll come alone, I promise,' she said, ignoring Luke's frown of protest.

He was driving as fast as he could, flashing his lights at the drivers carefully sticking to the speed limit.

'Can I speak to Oscar now, Martin?' Tess tried.

There was a pause. She could picture Martin, head to one side, considering. 'No,' he decided pleasantly. 'I don't think so. I think you should just get here as soon as possible.'

'I'm coming, I'm coming... I'll be there any minute.'

'I'll be waiting for you,' he said and cut the connection.

Tess stared down at the phone. She was trapped in a nightmare, jerked between Nell's horror and her own terror for her son. She couldn't think, couldn't breathe. Could it really only be a few hours ago that she had sat in the Museum Gardens in the sunshine? It didn't seem possible. Time itself was accelerating. Like a high-speed train that had pulled out of the station at normal speed, it was now rocketing uncontrollably along a track – no, along *two* tracks, past and present, with Tess torn between them.

She wanted to jam in her heels, to make it stop so that she could make sense of the terrifying blur of images flying past. They span jaggedly, like shrieks in her head, one vivid picture after another: Meg's face, stark with fear; Oscar, whispering in the background on the phone; Tom, his collar dark with blood; Martin, standing over his son, his hands full of her underwear.

The eerie implacability in his voice had frightened her. He had sounded like a man who had stepped past the point of no return.

'Hurry, Luke,' she said.

Luke kept his hand on the horn to warn the wandering pedestrians to move out of the way as the car hurtled along Monkgate, through the bar, careered down Goodramgate, and swung round towards the Minster. Tess was already opening her door as he came to a dead halt at the bollards blocking the way past the south transept. Before he could stop her, she was out and running blindly for Stonegate, careless of the tourists who turned to stare as she bolted past them.

Luke caught up with her as she reached the flat and bent over, heaving for breath. 'Tess, wait!' He pulled her round. 'Martin sounds like a psycho. I think we should wait for the police.'

'I'm not waiting for anyone. My son's in there.' Tess forced herself upright and scrabbled for her keys. Her fingers were as unwieldy as sausages.

'Then I'm coming in with you.'

'No! That'll just make him worse! You have to stay here and tell the police what's happening.' Desperately, she tried to get the key in the door one-handed but she kept dropping it, until Luke, grim faced but accepting, took it from her and opened the door.

'Be careful, Tess,' he said, and she took a breath as she stepped past him and closed the door behind her. It was shadowy in the narrow hallway and the image of Tom's body jumped into her mind with a scream of memory. She pressed her palms to her head as if she could physically push it away. She didn't have time for Nell now. She had to get to Oscar.

The stairs rose ahead of her. 'Martin?' she called. 'I'm here.'

The door at the top opened a crack. 'Are you alone?' he demanded suspiciously.

'Yes. I'm coming up.'

Martin opened the door as she reached the top of the stairs. He looked bizarrely normal in the clothes he had worn earlier. Tess was at the door before she noticed that there was something strapped to his chest, and her heart seemed to freeze in horrified disbelief.

Dear God, he had some kind of explosive device, and he was holding Oscar tightly by the arm.

He sounds like a psycho.

Oscar began to cry when he saw Tess.

'It's okay, pip,' she said, forcing down her panic and pinning a reassuring smile to her face. 'I'm here now. Martin, why don't you let Oscar go?'

'No.' Martin's expression was petulant. He dragged Oscar back to the front room, leaving Tess to close the door and follow. 'You only care about him.'

She closed her eyes briefly, fought for calm. 'He's just a little boy, and you're hurting him.'

'What about *you* hurting *me?*'

'I'm sorry if I've hurt you, Martin, but I'm here now.' She didn't want to look at the package on his chest. It was making the air shriek with danger. She had been afraid of Martin before, of his rage, of his silence, but she had never thought that he would do anything like this. 'Why don't we sit down and talk, just you and me like we said?'

'You don't want to talk,' said Martin, his handsome face sulky. 'You're just humouring me. You wouldn't even have come here if I hadn't brought Oscar. You don't want to be a family any more.' He didn't seem aware that Oscar's mouth was still trembling violently as he tried to control his tears.

Tess ached to snatch him up but she didn't dare. It was bizarre to be standing there in the familiar room, where everything looked just as it should except for her terrified son and her husband with a bomb strapped to his chest and a sheen of insanity in his eyes.

'I've done everything for you, Theresa.' Martin began to pace, dragging Oscar with him. 'I spoilt you, that's the problem. I gave you a beautiful house. I showered you with presents. I sent you flowers. I paid every bill. You had nothing to worry about, *nothing*.' He swung round, almost pleading. 'You didn't want for anything, did you? Did you?'

Tess licked her lips, her mouth dry. 'No, you were very generous.'

'And what do I get in return? Nothing!'

'Martin–'

'You never used to be this cold.' His voice broke. 'You used to love me.' He wiped the back of his hand under his nose. 'You don't love me any more. I booked us a beautiful holiday and you won't go.'

'I ... I didn't take time to look at it properly.' Tess struggled to pick her way through a minefield of lies and evasions. 'Look, why don't I make tea and you can tell me about it?'

Martin's mood swung viciously, without warning. 'Tea? *Tea?* Is that all you can suggest?' He pointed at his chest. 'Do you know what I've got here?'

'No.' Her throat was swollen with fear. 'I was ... wondering what that was.'

'It's a smart little explosive device. I put it together myself – one of the advantages of being in electronics.' He laughed wildly and Oscar winced. 'See this switch here? I flick this and poof! me and the boy and you and this grotty little flat will go sky high. So I suggest you stop wasting time with stupid suggestions about tea,' he said as the colour drained from Tess's face, 'and think about what you want to do.'

'You'd really kill all of us?' she whispered.

'At least we'd be together.' He was sweating, his eyes glazed, and she wondered what he'd taken. His mood was lurching from the vicious to the pathetic to the sly and Tess groped for a way, any way, to break through and make him realize what he was doing.

'We can be together here,' she said unsteadily, even as her flesh shrank with revulsion.

'That's what I want. That's all I want.' His eyes filled with pathetic tears. 'But I don't know if it's really what you want, Theresa. I just know that whatever happens we're going to be together, the way we're meant to be. The way you promised we'd be. Till death do us part ... but it wouldn't part us, would it? Not if we're together.'

Snivelling, he dragged his sleeve over his face. Tess struggled to think. She had to find a way out of this but Nell was too close. She could feel her scrabbling to break through and swamp Tess's mind with her own horror, but Tess couldn't let that happen, not when Oscar was whimpering and straining to get to her. His face was pinched with fear, his shoulders hunched against a blow.

Somehow Tess managed a smile for him. 'It is what I want, Martin,' she tried. 'Of course it's what I want. We'll be a family again. It'll be just like it was before.'

He stared at her, half hopeful, half sly. 'Do you mean that?'

'Of course.'

Pain was jabbing at her fingertips but Tess ignored it. She sank onto the arm of the sofa, trying to look relaxed, normal, and gave Oscar another smile that was meant to be reassuring but that probably looked ghastly. 'We're going home with Daddy. That's good news, isn't it?'

In the past Oscar would simply have nodded dumbly, but the weeks away from his father had changed him more than Tess had realized.

His voice trembled, but he was disastrously clear. 'Don't want to,' he said.

His timing couldn't have been worse, but Tess felt a flash of pride in him for standing up to Martin for the first time. There was an appalled pause before Martin jerked his arm furiously. 'You *don't want to*. Don't want to be with your own father? Is that what you're saying?'

'I want Mummy,' Oscar whispered defiantly.

Martin put his face down close to his son's. 'Well, you can't have her, because I want Mummy too, and if I'm not having her, nobody else is.'

Instinctively, Tess got up and took a step towards Oscar, but Martin saw her coming and pulled him back towards the window, away from her again. His face worked. 'I knew it! I knew it! You don't want to be a family again at all!'

Panic roared in her head. She needed to divert Martin's attention from Oscar, but she was too scared to think. Where were the police? But what could they do? As long as Martin had Oscar as a shield, no one could touch him.

'Martin, why are you doing this?' she said, her voice wavering all over the place.

'It's all your fault,' he spat at her, tiny flecks of spittle at the edges of his mouth. 'I gave you every opportunity to be reasonable, but you wouldn't.'

'I'm sorry,' she said. 'Tell me what I can do to make it better. I'll go on holiday. I'll go home with you. I'll do whatever you want.'

'It's a shame you didn't think that way before, isn't it?' Sweat was trickling into his eyes and he swiped it away with the back of his hand. 'A shame you didn't care about your marriage vows. Till death do us part. That *means* something, Theresa. It's not just words. I said them and I meant them. I'm not going to give up on my family the way you have.'

'That ... that's one of the good things about you.'

Tess's chest felt clogged and she was struggling to breathe, but she forced the words through. She had to try something and Martin had always been vain. 'You don't give up.'

His expression flickered and she pressed her advantage. 'And you'll do whatever it takes to do what needs to be done. That was a clever idea, bringing a bomb.' She almost gagged on the word, but at least Martin was listening and his hold on Oscar had relaxed at little. 'No pussy-footing around, just getting straight to the point.'

'I'd been indulgent long enough,' he said, but she could tell he liked the admiration she was forcing into her voice.

'Other men would have just given up when their wives left, but not you.'

'What was the point of whimpering to a lawyer?' said Martin. 'Lawyers are all talk. I always say actions speak louder than words.'

'I knew you would come after me. Nobody else would have been able to find me, but I knew *you* would.' Tess had no idea where she was going. She just knew that this was her first chance to make a connection with Martin, and she couldn't waste it. At least they were having a conversation. 'It would take more than moving to another city to stop you finding me, wouldn't it? I knew that was you in the flat, but I couldn't work out how you could have been there when I'd locked the door.'

'I had you watched right from the start.' Martin preened himself, remembering. He seemed to have forgotten Oscar. 'It's easy to get hold of a key when you know the right people. But then you changed the locks.' His smile thinned. 'You shouldn't have shut me out, Theresa. I had to get the key from your bossy friend, whatshername.'

'Vanessa.' Tess clenched her fists. Some friend Vanessa had been!

'That's it. I've been keeping an eye on her too. I thought she might be handy and it wasn't too hard to track her down once you'd told me she had Oscar. I had to listen to her yapping, but she couldn't wait to hand him over with a key. *She* knows what's right, even if she does need to shut up for five seconds so a man can think.'

'You ... you've gone to a lot of trouble.'

His face darkened. 'Yes, I have. That's your fault too, Theresa. You shouldn't have left me. That was a very, very foolish thing for you to do.'

'I know. I'm sorry.'

'Did you really think I'd let you go?'

Why hadn't she realized before how like Ralph he was? Tess looked at her husband with sudden clarity. Ralph, who had been crueller, less unbalanced and more sure of his own desires, but who shared Martin's need for utter control. Sex with Martin had been, in the end, a perfunctory business, but what if she could reach him by appealing to some of Ralph's more twisted tastes?

'It was stupid of me.' Tess swallowed, willing to try anything. 'But I knew you wouldn't let me get away with it. I need you to keep me in line, Martin. I've been reckless and stupid, and I need to be punished.'

She lowered her eyes submissively but not before she had seen his face light grotesquely.

'Only you have the right to do that.'

For a second she thought she had him, but a loudhailer crackled into life in the street below, startling them, and they both swung round.

'Martin Nicholson, this is Sergeant Jim Myers. I'm a negotiator with the North Yorkshire police. We're here to resolve this situation peacefully. We don't want anyone to get hurt. I'm going to ring you now. Please answer the phone so that we can talk.'

'Shit!' Wrenching the terrified Oscar by the arm, Martin scuttled over to the window. 'They've cleared the street.' He ducked back out of sight and chewed his lip while his eyes darted frantically around. 'Now what are we going to do?'

Tess was thinking frantically. The police didn't know about the bomb. Martin was already erratic and the stress of the police presence was only going to make him worse. She had to get Oscar out of there.

Martin's phone began to ring in his blazer.

Please, God, let the switch not be sensitive to vibrations, thought Tess. 'Let me get rid of the police,' she said to Martin above the sound of the phone. 'I'll talk to them, let them know you and I want to be alone.'

Martin's eyes flickered from side to side. His skin was sheened with sweat. 'They won't let us go.'

'They will. I'll tell them about the device, and that you want a car. They won't dare do anything as long as you've got that. You've got the whip hand, Martin,' she said urgently, moving closer to Oscar. She wasn't sure if he would buy her sudden attempt at collusion, but she had to try. 'We'll pretend I'm your hostage, and we'll go home. We'll be husband and wife again, the way you said, and no one will interfere.'

Martin's face was twitching. Abruptly, he pulled out his phone and tossed it to her. 'You tell them. We want a car. And nothing else! Don't let them pretend to be your friend. I know how these people work.'

'Okay.' Tess's hands were slippery on the phone. 'Hello? Yes, this is Tess Nicholson. We're all fine.' She kept her eyes on Martin's face while she spoke to Jim Myers. 'My husband has an explosive device and he's prepared to use it,' she said, finding it no problem to sound terrified. 'Please, just give him the car he's asked for and let us go.'

Martin gave her a nod of approval. He seemed to have calmed down and Tess risked covering the phone with her hand so that she could turn towards him, two conspirators together. 'We don't want the boy with us, do we? This is just between husband and wife. He'll just get in the way of my ... punishment.' She made the word sound as lascivious as she could and was careful not to look at Oscar herself. She needed Martin to believe that she was bound up in his fantasy.

Martin's face worked. He was torn, she could tell, but in the end the fantasy she offered won out. She had Nell to thank for that inspiration, Tess realized in a distant part of her mind. The image of Tom's lifeless blue gaze above his ghastly slit throat flashed across her brain again, and she squeezed her eyes shut briefly to push it away. She couldn't think of Tom, not now.

'All right, get rid of him,' Martin decided abruptly. 'But tell that lot outside I'm not taking off the bomb until we're safely away. Tell them I'm a security expert and I know what I'm doing.'

Tess was careful to conceal her relief as she relayed Martin's decision to the police officers waiting outside in Stonegate. She couldn't afford to remind Martin how much Oscar meant to her, so she didn't look at him. 'The boy's coming out,' she said. 'We don't want him with us when we go.'

She cut Jim Myers off before he could respond and laid the phone down on the table, still being careful not to make any sudden moves.

'I'll send him out, shall I?' she said, holding out her hand to Oscar but looking at Martin. 'Then we can be alone.'

There was a long pause and then Martin released his grip on Oscar's arm. With a small cry, Oscar stumbled over to Tess and clutched at her legs.

Tess longed to bend down and sweep him into a comforting hug, but she couldn't afford to alienate Martin just yet. So she contented herself with resting a hand on the back of his head and pressing him to her.

'Mummy and Daddy need some time alone together, Oscar,' she said. 'I want you to go downstairs and let yourself out the door. Can you do that?'

He shook his head against her thighs. 'Want to stay with you.'

'I need to talk to Daddy.'

'Come with me.'

'Oh, for fuck's sake!' Martin exploded.

Tess crouched down and kept her voice steady as she held Oscar away from her by the shoulders. 'Listen to me, Oscar. It's very important that you go downstairs – *very* important – so you need to be brave. There's a policeman waiting to see you outside. His name's Jim. Can you remember that?'

Oscar nodded miserably.

'Okay then.' Not looking at Martin, Tess took Oscar by the hand and led him to the top of the stairs. She wanted to tell him that Luke would be there, that he would look after him, but she didn't dare with Martin listening. But she pictured Luke holding Oscar, and the knot in her chest loosened a little. 'I want you to tell Jim that Daddy and I are fine,' she said instead, 'and that we're waiting for the car. Have you got that?'

Martin was looming beside her. There was no chance of making a run for it. Tess permitted herself a stroke of Oscar's hair and then she nudged him towards the stairs. 'Off you go, pip.'

Oscar put one hand on the wall and went down the stairs slowly, taking one at a time. When he got to the bottom, he hesitated and looked back up at Tess. For as long as she lived, Tess would never forget the look on his face.

'Go on,' she said, pressing her lips into a straight line to stop them trembling. 'Open the door.'

With agonizing slowness, he fumbled with the door while Martin muttered beside her, and Tess's throat closed when at last Oscar pulled it open. She saw a strong arm scoop her son to safety and then the door was shut once more.

'You spoil that boy,' said Martin.

In the front room, the phone began ringing again.

'Leave it,' said Martin. 'I'm not going back in there. They'll have snipers aiming for me. I know these guys,' he said again. His eyes were darting around and Tess was alarmed by how quickly the brief period of calm was unravelling into paranoia. She needed to find a balance again, to make him believe that he was just a man who wanted to be loved, that he just wanted his wife back.

Maybe buried deep inside Martin that man really existed, struggling to get past the man who needed to bully, to frighten and to control.

Now the police knew about the bomb, they would be working out a strategy to rescue her. Luke would be out there. He wouldn't abandon her. The realization settled strong and steady in her stomach. All she needed was to keep Martin calm and make sure the police could reach him.

She swallowed. 'We should keep the phone. They'll need to let us know when the car has arrived.'

Martin rubbed his temple. 'All right ... we'll get the phone, but then we'll move back.' He watched hawkishly as Tess picked up the phone from the table and grabbed her wrist when she came back. 'We'll go to your room. We'll be safe there.'

'Okay,' said Tess steadily. At least Oscar was safe. She held onto the thought. 'We can finish packing.'

'Packing?'

'To go home. You started packing for me.'

'Yes...' He frowned as if grasping at an elusive

memory, and rubbed his forehead again. 'Yes, I did...'

'Have you got a headache?' Tess asked. 'It'll take them some time to organize a car. Why don't you lie down for a bit? You could take that thing off,' she added casually. 'It must be uncomfortable.'

A shutter seemed to clang shut in Martin's eyes. 'Do you think I'm stupid?' he asked with quiet venom in one of those lightning-quick changes of mood that Tess had always dreaded.

'No, of course I don't.'

'I think you must do, or you'd never suggest that I *take off the bomb!*' His voice rose to a shriek and Tess couldn't help flinching. 'The bomb's the only thing that's making you stay here, isn't it? *Isn't it?*'

'N-no...' Tess stuttered.

'You sat in that ghastly tea room over the road and you told me you didn't want to go to the Maldives with me, and now I'm supposed to believe you want to pack while I take the bomb off and "lie down"?'

Martin's hand shot out and fastened around Tess's wrist. 'I'll show you *packing*,' he said viciously as he dragged her down the corridor. 'You wanted to be punished, I'll punish you!'

Sick with fear, she stumbled after him to her bedroom, pulling futilely at the cruel grip around her wrist.

Martin kicked open the door and then everything seemed to happen at once. A thick cloud of horror rolled out of the room and enveloped them, wrapping itself around their faces like a physical thing, cold and black and terrifying.

Ashrafar streaked between their legs with something between a screech and a yowl, making Martin, his mouth already open in terror, stumble and let go of her wrist. Tess watched as if in slow motion. She had time to think that if he fell on the switch they would both die, but the scream was blocked in her throat as the horror plucked her from the present and shoved her back into the past.

'No!' Nell groped for Meg's hand as she backed away from Tom in horror. She still didn't understand. She had been pitch-forked into a nightmare, and she was tumbling and flailing, not knowing which way was up in the new reality. She grasped at the thought that this was only a dream, but it was all too real. She had been in too many warehouses not to recognize the harsh aroma of white cloth as it permeated the hessian bales it was wrapped in and mingled with the sour, damp smell of the river that seeped underneath the doors and clung to the brick walls. Underfoot, the floor was packed earth strewn with straw, crushed and mouldy now, and the scent of it all was overlaid with the metallic smell of blood.

Tom's blood.

Beside her, she could hear Meg whimpering, inarticulate with terror. She should comfort her, Nell thought vaguely, but what could she say?

'Oh, my dear, you were right.' Ralph's voice behind them made them both spin round. He was standing next to Janet and observing them with delight. He clapped his hands and laughed at their expressions. 'It is better than the players!

You said it would be, and so it is!'

Still uncomprehending, Nell's eyes went from Ralph to Janet, who gazed adoringly up at him.

'Janet?' Her voice sounded rusty and unused, as if it belonged to someone else.

'Yes, Janet!' Ralph was gleeful at her disbelief. 'What a trusting soul you are, wife! You ran straight to the one person in York I account my soulmate.'

'*Janet?*' Nell whispered again as Janet leant towards Ralph and they kissed, a long, lascivious kiss. Nell could see their tongues thrusting into the other's mouth, twisting and twining, careless of the slobber of saliva, and when they broke apart, Janet's plain, sandy face was alight with gluttonous satisfaction. She smiled at Nell, a smile at once contemptuous and terrifyingly normal.

'You have no idea, do you?'

'I don't... I don't...' Nell stuttered.

'You don't understand? No, you don't. For once, wife, you are quite correct. You do not understand true pleasure. You have no appreciation of the exquisite torment of a soul in ecstasy. Janet understands. We were drawn to each other straight away, but you, you had to spoil it. You had to send her away. That was a mistake, wife. You are rather prone to mistakes, I find,' he added in a silky voice. 'And the biggest mistake you made was trying to run away with Tom. You will have to be punished for that.'

Janet sucked in a breath of avid anticipation, and Ralph chuckled, a light, inhuman noise that would have struck ice in Nell's core if she were not already so numb she couldn't feel anything.

'I trusted you.' Her voice as she spoke to Janet was empty of expression. She was almost surprised to hear the words coming out of her mouth. 'I saved you from him.'

'I didn't want to be saved!' There was a mad light in Janet's eyes as she thrust her face towards Nell's. 'Only with Ralph can I be myself. We understand each other. And you, you ruined it! We couldn't see each other every day any more. I had to go and live with that sot John Scott and be bedded by a man who thought to shove his prick in me was to show desire. There is a world of pleasure and desire that he and you know nothing of – *nothing!* You are married to a man who can show you the world, but do you honour him? No! You cringe and pule and weary him with the narrowness of your desires. Pah, what do you know of pleasing a man?'

'I know everything of pleasure,' said Nell, finding her voice. 'I love a good man and am loved by him.'

She couldn't look at the bales behind her where Tom lay, grotesquely dead. Her mind refused to accept that it was true. Surely this was a terrible nightmare, and she would wake in the great chamber in Stonegate before long.

Yes, that was all this could be, Nell told herself. She would wake and though Ralph might be snoring beside her, the knowledge that Tom was nearby and that they would be leaving soon would hum through her. Her lips would curve at the memory of him, of his hands warm on her skin and the laughter in his eyes and the desire, sharp and sure, that rose between them at every touch.

She even closed her eyes, willing wakefulness for once, but when she opened them again, she was still in the dank warehouse, and the smell of blood was rank in the air, a voice at the back of her mind shouting at her: *Fool! This is no dream. Tom is dead and all is lost.*

Nell wouldn't listen to it.

'What Tom and I have is not blessed by law, but it is strong and clean and true,' she said bravely. 'Do not talk to me of desire. I know what desire is, and it is not the unnatural appetites you share with my husband.'

'Well, which of us is the happier now?' Janet tittered. 'Oh, I wanted to laugh in your face when you knocked on my door that day and begged me to help you! As if I would help you dishonour Ralph so! But you, you were so sure I owed you, and you were right, but not in the way you meant.'

'You told Ralph what we meant to do.' If this was a dream, it was making a horrible kind of sense. No wonder Ralph had been in such a good mood.

'He was all for killing Tom there and then, but I persuaded him it would be so much more entertaining this way. To let you think you were going to escape...' Janet and Ralph laughed again, in fine good humour.

'You are mad,' Nell whispered.

'Mad? Are we so? We are not the ones who planned to shame our families, to run off with a pirate brother in the night.'

'You will burn in hell for what you have done this night.' It was Meg, her voice swooping and surging with fear. Her fingers were holding on to Nell's so tightly they were white to the bone.

Nell looked down at them and the pain of her daughter's grip digging into her flesh brought the truth crashing down at last.

This was not a nightmare.

This was real.

Tom wasn't going to spring to his feet and tell her this was only a trick. He wasn't going to save her from Ralph. He was dead.

'You have killed Tom.' Her voice was dull, deadened with delayed shock.

'Well, what was I to do with him?' Ralph asked reasonably. 'I could not have him making a fuss. And the world knows he sailed off on the ship. If he never returns to York...' He shrugged. 'Who will be surprised? York has done very well without Tom Maskewe these last few years; it will manage without him again. His mariner friend put up a little resistance, but I have learnt to deal with those who choose to put themselves in my way.'

'You killed him too?'

'He was an ignorant sailor.' Ralph waved a hand dismissively. 'No one will miss him. I will send my own man out on the boat and he can tip the bodies in the river. I have some goods arrived in Hull in any case. It will not be a wasted trip.'

Nell tightened her hold on her trembling daughter. 'And what of us?' she made herself ask.

'Oh, I think we should go home, don't you?'

What could she do? Nell was numb. Her mind couldn't grasp the enormity of Janet's betrayal. A frantic voice in her head kept telling her to do something, anything, but when she tried to imagine what it would be, all she saw was a blank. She couldn't scream. Janet had a knife at Meg's back and Meg herself had given up. She stumbled beside her mother, shuddering, beyond even tears now. All Nell could do was help keep Meg upright and pray for a miracle.

They retraced their steps through the dark streets. It was like pulling the wool out of the spindle, unwinding time remorselessly. The dogs barked again; their owners cursed and mumbled again. They went back through the passage, back through the door. Back up the stairs. No need to care for the creak this time.

Would the servants hear? Nell wondered. But even if they did, what could they do? Ralph would send them away and they would not dare say him nay. They must have heard Ralph beating her at night sometimes. They would be used to pulling the covers over their ears. They were sensible maids, both of them. They would turn over and go back to sleep.

'In the closet, I think,' said Ralph, businesslike.

Nell balked in the doorway. This room had held horror for her for so long, but she had never imagined a horror like this.

Too late, she woke out of her stupor. 'Wait,' she said, as if he would listen to her. 'Wait!' But Janet put a hand to her back and shoved her into the room. Meg followed, walking stiffly like a doll.

Nell remembered holding her when she was born, how her heart had swelled with love.

Her daughter, her child. God have mercy on her, it could not end this way.

Gathering her strength, she looked at Ralph. 'Do what you will to me,' she said straightly, 'but let Meg go.'

Ralph looked amused. 'But what I will for you, wife, is for you to suffer, and for that I need the girl. I have been too lenient with you before,' he explained almost kindly. 'I have stayed my hand, and let you grow rude and rebellious, so now I must find a way to really cause you pain, and punish you in the worst possible way, as you deserve.'

And his smile as he turned his pale gaze to Meg froze the blood in Nell's veins.

Chapter Twenty

'No...' What was left of her colour drained from Nell's face. 'She is your own daughter!' she whispered, terrified.

'I have never cared for her,' said Ralph, indifferent. 'It should have been Meg who died, not Hugh. What good is a girl to me? But *you*, she matters to you, does she not?'

'Let her go, Ralph.'

'I think not. I have some refinements to my technique I am eager to try. Bind her,' he ordered Janet abruptly, taking over the knife she held at Meg's throat to keep Nell quiet.

Janet bustled around, tying Nell's wrists and ankles together, and gagging Meg with brisk efficiency. Meg was slumped on a stool, her head hanging low, her eyes dull. Nell couldn't even be sure that she was listening. She barely reacted when Janet tightened the scarf around her nose and mouth.

'Now that Tom is dealt with, what is the worst you can imagine, wife?' Ralph stroked the edge of Meg's cheek with the back of the knife. 'Is it being shut up in the dark, or is there something worse than that, hmm?'

'You are a fiend. I think you must be the Devil himself.' The words, the worst she can think of, sounded bland. There were no words for the depth of her terror and disgust.

He tsked. 'Name-calling won't help. Now, if only you had Janet's appreciation for my skills ... but you always turned your nose up at me, didn't you? Even when you were a grubby brat. So beautiful and so strong... I longed to break your will, but you were a disappointment to me, I have to admit. You never understood what I needed.' He shook his head. 'I, Ralph Maskewe, was reduced to vagrants, to filthy whores and harlots who broke at the first blow.'

'It was you...' Nell managed. 'You killed all those girls?'

'I was disposing of them,' Ralph amended. 'Filth like that, corrupting our streets. I put them out of their misery.'

'Tell her about your first,' said Janet. She was circling Nell, knife at the ready. 'I like that story.'

'Oh, I was a bumbling beginner then,' he acknowledged with a self-deprecating tilt of his head. 'My mother was a devout woman and a good Protestant. She taught me early the tender power of a pinch or a slap, but then she died...'

His face worked with emotion. 'She was hardly cold in her grave before my father married again.'

'Tom's mother,' said Nell, grasping at the hope that if she could keep him talking long enough the madness would fade from his eyes.

'That papist!' Ralph spat. 'My father was in thrall to her. He should have made her change her religion, but no! He builds a priest hole, he re-panels his closet, he lets her harbour priests and say mass... He was a weakling!'

Nell did not remember Henry Maskewe as a weakling, but she was not going to contradict Ralph now.

'She had a psalter,' Ralph went on, momentarily lost in the past. 'She used to let me look through it.' He laughed scornfully. 'She thought she would convert me to the old religion, but I only wanted to see the image of the day of judgement.' His eyes held a faraway expression. 'I was so drawn to that page. I looked at what the devils were doing and I felt such a thrill. Ah, your senses are too dull ... I cannot explain it to you! Those screams, the blood, the pain ... it was so pure. I could feel it in my belly. I could feel it in my cock.'

He rubbed himself reflectively, and Janet chuckled, a feral sound, dark and loathsome. 'I knew what I wanted from a bedding,' Ralph said. 'I thought that dolt of a maid Joan would be grateful for my attentions, but no! Oh, she went through the motions, but I'd barely broken her in before she took herself off and drowned herself in the Ouse.'

A memory sliced through Nell's fear: she and Tom, at the staithe in the fog. *Joan never did any-*

one any harm except herself. She could remember her disbelief that anyone could do such a thing. Nothing could be that bad, she had thought, but she had been wrong. Poor little Joan, forced by Ralph to his unnatural desires. How she must have despaired of finding help. She had chosen death over Ralph, even though it condemned her to a grave at the crossroads with a stake through her heart.

'Then I had to look elsewhere.' Ralph sighed at the trouble he was put to. 'It was easy enough to find harlots. I didn't have to worry about marking their faces, but they weren't truly satisfying – no more than a momentary release. They would do whatever I asked if I paid them.

'And then there was you,' he said to Nell, who didn't dare take her eyes from the knife he kept at Meg's throat. 'But you weren't pure either, were you? Oh, there was pleasure in breaking your wild spirit, I'll admit, but Janet is the only one who truly knows what I need. She pleases me well, but still, there are times I crave for something more. Janet understands, do you not, my sweet?'

'I do,' she said with a grotesque simper. 'I know what you need, love. What you *deserve*.'

'Sometimes,' Ralph confided to Nell, 'she likes to watch, and tonight she shall.'

He lifted Meg's chin. 'I have been waiting for this a long time. Look how pure she is! How unmarked! The others were filthy whores, but this will be the culmination. How glad I am you decided to run, Eleanor, else I might never have had the chance to initiate our daughter into the delights of pain.'

'Sweet Jesù, no,' Nell whispered, beyond terror now.

'But yes,' said Ralph, pleased with himself. 'And as for you, wife, I have something special planned for you. You planned to insult and humiliate me.' He shook his head. 'That was a very bad mistake, and now you're going to pay.'

'I won't keep quiet if you touch Meg.'

'Oh, believe me, you will. You're going to be as quiet as the grave.' He threw back his head and laughed at his own joke, and Janet sniggered. 'You, dear wife, are going in the wall and you're never coming out. I'm going to shut you in the dark, and you're going to listen to what I do to your daughter, and you're going to die screaming in there.'

It seemed she was not beyond terror after all. It swallowed her, black, shiny, slippery. 'You are insane.'

'You think so? For that...' He nodded at Janet, who casually took Meg's little finger and snapped it back. Meg arched in agony but Ralph had his big hand over her mouth and no sound came out. Nell saw her daughter's eyes roll back over his palm, and her mind went dark with hatred.

'May all the devils in Hell torment you to the end of time,' she cursed her husband. 'May you be hounded to your death, and may you die in agony ten times worse than that you have made your own daughter suffer.'

Ralph waved her curses aside. He was in great good humour. Pain always made him smile. 'Gag her,' he ordered Janet and before Nell could draw breath to scream again, a filthy rag was slapped over her mouth and knotted firmly behind her cap.

Meg had fainted, and was slumped on the floor by the stool. Nell tried to hop over to her, but Janet pulled her back with the same casual inhumanity she used on Meg. How could she ever have thought of this woman as a friend? Nell wondered with an oddly detached part of her mind, the only part that was not blank and black with horror. How could she not have guessed that beneath that homely, ordinary surface lay a writhing mass of cruelty and madness?

Ralph was over by the fireplace, moving his hand over the wainscot. 'Who would have thought I'd ever be glad that papist persuaded my father to put in these priest holes? They are so cunningly concealed, you would never find them unless you knew where to look ... ah, here one is!'

There was a clunk, and a panel on one side of the fireplace swung open. In spite of herself, Nell's gaze was drawn to where the hole gaped obscenely black.

'No, no, no...' Shaking her head frantically, the words strangled by the rag in her mouth, she tried to back away, but she had forgotten that her ankles were lashed together. She fell heavily, and a bright shock of pain bloomed as her head struck the floor.

It had been freshly strewn with sweet smelling herbs. She had seen to it herself, not wanting Ralph to suspect that she was going. It was strange seeing the floor from this sideways angle with her skull still ringing from the impact. There was a tiny spray of meadowsweet right in front of her eyes. It was grey and dried and the leaves were withered. She remembered picking the flowers in the summer when they were feathery and white against their fresh green leaves, remembered holding the stems to her nose to breathe in their fragrance and then hanging them in bundles in her still room to dry. Shouldn't there have been a warning then, a prickling sense that these would be among the last things she would ever see?

For she was going to die. Nell knew that now, but still she struggled as Janet and Ralph tsked at how she had fallen and bundled her to her feet.

'I'll tell everyone you ran off with Tom,' Ralph informed her conversationally. Hopeless as she was, Nell resisted as best she could as he dragged her across to the fireplace. 'No one will look for you. They'll all have seen how you panted after him like a bitch in heat. Janet can come back and keep house for me ... yes, it will all work out perfectly.'

'What about the girl?' asked Janet, jerking her head at Meg, who had come round and was curled in a ball on the floor, keening as if she had lost her mind. As Nell profoundly hoped that she had.

Ralph paused, dropped Nell while he considered. 'The river?'

'Depends if you want to mark her or not,' Janet said practically. 'You can't pass her off as a whore and a vagrant. The coroner will ask questions, and you don't want no jurors nosing around. Leave her unmarked – you can say she killed herself after her mother abandoned her.'

He pouted. 'No marks, no fun.' He smiled down at Nell, showing all his big teeth. 'Besides,

I want her mother to be able to hear her suffer.'

'You could put them in together,' Janet suggested, eager to help. 'When you're done.'

'Too small. Ah, I have it!' Ralph clapped his hands. 'We'll use the secret stair.' He strolled over to the corner of the room by the window overlooking the garden and began feeling around for another hidden latch. 'Another papist alteration, but one I confess I have found useful when not wanting to advertise my night-time ... travels.' The teeth flashed again, bone white in the flickering candlelight, as a heavy click announced that the panel was open. 'A shame to close it up, but worth it, I feel. I'll get John Tyler in to brick up the door into the garden. He doesn't need to know why.'

Fastidiously, he brushed the dust off his fingers. 'Well, then, now that's decided, we can get on.'

Without more ado, he and Janet picked up a struggling Nell and bundled her into the priest hole. It was so small that the process was not without difficulty, but they managed with some shoving. At the last moment, Ralph ripped the bonds from her wrists.

'I like the idea of hearing you fighting to get out,' he told Nell. 'And you'll be able to hear exactly what I'm doing.'

And with a last gleam of his teeth, he closed the panel on her. A dull click as the wood slotted into place and Nell was alone in the smothering dark. The cobwebs clung to her lips and eyes, and the blackness licked its lips, slavering at the prospect of eating her up. But worse than all that was the inhuman cry that came from her daughter, left alone with the monster that was her father.

Even though it would please Ralph, Nell couldn't help herself from beating on the panel. She couldn't bear to listen, but she couldn't bear for her daughter to think that she had abandoned herself to her own terror without thought for Meg's. Her beating would bear witness that Meg was not alone. So she ripped at the implacable wood until her fingers were torn and splintered and behind the filthy rag that covered her mouth still she cursed Ralph and Janet from the bottom of her heart.

Meg was whimpering now, calling for her mother, her moans punctuated by the sound of Ralph grunting, and the slap of flesh on flesh. Every now and then he called out: 'Can you hear, Eleanor? Can you imagine what I'm doing to her?'

And she could. God help her, she could. Wrapped as she was in blackness, Nell could see with agonizing clarity: Ralph beating Meg. Ralph hurting Meg, stinging and slicing her tender flesh. Ralph forcing Meg to his vilest and most degrading pleasure while Janet groaned and shuddered with delight.

And Nell could do nothing. *Nothing.* She was trapped in the dark, with horror and grief and rage and despair and a desperate, wrenching guilt her only companions and she swore that she would pursue Ralph into Hell and beyond until her daughter was avenged.

She could hear Meg begging: 'Please ... please ... please...' but her cries grew fainter and fainter until Nell was straining to hear her. She continued to beat and tear at the wood, long after the only sounds were of the lash of the whip, and of Ralph and Janet gasping and groaning in ecstasy.

Finally, exhausted, depleted, Nell's ruined hands slid down the wood in despair. She would have slumped, but there was no room for her legs to do more than buckle, and the pain blotted out all but the most dreadful knowledge that speared dagger sharp through it all.

Her daughter was dead. Tom was dead. Nell was ready to welcome death, but horror had not done with her yet. It had its hands around her throat, and her heart jerked agonizingly as the darkness crushed her. It was pressing in, pressing on her mouth, on her ribs, on her mind, blotting out Ralph and Janet and even Meg at last, until there was only Nell, alone with terror and pain and the beast that was horror.

It suffocated her with its fetid stink. It gnawed at her flesh with its razor-sharp teeth, and fed on her belly, tearing at her entrails and clawing its way up inside her until it latched at last onto her heart and tore it apart with a bright shriek of agony that blotted out all awareness.

It was the only mercy shown to Nell that day.

Her eyes flew open with a wrenching gasp for air. He was backing away from her, bafflement and unease warring in his expression.

'What's happening?' he said, glancing over his shoulder, then back at her. 'Why are you looking so strange? What's going on?'

She was free! She raised a hand to her mouth but the filthy rag Janet had tied around her was gone. There was no tie around her ankles.

Her fingers were torn and bleeding, but she could breathe. She could *breathe*.

Exultation filled her, coursing along her veins with every breath, and she straightened like a leaf unfurling. The room was strange and everything was out of kilter, but the darkness had gone and the light was dazzling her eyes.

And the author of her horror was standing right in front of her.

'You,' she said softly. 'I told you I would follow you to Hell and beyond.'

'Stop it, Theresa!' His voice rose. 'Why are you talking like that?'

'Stop it? I will not stop. I will never stop until I have avenged my daughter!'

'Daughter? What daughter? What's wrong with you, Theresa?'

She threw back her head and laughed, a harsh sound that jangled through the clammy air in the room. '*You* are wrong! You are monstrous. What evil lives in your head that you would kill your own daughter?'

'Theresa, that's enough. I don't know what you're talking about, and I don't like it!' His eyes widened as they fixed on her bloody fingers. 'Christ, what's happened to your hands?'

A quaver of fear rippled through his voice, and she rejoiced in it

'Are you frightened?' she asked, stepping towards him, holding her ruined hands up before her so that he could see the blood. 'Is your belly turning to water?' she asked as he backed away before her. 'Is terror squirming up your throat?'

'Theresa, for God's sake!'

'Good,' she said, smiling. 'Now you begin to learn what it is like for your victims.'

'I don't have any victims! This has gone on long enough.' Gathering himself, Martin advanced on her, pure aggression, and caught her across the cheek with the back of his hand. The impact slammed Tess back into her body, and she doubled over, disorientated by the blow and the realization of who she was.

Martin stood over her, satisfied to be back in control. 'You asked for it,' he told her as if she had objected. 'I've wanted to do that for years, and I should have done it sooner. Now, what the fuck is going on here, Theresa?'

'You tell me, Martin,' she said, straightening again with difficulty. Tentatively, she dabbed at her cheek, but she looked him straight in the eye. She had died, survived the worst horror imaginable. There was nothing he could do to her now. 'What's that strapped to your chest?'

He was clearly taken aback by her change of tone. He didn't like her looking him at him like that. The bomb had done its work up to then. It had kept her conciliatory, eager to please, but now she was defiant again. 'I'll do whatever it takes to keep my family together,' he blustered.

'Including threatening to kill your own child?' Her own anger was feeding off Nell's. She despised herself for giving in to Martin's bullying for so long. She had put Oscar in danger.

'What's got into you, Theresa?'

'*What's got into me?* You've terrified my son and threatened to blow all of us to kingdom come and you ask me what's got into me?' Her eyes blazed, and she balled her fists as she stepped nose-to-nose with him so that she could jab her finger into the padding above the switch.

Martin flinched. 'Be careful, woman,' he said holding out his hands, palms upstretched to keep her off as he backed away, but Tess followed him.

'No, I won't be careful. I've been careful for years, tiptoeing around your obsessions, terrified of provoking you, not realizing that you can't be careful with someone whose mind is so small and warped and scared that he can't function without someone to control so he can feel big!'

'Theresa, I'm warning you, this thing will go off!' Martin was practically in the fireplace, and the tremor was back in his voice.

Tess ignored him. 'You're pathetic,' she said contemptuously. 'A strong man isn't afraid to talk and to listen, but you're too weak to do that. You decide to strap a bomb to your chest and threaten to blow everyone up instead. You know what?' she said, still jabbing at him. 'You go ahead!'

'You're crazy!'

His face was morphing, sliding grotesquely into Ralph's, and as his teeth grew and his lips thickened and the angle of his jaw changed, Tess felt Nell surge back into her. She was swirling in disgust and horror and hate. The air was thick and viscous with it.

She jabbed at him again and again until he stumbled back against the chest that filled most of the fireplace. His eyes were wild with terror at the strange voice coming out of her lips and the stranger looking out of her eyes. The air was pressing around them, like the suffocating darkness in the priest hole.

'Do it,' she said. 'Pull the switch and die.'

'You'll die too, you mad bitch.'

'I've died before, I can die again,' she told him. 'And I'll see you in Hell.'

Martin was scrabbling at the front of the device in terror. He was panicked now, beyond thinking, and there was a moment when everything went very still. Nell was sucked back into the past, and Tess found herself staring at the switch on the front of the device as Martin's finger moved inexorably towards it.

It was green, she thought in a strange detached way. That was all wrong. It should be red, surely?

And then she thought: I need to run.

It was hopeless. The knowledge that she was too late exploded in her brain, but she turned anyway. She flung herself round in slow motion and then there was a roaring in her ears and a great bang and she was falling, falling into smoke and darkness.

A great weight was pinning her head down. She was being crushed like Margaret Clitherow and panic fluttered behind her eyelids as she struggled to breathe.

'It's all right. It's over now.' A voice she recognized, but couldn't put a name to. A voice she trusted. A warm hand around her wrist.

Its grip was all that kept her from being dragged back down into the dark. She wanted to cling to it but there was something wrong with her hands. They were wrapped in bandages and she couldn't bend her fingers.

When she swallowed, her throat felt as if it were lined with sandpaper, and her tongue stuck horribly to the roof of her mouth. Forcing her eyes open, she saw a man sitting beside her and holding her hand. Above his beaky nose, his brows were drawn together and in spite of the steadiness of his grip, she sensed a churn of anger and fear.

Luke. The name spread like a drop of cool water over her mind.

She wanted to ask why he was so afraid, but it was too hard to string the words together.

'Thirsty,' she managed instead.

His expression cleared at her cracked whisper, and a smile that started right at the back of his eyes slowly spread over his face, dissolving the fear.

'You're back.' He filled a plastic cup of water and helped guide a straw between her lips so that she could drink without lifting her head.

Back? Tess's head was pounding. A sense of horror was prowling around the edges of her consciousness, but she wouldn't go there, not yet. As it was, her mind was swirling and stumbling occasionally over odd clumps of memory: Martin's eyes widening in terror; his fingers moving towards the switch; rage pulsating along her veins; Oscar's expression as he hesitated at the door at the bottom of the stairs.

The thought of her son brought her fully awake. 'Oscar?' she croaked.

'He's fine. He's with your mum.'

It was an effort to focus, and Tess still couldn't lift her head. Her eyes slid around as she sucked gratefully at the water. She was lying high in a complicated steel bed and attached to a drip. Bandages swathed both hands which lay on the cellular blanket. A bank of machines stood ready beside her and a curtain was pulled around, isolating her and Luke from the room beyond. It was the smell that made the connection first, though: an unmistakeable scent of antiseptic and tension.

'I'm in hospital.'

The corner of Luke's mouth lifted as he took the cup away. 'There's no getting anything past you, Sherlock. You had a nasty blow to the head and your hands are pretty torn up but otherwise they seem to think you're going to be fine.'

He hesitated. 'Not sure if I should be asking you this yet, but what do you remember?'

Her mind was sludgy, a dark, ominous river where memories lurked. Tess frowned with the effort of grasping at them. 'Martin was there...' Her eyes widened as she tugged one to the surface. She tried to struggle up but she couldn't use her hands and Luke pressed her back onto the pillow.

'Hey, just lie still,' he said.

'Oh my God, the bomb! The bomb went off!'

'No.'

'But I saw him pull the switch! I thought I was going to die. What ... what happened?'

'I think the police were hoping you could tell them that,' said Luke. 'We all heard a God-almighty bang outside and we just froze. It came out of nowhere. I thought that bastard had done it too. I thought he'd blown you both up.'

Luke's face worked and his fingers tightened around Tess's wrist. 'I thought I'd lost you all over again, Tess. I was first up the stairs, with the police shouting at me to stop, and I saw you lying on the floor in your bedroom with a sodding great block of masonry nearby, but I could feel a pulse and I felt...'

His expression cracked and he tipped forward to rest his forehead on the sheet beside her. He drew in a breath, let it out.

'I felt so fucking useless,' he muttered without looking up. 'Standing outside, knowing you were in there with him on your own, nothing to do but hold on to Oscar.'

Very gently, Tess lifted her poor, bandaged hand and touched his hair. She wished she could feel it, stroke it for comfort, like she did with Oscar sometimes.

'You weren't useless,' she said.

'I couldn't do anything to help you!' The words were wrenched out of him, flung at her almost accusingly.

'You did help,' said Tess. 'I needed to know that you were there for me, and you were. I needed to know you would keep Oscar safe, and you did.'

Luke lifted his head at that. With a twisted smile, he drew a tender finger down her cheek. 'I wanted to do more than that. I wanted to be a hero and save you, but you saved yourself.'

Her memory was coming back, fished up from the river piece by piece. She lay back against her pillows, glad of the quiet, of Luke's warm touch. It would hurt too much to shake her head. 'Nell saved me,' she said.

Luke gave her some more water.

'Go on,' she said after she'd drunk. 'What happened next?'

'Then the paramedics were there, shoving me out of the way, and the police bundled me downstairs, so I didn't get a chance to see much else, but I've taken pictures after bombs have gone off, and it doesn't look like that.'

'You mean it wasn't a real bomb?'

'Apparently it was but for some reason the detonator didn't work.'

Tess stared at him, wishing that she could rub her aching forehead. 'Then what exploded?'

'Nothing. It seems that the noise came from part of the fireplace collapsing. You were hit by a piece of it, but most of it fell on top of Martin. He's dead, Tess.'

Martin was dead. Tess looked at the curtain. It was a pale, listless green. Her husband was dead. She ought to feel something, surely?

'I'm glad,' she said uncertainly at last. It felt all wrong, but when she tested the notion for shock or horror or grief, all she could find was relief. 'Yes, I'm glad.'

'At first the police thought the collapse had been triggered by the bomb detonating, but now it seems that didn't happen, so no one can explain it.

'There's something else you need to know, Tess,' Luke said after a moment. 'When they inspected the fireplace, they found a skeleton of a body that had been wedged in a hole. They're going to do a post-mortem examination but it seems like it's very old.'

'Nell...' Tess let out a long breath as the swirling in her head juddered to a halt and the last terrible memories slotted back into place.

Luke leant forward, lowering his voice. 'What happened in there, Tess?'

He listened, grim-faced, as she told him about Nell's horrific end. When she had finished, the tears were streaming down her face and she was struggling to get out of bed again.

'I've got to tell the police to look behind the wall in the corner! They need to find Meg!'

'Whoa! Wait!' Luke tried to ease her back against the pillows as a nurse pulled back the curtain and frowned at the scene. 'The police want to interview you,' he said, 'so you can tell them then.'

'Now, what's all this?' said the nurse, bustling forward to take over from Luke. 'Get back into bed, Tess,' she said firmly. 'You've had concussion and you need to lie still for a bit.'

'I've got to get up! I need to talk to the police.'

'The police can wait until the doctor's seen you. And as for you,' said the nurse turning a stern look on Luke, 'what are you thinking of, getting her all upset?'

'Sorry.' He began to back away but Tess held out a bandaged hand to him. 'Please, Luke, you have to tell them! Make them look right now!'

He grimaced. 'Tess, what can I say? There's no damage to that part of the room.'

'I don't care. Tell them something. Anything! But make them look. Ralph said...' She gulped back the horror that still stuck in her throat at the memory. 'He said they would put her body in the secret stairway, but he was going to have the exit bricked up. She's still there, Luke.' Tess's eyes filled with tears of grief and rage. 'She was barely eleven, and she died in terror and alone. They have to find her! You have to make them!'

'All right,' said Luke, unable to bear the look on her face. 'I'll tell them,' he promised. 'We'll find Meg.'

A glassy, glittery frost lay over the ground and rimed the trees as they lowered the coffin carefully into the grave. The chill bit at her cheeks and Tess huddled into her coat, squinting into the bright winter light. Even in gloves, her hands holding the small sprig of rosemary were numb with cold. Her fingers, so raw when they had pulled her from the rubble, had healed miraculously by the time they unwrapped the bandages. The doctors couldn't explain it.

They had found Meg exactly where Tess had said she would be. Tess had wept when she heard.

Both bodies were sent for forensic examination, and when all the tests were done, Tess had lobbied for them to be buried together, with the garnet ring that had been found with Nell's skeleton. She had paid for the funeral. It was the least she could do for Nell, who had saved her from Martin.

Since that dreadful day, Tess had stayed firmly in the present, although it seemed to her that the past still echoed sometimes in the air. Every now and then she thought she caught a glimpse of a familiar face in the shadows. Out of the corner of her eye she would see the whisk of a skirt disappearing down an alley, but no matter how swiftly she turned to look more closely, it would be gone. Some days she would swear that the breeze carried the sounds and smells of the streets Nell had known. Then Tess would stop and strain her senses, but it was like trying to grasp the mist in her hand, and the next moment the wind would change and blow them away again.

She chose the sonorous words of the Order for the Burial of the Dead from the 1662 *Book of Common Prayer* for Nell and Meg: *Man that is born of a woman hath but a short time to live, and is full of misery. He cometh up, and is cut down, like a flower.* Tess let the words resonate through her. Nell had had her share of misery, but she had had her joys too.

Deliberately, Tess let herself remember Nell's happiest times. Walking alongside Tom eating hot pies. Hoisting her skirts to wade into the Foss and dig her toes into the soft mud. Lying in the long grass, cocooned in warmth and ease, her heart beating in time with Tom's. Holding Meg in her arms for the first time; spinning Hugh until he squealed with laughter. Sitting in her garden; dancing at Yule; laughing in the market.

Good times, ordinary times, side by side with the horror that was Ralph. Tess looked down at the rosemary in her hands and her throat ached for Nell's courage, for the way she had seized what joy she could from her life.

'Forasmuch as it hath pleased Almighty God of his great mercy to take unto himself the soul of our dear sisters here departed, we therefore commit their bodies to the ground.'

Luke stepped forward and dropped a sprig of rosemary onto the coffin.

When they asked her how she had known where to find the second body, Tess had demurred. 'Just a feeling,' she had said, and no one had pressed too hard.

There was still no explanation for why the fireplace had collapsed when it did. Tess thought she knew. Past and present had collided in the back room that day, and the huge burst of energy that had resulted had released Nell from her dreadful prison at last. When Tess came out of hospital, Luke had arranged for Pat French to conduct a service of deliverance in the ruined bedroom. For Tess, expecting drama and horror, it had been a quiet and unexpectedly moving ceremony.

The coroner's inquest into Martin's death had been thorough, but in the absence of any other evidence, he had had no choice but to return an open verdict.

Aghast at the damage to his flat, Richard had returned to York to oversee repairs and comfort Ashrafar who he persisted in believing was traumatized, although Tess had seen little sign of it. The cat had seemed perfectly normal to her, but Oscar had had nightmares when she tried to reestablish a routine, and she wasn't sorry to leave the memories behind when Richard announced that he was coming back. His academic interest had been roused by the skeletons in the priest holes and he was planning a whole new section for his chapter on murder in his book on Tudor crime. Tess was going to let him make what he would of the evidence. His story would not be hers.

She and Oscar had spent a few weeks with her chastened mother, who was horrified at what Martin had done, and once Tess had been granted probate on Martin's estate she had been able to rent a cottage in one of the villages outside York. Oscar went to the local school and had stopped asking to see Sam and Rosie now. For a while Vanessa had tried to pretend that nothing had happened, but Tess found it hard to forgive her for handing Oscar over to Martin, and once she had moved, Vanessa stopped calling.

Luke spent a lot of time at the cottage with them. Oscar missed him when he wasn't there, and Tess did too, but she balked at asking him to move in permanently. After being tied to Martin and Ralph, she couldn't stomach the thought of linking her fate to another man.

Once or twice they had discussed it. 'I'm just not ready,' she had said.

'That's okay,' Luke said easily. 'There's no hurry. I'm happy to go on as we are. It's fine, Tess.'

Now at the graveside, Tess looked at him. A scattering of people had come: the forensic pathologist who had examined Nell and Meg's remains, the archaeologists who were interested in the few artefacts found in the priest holes. Ambrose was there, and Richard, out of very different professional interests.

Luke was there for *her*. Luke who had believed her, who had been there when she needed him. Who still was.

Sensing her gaze, he lifted his eyes from the coffin and met hers, and in spite of the solemnity of the occasion, Tess felt lust curl in her belly. They were different still, and they argued, but Luke challenged, he didn't try to control. He helped, he didn't attempt to take over. She thought about the quick laughter they shared and the sharp spear of desire she felt at his touch. About the friendship that ran clear and true through every argument, and the sense of sailing into a safe harbour at last when she lay curled against him and listened to him breathing.

She thought about Nell and Tom, and how much they had risked for that. For them, the longing to be together had ended in tragedy, but that didn't mean it would be the same for her and Luke. Nell's story didn't have to be hers. Perhaps, Tess told herself, it was time to stop being afraid of the past and start living for the future. She would talk to Luke when they got home.

'Earth to earth, ashes to ashes, dust to dust; in sure and certain hope of the resurrection to eternal life through our Lord Jesus Christ,' the priest intoned and Tess stepped up to the grave.

As soon as she was out of hospital she had gone back to work on the assize court records. Only the week before she had come across an entry dated 1588. Janet Scott, widow, indicted for murder. Tess's hand had begun to shake as she transcribed and translated. An inquisition on the body of Ralph Maskewe, merchant, had found that on 31 October the said Janet had stabbed Ralph Maskewe to death with a dagger while they were lying together in bed.

Had some shared madness seized them, Tess wondered, or had Janet turned at last on her partner in pain? Either way, Ralph had been spared the lingering death Nell would have wished for him, but it had been sordid and, Tess hoped, painful. The jury had been in little doubt of their verdict on Janet. *Guilty*, was the clerk's laconic record. *To hang*.

Tess looked at the rosemary in her hand – rosemary for remembrance. Earlier that morning she had stood alone on Ouse Bridge and watched the sunlight striking diamond bright on the water that was Tom's grave as she dropped a sprig into the river in his memory. Now she let the rosemary fall gently from her hand onto the coffin where Nell and Meg lay together. She would remember them all.

'Rest in peace, Nell,' she said.

Epilogue

Murder in Merry England

The discovery last year of two skeletons found walled up in a house in Stonegate was a story that caught the public imagination for a while, and many theories were put forward about who they were and how they came to be there. These are questions, historians say, that can never be answered conclusively.

'The evidence can only take us so far,' says historian Richard Landrow, whose forthcoming book on Tudor crime will include a discussion of the Stonegate skeletons. 'Forensic examination of the two bodies established that they were both female and approximately four to five hundred years old. One was of a young girl between ten and fourteen years of age, and the other of a woman in her early thirties who had given birth. DNA analysis proved that they were related, so it's not

unreasonable to assume that they were mother and daughter, but we can't say for sure that was the case.'

Landrow points out that the forensic evidence, while compelling, is limited. 'We know that the young girl's hyoid bone was fractured, indicating that she was strangled, and she had a broken finger, but there is no evidence as to how the older individual died. There was some damage to the finger bones and, horrifyingly, it's possible that she was walled up alive and starved to death, but again, we can't be certain.'

Beyond that, Landrow says, everything has to be speculation. 'Stonegate was a high-status street in the Tudor period and there's no sign of malnourishment, which suggests that these two females were members of the civic elite.' However, the evidence from the artefacts discovered with the skeletons is confusing, Landrow admits. While some of the surviving objects such as buckles and fragments of girdles are clearly high status, the only ring found with the older skeleton was set with a cheap garnet. 'We would expect a wealthy woman of her age to be wearing jewellery of a much higher quality. It's a puzzle.'

Landrow, who lives in the house where the bodies were discovered and has a particular interest in the case, has been unable to identify them further. 'York has extraordinarily rich archives, but sadly we are still missing a lot of documentary material for the period, and there is no way to trace the ownership of this particular house.' Nor are there any accounts of two members of a family abruptly disappearing. 'It's possible that whoever was responsible for their deaths simply put it about that they had run away,' Landrow suggests. The bodies were hidden so successfully that it must have been done with the collusion of the head of the household, he thinks. 'As historians, we can speculate,' he says, 'but we have to accept that much of the past is unknowable and that there are some things that can never be explained.'

This horrific case shines a light on the darker side of England under the Tudors, says Landrow. 'Whoever they were, these two women died a horrible death that was most likely connected to domestic abuse.'

Today we are often horrified by the level of abuse and cruelty reported by the media. 'We tend to blame these on social changes and look back to a simpler and happier time,' Landrow says, 'but the fact is that "merry England" could be a brutal place, marked by violence at every level of society.'

Elizabethan England might have been the 'Golden Age' but the society that produced Shakespeare was also one that would press a pregnant woman to death for her beliefs. (Margaret Clitherow, a butcher's wife who lived in the Shambles, was executed in 1586 and canonized in 1970 as St Margaret of York.)

According to Landrow, casual violence was common on the streets, and an argument or scuffle could quickly lead to daggers being drawn. Vagrants were treated with particular brutality if they were caught begging in the city. They would be stripped naked, tied to the back of a cart ('the cart's arse') and whipped through the streets before being banished out of one of the city's four main gates.

In the home, too, says Landrow, abuse was prevalent. It was common to send children into service in another household, where they were supposed to be treated as part of the family but where it seems many endured brutal treatment, from beatings to worse. The suicide rate for children and adolescents in early modern England was far higher than today's, in spite of the fact that suicide was considered with a lack of compassion that seems to us shocking. Blamed for giving in to despair and the temptation of the Devil, the bodies of those who killed themselves were denied burial in consecrated ground and were commonly buried ignominiously at crossroads, and the belief that their spirits would return to haunt the living often led to the macabre practice of driving an iron-tipped stake through the heart of the corpse.

Leaving service to marry and train their own servants did not necessarily improve the lot of women. Wives had little recourse against abusive husbands. A man had the right to beat his wife, but not to kill her. Landrow cites the case of Alice Clarke, who was subjected to her husband's drunken assaults as well as to sadistic rituals when he would tie her to the bedpost and whip her. For women like Alice, Landrow points out, murder must have seemed the only means of escape.

'The poison of choice seems to have been ratsbane,' says Landrow, who has made a study of surviving assize court records for the period. 'In a world where there was no support for victims of domestic abuse, and women literally had nowhere else to go, it's surprising that there aren't more cases of wives murdering their husbands.'

For others, like the women who lived and died so horribly in the house in Stonegate, there was no escape. We will never know who was responsible for their deaths. Tess Nicholson, whose husband was killed in the explosion that led to the discovery of the bodies, thinks that they were victims of an evil and sadistic husband and father but admits that she has no proof. 'It's just a

Acknowledgements

Writing a book is a team effort. I am grateful as always to my agent, Caroline Sheldon, and to Louise Buckley, Wayne Brookes and the rest of the team at Pan Macmillan for their enthusiasm and encouragement. I'd particularly like to mention the copy-editor, Lorraine Green, who read the text so carefully and who made such perceptive comments.

For their help with *The Memory of Midnight* special thanks are due to Diana Nelson, Lisa Liddy, Steve Hodgson, and Ailsa Mainman, and to Jeanette McMillan who shared her memories of growing up in York.

Finally I need to thank all those friends who, as always, put up with the hair-tearing crises that accompany the writing of every book, and supply perspective, support or wine as required – often all three at the same time – especially John Harding, Stella Hobbs, Mary Hodgson, Steve Hodgson, Diana Nelson, Julia Pokora, Richard Rowland and Paul Sparks. I rely on them all more than they know.

The publishers hope that this book has given you enjoyable reading. Large Print Books are especially designed to be as easy to see and hold as possible. If you wish a complete list of our books please ask at your local library or write directly to:

Magna Large Print Books
Magna House, Long Preston,
Skipton, North Yorkshire.
BD23 4ND